THE WOODVILLE CONSPIRACY

BY THE SAME AUTHOR

The Pearl of France
The Queen's Spy
The Fair Maid of Kent
An Illegitimate Affair
The Epiphany Betrayal
The Making of a Tudor
Fire and Fleet and Candlelight

THE WOODVILLE CONSPIRACY

CAROLINE NEWARK

Copyright © 2023 Caroline Newark

The moral right of the author has been asserted.

Apart from any fair dealing for the purposes of research or private study, or criticism or review, as permitted under the Copyright, Designs and Patents Act 1988, this publication may only be reproduced, stored or transmitted, in any form or by any means, with the prior permission in writing of the publishers, or in the case of reprographic reproduction in accordance with the terms of licences issued by the Copyright Licensing Agency. Enquiries concerning reproduction outside those terms should be sent to the publishers.

Matador
Unit E2 Airfield Business Park,
Harrison Road, Market Harborough,
Leicestershire. LE16 7UL
Tel: 0116 2792299
Email: books@troubador.co.uk
Web: www.troubador.co.uk/matador
Twitter: @matadorbooks

ISBN 978 1803137 117

British Library Cataloguing in Publication Data.
A catalogue record for this book is available from the British Library.

Printed and bound in reat Britain by TJ Books Limited, Padstow, Cornwall
Typeset in 11pt Minion Pro by Troubador Publishing Ltd, Leicester, UK

Matador is an imprint of Troubador Publishing Ltd

MIX
Paper from responsible sources
FSC® C013056

In memory of Oriana and all who followed her
1989 – 2008

*"Now is the winter of our discontent
Made glorious summer by this son of York"*

William Shakespeare. *Life and Death of King Richard III*

THE FAMILY TREE
(SO FAR)

Edward the First, King of England, married Marguerite of France, and had by her issue, Edmund of Woodstock

♥

Edmund of Woodstock, Earl of Kent, married Margaret, daughter of Lord John Wake, and had by her issue, Joan of Kent

♥

Joan of Kent in her own right Countess of Kent, married Sir Thomas Holand, to whom she bore issue, Thomas Holand

♥

Thomas Holand married Alys, daughter of Richard Fitzalan, Earl of Arundel, by Eleanor of Lancaster, and had by her issue, Eleanor Holand

♥

Eleanor Holand married Thomas Montagu, Earl of Salisbury, to whom she bore, issue Alice Montagu

♥

Alice Montagu, in her own right Countess of Salisbury, married Sir Richard Nevill, to whom she bore issue, Kathryn Nevill

♥

Kathryn Nevill, daughter of Richard Nevill, Earl of Salisbury, married William Bonville, Lord Harington, to whom she bore issue, Cecily Bonville

CAST OF MAIN CHARACTERS

Cecily Bonville	Lady Harington, an heiress
Her mother	Kathryn, Lady Hastings
Her stepfather	William, Lord Hastings
John Zouche	a neighbour at Ashby
Mary Hungerford	Lord Hastings's ward
Cecily's cousins	Isabel, Duchess of Clarence
	Anne, Duchess of Gloucester
Lady Donne	Lord Hastings's sister
Joan Dinham	John Zouche's betrothed
William Catesby	a lawyer
The king	Edward IV
His brothers	George, Duke of Clarence
	Richard, Duke of Gloucester
The queen	Elizabeth Woodville
Her eldest son	Thomas Grey
Her daughter	Princess Elizabeth
Her brother	Anthony Woodville, Lord Rivers
Her sisters	Anne, Viscountess Bourchier
	Mary, Countess of Pembroke
	Catherine, Duchess of Buckingham
Duchess Cecily	the king's mother
Lady Stanley	Margaret Beaufort
Edith Dinham	in service to Lady Stanley
Lady Norfolk	widow of the Duke of Norfolk
Mistress Shore	a woman of bad reputation

PROLOGUE

CALAIS 1473

From where we stood at the edge of the trees it was impossible to be certain. At first I thought it a trick of the light, the kind of shape-shifting image you might see through a mist. But I was mistaken. This was no seven-headed monster risen up from the deep seeking children to devour for its dinner. This was as real as you or me.

As we crept closer we could just make out the body of a man lying half-submerged in the murky shallows at the foot of the bank. His head rested comfortably on a pillow of mud but his body was bent at a peculiar angle with one arm flung wide as if desperately reaching for safety.

'Is he dead?'

'I think so,' John said in a low voice.

John Zouche was our neighbour at Ashby and at fourteen, a year older than me.

On the left side of the dead man's face was a gaping wound where a sharp object had penetrated the skin, slicing through flesh and exposing a sliver of white bone. It was an ugly sight, made worse by the unseeing eyes which stared up at the sky as if in the moment of death the man had been seeking the gates of heaven.

'Perhaps he's a French spy,' John whispered.

I told him that was a particularly stupid remark. The man's jacket was of poor quality and his fingernails were torn, sure signs of a life not spent plotting in secret corners of a king's court. He'd be a servant who'd run away and missed his footing in the dark. The marshes around Calais were said to be treacherous, full of meandering streams and boggy hollows where a man might easily be swallowed whole. A wise person followed the causeways taking care not to stray but perhaps no-one had warned the dead man.

John crouched down to take a closer look.

'People say King Louis is full of guile. He might have sent a spy dressed like a common man as part of a cunning plan.'

'Next you'll be saying he's a spy for the Duke of Burgundy.'

'The duke's our good friend; he'd not spy on us.'

John was offended but should have remembered that friends can always betray you no matter how much they make of their closeness. Nobody spoke of my mother's brother, the faithless Earl of Warwick who'd rebelled against our York king and paid for his disloyalty with his life, but we all knew the story.

My uncle had once been the most powerful man in England, feted wherever he went until greed proved his undoing. People said it was unwise to dwell on the past and that the horrors of three years ago were best forgotten, swept out with the rushes like so much detritus. Perhaps they were right. In the privacy of her room my mother might shed tears for her dead brother but we were all loyal Yorkists now.

John inched further down the bank, clinging fast to a tangle of tree roots.

'We'd best search him. He might have incriminating papers on his person.'

Hanging on with one hand, he stretched out an arm in an attempt to pull the body closer but however much he tugged, nothing moved. Irritated by his failure he altered his position, leant over to gain leverage, lost his footing and fell headlong into the water.

There was a tremendous splash followed by a loud shriek from behind me. It was Mary Hungerford. She had evaded the watchful eyes of her governess and come tiptoeing across the clearing to see what John and I were doing.

Mary was my stepfather's ward, a miserable creature, seven years old and much given to snivelling. She followed me around like an unwanted puppy, whining in her reedy little voice that she wanted to be my friend.

'What are you doing?' Our governess's voice was shrill with fear, which was understandable. Think of the tragedy for her reputation if one of us drowned.

Within moments we were surrounded by my stepfather's men who were convinced we were the target of an enemy ambush. After some impressive cudgel waving and a great deal of shouting, they hauled John out of the water. He stood shivering on the bank while the men argued amongst themselves as to what they should do. It took them a ridiculously long time to reach the obvious conclusion which was to take John, dripping wet and covered in mud, to where my stepfather was talking to the master falconer in charge of his favourite goshawk. The bird's fierce yellow eyes were hidden beneath a black beaded hood but its curved beak, still dripping with gore, pointed menacingly towards me.

My stepfather looked unperturbed by this interruption to his morning's sport. I thought I saw a flicker of amusement on his face as he surveyed his sodden guest.

'You're fortunate my goshawk did not mistake you for a duck, young Zouche. I wager you'd not survive an attack from that quarter. Lose an eye most like, if not worse.' Everyone laughed as they always did when my stepfather said something amusing. 'However, seeing as you're in my charge, I'd best send you back to the castle. Can't take risks with a future Baron Zouche of Haringworth, can we?'

John stood, head bowed, shivering with cold. It was the humiliation which would hurt most, the shame of being made to look a fool. If he'd asked me I could have suggested a dozen better ways to retrieve a body but he'd not asked and I'd not vouchsafed the information. Like all boys of my acquaintance he thought he knew best, boasting of how important he was. Now my stepfather had disabused him of any notion of superiority. He was nothing but a foolish boy who should have been left behind with his tutor.

I knew John would prefer to stay with us but no-one contradicted the king's lieutenant in Calais. That would be most unwise. As my mother had told me on countless occasions, if a man wanted a favour, say an export licence or an earldom, who better placed to plead his case than my stepfather, William, Lord Hastings, the king's closest friend, the man who had the king's ear.

When he was at home with us at Ashby, the hall was full of men come to ask for my stepfather's help in opposing a challenge to their ownership of a piece of land or seeking justice for some wrong done to one of their kin.

And in matters touching the king or the queen's family my stepfather was said to be more than usually helpful.

John was hoisted onto a horse by one of the grooms while my stepfather gave orders to a group of men who looked none too pleased at having their day's fun curtailed by a young lordling unable to keep his feet on the ground. I could imagine them grumbling all the way back to Calais, taunting a miserable John Zouche for his stupidity.

'Let that be a lesson to you, Cecily,' said our governess in one of her many severe voices. 'Lord Hastings does not issue warnings idly. The marshes are dangerous. They are not like our parks in England. Calais may seem a merry town but the men of the garrison are there for a purpose, not to provide amusement for you young people. We are in constant danger from webs spun by the French king so you must be ever vigilant.'

'I understand,' I replied, sounding suitably contrite while keeping an eye on John and his escort fast vanishing amongst the trees.

At the disappearance of one of the few people she knew in this crowd of tall strangers, Mary let out a wail of distress. It was utterly shameful and if the nursemaids at Ashby had done their job properly, the child would know better than to make a fuss in company. Tears should be reserved for the privacy of the women's rooms, not shed in front my stepfather and his friends. I moved to one side so that no-one would think it was me making such a caterwauling.

Unsurprisingly, the noise irritated my stepfather, who looked up. 'What's the matter *now*?'

The tone of his voice made Mary howl even louder. She buried her face in the thick folds of her governess's skirts, snivelling and sobbing like an ill-bred village brat.

The woman began to apologise. 'Forgive me, my lord, the child is afraid. She has not seen a dead body before.'

My stepfather put a hand to his forehead. 'Dear God! Is that all.'

He knelt down on one knee in the dirt, seeming not to mind that his smart black hose would be ruined. He peeled Mary's hands away from her governess's skirts, then turned her round to face him.

'You know who I am, Mary?'

'Yes, my lord.' The words came out accompanied by a sniff, a sob and a hiccup.

'You remember how I told you I would be your guardian now that your father is dead?'

A nod followed by a subdued, 'Yes.'

'I said you would live in my house with my children and when the time came, I would find a suitable husband to care for you?'

Another nod. By now the tears had stopped, though her bottom lip was still trembling.

'So you see, little Mary Hungerford, there is no need to weep. Now, come, give me a kiss.'

She gave a wobbly smile, giggled, then threw herself into his arms like a dog reunited with its master after a whipping. It was disgusting. Next she'd be nuzzling his neck and licking his face.

I wanted to tell her he'd only bought her for the titles she'd bring to our family, that he didn't care for her one bit. She was a nobody, just the daughter of a man who'd been executed for treason on the orders of the king, and with a great-grandmother still living it would be years before she'd inherit her lands. I felt truly sorry for my brother who would have to marry such a girl but that is the way of it: boys must marry where they are bid.

My stepfather looked at me in the considering way he had as if he knew exactly what I was thinking. He was a clever man and my mother said he was kind, although sometimes I thought his kindness sadly misplaced. He gave me a small smile and the skin around his eyes creased with good humour.

'Well, Lady Harington, how do you fancy a run with your hawk?'

I beamed at him. I thought he'd forgotten but he never forgot anything. That morning he'd suggested we might go to the mews to see if Oriana was deemed ready. She was only a young goshawk and I'd spent hours learning how to handle her. She was darker than my stepfather's favourite hawk but I thought the black and white barring on her breast and her splendid white eyebrows, particularly beautiful. Her eyes were like molten gold with fire in their depths, which the master falconer said was extremely rare for such a young bird and promised a fine hunter. I'd been given a small black hood with a plumed crest for her to wear and considered Oriana the smartest goshawk of all.

I slipped my hand into the thick leather gauntlet which covered me almost up to my elbow, took a deep breath and extended my arm in order to keep my wrist steady. Oriana was surprisingly heavy but my stepfather said it was better to start with a fair degree of weight; besides, goshawks were best for hunting duck. At Ashby I had a little merlin whom I loved dearly but the master falconer said I was wise to have left her in England. Goshawks were better suited to the marshes.

The slight shock when I released Oriana from my wrist never failed to surprise me. My stepfather said it was like the jolt from firing a cannon. The excitement was tremendous. She flew past the trees like an arrow from a bow, swept low above the reed beds and, in a sudden burst of speed, slammed into a flock of unsuspecting ducks. Out on the marshes, the spaniels were held ready, waiting to retrieve the kill while Oriana flew back to me for her reward.

For the rest of the day we made great sport until a lowering sun in the west told my stepfather it was time to return for our supper. Despite a huge picnic dinner served on tables spread with white linen, I was hungry. As I climbed wearily onto my horse I wondered what we might have to eat and if there'd be dancing.

At the front of our procession two men carried our day's trophies securely tied to a pole. The ducks hung upside down, their feathered bodies swinging to and fro as if dancing a jig. The man in the stream would never dance another jig, never eat another dinner, never say his prayers and never again bed himself down to sleep.

Death had come without warning for the ducks, our goshawks snatching up their unsuspecting prey. Like the ducks, had the man not known how dangerous it was out here on the marshes.

1

ASHBY 1474

At first there was nothing to hear other than an excess of heavy breathing but when I lifted my head from the pillow I detected a noise from downstairs: a scurrying, banging and cursing which heralded our cook's arrival into the kitchen. The other girls were hiding beneath their covers, pretending to be asleep. Only Mary had her eyes open, but I had no wish to suffer her incessant chatter so I climbed out of bed and went in search of a yawning maid to help me dress.

I tiptoed silently down the stairs meeting no-one and slipped unseen out of a side door into the garden. I loved my stepfather's gardens at Ashby with their stately trees and sweet-smelling greenery but since returning from Calais my preference was to walk in the peace of the early morning. On my own there was time to think, impossible with a trail of stupid girls giggling behind me talking nonsense, shushed at regular intervals by our governess who had no idea how to keep them in order.

To my dismay two sets of footprints were clearly visible in the damp grass with none returning. That meant these people were still out there. Then I heard them on the other side of a hedge talking in low voices. Annoyingly I could barely make out what they were saying. I moved a little closer trying not to tread on the soft soil beneath the bushes in case I marked my shoes. A spray of spiky green leaves brushed against my face, tickling my nose and almost making me sneeze.

'You promised!'

That was my mother. I recognised her voice. She sounded angry which was odd because my mother was never angry. She had the disposition of a painted Madonna, calm and serene. There might be an occasional frown or a mild rebuke but nothing more. I wondered what had caused her to lose her temper.

'Ah Kathryn, you know there is nothing I can do.'

I nearly fell forward into the hedge. That was my stepfather's voice! My mother could not be angry with my stepfather. It was impossible. She was devoted to him. Their marriage was one of perfect harmony. Yet here she was hissing at him like a cat.

'Tell him, no.'

'I cannot do that.'

'Why? Is he more important to you than me?'

'My love, he is the king.'

There had been a time when I believed my mother the most important person in my stepfather's life. She was the woman he'd married for love, an earl's daughter, widow of a lord who'd died fighting for the king and an excellent match. But their marriage was founded on so much more.

That was my belief until the events of four years ago showed me how wrong I was.

She might be his beloved wife and mother of his children; he might entrust her with the care of Ashby when he was away from home; he might kiss her in that lingering way I'd seen other men kiss their sweethearts;

but the king's needs and desires would always come first. When disaster struck England it was not the king my stepfather abandoned but my mother.

He fled and we were left behind not knowing where he'd gone. We were terrified of the danger we were in when all we had to keep Ashby safe was a not-yet-finished defensive wall, a fanciful plan for great towers, and a depleted guard comprised of nothing but elderly men and young boys.

'We must pray your Uncle Warwick will think to protect us from his new-found friends,' my mother wept. 'I would not have my children burned in their beds by a Frenchman.'

The picture she painted was of a country torn apart, neighbour fighting neighbour, cousin pitched against cousin, a land brought to ruin with a king fleeing for his life.

I was ten years old and understood nothing of the prolonged and bitter conflict between the great families of England. I was ignorant of how my mother's treasonous brother had reignited a cause once thought lost, giving King Louis an opportunity to meddle in the affairs of his enemy, the York king.

All I knew was an ice-cold fear which engulfed me each night as I lay in my bed unable to sleep. Every creak of a floorboard or clank of a pail was the sound of a hired killer brought from France by my uncle in his bid to steal back the throne for Mad Henry, the failed Lancastrian king. I imagined a man scaling our walls, insinuating himself through an unguarded window, silently climbing the stairway. I could sense him creeping about in the darkness of our room, feel his fingers wrapped round my throat so that I couldn't breathe, his dagger ready to plunge into my breast.

My mother spared me nothing when I confessed my fears, 'It is not only the men. Mad Henry's French queen would slit your throat herself if she got the chance. She is an evil woman. I pray you never fall into her hands.'

During that long cold winter we cowered inside our house, too fearful to venture beyond the walls of Ashby. We were desperate for news but despaired when we heard that Mad Henry was back on the throne with my uncle at his side.

'They will declare my husband a traitor and confiscate his lands,' my mother wept. 'We shall be left with nothing.'

I tugged nervously on her sleeve. 'Perhaps my stepfather will return.'

'If he returns, they will kill him,' she said flatly.

It was almost a year before my stepfather came back to Ashby, welcomed by my mother as if his absence had been nothing more than an unremarkable interlude, not one involving flight, exile, danger and a series of desperate battles to regain the throne. My mother knew that God had set her husband above her and her duty was to serve him as best she could. So there were no tears, no recriminations, no indication that she and his children had been terrified for their lives and that I, his stepdaughter, was still unable to sleep at night without a maid in her bed and a guard on the door. If he prized his king above his wife who was she to complain.

Yet here she was, complaining loudly.

'I would remind you, my lord, of your solemn promise. You said this would not happen. Were you lying? Is it only to your king that you remain true?'

There was a lengthy pause followed by the rustle of crushed brocade and the sound of a half-strangled sob. I had observed, with the prurient interest of a growing girl, the way my stepfather handled my mother. On the rare occasions they disagreed he persuaded her to his way of thinking, not by shouting like another man might do to his wife, but by gentling her as he did his favourite horse.

There was no doubt in my mind that I was the reluctant witness to an embrace designed to quell any resistance followed by a long slow loving caress and a passionate kiss. My stepfather had my mother's measure. The pattern never varied and my mother always capitulated.

The sound of a small cough came from behind me. I spun round, guilty at having been caught eavesdropping. A man, perhaps thirty years old, dressed in black with a cap on his head, was standing not four feet away but he was not someone I recognised. The previous evening my stepfather had ridden in like a visiting emperor with fifty men in his train This, I presumed, was one of them.

The man removed his cap, uncovering a head of neatly combed dark hair. and bowed politely. 'My apologies for disturbing you, Lady Harington.'

He knew who I was but who was he and why was he here.

'My name is William Catesby.'

A gentleman. That told me nothing.

'What do you want, Master Catesby? Is it your practice to creep around other people's gardens?'

His smile was thin, barely more than a twitch of the lips.

'Lady Harington, forgive me, but if you wish to know what is being said you would do well to move further forward to where there is a gap in the hedge.'

I felt a slight blush rise into my cheeks and said hastily, 'You are impertinent, Master Catesby. What makes you think I am interested in what other people are saying?'

His smile widened a fraction. 'Your shoes are caked with mud. I doubt a lady of your quality would risk her shoes unless what was being said was of importance to her.'

'You are wrong, sir. I do not care what is being discussed by my mother and Lord Hastings. It is none of my business.'

He took a step sideways and picked a sprig of leaves from the hedge and lifted it to his nose. 'Perhaps you *should* care, Lady Harington.'

'Why do you say that?'

'What if it is your future they are discussing.'

He tucked the sprig of leaves into the purse at his belt.

I smiled in the disdainful way I'd rehearsed in front of my mirror. 'You are wrong, Master Catesby. My mother and Lord Hastings are in complete agreement as to my future. There is nothing to discuss.'

My mother once told me how my stepfather had refused an offer from the Earl of Pembroke of a marriage for me with his son – "Not good enough for Ceci," my stepfather had declared. "Too new to the title. I shall find a better match."

'Are you certain?' Master Catesby said quietly.

For the first time in our conversation I felt at a disadvantage. 'Do you have other information?'

He smiled more broadly. 'Lady Harington, information has value. It is a highly prized commodity. Why should I tell you what I know?'

'Why should you not! You started this conversation, not I.'

He laughed. 'So I did.'

I looked at him more carefully. In the early spring sunshine, I could see that his clothes, although clean and probably costly to a man like him, were not of the best quality. His doublet had a slight sheen which betrayed the thinness of the cloth and his boots, though well-polished were also well-worn. I was unable to place him and wondered who he was.

'What business do you have with Lord Hastings? You seem to know him yet I've not seen you in his company.'

'I am a lawyer, my lady. I serve Lord Hastings in that capacity.'

So Master Catesby was a lawyer. I should have guessed. Whenever my stepfather was home, there were always two or three of Master Catesby's ilk slinking around with satchels full of documents. Even our servants knew that each time Lord Hastings acquired another grant from the king there was work for his lawyers. It was their job to sort out the intricate details of wardships and deal with problems arising from leases and fees. A whole room at Ashby was devoted to their toiling, crammed full of dozens of clerks and unending piles of paperwork.

'Do you discover much information for Lord Hastings while lurking behind hedges?' I enquired.

'Naturally, otherwise there would be little reason to continue the practice.'

'Is this information of benefit to your lord?'

'It is of benefit to me and I always use my best endeavours for my lord. But in this particular instance I thought to do you a kindness, Lady Harington.'

'Why would you do that?'

He smiled in that thin way he had. 'I do not know. You do not seem particularly grateful.'

On his last visit I had overheard my stepfather tell my brother that a lord should always judge a man first on his usefulness and only then on his rank. That way he would be certain of surrounding himself with men who would serve him well. It seemed to me the same words could apply to a clever woman. Perhaps there would be an advantage to me in knowing a man like Master Catesby. It was possible he might be of use.

'Tell me, Master Catesby, in your search for information do you also read other people's letters?'

He raised his eyebrows, surprised at the directness of my question. 'Naturally there are occasions when I am asked to give my opinion on Lord Hastings's correspondence. The meanings in letters he receives are sometimes obscure. Another man's advisor may try to pull the wool over my lord's eyes. Is that what you wanted to know?'

'You know it is not.'

'I hope you are not suggesting that a humble servant such as myself would stoop to read what another man has written, without my lord's permission.'

'It is no worse than eavesdropping on what he says.'

He touched his forehead in a gesture of a point well made. 'You argue like a lawyer, my lady. And you are correct. But you must understand that to pick up a piece of correspondence not intended for your eyes is harder to justify than to be passing by on the other side of a hedge.'

This time I laughed. 'I shall remember that and give up searching for my mother's letters.'

He bowed. 'I must take my leave of you, Lady Harington. Talking with you has been an education.'

I nodded, giving him permission to withdraw.

As he made to go. he stopped and turned round. 'I nearly forgot my purpose in coming into the garden. My wife, Meg, sends greetings and asks to be remembered to you. She has many pleasant memories of Ashby.'

My eyes widened. John Zouche's sister Meg was older than me but for a few months one summer we'd been close in the way girls often are, doing everything together, not wishing to be parted for a single moment. But by the following summer she had left home to be married and our friendship had withered and died. I thought it odd Meg's husband should be a man like Master Catesby. As the sister of a future Baron Zouche of Haringworth I would have expected her to make a better marriage.

Next morning my stepfather sent word that he wished to see me in his Great Chamber, the room where he entertained his most important guests. The girls were undecided if this was a summons to be in awe of, one which might result in some unimaginably marvellous consequence, or if, more likely, it was one to be feared.

'What have you done?' breathed a wide-eyed Mary. 'Will he have you beaten?'

'He is my stepfather. I am often invited to sit with him,' I lied, tilting my chin to show them my superiority.

In truth, I rarely saw my stepfather. He was a busy man, seldom at home with my mother. His work for the king meant spending many months at court where he performed important duties as royal chamberlain, planning entertainments for the king and his friends. For much of the year he was in Calais, organising the garrison, keeping an eye on the merchants of the staple in case they cheated the king of his taxes, while watching, from afar the machinations of King Louis. I'd seen for myself how hard he worked.

My mother said most of her husband's days were passed on the back of a horse or the deck of a ship. She made it sound as if there was no time for jollity yet I'd observed him in Calais making merry with his friends and with the wives of his friends. I was beginning to wonder if he missed us at all.

The Great Chamber above the parlour was smaller than the hall but very much grander. Like most houses, our hall had a hearth in the middle of the floor which kept everyone warm but allowed wreaths of smoke to drift around the room and up people's noses and into their eyes. In his own chamber, my stepfather had followed the latest fashion in building design and installed a huge rectangular fireplace with a carved overmantel. Here, smoke from the fire rose gracefully up the chimney and did not blow back into people's faces.

The walls were covered with beautiful tapestries brought back from one of his trips to Calais, and placed around the room were his great bed, some good solid tables and chairs and two large chests.

My stepfather stood to one side of the hearth watching my mother who sat on the other side looking at her hands which lay in her lap. I noticed with surprise that he'd given her his best chair. She turned her face towards me. I could see at once that she'd been crying; her eyes were red-rimmed and her face had that puffy look which plagues even the prettiest of women when they weep. Whatever their quarrel in the garden had been about, it was not resolved.

I curtsied to my stepfather, giving him an obedient greeting as this was the first time we'd met that morning. He smiled but did not invite me forward, a hint of wariness lurking behind his eyes. Obviously what was about to be said was causing him concern. I waited, hands clasped neatly in front of me as I'd been taught. His gaze flickered sideways to my mother, then back to me.

'Good news!' he said heartily, in a manner which would not have fooled a five-year-old. Whatever news he had was not to his liking and most definitely not to my mother's. I ventured a small smile, for the moment willing to be complicit in whatever was about to be discussed.

'You are to go to court,' he said. 'The queen wishes to see you.'

The queen! A little tremor of excitement ran up my spine. The queen had asked for me. Me! Not my mother, not one of my aunts, but me.

I'd never seen the queen but my stepfather's sister, Lady Donne, who served at court, had told me about her. Elizabeth Woodville was the fairest woman in all England, a Lancastrian widow plucked from obscurity by the king to be his queen. People said it was a whirlwind love affair: him newly come to his throne, her with nothing to recommend her but the old grey gown she stood up in. So great was his desire to make her his wife, they'd married in secret, telling no-one, not even his councillors. She may not have been of noble birth, Lady Donne explained, but she was pious, clever and fertile – all highly desirable assets in a queen.

My cousin Isabel had a different opinion. The king had been bewitched. He should have married a French princess, or a young woman from one of the other ruling houses of Europe, not a scheming Lancastrian drab with two children. But Isabel was Uncle Warwick's daughter and had probably had her ears filled with poison by Mad Henry's queen.

'Shall I go with you?' I asked my stepfather, thinking how important I'd feel with my hand on his arm,

'No, your lady mother will take you.'

That was a surprise. My mother never went to court. When I was little I thought perhaps she did not know the way. Later I wanted to ask why she did not wait on the queen like my stepfather's sisters. Did she not want to go or did my stepfather not want her there. Whichever it was, while my stepfather dined and made merry with the king and the queen, my mother remained at Ashby caring for me and his children.

'Am I to have a new gown?'

I looked towards my mother who had said nothing.

My stepfather laughed. 'Why not? You and your lady mother shall both have new gowns. I want my women to be the best-dressed ladies in England.'

He glanced at my mother once more but her approval of his plan was not for sale, at least not for the price of a couple of new gowns. Most women could be seduced by a gift of beautiful new clothes or a glittering jewel. I wondered what he would offer her next. Perhaps his generosity might stretch to a new mare, complete with jewelled bridle and engraved saddle. In any exchange with a man, a clever woman always holds out for as much as she can get and my mother was an exceptionally clever woman – just like the queen.

I passed a wonderful afternoon with my mother and our seamstresses, surrounded by swirls of figured silks, bolts of patterned brocades, velvets of every colour and piles of exotic furs. My stepfather knew about the latest fashions which he'd observed in Flanders during his exile and had ordered the very best of what was available to be brought to Ashby. He had an intimate knowledge of women's clothing and how it should be worn which surprised me but was no surprise to my mother.

'Of course he knows,' she said. 'The Burgundian court is considered the most sophisticated in Europe. You have to remember, Ceci, your stepfather was with the king in Flanders for several months. Naturally there were women who flattered them with their attentions. He will have seen at close quarters the magnificent silks and satins of their gowns, measuring the depths of their necklines with a man's eye.'

I tried to imagine my stepfather in the guise of a master tailor, examining how many layers of clothing a woman might wear, inspecting the cut of each long silken sleeve and appraising the exact shade of blue to match with the dark red of a woman's kirtle. He would have stroked the dark fur linings of each garment, gauging their softness as well as their worth, and naturally he would have scrutinized the black velvet collars and jewels worn by a women at her throat. Being an engaging companion, he could easily have persuaded a woman to raise her veil or allow him to remove the padded roll she wore as part of her headdress, to study exactly how it was contrived. It was no wonder he was so knowledgeable.

2

WESTMINSTER 1474

It was late and I was unable to sleep. I snuggled close to my mother in the bed we shared in my stepfather's London house as she began her story.

'Once upon a time there were two girls, both pretty, both obedient and both blessed with families who loved them. When the two girls reached an age when a young woman should marry, their parents found good men to be their husbands.'

'Were the husbands handsome?' I asked, wanting this story to be a perfect one.

'Would it make any difference?'

'It is said that men who are misshapen reflect the evil in their nature.'

My mother smiled. 'They were not misshapen, of that I can assure you.'

'Good.'

'In due course, God blessed the two young women and their husbands, who were not in the least misshapen, with children. One couple had two sons the other a single beloved daughter.'

I moved closer to my mother's warm body. That was like me: a single beloved daughter. My mother might have other children, but I was the first, the best, my dead father's only child.

'The sun shone, crops in the fields flourished, cattle grew fat and the future looked set fair for our two young couples. Then tragedy struck. War broke out, the families were on opposing sides and both young husbands were killed.'

'Oh no!' I whispered. 'I thought they would live happily ever after.'

'Alas no,' said my mother. 'It is not that kind of story. Now we have two young widows who returned home to their families to grieve. And grieve they did. Many tears were shed because doubtless both young women had truly loved their dead husbands and worried for their fatherless children.'

'What happened to them?'

'The victorious family were favoured, speedily finding a new husband for their young widow: a wealthy lord with excellent prospects who would care for her and her little daughter.'

'It *is* me!' I said, delightedly. 'I am the little daughter. My stepfather is the lord with excellent prospects.'

'If you say so,' said my mother. 'But it never does to be too hasty. What of the widow with two sons? What of her prospects? Her family had been on the losing side in the war so there was no brilliant marriage for her. Was she to spend her days plying her needle, mending other people's sheets?'

'I doubt anyone would marry her.'

'True enough. There were few young men to be found and certainly not one who would marry an impoverished widow with two small sons. But the widow was a clever young woman, some said suspiciously clever. It was not natural for a woman to know things that she knew. She sang a little song to herself, combed her hair and put on a clean gown. Then she took her two boys by the hand and walked to the road which passed near her parents' house and there she waited under a tree. It was Maytime, the sun shone through the leaves making patterns of golden light on the ground and if she listened carefully she could hear the sound of voices singing. But she took no notice. Something told her she must wait. Then, who do you think rode by?'

'A man with a bag of magic beans.'

'No,' laughed my mother. 'Although it might have been better if it was.'

'An evil duke disguised as a miller.'

'No, although disguising is part of every man's nature and this man was no exception.'

'Who rode by?'

'A king. Just imagine! With one snap of her fingers, the young widow had caught a king in her snare. It might just as easily have been a miller or a man with a bag of magic beans. But it wasn't; it was a king.'

'And he fell in love with her.'

'You could say that. Certainly with another snap of her fingers she had a gold ring.'

'He married her?'

'He did.'

'And they lived happily every after.'

'That we do not know. Her story is only half written. Perhaps someday you will help write the other half. Now, close your eyes and go to sleep.'

That night I dreamt of the young woman who'd snapped her fingers and caught a king, imagining who I might catch if I snapped my fingers.

Next day my stepfather sent his barge to bring us to the royal palace at Westminster and for the first time I had sight of the magnificence in which the king and queen and their children lived.

The outer courtyards of the palace were vast. To one side were gardens stretching down to the water's edge, on the other, some ancient stone buildings and an enormous chapel with lancet windows. One of my stepfather's servants accompanied us through into an inner courtyard where men and women could be seen strolling in cloistered walkways. We then passed under a gated arch into a yet smaller courtyard and climbed up a set of wide stone steps. At the top was a doorway, guarded by men dressed in splendid red and white tunics who obligingly stood aside to allow us to enter.

Within the palace everything glittered. Walls were brightly painted with scenes of hunting where horses seemed almost alive and men with hounds strode purposefully through trees in pursuit of a distant white stag. Above our heads soared a dark blue ceiling decorated with silver stars.

I followed in my mother's wake, frightened I might lose her in the jostling crowd. Hundreds of people thronged the hall: servants, guards, clerks garbed in black, a bustling cleric followed by a train of small boys, men resplendent in rich silks with velvet robes lined with fur, and women wearing what I knew must be the latest fashions from Burgundy. It had been a wise move for my stepfather to order us new gowns. It was obvious that if you wanted to be noticed at the king's court, you had to be exquisitely dressed.

As we advanced deeper into the palace, the rooms became more magnificent, the people fewer, until at last we reached a huge double door, painted blue and red and gold and studded with gilded nails. Two tall men in royal livery stood, with halberds crossed, guarding the door. The servant murmured our names and the guards stepped back. Two men appeared from nowhere and threw open the doors to let us pass through.

Inside the room everyone continued their conversations. To my disappointment, they didn't look up to marvel at our arrival, although one man nearest the door treated us to a curious stare.

A large man in a black hat and black silk robe, announced our names: 'Kathryn, Lady Hastings and Cecily, Lady Harington'.

His booming voice caused people to draw back, some craning their necks to see who we were, while one or two women twitched their robes out of our way as we advanced slowly down the length of the royal chamber. First my mother, dressed in deepest crimson silk brocade, her robes sliding easily over the decorated floor tiles; then me, horribly aware that my new satin slippers were pinching my toes. Surely my feet hadn't grown in a week!

I was incredibly nervous, wishing I could reach for my mother's hand. Did the neckline of my new blue gown display too much of my kirtle? Perhaps my mother's maid, in her enthusiasm, had plucked my hairline too far back. Were my sleeves too tight? Too long?

I remembered my mother's instructions: say nothing unless the queen asks you a question. Then you may answer. Remember who you are: you are Cecily, Lady Harington, a great heiress in your own right.

Just at that moment, I did not feel like a great heiress; I felt like little Ceci from the nursery who barely knew how to behave in front of her stepfather's guests.

There was no opportunity to look around as I had to concentrate. Each step must be measured, not too long, not too short. I must not lag behind my mother like a poor relation apologising for my existence, yet not walk so close that I accidently bumped into her; or worse, trod on the hem of her gown. Three steps was the correct distance between us. I must keep my head up and my eyes lowered as it was not acceptable to stare at the king and the queen. When I thought no-one was looking I risked a peep but caught sight of Lady Donne frowning at me and promptly lowered my gaze to my slippers.

My mother had been born to this life. She was the daughter of an earl and knew exactly how to behave, but I, despite my importance, was ignorant. The closest I'd come to meeting truly great people was when I'd attended my stepfather in Calais and I was unsure how many of them were of much importance. It was not as if I'd had an opportunity to meet King Louis or the Duke of Burgundy. Besides, Lady Donne said, protocol in Calais was much less strict than in royal palaces; she feared my stepfather allowed behaviour that was disturbingly lax.

I had wanted to believe the queen was no more good-looking than my mother but I soon realised that was impossible. I'd never before seen a more beautiful woman. She had a heart-shaped face with a pointed chin and a small straight nose. Her skin was luminous with a slight blush on each cheek. Her eyes were slightly tilted but well-spaced with wonderfully arched eyebrows. She had a smooth high forehead and the most delicate ears I'd ever seen on a woman. Reluctantly, I had to admit she was even more beautiful than the painting of Our Lady in the church at Ashby.

If Lady Donne was to be believed, the queen had been picked by the king for her ethereal beauty and ten years of marriage had not diminished her looks by one jot. From where I stood there were no wrinkles or blemishes to be seen let alone a sagging chin or wisp of grey hair. That the king still desired her, Lady Donne had confided to my mother in a conspiratorial whisper, was evidenced by the regular arrival of the queen's babies in the royal nursery. So far there had been six: two princes, three princesses and one poor little mite who had died.

I watched the queen's eyes for some sign of pleasure at our approach but was sadly disappointed. Her face remained serene, without a flicker of a smile, as if her features were carved from alabaster.

As my mother sank to the floor in a swirl of dark crimson, I saw a man sitting beside the queen. He was whispering something in her ear. Mercy! This must be the king! Another glamorous personage: tall, long-legged, broad-shouldered, dressed in white satin and more handsome than any other man in the room. He resembled the brave hero in every book of romances I'd ever read.

The queen murmured a reply, barely moving her red-painted lips. At the sight of my mother, the king sprang up and came striding down the room. I felt my heart thud painfully against my ribs, I'd not expected him to be so familiar. I thought he'd remain on his throne on the dais regarding us with disdain. I'd not imagined him coming so close.

He seized my mother's hand in his, raising her up as if she was a valued friend. For a dreadful minute I thought he would clasp her in his arms.

He stood close, as close as a lover. 'My Lady Hastings. At last!' he breathed.

My mother's voice was cool, almost distant, certainly not that of a woman greeting a lover. 'Indeed, your grace. It has been a long time.'

The king's mouth was close to her ear, so close that none of the other people in the room could hear what he was saying; but I was only a step behind my mother's skirts and could hear every word.

'Far too long, my Kathryn. I have missed you,' he murmured in a low cozening voice.

I was no fool. This was the king, a man anointed by God to command, to rule, to order; to be set above us mere mortals; this was not a man to stand as close to my mother as my stepfather would, or say words like those my stepfather used when he wanted my mother to oblige him. If this was how the king spoke to my mother, how might he speak to me!

I gulped, more worried than ever about the depth of my neckline which in spite of the white satin partlet revealed too much of my skin for my liking.

My mother's voice remained steady although she must have felt awkward at having the king speak to her so intimately, and in public. Even my stepfather waited until he and my mother were in our private rooms before using endearments.

'I am certain your grace has been far too busy to consider my welfare,' she said.

I watched as his mouth curved in an engaging smile. 'Ah, Kathryn, you know that is not true. Your welfare has ever been close to my heart.'

'I am honoured, your grace.'

His voice dropped lower still. 'Do you not still think of me?'

I was bewildered. I understood that men used the conventions of courtly love to declare an interest in a young woman, writing verses in praise of her lips or her eyes in the hope of gaining her favour; but this was the king declaring an interest in my mother. However, I was not a child and recognised a man bent on flirtation when I saw one.

'At Ashby, we pray daily for the continued good health of your grace and of her grace, the queen,' my mother replied.

The king's eyes danced mischievously. 'As do all my subjects. But you must know the prayers of some are more welcome than others. Yours, in particular, I treasure.'

My mother bowed her head and calmly withdrew her hands, declaring as clearly as if she had used actual words that a flirtation with the king was not something she would allow. I thought her incredibly brave. Or incredibly foolish. I was unsure which.

Stepping lightly to one side, she said, 'Your grace, may I present my daughter, Cecily, Lady Harington.'

My great moment had arrived. I lowered myself into a curtsey in front of the king, hoping I would not disgrace myself. As instructed, I kept my gaze on the floor. Through my lowered lashes I could see a pair of soft, white leather boots with sparkling silver buckles and, above them, the royal hand bidding me rise.

'As pretty as her mother.'

I blushed at the compliment.

'A dutiful daughter,' my mother remarked in a voice which did not invite further compliments.

'A dutiful subject, I hope.'

'Would any of our family be anything else, your grace?'

'You were not always so obliging, as I recall,' he murmured, smiling into my mother's eyes and ignoring me.

'In those days I did not have a husband to remind me of my duty,' replied my mother stiffly.

'What does your duty tell you now?'

My mother hesitated. 'That whether I like it or not, a king's desires are paramount.'

The king ceased smiling but his eyes were still warm. 'Kathryn, this is a favour. You must know I'd not force you to something which would not be of benefit.'

'Do I?'

'Your daughter will gain by this.'

I pricked up my ears. This favour was something to do with me.

'So Lord Hastings tells me,' my mother replied in the same measured tone of voice.

'I'm sure William has explained the advantages of our arrangement?'

My mother seemed to have forgotten royal protocol, looking straight into the king's eyes. 'Advantages to whom, your grace? It appears to me there is little of benefit to my daughter or to me or to Lord Hastings in this arrangement.'

The king gave an uncomfortable laugh. What my mother had said was not to his liking. I wondered how she dared question the king's motives.

'Come Kathryn, most people would disagree. She will be welcomed as a valued member of the queen's family.'

'Oh, I am certain she will. I have been assured by Lord Hastings that her grace will treat my daughter most kindly.'

To my annoyance, mention of the queen must have reminded the king that a private whispered conversation with my mother in front of the whole court would not be approved of by his wife. All of a sudden he turned and in a hearty voice proceeded to introduce my mother and me to the queen. Now I would have to wait to find out what this arrangement was and how it concerned me.

The ethereal beauty on her elegant throne barely moved a muscle as my mother and I lowered ourselves down to the floor. As I rose she gave me an appraising look out of a pair of limpid brown eyes and honoured me with an almost imperceptible nod. This was to be my welcome to her world.

I had no real understanding of this woman. Who was she, this perfect alabaster beauty who had asked to see me? All I knew came from snippets of overheard kitchen gossip and snatches of grown-ups' conversations.

If Cousin Isabel was to be believed, the queen was a witch, born from a long line of witches, a scheming enchantress with fingers dipped in her enemies' blood; a woman to be feared.

My mother's friends were mostly careful about voicing their thoughts, as people had learned to be these past few years, but there'd been one hard-faced dowager determined to have her say. "Those Woodvilles are an unscrupulous family," she'd declared. "Always were. Saw an opportunity to enrich themselves and grabbed it. Used their daughter to lure a love-struck young man into matrimony."

But to the village girls at Ashby she was Dame Elizabeth Grey, a poor young thing, grieving in her widowhood, who'd been smiled upon by a king? "Like a miracle, 'twere," they said. "Could even 'appen to you, Lady Cecily."

According to Isabel, a rumour running round the courts of Europe said the widow had pulled a dagger on the king to protect her virtue, and he, unwilling to lose the prize slipping from his grasp, had carelessly promised marriage. The king of England trapped by his own lust, and by a commoner. It was a great joke.

But as to who she really was? The answer was as opaque as ever. Her beauty was not fashioned from alabaster as I'd first thought but was a very human beauty; one framed by a veil of fine white gauze, so delicate as to be almost transparent. Beneath her gown of dark green velvet, her small breasts rose and fell as she breathed, gently disturbing the heavy gold collar at her throat and the gold embroidered revers of the gown sliding over her shoulders. Her headdress, worn fashionably far back, exposed a broad forehead with her hair, a mere mist of gilded threads, shimmering from gold to brown to tawny red, as the candlelight flickered.

Here, in her private room, the queen was surrounded by her ladies. These were high-born women, chosen to serve and keep her company. I knew from Lady Donne that the faces in the room would constantly change, each woman also having duties to husband, home and children. Isabel said there'd been a mad scramble for places. Despite what everyone thought of the witch herself, serving a queen was considered an honour and everyone wanted to be close to the king.

The women were beautifully gowned, mostly in muted greys or blues; rich cloth, exquisitely embroidered, but not so grand as to rival the queen. Other than Lady Donne, I recognised no-one. For a while the queen made polite conversation with my mother but, judging from their unsmiling expressions, the exchange was chilly. Then with an expertise born of practice, she waved her fingers, murmured a few words, and suddenly she and I were alone. With a lurch of panic I saw my mother disappear with Lady Donne. I had been abandoned!

"Say nothing unless you are spoken to," my mother had instructed.

"Say nothing, her grace will lead the conversation," Lady Donne had advised.

"Say nothing," Isabel had warned. "It is wiser."

Panic ran through every part of my body as I wondered what I should do.

'Lady Donne tells me you paid a visit to our outpost at Calais across the sea.'

The slight inflection and expectant pause told me I should make a reply.

'Yes, your grace.'

'Did you enjoy the experience?' The queen's voice was surprisingly low-pitched for a woman.

Meg Zouche once told me that men admire women who speak in low, rich tones. At the time she'd been practising to make her voice sound resonant and compelling but had merely succeeded in producing deep rumbling growls.

'Very much, your grace,' I said, trying to imitate the way she spoke. 'Lord Hastings ensured we had a merry time.'

The royal nose gave an elegant sniff. 'I had forgot Lord Hastings commands the garrison. There was a time when Calais was in the care of my brother, Earl Rivers. But of course, times change and not always for the better. However Earl Rivers now has a far greater responsibility than the command of a town full of cloth merchants and unruly soldiers.'

Another pause. I'd heard of Anthony Woodville, Earl Rivers, the queen's eldest brother, a man of letters and a great jouster. Cousin Isabel said he wore a hair shirt beneath his robes in penance for having a witch as a sister. My mother said he was a contradictory man. My stepfather, oddly, was silent on the subject of Anthony Woodville.

'Earl Rivers must be very clever,' I said in what I thought a triumph of diplomacy.

The queen's eyebrows lifted slightly. 'Naturally he is clever. My father wished all his sons to have the best available education.'

"Do not mention the queen's father," my mother had advised without further explanation.

Lady Donne had been more forthcoming. "Your Uncle Warwick had the queen's father executed. Be careful what you say."

Cousin Isabel had said darkly, "Blood has been spilled. One day she will seek revenge."

I swallowed hard and said nothing.

The queen gave a smug maternal smile. 'My son, the little Prince of Wales, lives at Ludlow in the Welsh marches. Earl Rivers has the position of governor there. It is a great honour to manage the education of the heir to the throne but of course my brother is eminently suited to such a task. His grace, the king, knows, as do I, that our son could not be in better hands.'

So, Earl River's hands were deemed more capable than my stepfather's, and the queen did not approve of the removal of Calais from her brother's remit. That much was clear.

Thoughts of her brother clearly warmed the queen's mood because she smiled at me. 'You are nearly fourteen, Lady Harington. Do you hope for a husband soon?'

I blushed. 'My stepfather has said he will find me a suitable marriage, your grace.'

Her eyes changed colour. It was most odd. One moment they were the colour of soft warm fur, next that of rain-washed cowhide in the killing ground at Ashby.

'I am sure Lord Hastings is adept at making advantageous bargains for his family,' she said crisply. 'But a man cannot always have what he wants, can he?'

'No, your grace.'

'He has not told you of his intentions?'

'No, your grace. But I believe he has discussed them with my mother.'

'Does your mother approve his plans?'

'My mother always does as my stepfather bids.'

'As a wife should and we know Lord Hastings is a remarkably persuasive man. The king finds himself quite unwilling to part with him. I'm surprised your mother does not follow Lord Hastings to court.'

'My mother has duties, your grace.'

'As do we all.'

Having disposed of my marriage prospects, the queen turned to my family. How often did I see my cousins and were we close? What of my aunt, Lady Fitzhugh? Had I heard aught of the poor Countess of Oxford in sanctuary in St Martins? As my kin were all from my mother's side of my family, they were Nevills by birth. Being queen gave her licence to probe into these private matters but I found her questions frightening. Why did she want to know?

"She will discover everything about you; then she'll have you in her power," Isabel had warned.

After a few more minutes of difficult conversation where the queen asked about my devotions and my schooling, the ordeal came to an end. I heard the patter of feet and the sound of childish laughter as the women returned, bringing with them two small girls. They were about the age of Mary Hungerford, not long out of the nursery, both fair haired, both pretty and wearing identical white silk gowns. They must be two of the royal princesses.

At the sight of her daughters, the queen's face broke into a genuine smile, the smile of a mother pleased to see her children. The girls bobbed a curtsey to their mother and settled themselves happily on cushions at her feet. After a while one of the women produced a lute and proceeded to play a tune while the little princesses danced for us. The elder, Princess Elizabeth, danced elegantly, like the ladies I'd seen perform the baasedance in Calais.

When the dance was finished and we had applauded, she whispered something to her mother.

'If you like,' said the queen.

The child came and asked if I would care to dance with her.

If her mother was distant and reserved, Elizabeth was nothing but open and friendly. She tilted her head slightly to one side and smiled sweetly.

'Thank you, I should be delighted,' I said, smiling back.

Perhaps it was the dancing, or the little princesses, or simply the passing of time, but when I returned to my seat, breathless and flushed from my exertions, the ice between the queen and my mother had begun to melt.

A little later the king came in with several men, some young, some old. Judging from the ease with which the queen's women treated the invaders, smiling and teasing the younger men, I assumed this was a regular occurrence. The king called for livelier music and proceeded to romp around the floor with his daughters, making everyone laugh including the queen.

When the dancing was finished, the king ruffled the hair of the two young princesses, then came and sat beside the queen. He smiled at her. An uxorious husband, I thought. As Lady Donne had said, he still loved his wife.

'Making friends?' he enquired.

'Lady Harington has been telling me how Lord Hastings is finding her a husband. Did you know that?'

The king gave the queen a bland smile and said smoothly, 'As you know, my dearest, William tells me everything.'

'I thought it was arranged.'

'It is. Do not fret.'

'Good,' she said, smiling at him.

A damp April dusk was falling as we travelled back to my stepfather's house. The tide had turned so the river was running out towards the sea as if there was no time to lose. It must be odd to live on a river that ebbed and flowed like this, with vast expanses of stinking mud one moment, water lapping greedily at your walls the next. Our rivers at home flowed in the same fashion all the time, not rising and falling like the Thames.

My mother sat with her gloved hands tucked inside her cloak, warmed against the evening chill. She stared silently out over the water.

'The king was very merry,' I ventured at last.

'The king is always merry.'

'I thought he would be terrifying.'

My mother paused as if remembering a time when she'd known the man who was now king, when they'd been young cousins playing together. She rarely mentioned their kinship or the days when she was a girl in Yorkshire.

'Your stepfather says he has a temper but he is mostly good-natured; men like him for it.'

'And women?'

My mother laughed. 'I doubt there is a woman in London he's not kissed.'

'Do they like that?'

'They do. Whether their husbands approve is another matter.'

I thought my stepfather was a man who might well not approve.

'Why did the queen wish to see me?'

My mother regarded me seriously. 'Do you not know?'

I shook my head. 'No. She asked me questions but that was all.'

There was a slight pause before she said in the lightest of voices, 'She wants you as her daughter-in-law.'

I stared with my mouth open.

'Her daughter-in-law?'

'Yes. She wishes to marry you to her son.'

I thought of the queen's children: three young princesses and two even younger princes. My heart leapt at an impossible thought.

'He is only four years old!'

My mother gave a short laugh. 'Do not imagine she wants you for one of her darling princes. No; you have been chosen for Thomas Grey, a son of her first marriage.'

'But my stepfather said …'

'It matters not what your stepfather said. He and I did not want this for you but it seems our wishes count for nothing. The king has decided to give the queen what *she* wants and what she wants is you.'

But why me? And who is this Thomas Grey?'

'I told you, he is a son of her first marriage. His father was a Grey of Groby, a Lancastrian family.'

'Is it a good marriage?'

My mother shrugged. 'The young man himself is nothing, the father was nothing. But when your mother becomes Queen of England you are transformed overnight from dross into precious metal.'

This could not be. As a child I'd been told I was a prize to be won, that men would flock to ask for my hand for their sons. Had not my stepfather turned down the Earl of Pembroke himself as not being noble enough. I'd expected a duke not a young man whose father was nothing.

'Why me?'

'Can you not guess?'

My thoughts skittered around all over the place causing my belly to flutter and my heart beat faster. Of course I knew why. It was obvious. There was only one reason why the queen, who had never so much as set eyes on me before, would want Lady Harington.

'It is because of Shute.'

'Yes,' my mother said levelly. 'It is because of Shute.'

3

ASHBY 1474

From the time I was a little girl I knew that what made me special was my inheritance. "The richest heiress in all England," my stepfather used to say approvingly as if I had done something clever to deserve such wealth. My mother would sit me on her knee and tell me stories of Shute, the manor house where she'd lived with my father and where I'd been born. Of course there was much more to my inheritance than this one little manor house in Devonshire but it was Shute, set amidst the valleys and hills of the South West, which captured my childish imagination.

Six months after I was born, my father, my grandfather and my great-grandfather were killed fighting for the York king. Their deaths meant that the whole of the immense Bonville and Harington inheritance fell into my lap. Although I'd seen none of them, I knew I owned valuable properties all over Dorsetshire, Devonshire, Cornwall and Somersetshire as well as several in Yorkshire and Lancashire and Cumberland. To add to my worth, I had inherited my father's title. I was Lady Harington in my own right. A man would have to go far before he would find a marriage prize as valuable as me.

I had been so busy concentrating on my own desirability I'd given little thought to the man I would marry. I had believed my visit to Calais was to show me to a son of the Burgundian ruling House but it turned out the duke had no sons, only a single daughter who would inherit the duchy. Our king had given his sister to Duke Charles, hoping the duke's third marriage would produce a son, another link in the chain to encircle France, but everyone had been disappointed.

'Barren,' Lady Donne had whispered, condemning the new Duchess of Burgundy to the slaughter ground like a cow that had failed to breed.

I'd dismissed the possibility of a French marriage. Their king was fabulously wealthy and had a son, but France was our enemy and Louis a duplicitous villain. Besides, what woman would wish to marry a man hostile to our good friend, the Duke of Burgundy, prince or no.

'Lady Harington.'

The voice was unmistakably that of William Catesby, still wearing the same dusty black garments but with an elegant velvet cap which I did not recall from our last meeting. He was standing in the shadows by the Ashby chapel. I had the distinct feeling he'd been waiting for me. He bowed politely, removing his cap.

I hesitated, wondering what it was that he wanted.

'Master Catesby.'

He gave a small smile. 'May I offer congratulations, my lady.'

Naturally he knew about my marriage to this Thomas Grey person. He'd probably read letters relating to my stepfather's wardship powers and overheard private wrangling between the queen and my stepfather over the price. I would have liked to know how much she was paying for me.

'I thank you, Master Catesby.'

'A good marriage.'

The very slight uplift at the end of his remark in what was otherwise his usual monotonous tone made me wonder if this was a statement of fact or a question. Was he asking if I was pleased with this marriage.

'I shall be the queen's daughter-in-law.'

'You will indeed.'

'With access to the queen's family.'

'That is true.'

'A young woman who will be able to bring certain matters to the attention of the king if she should so wish.'

Master Catesby smiled at my display of self-importance.

'That would certainly be of great value to any man.'

'A young woman who could, if she chose, become a most useful patron.'

'And friend.'

'Are you proposing we should be friends, Master Catesby?'

His smile thinned. 'My lady, I would not be so presumptuous. The young man is already an earl; you will be a countess and far above me. But I believe we might, in time, perhaps be of use to one another.'

'You do?'

'May I give you some advice, my lady?'

I was curious to know what sort of advice Master Catesby thought he could offer.

'If you wish.'

'In the courts of kings, people rarely speak truth to power. It is far too dangerous. You will hear men say words presented as truths which are lies. Women dissemble, smiling as they plot the advance of their husbands or sons at another's expense. The past is only a small step away and grudges have spent a long time brewing.'

'Very interesting, Master Catesby, but what does that have to do with me?'

'I would urge you to be careful. Trust no-one. Guard your tongue.'

'You make it sound as if I am walking into a bear pit.'

'The bears will come disguised as lambs. Not even the cleverest of women will be able to tell the difference.'

I laughed at the picture he painted: a bear pit full of lambs, claws sheathed, sharp teeth hidden, no-one being any the wiser, not even the dogs.

'That is very amusing, Master Catesby but I must bid you farewell. I have urgent business with my mother.'

He gave another of his little bows. 'I wish you good fortune in your new life, Lady Harington. My wife sends her greetings.'

I nodded. 'Please give Meg my greetings. Tell her I hope to see her once I am married.'

I took two steps, then turned back. He was still standing there, staring in my direction.

'Master Catesby!'

'Yes, my lady?'

'What do you know of my betrothed?'

He smiled as if he had just won a wager. Perhaps he knew I would ask. After all, who else was there who would tell me the truth.

'I regret I am unable to tell you what the young man is like now. All I know of Thomas Grey is that some ten years ago his grandmother tried to deprive him of his rightful inheritance.'

'His grandmother!'

'Lady Ferrers of Groby.'

Groby was close to our summer house at Kirby Muxloe but we had little commerce with our neighbours.

'How do you know?'

'Letters, agreements, business arrangements written down and later forgotten. We lawyers have access to a great deal of information if we care to look diligently, and as I told you before, knowledge has value.'

'What happened?'

'The boy's mother wanted to petition the king but had no means of access.'

'That is ridiculous; she was the queen.'

'Not then. At the time she was a widow, a Lancastrian widow at that, plain Dame Elizabeth Grey.'

'Then the king saw her and made her his wife.'

'No. She approached her neighbour, Lord Hastings, your stepfather, and begged for his help.'

'And *he* brought her problem to the king's attention.'

'No, it did not happen like that.' He paused, waiting to see if I was clever enough to understand the course of events. I thought of how my stepfather did business, the favours he got for people, the positions, the privileges, and how they rewarded him.

'What did he ask in return for his help?'

Master Catesby smiled approvingly. 'Somewhat more than Dame Elizabeth was expecting. A share in the rents and profits of the lands recovered until the boy was twelve years old and a marriage between the boy and a daughter of his.'

'Me?'

'Oh no, Lady Harington. You were far too valuable a prize for Lord Hastings to waste on a son of Dame Elizabeth Grey.'

I thought of the queen's apparent dislike of my stepfather and wondered if this was the cause: a hard bargain when perhaps she had expected a little kindness.

'How soon afterwards did she marry the king?'

Master Catesby looked at me as a tutor might gaze on a particularly apt pupil. 'A month or possibly less. It is said, and I have no reason to believe it is not true, that theirs was a Mayday marriage.'

'What happened to her arrangement with Lord Hastings?'

He spread his hands wide. 'Gone with the wind. When a woman becomes your queen, a wise man forgets any claims he has on her, particularly if a degree of coercion was involved in the bargaining.'

'And now I am to marry her son.'

'A clever woman's idea of justice, do you not think.'

Not knowing what to think about a queen's justice was perhaps natural; I was after all only fourteen years old. But I'd been raised to know my position and knew exactly what to say to a man like William Catesby. He believed I was being used by the queen as a tool of retribution against my stepfather, whereas I knew better.

'I have been assured her grace will treat me like a daughter, Master Catesby. Why should she not? I have been chosen. I am not some idle piece of flotsam plucked from the waters to benefit the queen's son; I am Lady Harington, a great heiress, a young woman deserving of every honour to be heaped upon her shoulders. If I am a countess this year, then that is only the beginning. With me to advise him, my husband cannot fail to prosper.'

He smiled, bowing his head in acknowledgment, his shadow on the grass shortening as if in recognition of my superiority.

'I beg your forgiveness if I have offended you, Lady Harington. I merely wished, as a friend you understand, to give you some advice. I would urge you to watch your step. There are many things you do not know.' His voice was oily with a sly knowingness but I took no notice. I stuck my chin in the air. This man was no friend of mine. A lawyer would always be a servant, and I was used to dealing with servants.

'I am well informed, Master Catesby. Have no fear. I know exactly where to tread.'

I turned around, and set off in the direction of the parlour, my head held high and my gown swirling about my legs like a ship's sail billowing confidently in the wind.

4

WESTMINSTER 1474

I wore red on my wedding day, that rich deep crimson favoured by women who can afford the extravagance. My gown was stitched from a dozen ells of Florentine figured silk, imported from Calais by my stepfather. The sleeves were tight, the gold embroidered band beneath my breasts, even tighter. In accordance with the latest Burgundian fashion, the neckline displayed a teasing glimpse of my black silk kirtle while at collar, cuff and hem I wore *gris,* the blue-tinged winter-harvested fur of the northern squirrel, highly prized and extremely costly. My hair lay combed out across my shoulders as befitted a bride and the only jewel I wore was my mother's gold and ruby ring, a wedding gift to a beloved daughter.

'It was given to my great-grandmother by the princess who was a granddaughter of the first Edward. Your grandmother said the ring once belonged to his queen, the Lady Marguerite, but where it came from before that, nobody knows.'

My mother seemed sad so I kissed her and said I would remember her in my prayers.

'Make sure you do, my daughter. And remember the lessons you have been taught. Be kind to your husband, be loyal, but most of all, be obedient and do your duty as a wife.'

To my satisfaction, my cousin Isabel was there to see my triumph. Isabel was married to the king's brother George, Duke of Clarence, the brother who'd joined my Uncle Warwick in rebellion but had quickly changed his mind. "Smart move," John Zouche had said. "Saw which way the wind was blowing and jumped ship like a rat before the vessel sank."

George was a short man, no taller than his wife; brown-haired, with a discontented face and none of the easy charm of his brother. I would have pitied Isabel but she was as prickly as a thorn bush. She was older than me and having once had her husband branded a traitor made her overly snappy.

'Goodness, Cousin Ceci,' she said as she helped prepare me for my entrance. 'Lady Harington today, Countess of Huntingdon tomorrow. Where will it end?'

'Duchess?' I said smiling.

Obviously the wrong thing to have said as Isabel glared at me. 'The king will never give that woman's son a dukedom. Dukes are of the blood royal. They don't crawl out of some village manor's privy pit.'

My prospective husband's lack of noble pedigree was a distinct blot on the page of my contentment. The details had been impressed on me by my mother who, as the daughter of an earl, knew everyone's origins. Thomas Grey's paternal grandfather had been a Grey of Ruthin, the grandmother, Baroness Ferrers of Groby. Nothing there to warrant the grandson being made an earl. His mother, the queen, was born plain Elizabeth Woodville, daughter of an obscure squire whose marriage to the Duke of Bedford's widow, Jacquetta, had brought him to the attention of mad King Henry.

'What you must never forget,' my mother had said, 'is that Jacquetta Woodville, came from a long line of women born with silvery scales. She was part woman, part serpent, a descendant of Melusina, the river fairy. Your Uncle Warwick tried to have her burned as a witch. He believed her a dangerous woman. What none of us know is how much of her learning she passed to her daughter and how much of a threat that daughter is to anyone who opposes her.'

So the widowed Dame Elizabeth Grey might, beneath that fabled beauty, have charms denied to mere mortal women. If she had not stood under that tree on the road to Northampton one springtime morning ten years ago, the king would never have seen her and made his wife. A turn of Dame Fortune's wheel or a calculated enchantment? Whichever it was, it meant the son was marrying me, the greatest heiress in the land. I looked down at my slippers, crimson and gold to match my gown: crimson the colour of pigeon's blood dripping onto the floor, gold the colour of the king's personal emblem the sun in splendour, and nowhere the silvery flick of a serpent's tail disappearing into the water.

'You're younger than I expected,' my husband said bluntly.

We'd been put to bed like a pair of small children, in a bed the size of a battlefield. I eyed him nervously, unsure what to make of this half-naked intruder in my bed.

'I am fourteen.'

'A young fourteen. I'd imagined you older, more ...' He let his eyes roam over my body in a way that in any man other than a husband would have been wholly inappropriate. '…more shapely.'

I remembered Master Catesby's advice and bit back the retort which sprang to my lips, knowing that a good wife suffered in silence no matter what a husband might say or do. This husband looked amenable but I was piqued he'd not bothered to interest himself in the young woman he was to marry. It was not as if *I* was the nobody. *And* I knew a great deal about him.

In the weeks since I'd discovered the identity of the man I was to marry, I had made it my business to listen and learn.

'There are women,' Lady Donne had whispered to my mother, unaware that I was sitting quietly in the window embrasure.

'He is a young man,' my mother had remarked, peaceably.

''Indeed, indeed! Nobody minds a carefully managed encounter if a man cannot be chaste. But so many!'

'Exaggeration, for sure.'

Lady Donne's voice lowered to the point where I could barely hear what was being said. ' …a young woman for his private use … a house in Clerkenwell.'

My mother had tutted. 'Not what we want, not in the early days. Best let them get acquainted. I'll ask William to see if she can be paid off.'

Lady Donne had nodded her head.

So this husband of mine was experienced with women, unsurprising with a mother prepared to importune herself at the roadside like a common whore.

My initial impression had been of a tall man with dark brown hair, a pleasant face and intimidating shoulders who looked nothing like his mother yet now, sitting so close together, I realised that his eyes had the same uncanny knack of changing colour.

'You seem a pretty little thing,' he said pleasantly. 'I expect we shall do well together. What do they call you?'

'Cecily, my lord.'

'Ha! Like the old Duchess of York. You've met her?'

'No, my lord. I have not.'

Duchess Cecily was the king's mother, a York to the tips of her fingers. Isabel said she'd been outraged at her son's foolishness in marrying the Grey widow and refused to attend her daughter-in-law's coronation.

'You should not call me "my lord" when we are being private, you may call me Thomas.'

'Yes, Thomas.'

The servants had left a jug of wine and two cups for my husband's use. He climbed out of bed and poured himself a cup.

'Wine?'

I shook my head. 'I thank you, no.'

He seemed surprised at my refusal. 'My mother thinks wine best for a young bride on her wedding night,' he said pouring another cup and holding it out to me.

So I was to be under the queen's command even here in our marriage bed. Not content with taking my inheritance, she wished to make me her puppet. I took the cup and raised it to my lips, wondering if she'd done this to the first one.

My husband looked pleased at having an obedient wife.

'Is it true you had another wife?' I asked, feigning innocence.

'Yes, it is true. Why do you ask?' he said climbing back into bed.

'Is she dead?'

'Yes, of course she is dead. I'd hardly be marrying you if she was still alive.'

'Did your family have her killed so you could marry me?'

He spluttered into his wine and nearly dropped the cup.

'Good God! How dare you make such a foul accusation!' His cheeks turned a blotchy red with fury and for a moment I thought he would strike me but he must have thought better of a show of violence on our wedding night. 'She died of a fever,' he said slowly.

'That must have made you sad. Was she very old?'

'She was a child. Younger than you, barely twelve.'

I waited to see if he would tell me that they had not lived openly together as man and wife but he said nothing. Perhaps he had looked upon her as a man might regard a purse full of gold, an entry in his accounts ledger, nothing more. Losing a fortune would make a man angry, not sad. I wondered, had he been angry?

'Was she an heiress?'

'Yes and a more valuable one than you, madam.'

I knew all about Thomas Grey's marriage to the Duke of Exeter's daughter and the fortune he'd hoped to acquire. My stepfather had told me. I also knew, through the good offices of Master Catesby, how the queen had secured my lands for her family no matter what might happen to me in the future, even if I should die. "A clever woman is never caught out twice," he had murmured softly, explaining how the legal complexities might have been arranged.

You'd have thought the whole court had got married there were so many jousts and feasts and entertainments next day. Everybody stared at me, all wanting to know about the wedding night. I heard whispered stories of one girl who'd fled the marriage bed in horror at the sight of a naked husband and of another so besotted after one night's enjoyment, she'd been driven mad when her loved one abandoned her.

The queen was especially gracious, asking was I comfortable, was I hungry, would I perhaps prefer to sit closer to her. It was all very pleasing. My husband acquitted himself well in the joust, though not as well as his uncle, Lord Rivers, who received the victor's purse from the queen and a garland of flowers from me.

My mother, for once present at a court event, asked tentatively if I was well.

'Perfectly,' I said with a smile.

'Was he …?'

'Yes.'

'He didn't …?'

'No, her didn't.'

With a nervous kiss she moved away, anxious yet reassured. Cousin Isabel wafted by in a green silk gown which did nothing for her complexion. 'Did he?' she murmured.

'Oh yes,' I said, with a smile as secretive as hers.

'He was very drunk.'

'Did you think so?'

'Yes. Even George remarked on it.'

George, I'd heard, was a sot, seldom completely sober, prone to muttering treasons under his breath and bewailing how his brother, Richard, had stolen half his wife's fortune.

The only woman who had the courtesy not to enquire as to my health or my wellbeing was Lady Donne. It was as if she knew so had no need to ask.

'Don't be afraid,' my husband had said. 'I'll not hurt you.'

It was a lie. He did hurt me though not very much and afterwards he held me in his arms which, in a way, was kind.

'Is that it?' I said when he finally finished his assault.

He lay back, breathing heavily as if he'd just run up a flight of stairs. 'Yes. I don't suppose you enjoyed it. Wives mostly don't.'

The following nights were an improvement on the first. He was less impatient, I was more obliging and was beginning to see there might be possibilities in having a husband. Not only was his body long and lean and his skin firm to my touch but I enjoyed the warmth of him and the male smell of soap and fresh linen which reminded me of my stepfather. I liked the way he kissed me, firmly on my mouth but not too roughly, the taste of wine mellow on his lips. The first time I kissed him back he seemed surprised as if a hint of desire on the part of a wife was not what he expected. He moved his face away and looked down at me. I smiled sweetly. This would be easy, I thought. I was beginning to get the measure of him.

He will lead and you must follow, I'd been taught. A wife's duty is to obey her husband's commands.

If we were to be a pair of oxen yoked to the plough it would be considerably more comfortable if we both pulled in the same direction. As I gazed at him, his face relaxed in sleep, his breathing slow and steady, I knew we would have a good marriage. I would make certain of that. But it would have nothing to do with my dutifully following three steps behind him. If we were to progress he would have to do what *I* wanted. My task was to ensure that he would want it too.

We had been married four weeks when the vomiting began, an inconvenience, but one I should have expected as my husband's attentions had been not only punctilious but enthusiastic. I told no-one and swore my maid to secrecy.

'Have you spoken to my mother?' enquired my husband one evening after enjoying himself in our bed, the one place I was content to let him lead. Why would I use whore's tricks to keep him amused? I was not like the woman he had kept at Clerkenwell who was doubtless obliged to earn her keep? I was his wife.

As a wife I knew he found me an ideal companion: always available, always amenable, always desirable. The kind of wife any man would want. As for me, those four weeks were long enough for wifely duty to become an increasing pleasure. But I was not about to tell him so and doubted he noticed as he concentrated on his own gratification. I was no lovesick fool and could ill afford to lose my heart to a husband. That would have been extremely unwise. Husbands could not be relied on. Fickle, faithless and foolish, the old women at Ashby used to say; "Best used for breeding like the village bull," they'd cackle, with a sideways glance at the handsome brawny blacksmith.

'I speak to your mother every day,' I said innocently, wondering could he count.

He hesitated. He was unsure and I was not about to tell him, not until I'd decided if some advantage could be gained by remaining silent. He frowned, unwilling to pry further into the ultimate mystery of a woman's body. He chewed his lip, wondering how to ask and yet not ask.

'You know the king is taking us to war?' he said eventually. 'Each man will want to be sure of an heir before risking his life in battle.'

I opened my eyes wider, ignoring the flutter of panic in my belly at the thought of my husband dead on a battlefield, inching closer until my legs touched his, my satin ribbons teasing the skin on his bare shoulder. I laid my fingers on his chest.

'If anything should happen to you, your mother will marry me to your brother. She will say ours was not a true marriage, she will swear you left me untouched.'

My mother had told me of the arrangement insisted on by the queen at the time of our betrothal, a sly deal so that my inheritance would not slip out of her hands. The decision was considered of such importance that parliament had to agree. So there it was, written in black ink in the hand of a clerk in parliament that if the Lord Thomas Grey were to decease before the marriage was consummated, Cecily, Lady Harington would marry Richard Grey, his brother.

'I shall not die,' he said with all the bravado of a young man whose experience of battle was negligible but thought he knew everything about war.

'Are we to fight the French?'

We were but I thought I'd allow him the pleasure of telling me.

'Of course we are to fight the French.'

'Is that wise?'

'Not only wise but necessary. We own France. The king says we must take back what is ours.'

I knew more than my husband about the king's long march towards war. For three years my stepfather had been forging alliances for the English king with Burgundy and Brittany; three years in which archers had been promised and territory demanded as the price of agreeing to fight against King Louis. I'd heard my stepfather tell my mother how the Duke of Brittany had hesitated, frightened of the French king's huge armies; the Duke of Burgundy had vacillated, resenting every one of our king's demands; and the English parliament, as always, had complained about the amount of taxation.

'Your half-sister's betrothal brings the king an advantage,' I remarked, remembering the previous day's discussion in the queen's rooms.

The contract of betrothal with the king's little daughter and the Scotch king's son had been signed. There would be peace between England and Scotland for a lifetime and when the children were older, a marriage. The king would no longer need to look over his shoulder each time he wished to wage war in France.

Thomas seemed surprised at the news. He paid little or no attention to what happened in the king's council or in the chambers at court. He was idle and pleasure-loving, an easy man to live with but not one to trust in a crisis. He had lived through the dangerous years when my

Uncle Warwick had rebelled yet seemed to have learned little. If he was to become as important to the king as his uncle, Earl Rivers, I would have to teach him how to gain influence. Since childhood I had watched my stepfather and knew plenty about attracting men to your side.

The following night, to divert my husband from further questioning about the state of my health, I asked how the king intended to pay for his war.

'The king's revenue is not your concern,' he said, trying to burrow his way under the folds of my nightgown.

'Lord Hastings says wars are ruinously expensive.'

'I choose not to listen to Lord Hastings. Ah!' His initial reconnoitring had paid dividends. 'By Christ!' he whispered, his voice thickening with desire.

To please him, I wriggled a little, showing just how much more exciting our encounter might be if he chose to venture further. Which he did. The result of his success amidst the profusion of my Florentine silk led to a lengthy pause in our conversation.

'My lord,' I murmured, once he lay panting, collapsed at my side.

'Mmm.'

'What if the king does not have sufficient for his war?'

He lay back against the pillows, content, and told me of the king's novel way to raise money. 'He inveigles money from the rich. He plucks their feathers, yet they do not squawk.'

'How so?'

'A Suffolk widow gave him ten pounds, then doubled her contribution when he kissed her.'

'For shame!'

'Would you not double your stake for a kiss?' he enquired, smiling.

'From you, my lord, for sure,' I said, blushing prettily.

'Not from your king?'

'I would not know where else his lips had been.'

He roared with laughter and said what a clever little thing I was and how wise he'd been to marry me.

It had not taken much cleverness to know that the king was a philanderer, a man who pursued his pleasures wherever and whenever the fancy took him. There was a small child in the palace, the servants called "the lord bastard". I'd seen him once with a servant woman, a small boy dressed in black velvet. Nobody mentioned him and soon after I arrived at court, he disappeared.

The king's roving eye was known to everyone in the queen's chamber but the queen, wishing to uphold the reputation of the family she'd done so much to acquire, would allow no hint of scandal to seep out. The king regularly visited her bed, as Lady Donne had said, however people speculated on what other beds he also visited.

Discretion was required from us all, yet the court leaked like a sieve. Kitchen boys laid bets on who would be the king's next conquest while gentlemen's sons who served at table sold their stories of roistering in the city stews to the highest bidder. So much lewd talk was bandied around it was hard to know what was true and what was invention.

'My son informs me you have been unwell,' the queen said as we played ninepins in the long gallery one afternoon.

'A little discomfort, your grace,' I said, taking careful aim, wondering had my maid disobeyed my orders.

'You did not think to tell me?'

'I thought it too soon, your grace.'

'It is never too soon for good news. A wedding night baby?'

'I do not know, your grace.'

'A woman always knows, my dear Cecily. Remember there are to be no secrets in our family. If you are afraid, it is only natural but you need not fear for I shall take the greatest care of you. This will be my first grandchild.'

'Perhaps our baby could be born Shute,' I suggested to my husband thinking of the queen's desire to smother me with kindness.

'Shute? Where's that?'

'In Devonshire. It is part of my inheritance. We could make it our summer home.'

He frowned and I realised. I'd made a mistake. It was too soon to talk about Shute, far too soon.

'This is your home. Next year we shall move to Bradgate. Build a house. But my mother says you are too young yet for the responsibility. You must first learn correct ways. Besides, the revenue from your inheritance goes to my mother.'

'Forgive me husband, but should the rents not be yours?'

'What a fuss you make. My mother has them until you are sixteen. It is perfectly normal.'

Normal it was not. Fourteen was the age at which rents from my inheritance should go to my husband for our use. Master Catesby had explained it to me. This sounded like another piece of sharp practice by the queen.

5

WESTMINSTER 1475

A man breathes danger every moment he is on the battlefield, or so he would have us believe. Yet a woman's life is equally imperilled during childbirth. Naturally we women are not praised for recounting endless stories of the horrors we endure in the birthing room: the blood, the heat, the stench, the clutching of holy relics and invocations to Our Lady, the screaming and the pain. So my conversation was carefully limited to how, after a little discomfort and a few hours of travail, I gave my husband what I had promised him – a son: a large lusty boy, the best bawler in years, the midwives said.

Four weeks after the birth, the king made my husband, Marquess of Dorset, and I became a marchioness. It had taken me less than a year to achieve the first step in our upwards path and I was vastly content. I had my baby brought to me and informed him of our success. Disappointingly, he seemed unimpressed, blinking solemnly, then letting out a great howl.

I had spent the months of my increasingly swollen belly, whispering to my mother-in-law of how much my husband deserved a reward from the king, what an honour it would be for the father of her first grandchild. The day after I heard the news, my husband came to visit me. I was still confined in that dreary stuffy room insisted on by his mother as suitable for a woman in the weeks surrounding the birth. Men were not supposed to venture across the threshold but my husband, careless of protocol, chose to disobey.

'He's got my nose,' he said peering uncertainly into the cradle.

'He's got your lungs.'

He laughed. 'And what of you, my little wife? You look well. How much longer will they keep you here?'

'Two more weeks.'

'That is a very long time. Are you certain it is that long?' He cast a glance at the rumpled bed. 'Perhaps we could …?'

I favoured him with lowered eyelashes, a quick glance upwards accompanied by the glimmer of a mischievous smile.

'Your mother would disapprove, my lord.'

'My mother need not know.'

The outrageousness of his suggestion surprised me. He never disobeyed his mother. 'My lord, someone would tell her. Besides, it is too soon.'

I turned my face away as if unwilling to talk of such matters, even to a husband. He shrugged his shoulders, backing away from the unsavoury realities of childbirth.

He reached out his hand and gently stroked my cheek. 'Perhaps you could please me in another way.' He began to smile. 'You remember?'

Yes I did remember but what we'd done when I was a new young wife was not, I thought, suitable for the mother of a man's heir.

He sighed. He'd not expected me to say yes. He'd been tempted by the sight of me, flushed and pretty, wearing an invitingly loose gown. However I had no intention of risking the loss of my mother-in-law's favour. I had worked hard to get this far and my success had already resulted in her relinquishing my inheritance into my husband's hands.

'Beautiful,' she had cooed over our little Edward, tickling his belly and carefully counting his fingers and toes. My own mother had held the baby close, her cheek against his downy little head, saying how she wished my father had lived to see his grandson, how proud he would have been of me and how much she still missed him. Personally, I thought my son a fine specimen, if horribly noisy.

Instead of a seduction, my husband contented himself with describing to me in great detail the town house he'd acquired to supplement his new dignity as Marquess of Dorset. Then he told me how Lord Dinham had ships patrolling the Narrow Sea to protect the crossing of the king's army to Calais.

'You should see the guns we're taking. Monsters! Each one mounted on a chariot. And a thousand stone cannonballs.'

'Very impressive,' I murmured, wondering if the Suffolk widow's twenty pounds had been spent on arrows or cannonballs.

'The king is taking a wooden house covered in leather so that he will sleep in comfort and a robe of cloth of gold with a red satin lining for his coronation at Rheims.'

This expedition was beginning to sound more like a royal progress than an advance towards war.

'Who is going?'

'Everyone except old Westmorland.'

'The king's brothers?'

'Of course.'

I did some quick calculations: five dukes, one marquess, seven earls and sixteen barons. There would be dozens of non-noble captains, hundreds of men-at-arms and thousands of archers. England would be drained of its men. In the circumstances I thought a little feminine fragility might be in order as men appreciated delicate women.

'Husband, who is to defend those of us left behind should an enemy come?' I allowed a small break in my voice to show him I was afraid.

'The council, of course. Arundel and Essex will remain.'

'Who will represent the king?'

'My mother.'

Kings died in wars. No matter how many cannonballs or portable wooden houses a man had, no matter how fine his coronation robes, a king could still die. Look at the fifth Henry, victor of Agincourt! It was said he had died whilst campaigning in France. I shivered. If the king died, who would be king? Surely not my husband's mother.

When summer arrived it brought rain. Not gentle showers moistening and swelling the crops but cold relentless downpours which turned farmers' fields to marshland where nothing would flourish but bog myrtle. Water streamed from sloping roofs onto flooded streets, culverts and ditches overflowed, animals drowned and bridges were washed away. It did not feel like summer at all.

By early August the king and his friends had long since departed overseas. I imagined them in Calais, plodding through sticky mud, their cloaks saturated, knee-deep in water, unable to tell where the causeways were; horses slipping, men cursing, and all the time nothing ahead but a solid curtain of rain falling from a sky the colour of old pewter.

In the depths of the palace, far from the sound of rain, the queen's chamber was full of damp and worried women. Three of the queen's sisters had arrived to take their places, a welcome splash of colour to lift the gloom which pervaded the gathering. Viscountess Bourchier sat next to the queen. The two were of an age though I doubted the king would stop his horse on the highway for the middle-aged viscountess. She had a discontented mouth, her eyes suspicious of me and my place amongst the queen's ladies. I thought her jealous of her sister's success. My mother, who had been one of six sisters said most sisters left to their own devices, fought like cats.

The Countess of Pembroke who sat at my side, deliberately ignoring my presence, was only a few years older than me. I wondered did she know that my stepfather had rejected her husband as unsuitable for me? Another woman's leavings would not please the countess but then I doubted the earl did either.

According to Lady Donne, who had it directly from my stepfather, the Earl of Pembroke was a disappointment to the king. Not the man his father was, unable to keep order in South Wales where he'd been installed to see off threats from Mad Henry's half-brother, Jasper Tudor. Then there was the matter of children. So far no sign and the countess was not getting any younger. Eventually, curiosity got the better of her and she asked about my son. I marked the note of envy in her voice.

Next to the countess, taking pride of place, was the young Duchess of Buckingham, another cool Woodville beauty and at seventeen the youngest of the queen's many sisters. Married whilst still a child to Harry Stafford, Duke of Buckingham, it was said her husband disliked her family. The duchess too, I reckoned, as she had the look of a dried-up virgin.

'Beautiful, are they not?' murmured a voice in my ear. 'I see you are admiring the queen's sisters.'

I recognised the voice. It was Lady Stanley, wife of hatchet-faced Lord Stanley, steward of the king's household. She was a diminutive woman, more the size of a child, with a sharp nose and pale skin. Very strict, Lady Donne had said, and very devout.

'They are,' I agreed, politely.

There was an expectant rustle in the chamber, like hens flapping in the confines of a coop, as the queen prepared to read out the latest letter from overseas. The king, to my surprise, was a dutiful correspondent. After all these years and all those children, I thought he would have better ways to occupy his time than writing to his wife.

'Our dear kinsman, the Duke of Burgundy has joined his grace, the king.' She looked up, smiling.

'Has he brought his army?' the Countess of Pembroke asked anxiously. She must have heard the rumours that Burgundy was otherwise busy, laying siege to an insignificant little town near Kologne in direct defiance of his treaty obligations.

The queen bent her head to her letter. 'A small personal retinue.'

Hands flew to mouths as a stifled groan swept the room. What good was a small personal retinue to anyone! We needed the duke to bring his army.

'What is to happen?' the Countess of Pembroke whispered to her sister, the duchess.

'The venture will be abandoned,' the duchess said firmly, all at once an expert on military tactics.

The viscountess glared at the duchess. 'Nonsense! His grace will press ahead.'

'As I would expect,' the queen agreed. 'Our men are to advance eastwards through the duke's territories to Péronne, then into France'

'Is it true your grace's uncle, the Count of St Pol, has promised to deliver the town of St Quentin into our hands?' Lady Stanley enquired. She was a woman who clearly received intelligence from her husband.

The queen gave a glacial smile. 'So his grace, believes.'

I too had heard of the Count of St Pol's promise, but I'd not trust an uncle of the queen, neither would I trust the Duke of Burgundy. In Calais, men had whispered of the duke's vices, of the poor neglected English duchess, untouched and childless. How could such a man be trusted? He would want glory on his own account, not gained by acquiescing to the personal vanity of his English ally.

I had to admit that my stay in Calais two years earlier had opened my eyes to the duplicitous nature of men. I'd been present when a prideful Burgundian envoy was presented to my stepfather and seen how they pretended to be friends. I'd overheard conversations, not understanding the words but noting the way men spoke, how their eyes shifted slyly from one side to the other as they lied. And peeping out of our chamber door late one night, I'd seen a half-clothed woman, ease her way out of my stepfather's room, hair loose over her shoulders and a low-pitched giggle on her lips as she ran quickly past the guards. I'd not told my mother. I'd not told anyone.

I intended to be a good wife, to manage my husband's affairs while he was away in the way my mother did at Ashby. But I was told I was too young, too inexperienced, that my mother-in-law and my husband's men, would take charge. All I was permitted to do was play house like a little girl, organising my new rooms to my requirements. I knew the queen would have a spy set in my household but that was of no consequence as I paid an obliging maid in royal service to keep her eyes and ears open on my behalf. My husband believed what he was told by his mother but I'd learned Master Catesby's lessons well and preferred to have my own sources of information.

In Calais I'd discovered how people liked to talk – all kinds of people, not just great lords. Servants passed on details of what they heard whilst serving at table; a man's valet would be privy to what his master said while helping him into his doublet; shopkeepers repeated conversations between their customers and ships' captains had gossip from foreign ports. Trade seemed an excellent way to discover a man's intentions. Envoys who came to broker a peace deal might lie, but in the buying and selling of cloth, untruths were quickly discovered. I reckoned the merchants of Calais knew as much about the French king's plans for war as my stepfather did.

With whatever funds were available to me I resolved to pay men to go where I could not. Above all, I wanted to know what was being said.

'I have here a list of suitable women for your companions, my dear Cecily,' said my mother-in-law in her most honeyed voice.

'Thank you, your grace,' I replied, running my finger down the names – no-one I knew. 'May I suggest two other young women who I believe would prove satisfactory, your grace?'

She eyed me as if I'd suggested importing a couple of sluts from the alleyways into my household.

'Are they known to us?' she said sharply.

'I do not know, your grace. My mother's neighbour, Lord Zouche, is soon to marry. His betrothed is a sister of Lord Dinham. She is a few years older than me and would, I think, be a suitable companion.'

I smiled sweetly, thinking what a pleasure it would be to have Joan Dinham in my household. My mother knew the Dinhams from the days when she'd lived at Shute and spoke fondly of the sisters.

The queen tapped the arm of her chair. 'His grace approves of Lord Zouche, and the Dinhams are well known to us. I see no reason why not.'

'Thank you. Lord Zouche has a sister. Do you think she too might be suitable?' I could imagine nothing more enjoyable than to have Meg as a companion.

'A sister? Unmarried?'

'No, your grace. I believe she is wed.'

'We would need to know more about the husband. You cannot have just anyone in your household, Cecily. My son is a man of importance. Now as to the other names.'

I had won a small victory but knew there would be more skirmishes ahead. It would take a lengthy campaign to wrest control of my husband from his mother. With Thomas's father dead, she'd had the ordering of him when he should have been learning independence in another man's household. As his mother she considered he owed her a higher duty than he did to me, his wife. I had been purchased for my inheritance, not to direct her son and most certainly not to select unsuitable young women for my household.

6

BAYNARD'S CASTLE 1475

Our house fronted the river not far from Paul's Wharf where the best houses were. It had two large halls and a number of private rooms, all with fireplaces like the one my stepfather had installed at Ashby. There was a kitchen with the usual offices and storerooms as well as a bakery and a brewery. There was also a range of low outbuildings next to the courtyards with a number of stables and barns.

From one of the upper windows I could see Baynard's Castle, the old Duchess of York's townhouse. According to Cousin Isabel, Duchess Cecily had retired to the York castle of Fotheringay after her son's marriage to avoid meeting the queen and was seldom in town.

I did not expect to have sight of her but one Thursday my servants reported horsemen and wagons arriving at Baynard's Castle and later, a handsome carriage, complete with outriders and men-at-arms. It was not long before a man dressed in York livery brought a note asking me to pay a visit. The duchess had returned and wished to see me. A scribbled addition to the bottom of the note said my two cousins were visiting their mother-in-law and required my presence to relieve the tedium.

With an array of new garments at my disposal, I now had my pick of gowns. I selected an apple-green silk with a dark red kirtle. The dark green henin covered in gold thread embroidery and a floating veil made me look truly elegant. I wished my husband was here to see how fine I looked but he was plodding through the mud and rain of Flanders, hopefully thinking of me and not of some trollop he'd acquired in Calais.

I had my maid adjust the mirror so that I could admire myself. Very suitable, I thought. Not too gaudy for the old lady, yet fashionable enough for my cousins. A warm hooded riding cloak of best Flemish cloth placed over my shoulders because the summer afternoon was chill, and I was ready.

Baynard's Castle was very grand, rebuilt by the old Duke of Gloucester whose reputation as a man with an eye for beauty, was legendary. It was large but I thought the stone wings of the castle with their many windows should have been set square rather than running away from each other like a row of houses on a hill.

Seen from the river it was forbidding: a malevolent phalanx of mighty towers rearing out of the river with a single watergate giving access to a dark tunnel which led into the bowels of the castle. It looked like what it was – a fortress built for defence.

My husband said nobody needed a house like Baynard's Castle nowadays and possibly he was right. After my uncle's failed rebellion, the country was at peace. Mad Henry was dead, his only son dead, his wife, disgraced and exiled. How much better to have gardens and orchards than cannon loops and arrow slits. Surely Venus was preferable to Mars.

Yet perhaps one should be careful. My mother said no king should take his crown for granted. At any moment a greedy brother or an exiled prince might appear at the head of an army to snatch it from his grasp.

I followed an elderly steward through the great hall casting my gaze at the tapestries hanging on the walls. Not the kind I would have chosen. They reeked of a time past, glories long forgotten, great battles and mighty conquerors, blood and gore and death. Too much destruction.

My cousins were waiting for me in a little parlour at the top of a long flight of stairs. They seemed pleased to see me.

'Our mother-in-law says she will meet with you shortly.' Isabel was openly admiring my apple-green silk. 'Where did you find that?'

'My stepfather knows a man.'

Isabel laughed. 'Lord Hastings knows everyone.'

'How is your baby?' Poor Anne, still childless after three years of marriage.

The king's younger brother, Richard, was a sober man who said little. He might be dutiful but I doubted he'd be much fun as a husband, not like Thomas who enriched my life in a way I did not quite understand. Richard had the north to rule for the king so he and Anne were mostly at Middleham in the faraway reaches of Yorkshire where my mother had spent her childhood. From the stories I'd heard, I was glad to have lived at Ashby.

I told Anne about my Edward and Isabel told me about *her* Edward. After six years of marriage, Isabel had at last given her husband a son, born in the late winter. I smiled pityingly. With God's blessing, I had achieved success in only nine months. Perhaps it was because my father had died fighting for the king whereas Uncle Warwick had died in open rebellion. I felt truly sorry for both my cousins.

'George is immensely pleased,' Isabel said defensively, noting my cousinly smirk. 'Royal descent on both sides. York and Nevill. What could be more illustrious. I pity the king yoked to his old grey mare.'

'Hush, Izzy,' you should not speak ill of the queen,' Anne said, always anxious to be a peacemaker.

'Why not? She speaks ill of us all the time.'

'Nevertheless, she is kind.'

'Kind! You think she feels kindness after what our father did to her father?'

My eyes flicked between the two of them, wondering which one was right. My mother had told me how Uncle Warwick ordered the execution of the queen's father and brother without so much as a trial. Nobody liked to say it was murder, but it was.

'It might be wiser to guard your tongue,' I suggested, but discretion was not Isabel's way. She preferred a direct attack.

'Has it not occurred to you, Ceci, that Thomas Grey's father might have skewered your father. If so, not even being a marquess would endear him to you.'

'My husband is a good man,' I said, unwilling to have Isabel slander Thomas, hoping she knew nothing of the woman in Clerkenwell.

'Your husband is a nobody. His mother is a nobody. But however mean your husband's lineage, at least you have the comfort of a Nevill for a mother.'

'And a loyal Bonville for a father,' I retorted.

Fortunately, before we resorted to hair-pulling, one of Duchess Cecily's men came to say her grace was ready to see me.

The room was large but ill-lit, its corners lost in shadows. In the air hovered a faint odour of decaying flesh, overlaid with the dry acrid scent of cinnamon. Perhaps Duchess Cecily carried relics of her dead husband about her person, hidden beneath her bodice or sewn into her trailing sleeves: a lock of hair snipped from his severed head or a finger nail rattling in a tiny box. She looked like a woman firmly anchored to a past littered with dead bodies.

She sat rigid, regarding me, her eyes gleaming like a pair of tiny polished beads. Her spotted hands gripped the carved arms of her chair as if she feared falling sideways. She was old, held together, like all women her age, by stiffened buckram and the solid stitching of her garments. There was no allowance for fashion. She wore a horned and rolled headdress of the kind long abandoned by my mother. The cloth of her gown was exquisite: dark green and gold patterned brocade lined with what looked suspiciously like ermine; cut high at the neck but falling in easy folds over her soft leather slippers. Behind her, in muted greys, were her women, pale faces, fading away into the blackness.

She watched while I curtsied. I dropped a little lower than was required which I knew would please her. Old ladies appreciate politeness in the young, and to her I must have seemed a mere babe-in-arms.

'So, you've come.'

A murmur and a graceful incline of my head in acknowledgment.

'Look like your mother.'

'So I've been told, your grace.'

'Never knew your father. You've the look of a Neville: eyes, nose. Won't get you far these days; not with *her*.'

I waited to see what she wanted. Was I being inspected for a higher purpose, some devious reason for this summons?

'Promised your grandmother I'd keep an eye on you. Hear they've married you to one of her boys.'

'Yes, your grace.'

'Hmmph! Leastways he's trueborn, not like that clutch of little bastards she's given my son.'

I'd been warned the old duchess still refused to recognise her son's marriage to the queen and, as such, was not welcome at court.

'I remember the day she arrived. Seven sisters trailing behind her, all unmarried. Every mother with a daughter, despaired. Knew she'd snap up the best of 'em – which she did. Told him it was a mistake but he'd not listen.'

The litany of complaints was well-ploughed ground but I listened politely while she tore the queen to shreds, strip by strip, thread by thread until all that remained were the fragile bones of an amoral slut who'd used witchcraft to ensnare a virtuous son of York.

I wanted to say all men were beguiled into marriage one way or another, with contracts promising wealth and prestige or sweet words offering to assuage carnal lust. What man does not look upon his betrothed and count the fat acres of her dowry or imagine the pleasures of his wedding night? But no words from me were required to assist the duchess in her demolition of her son's wife although I was tempted to remark that, beguiled or not, the king's marriage was sound and could not be set aside. Wisely, I said nothing until at last she ran out of bile.

For a moment there was an expectant silence while she regained her strength.

'They tell me you're clever. Are you?'

'I believe so, your grace.'

She snorted, her laughter ending in a bout of coughing which required elderly women with bowls and cloths to appear at her side. She waved them away into the shadows.

'So no fool?'

'No, your grace.'

'Love your husband?'

'Naturally.'

Her gaze was steady. I was being scrutinized; sized up, weighed and categorised. Was I a wise virgin or a foolish one? She nodded.

'Hmmm. You may fool him but you don't fool me. You're too smart to fuss and fumble over a man in fine silks with a pretty face.'

'If you say so, your grace.'

She beckoned me forward.

'Does he treat you right?'

'I believe so, your grace. I have no complaints.'

'Got a child, I hear?'

I smiled. 'A boy.'

'Healthy?'

'Yes, your grace. The image of his father.'

This time she almost choked with laughter but her women didn't move.

'See I don't need to worry about you. You're a match for her. Serve her right for choosing you. She *did* choose you, didn't she?'

'Yes, your grace; I was chosen.'

'Wanted your inheritance?'

'I was a valuable prize.'

'Ha! Is that what they told you? Now listen to me. You be careful. They're a close-knit family. You may think he's yours but he'll tell her everything. Anything you let slip will find its way to her ears so don't go spilling your secrets onto your pillow.'

'I have no secrets to spill, your grace.'

Up went the eyebrows – neatly plucked in an old woman's vanity.

'Is that so? No secrets, eh? Just as well. A secret shared is no longer a secret. Might as well nail it to the church door. And remember: a woman with a secret is a danger to somebody.'

At the beginning of September, the rain stopped and the men returned home. The campaign had ended, not in a huge victory, not even in a small one, but in a fudge. The great harvest of rewards which the king had promised to reap for his army, filled storerooms with gold for the wealthy but failed to provide lesser men with enough spoil to see them through the winter.

As Joan Dinham said, a week's whoring and drinking in Amiens did not buy bread for a man's family. Joan was an outspoken young woman, a little older than myself but who never forgot I was a marchioness whereas she was not yet a lady – not until John Zouche named the wedding day.

Naturally, the queen claimed the king had chosen wisely, avoiding bloodshed while forcing Louis to fill the purses of Englishmen to repay us for his insolence. But scratch the surface and a different story emerged: one where the French king divided his enemies, bribed the English nobility and fawned over the queen's husband like an eager brothel keeper.

We'd been betrayed on all sides. The Duke of Brittany had dithered; the Duke of Burgundy had reneged on every one of his promises, stamping off in a fury; and the queen's uncle, the Count of St Pol, had failed to deliver St Quentin into our hands.

On a bridge at Picquigny the two kings had met and agreed a truce to last for seven years. The gates of Amiens were flung open to the English; wine flowed, pensions were paid, kisses were exchanged and the English departed peacefully back to where they'd come from. The victor of Agincourt would have despaired.

'Do you not think it shameful?' I asked my husband, thinking how much I would like to be kissed properly, something he had so far failed to do.

There had been formal greetings in front of the whole court, followed by days of feasting and entertainment; then another formal greeting at our house where the servants lined up in the yard to welcome home their lord. There was urgent business to attend to and senior men of the household to be consulted; letters were dictated and visitors pacified.

Late that evening, once the servants had seen to my husband's requirements and taken out the candles, we were finally alone. Foolishly, I longed for him to take me in his arms.

'Shameful? Nonsense! An honourable peace.'

'I cannot believe Louis agreed.'

'Scared witless!' He laughed. 'You should have seen him on the bridge, hiding behind his trellis, trembling like a girl. Terrified he was. Thought we'd come to murder him the way his father murdered the old Duke of Burgundy. I almost split my new doublet when the king bowed right down to the ground. That showed Louis. You could see him wondering if a York king was truly God's anointed or was it a trick.'

'No trick, just theatre,' I said, thinking of my father who'd died to put this preening York king on his throne.

'I am one thousand crowns the richer.'

I smiled as if his prize had been won in single combat not with a cynical gesture by the French king .

'What of the coronation at Rheims?'

I wanted to keep him talking while I controlled my longing. It was unworthy. I was a wife. I was not a common Calais doxy to display my appetite lying naked on our sheets – though such a thought had occurred to me.

He stripped off his robe and climbed into bed. 'I had forgot how pretty you are.'

I hugged the compliment tight. 'Prettier than the women in France?' I teased, wanting to ask how many there'd been and had he thought sometimes of me.

'Much prettier. D'you know, Louis invited us to Paris to dine with the ladies. Even offered the Cardinal of Bourbon as our confessor. Said he was a jolly fellow who would absolve us from sin if we committed any.'

'Did you enjoy your visit?' I held my breath, thinking of the many sins a careless husband might commit in the arms of the painted ladies of Paris.

'Didn't go. Louis changed his mind. Thought if we got to Paris we might never leave.'

I laughed, wanting him to promise he was true to me, would always want me more than any other woman, but he was too busy reacquainting himself with my charms. Soon I forgot my mask of wifely indifference and abandoned myself to the joy of what passed between us in bed.

Afterwards, I watched as he lay sleeping, the same way I watched my baby son, wanting to keep him for myself, protect him from harm, mould him into the man I needed him to be. I knew now I'd been mistaken. I had thought Thomas wanted to detach himself from his mother's skirts and she was refusing to let him go. But Duchess Cecily had shown me a different Thomas: a small boy seeking comfort at his mother's knee; a boy supplanted by a younger, favoured, princeling; a husband whose grasp was not secure, who feared the loss of his position in his family.

If this was true, I would have to play many parts: not only the wife and the lover but also the mother. A complicated task for a young woman of fifteen years, but one which, in my pride, I was certain I could perform.

In the days that followed, I discovered that every one of the king's friends had received a fat pension from Louis. My stepfather received the most: two thousand crowns a year. My mother told me, quietly so that no-one else would hear, that when asked, my stepfather had declined to give a receipt.

I laughed. 'How clever of him. Now no-one can say he was bought off by the King of France.'

'The king's brother, Richard, refused a pension.'

That did not surprise me. Anne's husband, the humourless Duke of Gloucester would not dirty his hands with the French king's money – far too principled.

'What of Isabel's husband?'

My mother laughed, stretching out her hand, palm upwards.

I grinned. 'He stands with the king.'

'Shoulder to shoulder. George may be greedy and a little foolish but he knows he must show himself loyal. He has betrayed his brother once, he cannot risk doing it again.'

'There are those who regard this agreement with King Louis as failure, not victory,' I remarked, thinking of poor Isobel saddled with a one-time traitor for a husband.

'True,' my mother agreed. 'But warfare is not all glory, my daughter. You should count your blessings. Your husband has come home to you – mine did not.'

As well as disagreements over who had gained the most from the king's French campaign, the return of our men brought other problems, notably a greater awareness of my mother-in-law's role.

'I wish to send a gift to the queen. I want her to think well of me. What do you think she would like?'

Joan thought for a moment. She was fast becoming invaluable, my eyes and ears in all matters, sometimes my conscience, always a wise friend.

'A jewel.'

'I have nothing as fine as the ones she already has.'

'A piece of music.'

I shook my head. 'Too insubstantial.'

'A special dish from the kitchen.'

I laughed. 'She is no glutton.'

'An illuminated manuscript.'

I clapped my hands. 'Perfect! I shall ask my stepfather for advice. If I had the funds I would commission a triptych like Lady Donne's husband has.'

Joan's eyes widened. 'My sister Edith, says it is more than beautiful.'

'Is she the sister who serves Lady Stanley?'

'She is and she tells me she remembers holding you when you were a baby.'

'She knows Shute?'

I felt a familiar longing at the thought of the house which now lay in my husband's hands. My father had lived at Shute with my mother. I was born there but could only visit if my husband permitted. So far he had not – too far, too much to do, your duty is here with my mother, with me, with our son; why in God's name would you want to go there!

Joan smiled at the expression on my face. 'It's only Devonshire, Marchioness, not Paris or Bruges, nowhere grand. Only a little manor house set amongst the trees.'

Yes, but it was *my* little manor house set amongst the trees.

If autumn brought an indifferent harvest which failed to salve our men's injured pride at the king's tame surrender to King Louis, winter hefted in with north-easterly gales and bawdy French ballads of how the English had been driven out of France with venison pasties and fine wines. Shutters rattled, men grumbled and women, recalling the enthusiasm with which their husbands had returned from overseas, began counting the number of weeks on their fingers. By the time a December frost turned the fields at Southwark white, I was wrapped in my warmest fur-lined robe, calling for more logs for the fire and carefully unpicking the seams on my gowns.

7

WINDSOR CASTLE 1476

The last day of our Christmas revels brought my mother to court, an unexpected pleasure along with the fire-eaters. acrobats and foolish games.

'I hear the Duchess of Buckingham complains the roads are dangerous,' she remarked, greeting me with a kiss. 'She fears the sight of dead men on gibbets.'

'Perhaps she'd rather they were at large to waylay her carriage.'

We were sitting on a cushioned bench in the window embrasure, as private a place as was possible in a court hungry for enjoyment.

'She says she is in mortal fear of the Duke of Burgundy.'

I smiled. I too had heard the duchess's wailings.

'Mother, Burgundy may wish to foment trouble. He may even have his eye on the English throne. But I doubt he will march to Maxstoke intent on rape and pillage.'

Judging from her frown, my mother disagreed. 'As women, we cannot know what men will do.'

In one way she was right, men's minds were a mystery, especially my husband's.

'Is Mary Hungerford not with you?' I asked.

My mother arranged her face with downturned mouth and tragic eyes. 'Weeping because she has no invitation.'

'She is far too young for court.'

'So I have told her but she hears Princess Elizabeth is with the queen and Mary is the same age.'

'Let us hope she improves before she marries my brother. He will not want a weeping wife.'

My mother tapped my hand. 'People do not improve, they merely become adept at hiding their true feelings.'

She nodded in the direction of the king. He was talking to a pretty young woman in yellow damask, not someone I recognised – a city alderman's wife perhaps. I let my gaze drift to where the queen sat with her sister, the viscountess, half her attention fixed on her husband's latest flirtation.

'Has he always been like this?'

My mother smiled. 'Have you not heard the story of the prince who searched for true love?'

'You know I have not.'

She laid her hands in her lap and began her story. 'There was once a king who planned to marry his son to a foreign princess. A peace treaty and a vast dowry were offered, but the bride was said to be ugly so the prince was reluctant. The father gave his son a month to find a bride more suited to his fancy, otherwise the wedding would go ahead.

'Only a month?' I said, thinking that barely enough time to ride round Essex.

'It was a small kingdom,' explained my mother. 'The prince rode off and on the second day stopped by a river to water his horse. In the shallows stood a young maiden, struggling with a heavy bucket. Being a chivalrous young man and liking the look of the girl, he waded into the river to help. Once he had both girl and bucket brought to safety, he gazed at her bare legs glistening with drops of water and thought what any young man would think. "Come sit with me awhile," he said. The girl, knowing no better, sat beside him on the grass.'

'Did she have no governess?'

'A father whose daughter fetches water from a river is not wealthy enough to employ a governess. There was no-one to mind her and it was not long before the prince had bargained for a kiss. "Let me lie with you," he whispered, feeling the stirrings of what he thought was love. "Oh no sir, my father says I must not lie with a man till I be wed," she giggled. "Then we shall wed," said the prince, thinking how wonderful it would be to have this enchanting young creature in his bed each night. Knowing no better, the girl agreed.'

'A hedgerow wedding?'

'Who knows. But when a chill evening breeze stole over the lovers, the prince jumped to his feet. "I must away," he said, thinking the girl not really that pretty and, underneath her woollen shift, her body not that clean. "Remember me!" he called gaily as he rode off into the sunset. The girl *did* remember him because her belly swelled with the harvest and her father cursed her for a fool. But the damage was done. The prince did not return and she had no idea who the handsome stranger was.'

I laughed. 'Her mother should have taught her better.'

'Indeed, but we are not concerned with the girl. A week later the prince happened upon a small manor house. At the door was a young woman possessed of an ice-cold beauty, the kind that hot-blooded young men long to melt. She offered him hospitality for the night for he was clearly a man of high birth. Later that evening he pressed her for a kiss. She hesitated. "I burn for you," he said, thinking how much he wished to lie with her. Eventually she allowed him one chaste peck on the cheek. "No more," she said, "It would not be right." "Marry me," said the prince recklessly, thinking he would go mad if he did not get to possess this fascinating creature. "Very well, tomorrow we shall find a priest," she said.'

'A sensible young woman.'

'You would think so but let us see what happens. "I cannot wait," said the prince, but the young woman firmly bolted her bedchamber door, leaving the prince alone. Next morning they were wed at cockcrow so that the prince could lie with his ice-cold beauty. But, like others before him, he found that ice is not a comfortable bed companion and unfreezing the young woman's reluctance rewarded him with only a tepid response. He had expected more so decided she was not for him. He bade her a courteous farewell, promising to return, and went on his way.'

'What did she do?' I asked, thinking I would not have given in to this young man.

'She was very devout. Perhaps she prayed for his return, perhaps for forgiveness of her sins.

'She had committed no sin.'

'She wished to give herself to God, not to a handsome young man. She longed for a life of prayer and seclusion but was betrayed by her bodily desires. Perhaps she felt unclean.'

'The prince betrayed her,' I said firmly. 'What happened next?'

My mother smiled. 'The prince searched high and low throughout the kingdom but nowhere could he find a young woman who was both beautiful and to his taste. Then three days before his time was up he met a young woman standing by the wayside. She was the most exquisitely beautiful woman he had yet seen. After learning that her father was a lord, he kissed her and asked her to lie with him. She refused, saying she would not dishonour her father's name. Desperate to possess this beauty, the prince offered marriage.'

'Again!'

'Yes again. And once more the young woman accepted. But this young woman was no fool. She brought to the church next morning, not only a priest but also her mother.'

'How wise of her,' I said.

'It was. The consummation of this marriage was all the prince could have wished for, so much so that he completely forgot the ice-cold beauty and the girl by the river.'

'And the others. There *were* others, surely?'

This time my mother laughed. 'Yes, I am certain there were others because, as we know, a man's true nature never changes.'

'Was the king satisfied with his son's choice?'

'What do you think?'

'I think he was angry but there was nothing he could do. He should not have allowed his son to search for his own bride. That was foolish.'

'Perhaps. But think for a moment. It may be the prince and his beautiful wife lived happily ever after?'

I thought of this careless young man leaving a trail of broken promises in his wake, satisfying his own desires, heedless of the damage he'd left behind.

'I think that a man who has pursued beauty and true love three times might be tempted to do so again,' I said slowly.

'And again,' laughed my mother.

I looked across the floor to where the king had moved closer to the young woman. She was blushing. He had one hand on the upper part of her sleeve while the fingers of the other hand were gently teasing apart the grey fur at her neck. The husband had wisely made himself scarce.

'He does not ask for you?'

My mother smiled. 'No, nor will he.'

'You are very certain. He finds you desirable.'

'Maybe he does, but we are old friends.'

I wanted to ask had there been more between them when she was young but found I could not. Some things a woman keeps private. If she had wanted me to know, she would have told me.

'Will he send for me?'

'No.' There was no hesitation.

'He would not shame my husband.'

My mother shook her head. 'He knows your husband would look the other way but he also knows your stepfather would beat him to a pulp.'

Soon it was February, the coldest time of year. Days were short, nights were long, and our gathering was one of great sadness. The king's elder sister, Lady St Leger, once Duchess of Exeter, had died in childbirth and we had returned to Windsor for her burial.

The previous summer, after the king's great expedition, the Duke of Exeter had not returned home from France.

Fallen into the waters of the Narrow Sea, it was said. How careless! And how little he'd be missed. But the other story was that the king had ordered the duke thrown overboard. Couldn't swim. Praise be!

Now his one-time wife was dead. I wondered if they would meet in purgatory and what they'd say to each other. Or were the dead in purgatory not permitted to speak.

As befitted a duchess, Cousin Isabel's accommodation was grander than mine: a vast chamber decorated with rich tapestries and a large high bed, hung with red velvet. Her maidservants were barely visible, two bent backs huddled at the far end of the room, endeavouring to catch what meagre light was afforded by the narrow window, doubtless mending one of Isabel's many gowns.

My cousins sat with their dark heads close together like a couple of old women exchanging recipes for potions. They were dressed in mourning clothes suitable for this sombre occasion.

'The Duke of Norfolk is dead,' said Anne' raising her face to mine, her eyes misted with tears, her lips trembling.

Mercy! A second death, so soon after the first! I shivered. The old women at Ashby said death always came in threes.

'How did he die?' I asked, wondering who was to inherit.

Anne shook her head. 'It was sudden. There was no warning.'

'I do not remember him as old.'

'Nor he was; he was in his prime.'

'You see,' Isabel said, her voice sharp with fear. 'It has begun.'

'What d'you mean? What has begun?'

They neither of them spoke. There was something odd here. People did not die of nothing. There had to be a reason. I wondered what had happened to the duke.

Norfolk. A vague impression of a tallish man with a beak of a nose; earl marshal; a Mowbray. My mother had a tangled kinship to his wife, the duchess. She was a Talbot, daughter of the old Earl of Shrewsbury who'd died in the French wars. Her mother was half-sister to Uncle Warwick's wife. I knew there were other strands of kinship but, for the moment, was unable to unravel them.

I turned to Isabel. 'Has your husband had some intelligence? Gossip, or whispers?'

'Yes, but I cannot tell you. I know nothing for sure.'

'The poor duchess,' Anne sniffled. 'All she has left is her daughter.'

'No son?'

Anne shook her head, dabbing at her eyes with a handkerchief. 'My husband says the queen wants the daughter for the younger of her two princes.'

'Such haste!' There was something indecent in the snapping up of a child with the father not yet cold in his grave.

Anne was practical. 'A great fortune is at stake.'

'Are there no other heirs?'

Anne's thin shoulders drooped. 'I do not know. Lord Howard is kin. He may have a claim.'

'If I were Lord Howard I would forget any claim I might have,' Isabel said fiercely. 'If I wanted to remain alive I would keep quiet about my so-called kinship with the Duke of Norfolk, pretend it never existed.'

She was right. My mother-in-law would not look favourably on other claimants. But inheritance was a matter of law, not of a queen's preference. Master Catesby had once explained the rules to me, how, in certain circumstance the law was flexible and could, if justice was to be achieved, bend like a willow rod. But it could not break. If Lord Howard was in the line of inheritance, no amount of devious dealings or beguiling sweetness on the part of my mother-in-law would have any effect.

'What about you, Ceci?' enquired Anne, her eyes gazing longingly at my thickened waist. 'When is it to be?'

'Early summer.'

'You and a dozen other women of my acquaintance,' Isabel remarked sourly. 'How blessed you are!'

'Is your husband pleased?' Anne enquired.

I thought of Thomas's pleasure at my news and the celebrations which had lasted well into the night in certain establishments frequented by my husband and his rowdy friends. My informant reported drunken singing and a variety of accommodating women. There were complaints from neighbours and arrests made in the streets. Next morning several young men in torn silks were hauled out of one of the city lock-ups, with a handful of coins, a tugged forelock and a promise of silence.

'He is pleased,' I said, knowing that my mother was right – a man's nature did not change, no matter how much I wished it would. I put out my hand and grasped Anne's fingers. 'It will happen for you, Anne. I know it will.'

'I pray so.'

'You must not give up hope.'

But hope looked as if she had fled this past year, defeated by a long, dark winter in Yorkshire. Perhaps it was the same long dark winter which had defeated the Duke of Norfolk. Or perhaps it was something else.

8

FOTHERINGAY CASTLE 1476

Deep in the vastness of the church at Fotheringay there was a shuffling, rustling, whispering noise like the murmur of leaves disturbed by a sudden breath of wind. Candle flames dipped, heads turned and in through the great west door came the first of the coffins.

This was no ordinary funeral of a lord but one ordered by the king for his dead father, the Duke of York, and for his brother, Edmund. It was fifteen years since they'd died, a mere heartbeat in some people's memory, but my mother thought it unwise to dig up these old bones lest they disturb the enmities of the past.

In the battle where they and my own father had fallen, the queen's family were the enemy. Sir John Grey, her first husband, had fought for Mad Henry and his she-wolf queen. There were many who remembered those times, who grieved for lost fathers and brothers and sons, who named them each night in their prayers. These same people would never forgive and never forget. My mother, a most forgiving woman, thought it foolish to add fuel to their fires.

I suppressed a yawn. My second son, little Anthony, was barely two months old and I was still plagued by weariness. We had been waiting at Fotheringay for more than a week while the funeral procession wound its long slow way from Pontefract. I wished I was lying down with my feet propped up on a stool, not standing in a church on cold stone flags.

For days, rumours had reached us of the magnificent effigy of the dead Duke of York kneeling on top of his coffin as if in prayer, eyes open, gazing upwards at an image of Christ, an angel holding a crown above his head. As the coffin was carried up the aisle into the chancel, I heard tiny gasps as those beside me saw the duke, displayed in all his glory like the king he should have been. Someone was sobbing softly.

Next came the coffin of Edmund, Earl of Rutland, cut down at the age of seventeen beside my eighteen-year-old father – two young men who should not have died. Behind the coffins came the king, weeping, dressed, like the effigy of his father, in robes of dark blue furred with ermine. He was followed by his brothers, my cousins' husbands: George, Duke of Clarence and Richard, Duke of Gloucester.

After them came the Archbishop of York, a dozen bishops, a multitude of earls, lords and other mourners, all dressed in black. Occasional glimpses of colour gleamed amidst the darkness as the Garter King of Arms and his heralds took their places. By now everyone was weeping. The queen made great reverence to the coffins but I noticed her eyes were quite dry.

At the banquet next day, I was seated next to Catherine, Duchess of Buckingham. She was by far the most beautiful of the queen's sisters. With her pale skin and silvery fair hair, she looked as fragile as a treasured piece of Venetian glass but in my considered opinion my Lady Buckingham was as tough as an old leather boot.

Her dark green brocade gown was of the best quality and the deep neckline with its white silk piece edged with gold embroidery, exceptionally becoming, but there was still no sign of anything but a kirtle beneath the folds of her skirts.

'You are well, Lady Catherine?' I enquired sweetly.

She turned her head slowly in my direction. Her eyes narrowed as her pale red mouth curved into a mean little smile.

'I hear you have given our Thomas another son,' she said, equally polite.

It was odd how the queen's sisters all spoke of my husband as if he was one of their chattels, merely lent to me for the getting of heirs. As far as Lady Catherine was concerned, I had no claim on him, no rights to his attention or his favour, I was nothing but a vessel for sons.

'We named him Anthony, for your brother, Lord Rivers,' I said, wanting her to believe I had been party to the decision, not ignored now that my role in the production of this new addition to the queen's family was finished.

Naturally I would not tell her of the row over the child's name. I had wanted William, for my father and step-father but was over-ruled by the queen who insisted her brother should be godfather. Naturally the child would be named for him, there was no question of any other name. It would be an honour, she said, although for whom I was unsure. I had complained to Thomas who had merely shrugged and said I should not make a fuss; Anthony was a perfectly acceptable name.

'You must long for a daughter,' said the duchess, inferring that two boys was not what a woman would want.

'If God blesses our marriage with sons, why would I wish matters otherwise?' I said with a superior smile.

She wrinkled her nose as if an unpleasant smell had wafted up from her plate of fish. 'You consider your marriage blessed?'

'Naturally,' I replied. 'Do you not consider your marriage to the duke, blessed?'

She looked as if she wanted to strangle me. 'The Staffords are one of England's greatest families. We have always been close to the throne. God shows his blessings to us in many ways.'

'Close to the throne! Oh but I have not seen your husband. Is he here?'

'Of course he is here. Where else would he be?'

'I thought perhaps after his little disagreement with the king last year ...' I let my voice tail away as if not caring to discuss a quarrel between the king and one of his nobles.

'Who says there was a disagreement?'

'I thought, well, we all thought that now the young prince resides at Ludlow, I mean it seemed natural. We all expected your husband would sit on his council. He has interests in the Marches so it would be natural, would it not, but Thomas tells me it is not to be. We hear it is the queen's Woodville kin who will make the decisions. Does that not worry your husband?'

It was well known that the king and the wealthy young Duke of Buckingham had fallen out during the French campaign but none of us could discover why.

'You are wrong,' she spat.

I lifted my shoulders in an elegant shrug. 'Perhaps I was misinformed.'

'You were and I would advise you, Lady Cecily, to keep your nose out of my husband's affairs.'

With that she turned her back on me and began talking to the woman on her other side.

'I think you have made an enemy,' whispered Anne who was seated on my right.

I grinned at her. 'Lady Catherine is angry because my husband is favoured over hers. That is all. It seems the duke has not yet learned that if you wish to progress you must have the king's favour. Also, she is jealous. She wants a child.'

Anne placed her hand protectively over her belly. 'Poor woman. I pity her.'

I touched her arm. 'Your husband has no need to worry; he is the king's brother.'

'Richard is loyal,' she said, clearly anxious to reassure me.

'And the king has rewarded him for his loyalty.'

It was Richard, Duke of Gloucester who'd been chosen by the king to accompany the cortege from Pontefract to Fotheringay. Some foreign envoys present at the reburial of the king's father, wondered why that particular honour had not gone to the Duke of Clarence, him being the elder of the king's two brothers, but most people understood that a beloved brother once turned traitor would never be wholly trusted again. No matter the embraces, kisses and warm words, George, Duke of Clarence, would always be suspect. Besides, everyone knew the queen hated him.

Anne sighed. 'I wish it was the same for Isabel.'

'Is her husband out of favour?' I nearly said "again" but thought it unkind.

Anne's eyes were worried. 'George is not an easy man. He bears grudges. Isabel says she must walk on eggshells not to arouse his temper.'

I smiled. 'Enough of the king's brothers. What of your baby? When is the birth?'

Her face lit up with genuine pleasure. 'November, we believe.'

And Isabel?'

'Also November. Sadly, neither of us can be with the other. I would have dearly liked her to be with me.'

Isabel was at the top of our table, squeezed between Viscountess Bourchier and the Countess of Pembroke. She had eaten nothing and looked unwell.

'Is she ailing?' I whispered to Anne, as two men bearing a huge salmon on a silver platter on their shoulders walked slowly up towards the dais.

Anne leant a little sideways, cupped her hand over her mouth and whispered, 'She is afraid.'

'Of what?'

'Poison.'

I blinked in surprise. 'Here? At the king's table?'

'Shhh!' whispered Anne, looking around fearfully in case someone had overheard.

'Anne, that is ridiculous. Why would anyone wish to poison Isabel?'

Anne shrugged. 'We are our father's daughters.'

'Nobody will poison Isabel for being her father's daughter. Why would they? What would they gain?'

For a woman close to the throne there might be a dozen men willing to slip henbane into a cup of wine but after the death of Uncle Warwick, Isabel was no threat to anyone. Was it George trying to rid himself of his wife? Stranger things had happened and Isabel had not brought George the crown he'd expected when he married her. I looked to the top table where the king's two brothers sat: Richard sipping his wine but George, leaning back, arms folded, his plate of food, like his wife's, untouched.

Anne put her mouth to my ear. 'She says she is careful but what if she's right? What if someone *is* trying have her killed?'

Her words were like an echo from the past. I thought back to our meeting in February at Windsor when Isobel had said Lord Howard should be careful. She had believed there would be danger if he advanced a claim to the Norfolk inheritance She'd not said the words but she meant us to understand that the queen would somehow have him killed. But my mother-in-law had no reason to kill Isabel. Isabel posed no threat.

Back in my room, I dropped, exhausted, onto a chair while a maid unlaced my gown and removed my shoes. Joan was fingering some jewels she'd laid out on a table. I'd not yet decided which ones to wear that evening. She picked up a topaz surrounded by a cluster of diamonds, then put it down again.

'Is something amiss?' I asked.

She hesitated. Clearly something was on her mind.

'Joan, you'd better say what you're thinking otherwise you might swallow the words, then you'll choke, You've no need to worry. I'm not going to bite off your head.'

She shrugged. 'It may be nothing.'

'I doubt it. You never bother me with trifles. That is why I keep you with me.'

She laughed. We were easy with each other and I was well aware of her usefulness. My maids would tell her things they would not dare tell me and she was friendly with most of the women who served the queen's senior ladies. I learned many secrets whispered in corners of the queen's rooms. I suspected she had learned her skills in Devonshire, in that little manor house at Nutwell with her sisters.

In my mother's stories, Nutwell was a magical place, where the sky was always blue, the river sparkled in the sunshine and birds flew up in white plumes from the trees. Like Shute, Nutwell inhabited a kingdom where nothing bad ever happened, where no-one had heard of Mad Henry and the tribulations of a York king.

'You have heard something?' I enquired.

Joan bit her lip. 'It may be nothing. It is only maids' tittle-tattle. You know how they gossip down in the laundry when they've nothing better to do. They think they are being secret but sometimes their whispers float away through the air. I would not want you to give the story credence because these girls are not wholly to be trusted.'

'Perhaps you should let me be the judge. What did you hear?'

'The mistress of one of the maids has been given a piece of information.'

'Do we have a name for the mistress?'

'The Lady Isabel.'

'The Duchess of Clarence?'

'Yes, that is why I thought you should know.'

'Do we know what this piece of information is?' I asked.

Joan shook her head. 'No, but the girl fears for her mistress if the queen should find out.'

'It must be a very powerful piece of information,' I remarked, wondering what Isabel had been told and why it was of interest to the queen.

'I'm sure it is nothing but silly gossip,' Joan said, looking as if she did not wholly believe her own words.

Already I could feel a coldness, a fear of something unknown, a malevolent creeping danger. First Isabel fearing she was to be poisoned, now a piece of dangerous information.

'Do you know any more?'

'No and I'm sure it is nothing,' said Joan, laying the jewels back in my casket. 'I'm sorry I bothered you with something so foolish.'

'I doubt it is foolish. I think it may be of great importance but I cannot fit it into the puzzle of what I already know. What of the other maidservant, the one the girl was talking to?'

'I did not recognise her voice.'

'Do you know the name of her mistress?'

'No. Forgive me, I have failed, bringing you nothing but crumbs from a half-baked loaf.'

'Joan, you never fail me. I know more than I knew before.'

She got up, holding the casket. 'Shall I return this to your chest?'

I nodded, thinking of Isabel. The last time she had spoken of danger was last winter at Windsor when we'd gathered for Lady St Leger's funeral. Then it concerned the death of the Duke of Norfolk. I'd heard nothing more about the duke's death. No-one knew why he'd died or why the death had been so sudden. It was said the duchess was not with him when he died but was at Norwich.

What we did know was that the duke's heir, his five-year-old daughter, would shortly marry the younger of the two princes. As soon as the children were a little older, there would be a wedding. The queen, having pressed the king for the match, was pleased with the arrangement, but the girl's mother was said to be unhappy. Could this dangerous information have something to do with that?

9

KIRBY MUXLOE 1476

Our little cavalcade rode towards Kirby Muxloe along winding roads which were often nothing more than narrow dirt tracks. We splashed through shallow fords and picked our way carefully around tangles of undergrowth blocking our path. As soon as we were out of sight of Fotheringay, I pushed my hood back from my face and laughed for joy, glorying in the unexpected freedom of having my husband to myself for two whole days. It had been decided that the queen and her daughters would accompany the king and the court back to London while Thomas would escort me to my stepfather's house for a visit to my mother.

By noon, the day was unbearably hot. Birds in the woods had fallen silent and my senses were drowsy from the scent of honeysuckle. Near one of the villages, the smell of warm meadow grass ready for scything hovered lazily in the shimmering air. It would soon be time for haymaking. There were strips for the villagers to grow wheat and barley but most of the open ground was rough pasture where a few cattle grazed peacefully in amongst the weeds and bracken at the edge of some trees, their tails flicking away armies of buzzing flies. They were watched over by a tow-headed boy who sat on a log, idly whittling a stick.

From my saddle, I could see onions and peas growing amidst a profusion of burdock and willowherb in a woman's cottage garden, fenced off from some scabby chickens pecking nearby. A small child in a cap had been set to mind them but had gone to sleep with her thumb in her mouth.

People stopped what they were doing to watch us ride by. The women waved at the sight of a handsome lord and his pretty young wife, though I doubted they knew who we were. Thomas's banner was not yet well-known in this part of Leicestershire, unlike my stepfather's. Everyone knew Lord Hastings. But we wore silks and velvets, had fine horses with jingling bridles which was enough for the common people to raise a cheer.

We passed a night at the home of one of my stepfather's tenants, an elderly man in a faded red doublet who was overcome with the honour of entertaining the marquess and his wife. The woman of the house, clearly dressed in her best gown for the occasion, was younger than her husband but equally in awe of us. After a few hesitant words and a couple of awkward bobs, she showed me our room and offered her own maidservant to assist me. I said there was no need as my girl would see to the bringing in of my belongings. The woman gave another curtsey, a "thank'ee, m'lady", and scuttled away.

There was no magnificence here: the furnishings were plain, the single chest sturdy, the room remarkably small. It quickly became apparent that our hosts had vacated their own tiny room for their guests, forcing Thomas and me into unaccustomed proximity.

'I had forgot people lived like this,' whispered Thomas as we lay squashed together on the sagging mattress, an inch away from an outside wall, listening to the banging of unfamiliar doors and the rattling of distant bolts.

'You have become over-mighty, husband,' I giggled, thinking how much I enjoyed sleeping so close. He had tucked me into the curve of his body, his cheek warm against mine.

'My brother and I used to sleep like this.'

'At your father's house at Astley?'

'No, later, at Grafton.'

'Do you remember your father?' I asked, curious. Thomas never spoke of his father nor of his childhood. The little I knew of his life before we married, I'd gleaned from my mother-in-law's sisters.

He gave a weary sigh. 'When people ask, I tell them how my father sat me in front of him on his great warhorse; how he gave me a wooden sword, telling me that one day I would be a knight like him; how he knelt in front of me, giving me the care of my mother while he was away. They say how fortunate I am to have those memories but, in truth, I remember nothing.'

'Nothing at all?'

He shook his head. 'Only other people's memories, small doings they pass on as if offering me a gift. But these are mere crumbs. My mother told me what a great a man he was, how he died doing his duty but I cannot see him. I imagine him riding off to war. bright colours fluttering, armour shining, but where his face should be there is just a blur. I want to remember. I try to picture his smile or the way his eyes would have creased when he laughed, but there is nothing there.'

This was a pain I could understand. I, too, had no memories of my father. Sometimes I would catch a glimpse of a visitor at court and think: my father looked like this. Once, the sight of my stepfather cradling my little half-sister made me certain I remembered my father holding me in his arms.

'How old were you when you came to court?' I asked gently.

'Nine.'

I smiled at the thought of nine-year-old Thomas Grey, a small replica of the man lying beside me. 'It must have seemed like a miracle to you.'

'I hated it,' he said quietly.

'How could you hate it? You had everything.'

He paused, then said stiffly, 'I was not made welcome.'

'By whom?'

'Others.'

There was something odd here. The queen would have ensured her two Grey boys had the best care. She would not have abandoned them to the ministrations of indifferent strangers.

'Which others?' I asked.

He shifted over onto his back, his eyes open, staring up at the plain cloth tester above our heads.

'The king's brothers, George and Richard.'

I'd seen enough of my half-brother's spitefulness to smaller boys at Ashby to understand how it must have been for Thomas. There would have been pinches, kicks, tale-telling, endless petty cruelties meted out to an unwelcome intruder.

'Did you not fight back?'

He gave a hollow laugh. 'They were older than me.'

It is the same in the schoolroom as in the chicken yard: the biggest and strongest rules the roost; the smaller ones get bullied unmercifully.

'What happened?'

'I survived. We grew up. The fighting stopped.'

He put out his hand and gripped mine. At that moment, in that stuffy little room under the eaves, I felt more a married woman than I had for the whole of the past two years. Since our wedding day, Thomas had given me many valuable gifts; he had discharged his husbandly duties with kindness and fathered two healthy sons; I had attended court on his arm, recognised by everyone as the wife of the king's stepson, the marquess. But all that was of little consequence compared to the glimpse he had just allowed me of the real Thomas Grey.

The pretty manor house at Kirby Muxloe in the wooded country near Leicester was where my stepfather brought my mother after their marriage, where I took my first steps and learned my first prayers. Sir Leonard Hastings, my stepfather's father, had been a landowner who hailed from Warwickshire. He'd fought with the Duke of York in the French wars and before that, at Agincourt. It was even rumoured he had drops of royal blood in his veins. It was he who had first leased Kirby.

When the king gave my stepfather the Earl of Wiltshire's grand house at Ashby, Kirby became our second home, used when my mother wanted respite from the constant comings and goings at Ashby. Kirby Muxloe was tranquil, except when my stepfather came visiting with a great train of followers. Then, my mother would sigh deeply, set aside her sewing, call for the steward and set to working out where the men would sleep.

Fortunately for her, Thomas and his men stayed only one night, departing the following morning for London. I bade my husband farewell with something like regret, wishing we had more time together.

'Why does my stepfather not approve of my husband?' I asked my mother as we walked from the courtyard into the pleasure garden.

My mother eyed me in the critical way mothers do. 'He wanted a duke for you. He thought with your fortune you should be a duchess. But, as you know, the queen intervened.'

'And there was a shortage of dukes in the marketplace.'

'Also, he views Thomas Grey as a rival. The king has allowed your husband increasing influence in these parts. He is treading on your stepfather's toes.'

'Thomas is much admired,' I protested, remembering our hosts of the other night. 'People say he is good-looking.'

'Oh Ceci, a woman does not keep a horse because it is good looking. If she did she might likely end up in a ditch.'

Mary Hungerford, who was all ears, listening to our conversation when she should have been arranging games for the younger children, said, 'I like the marquess. When I smiled at him, he smiled back.'

My mother stifled a laugh. 'Mary, a man who smiles at a young woman when she is already betrothed, is not to be trusted.'

Mary's eyes filled with tears. 'He likes me; I know he does.'

I tweaked her ear in a sisterly fashion. 'Don't matter. The marquess is married to me. He is not free to like you. Just remember that and keep your smiles for my brother.'

Mary pouted. It was well-known that she did not care for my brother. But they would marry soon whether they liked each other or not. Perhaps then things would get better.

'How hard it is to be young,' my mother whispered.

We watched the children play a catching game with a ball. My stepfather's ward, the young Talbot heir who'd been purchased as a future husband for my little half-sister, refused to join in the game. He was poking at some small creature in the bushes.

'Do you trust your husband?' enquired my mother.

I bit my lip, wondering how much to tell her, not wanting to be disloyal. 'I do not know. Sometimes he disturbs me.'

'In what way?'

'When we first wed, I thought I had the measure of him. Now I am not so sure.'

'Do you love him?'

'Oh no,' I said quickly. 'I am not so foolish as to love him. I know what he is.' I shrugged, feeling a chill little breeze blowing across the grass. 'If he is not exactly what I want, then I shall change him.'

My mother laughed. 'Brave words!'

'Surely It must be possible to make a man more to your liking.'

'Perhaps, but if that is your plan you will have to fight his mother every inch of the way and she is a formidable adversary.'

I remembered the queen's insistence on my baby's name, then shivered, recalling Anne's words at Fotheringay.

'Mother, do you think the queen would have someone killed?'

My mother raised her eyebrows. 'Killed? I presume we are not talking the king's justice here.'

'Would she have someone killed so that no-one would know it was done on her orders?'

There was a long silence while my mother considered the question. 'Why would the queen do such a thing? She would be taking a terrible risk. What would she gain?'

'Do you think it possible?'

'It might be. She would have to have a good reason. Perhaps if she considered herself threatened in some way.'

'She might do it.'

'I suppose a woman who charms her way onto a throne might do anything.'

'Even kill someone.'

There was a slight pause; then my mother said in the same tone of voice she employed when telling me to come for dinner. 'I once killed a man.'

'You?' I gasped.

'Yes.'

'When?'

'Oh, a long time ago. Before you were born.'

'But how?'

'With a knife. I slit his throat.'

I could not believe what I was hearing. 'You slit a man's throat with a knife?'

'I did. The knife was tucked in my belt. My Uncle Fauconberg gave it to me, said I might need it one day.'

I was so shocked I did not know what to say.

'Who was he, this man you killed?'

'A nobody, just one of God's creatures, But I took his life which was a sin.'

'Why did you kill him?'

'He was attacking someone I cared for. He would have killed her but I killed him first.'

My mother had this uncanny ability to surprise me. She was a calm woman, a peaceable woman. I could not equate her with being a murderess.

'Was this in Yorkshire?' From stories I'd heard, there'd been dreadful doings in Yorkshire during my mother's childhood. I could imagine some sort of affray: my mother in the street, terrified, attacked by a mob.

'No, it was at Shute.'

'*My* Shute?'

My mother smiled. 'Yes, your Shute. Shute Manor which is part of your inheritance. Oh Ceci, do not look at me as if I'm a monster. Times were different. There was violence everywhere and Shute was under attack from the Earl of Devon's men. I'd already seen a friend dead on the road in a pool of blood and an old woman tipped out of her bed by robbers. What would you have had me do? Run away?'

'No, but …'

'I pray you never have to face what I faced, the choices I had to make. You cannot imagine how terrible it was. I lost my husband, my father, my favourite brother and my father-in-law in one day. A month later your Bonville great-grandfather was murdered by Margaret of Anjou. My husband's family were regarded as traitors. I was to be turned out of my home and had nowhere to go. You were the only comfort left to me.'

'How did you survive?' I asked weakly.

Your Uncle Warwick had me brought to London, to his house. And if you are ever tempted to think the king puts money before honour, you should remember that, if nothing else, he has brought us peace.'

'And the queen? Has she brought us peace too?'

My mother sighed. 'There are people who said a marriage between a York king and a Lancastrian widow would unite the country but there are many who despise her, not for what she represents but for who she is.'

'So, what should I do?'

My mother stopped, took my hands in hers and looked me straight in the eye. 'I do not know what it is you have been told and I do not wish to know. But I advise you to be careful. Keep whatever suspicions you have to yourself. Tell no-one, because if there is a battle between you and the queen, you will lose and your husband will not help you. His loyalty will be to her, first and always.'

'My stepfather would not allow me to be harmed.'

'Your stepfather would be powerless.'

'But he is close to the king.'

'The queen is closer.'

I stood, staring uneasily across to where the children's game had descended into howls and recriminations.

'You think I should do nothing.'

'Come with me.'

She led me back through the garden into the low-ceilinged hall and up the narrow stairs to her private rooms. She knelt down in front of one of the small chests and lifted the lid. After a few minutes of searching she found what she was looking for: a small knife in a leather sheath.

'Take it,' she said. 'You will feel safer.'

10

WINDSOR CASTLE 1476 – 1477

I followed my mother's advice and told no-one of my suspicions. How could I when I was surrounded day and night by my mother-in-law's confidantes. One ill-advised remark, one careless observation, even to a maidservant, would have sent them scuttling to whisper my words into the queen's ear. None of them were to be trusted. Joan was the only person who might have guessed what worried me but she was too taken up with arrangements for her forthcoming marriage to John Zouche to pay attention to my brooding silences.

In my mother-in-law's presence I was a model daughter-in-law. I kept my head dutifully lowered and, if asked a question, answered politely. I played cards, smiled sweetly, laughed at her jests and allowed none of my misgivings to show in my face. I thought my dissembling perfect until one morning when I lifted my head from my sewing I found her gazing speculatively at me as if wondering what I was thinking.

Summer made way for autumn. The harvest was good, people sang in the streets and men said how the York king, God bless him, had brought them luck. With food in their bellies and sun on their backs why would anyone think about winter frosts or the price of a loaf.

I counted the days, dreading what might happen, praying both my cousins would come safely through their months of confinement. Childbirth is the most dangerous time in a woman's life, when we give ourselves into God's hands, pray our midwives are skilled and stay sober, not like the old crones at Ashby who were always drunk by noon.

By the time the court moved to Windsor for our Christmas entertainments I was unable to rid myself of a nagging feeling that all was not well. I'd heard nothing from Anne but was not greatly concerned. Being winter, a letter from Yorkshire might take several weeks to reach Windsor. Snow drifts vould block roads or floods wash away bridges – anything might have happened. But Warwick Castle? I tried to remember how far it was. Two days ride, maybe three because hours of daylight were short in December.

It was only a few weeks since we'd celebrated the birth of another son born to the Duke and Duchess of Clarence, a boy named Richard for his uncle. I'd thought to recall my man but some inner doubt persisted so I left him where he was, a low-born servant with an unusual skill, working unnoticed by those he was set to spy on.

The letter came late on the eve of the Nativity, the messenger entering through a side door, stealing quietly up the back stairs so as not to be seen. Acting on my orders, my maid admitted him to my rooms, then sent word to tell me he'd arrived.

I'd paid well for this information, far more than I could afford, yet now it was here in my hands I was at a loss to know what to do. My fingers fumbled as I unfolded the note. I peered, trying to make out what was written. The man was unskilled with a pen, the writing crabbed, with several blots and in one place he'd scratched a hole with the point of his quill. But the meaning was clear:

"Lady Isabel died this morning. The child is not expected to live."

Outside, daylight was dying. Nothing remained but a single streak of vermillion merging slowly into the purple blackness of night. Two servants came, bringing candles but I sent them away. A log in the hearth crumbled to ash. Already I felt chill creeping into my bones.

I unfolded the note again, praying I had misunderstood but the words were the same. I thought of my mother at Shute all those years ago, learning that my father was dead: her husband, her father, her brother and her father-in-law – all gone in an instant with no warning. How had she survived such a blow?

Isabel was my cousin. I was unsure how much we liked each other but that was unimportant; she was family and family must be cherished. Without family there is nothing in this world.

Tomorrow or the next day, when a rider came from Warwick, there would be an official announcement and the usual formalities: requiem masses, prayers, notices; and afterwards tears, questions and regrets. But tonight I would grieve alone. Once more I let my fingers trace the written words.

The door opened. I heard Joan walk softly across the floor. She came and knelt beside me. It was a relief to feel her hand on my arm, hear her voice murmur quietly, 'Is there anything I may do?'

Dumbly, I passed her the note. She read it, gasped as her hand flew to her mouth.

'I did not believe her,' I said sadly.

Joan's words were comforting. 'You were not to know.'

'How could this happen?'

'It is the fate of women. She knew the risk. We all do.'

'She was frightened. She left court because she feared someone wanted her dead. Now she is gone.'

I began to weep. Joan put her arms around me and held me while I sobbed for my cousin: twenty-five years old, barely a life.

On the Feast Day of St Stephen, the passing bell began to toll, a mournful dirge letting the whole castle know someone had died. Joan's sister, Edith, arrived at the door before my maid had finished combing my hair. Edith was older than Joan but they looked remarkably alike: the same round Dinham face and dark unruly hair. She served Lady Stanley and was married to a man in her household.

I quickly wiped away any tears. Edith gave a neat curtsey and said. 'Lady Cecily, I have been sent to find you. The queen has just received word from Warwick Castle. It is the Lady Isabel, may God preserve her soul. Dead four days since. Such a tragedy. The king has ordered a requiem mass for his brother's wife and her grace wishes you to accompany her to the chapel.'

With another curtsey and a swirl of grey skirt, Edith turned on her heel and was out the door.

'I cannot face her,' I said.

'You must.' Joan was firm.

'You could say I was sick.'

'It is a royal command. If you refuse, it will look very peculiar. Do not forget who she is.'

'As if I could, surrounded by her coven.'

'Marchioness, please be careful what you say.'

She was right. Caution must be my watchword, now more than ever. Remembering my mother's advice, I washed my face, changed into a black velvet gown and, with Joan walking two paces behind me, went to find my mother-in-law.

The burial was to be at the abbey at Tewksbury, where Isabel's body now lay in state in the middle of the choir. I had wanted to go, to say farewell and to question Isabel's women about what they'd seen. but it was impossible. My mother-in-law was due to go into confinement and had ordered that I remain with her. She said she found my company restful. I fretted but knew a burial would have not been the place to cast doubt on how my cousin died and Isabel's women would likely have been too frightened to tell me anything – why put your head in a noose. All I could do was mourn my cousin alone.

I turned to Thomas for comfort.

'I am lonely,' I said in a small voice. 'Isabel was like a sister to me.'

He patted me awkwardly, as if unsure how to manage a tearful wife.

'You will find someone else,' he said briskly. 'There are my mother's sisters and all her ladies. You are surrounded by women.'

I touched his shoulder tentatively. 'It is not the same.'

'Perhaps you should visit the children?' he said, climbing out of bed before there were more tears.

'We could both go,' I said, without much hope.

He shook his head. 'You know I cannot. The king needs me.'

I wanted to say, I need you but husbands did not wait on their wives. Husbands had duties and Thomas's was to be at court, keeping the king amused.

Last year, when I'd been confined at Bradgate, I'd heard there were hunting parties and picnics while visiting the houses of other men. Neighbours and local townsmen were invited together with wives and daughters. People spoke of how affable the king and his intimate friends were, how much they'd enjoyed themselves.

My mother-in-law did not attend these gatherings, preferring to remain with her children at one of the king's palaces. In those long summer days I doubted my husband thought of me at all, not when temptation beckoned from every sunlit glade or leafy bower and I was a hundred miles away.

I told myself it was of no consequence. I did not love him. As long as he treated me well as his wife, that sufficed. But when he patted the top of my head like an absent-minded father, then called for his valet to bring his clothes, I felt lonelier than ever.

The weeks shut away at Windsor with my mother-in-law and her chosen companions were interminable. Her rooms were hung with thick tapestries and with doors closed and not a chink of daylight to be seen, the air grew hot and stuffy. We had left the outside world behind, but what was supposed to be a tranquil existence, a time passed in prayer and contemplation, quickly became a privy pit of female spite.

The momentous news that the Duke of Burgundy had died, whispered at the door by a maid bringing fresh linen, produced a bitter row between the queen's sisters. In the end, Viscountess Bourchier exercised the privilege of age over rank and informed the queen, in the gentlest way possible, that her kinsman was dead, while Lady Catherine sulked in a corner like a child denied a treat.

Even after the queen gave birth to a healthy baby boy, and the subsequent excitement of the baptism in St George's Chapel, the bickering continued.

'I thought you had run away to Calais with Lord Hastings,' Lady Catherine murmured, sidling up to me.

The duchess enjoyed trying to provoke me but with a dozen other ladies within earshot and the queen resting on her day bed nearby, most of our exchanges were conducted in low acrimonious whispers. Today her chosen weapon was the Duke of Burgundy's unexpected death and its repercussions.

'Are you not concerned, Lady Cecily? Now that Burgundy is dead, my husband says King Louis will cease paying Lord Hastings a pension. Why would he?'

I smiled at her, thinking what a foolish young woman she was. 'Lord Hastings is not in the pay of the French king, Lady Catherine.'

'That is not what I heard. My brother says Lord Hastings would sell Calais to the French king if the price was right.'

Lord Rivers, having once been captain of Calais, could

doubtless compute the value of our overseas' outpost down to the last shilling.

'Lady Catherine, my stepfather is loyal to our king as you well know. He would no more sell Calais to Louis than he would sell him your husband, though I doubt the French king would pay much for an unfavoured English duke.'

With that I turned my head and began talking to Lady Stanley.

Upon hearing of the death of Charles of Burgundy, my stepfather had been dispatched to Calais. The king's sister and her stepdaughter, the new duchess, were in fear of their mighty neighbour. They had appealed to the English king for help, lest Louis should overrun their territories.

My stepfather was to arrange for Lady Donne's husband and a Doctor John Morton to visit Paris. Doctor Morton was a plump little man, clever as a fox, a Lancastrian turned loyal Yorkist, a priest and a lawyer. Master Catesby said he should not be underestimated.

Nobody said, but I thought it probable, that their orders were to ensure that the English king's pension would continue to be paid. My stepfather was pleased to receive gifts from King Louis but the queen's husband, with his lavish tastes, would be seriously inconvenienced if the flow of money, wine and extravagant gifts ceased. With Burgundy no longer a threat, Louis might just decide his money would be better spent elsewhere.

There was a sudden bustle in the room as the senior nursemaid arrived with the queen's baby. I wondered if the birth of another prince meant my child, too, would be a boy. Was there a fashion for boys in the same way there was a fashion for tight sleeves or deep necklines? And how odd of the king to choose his brother's name for this third little prince.

'George is eyeing Burgundy,' Lady Catherine whispered.

'Forgive me,' I replied, turning round. 'Did you say Burgundy?'

'Yes. He wishes to marry the daughter, the new duchess. Now the father is dead, the duchy is hers. George fancies it being his.'

I gave her a chilly look. 'My cousin is barely cold in her grave. It is indecent to think of remarrying so soon.'

'Oh come, Lady Cecily! Do you imagine our Thomas would hesitate for one moment if anything should happen to you – which of course we all devoutly pray it will not.'

'The king would not permit such a marriage.'

She gave a cat-like smile. 'My sisters tell me George failed to get permission when he married Lady Isabel. But doubtless considerations were somewhat different when your wife's family is plotting treason.'

'Lady Catherine, that was a long time ago. The king has forgiven his brother. You would be wrong to rake over cold ashes.'

She leant closer and whispered into my ear, 'What if the ashes are not cold? What if there is a spark hidden somewhere, just waiting for a man to arrive with a little pair of bellows? What then?'

Indeed! What then? But George would not have known the Duke of Burgundy would die. He would have had no reason to poison his wife. He was not the cause of Isabel's death, of that I was certain.

After the celebrations for the queen's triumphal return to court, I was permitted to leave for London. Lady Stanley said she was sorry to see me go as she valued our friendship. I was surprised, considering us no more than passing acquaintances thrown together during the weeks of the queen's confinement.

Lady Stanley was a woman fast approaching her middle years, prone to exhausting bouts of piety. Two days earlier she had confided in me how much she missed her son whom she had not seen for six years as he was in Brittany We had enjoyed an interesting discussion on how the duty of a wife to a husband might be at odds with the duty of a mother to her child, but that was all. It was not the beginning of a life-long friendship.

'She thinks her son should be king,' remarked Lady Catherine, idly picking up a piece of scarlet ribbon which I was about to put in my chest.

'Who?' I said, startled.

'That old hag, Lady Stanley.'

I leant over to retrieve the ribbon which she'd thrown onto the bed. 'Lady Stanley is not old, Lady Catherine.'

'Always with her nose in a book.'

'It is her prayer book.'

'Sanctimonious fool!'

'Lady Catherine!' I exclaimed. 'You cannot say that about Lady Stanley. She is a good woman.'

'Where did you get this?' she asked, holding up a length of pale blue silk.

'Thomas gave it to me, not that it is any business of yours.'

'She is a Beaufort?'

'Lady Stanley?'

'Yes, did you not know? Her great-grandfather was a son of old King Edward.'

A Beaufort indeed! So that was why Lady Stanley's son was in Brittany. A Lancastrian Beaufort in the direct line to the throne – or as direct as one can be with a touch of bastardy in the mix! There'd be no favours from a York king for Lady Stanley's boy, certainly no earldom. He'd be lucky to have a single manor for his livelihood.

'Cannot Lord Stanley arrange his son's return?'

Lady Catherine laughed. 'He's not Stanley's son. He's a Tudor, half-brother to Mad Henry. It's no wonder Lady Stanley keeps him overseas. Just think what the king might do if he got his hands on her little Tudor – roast him for dinner, I warrant.'

'He'd not do that,' I said, thinking of the affable nature of our York king.

'You're a fool, Lady Cecily. Of course he would. Who d'you think did away with Mad Henry.'

With that parting shot she waved her hand and was gone. Lady Catherine was known to be light-fingered so I counted the ribbons I'd laid on the table.

I enjoyed the walk from the castle, down the cobbled track to the river, all the more for knowing that soon I would be shut away again for the weeks of my own confinement. It was early morning but already the sky showed a wash of delicate blue with a lemon-coloured sun peeping above the horizon. The river sparkled silver in the sunlight, the trees were greening nicely and the crop fields gleamed a deep golden brown where ploughmen and their oxen had been busy.

A steady stream of carts and wagons passed me, making their way up the hill to the castle. The men tipped their hats in acknowledgement, one or two calling a greeting. I waved back, pleased to feel the morning air fresh on my face.

As I neared the landing stage I saw a familiar figure with a leather satchel on his shoulder. It was Master Catesby. When he saw me, he made a bow.

'Marchioness, how fortuitous. I did not hope for this pleasure.'

I felt my cheeks grow warm at the compliment. I inclined my head, returning his smile. 'Are you at Windsor on business, Master Catesby?'

'A lawyer's commission takes him into the chambers of the highest in the land, my lady.'

I gave a little gasp of surprise. 'Goodness me! How important you have become. Did you see the king?'

He gave a rueful smile. 'Alas, no; merely a royal official.'

'Not so important, then.'

He laughed and shook his head. 'I remain, as ever, a humble lawyer, ready to serve.'

'Are you for London?'

'I am. I must return to Westminster. I have work for a client that needs my attention.'

'Then we are making the same journey. Perhaps you would care to accompany me, that is if your newfound fame does not prevent you from sharing a barge with a mere lady marquess?'

He bowed gravely. 'Thank you, my lady; I should be more than pleased to accept.'

One of the servants called up the Dorset barge and Master Catesby stood aside while I was handed in and seated under the canopy. My maid brought a cushion for my back as the seat was somewhat uncomfortable for a woman with a large belly who expected a baby before midsummer. Once I was settled, Master Catesby clambered in and sat facing me, placing his satchel on the bench beside him. His boy and my maid perched themselves on the servants' bench tucked behind my seat,

'What of your brother-in-law's wedding?' I asked, as the men took up their oars.

Master Catesby nodded. 'A fine affair. The bride looked beautiful as brides must but please, do not ask me to describe what she wore. My wife says I have no eye for details of fashion and fail miserably in my attempts. Lord Zouche was sorry you were absent.'

'So was I but, as you know, the queen's desires come before mine.' I tried to make light of my disappointment at missing Joan's wedding.

'Another boy, so I hear.'

'Another prince for England. And how is Mistress Catesby? Is she well?'

He smiled. 'She has given me another daughter.'

I had never before thought of Master Catesby as a tender husband but it seemed genuine affection flourished between him and Meg, a rare commodity in marriage.

By now our barge was headed downstream, leaving the king's grey castle on the hill to disappear into the distance.

Master Catesby gave a little cough. 'I described our meeting as fortuitous, my lady. If you will permit I should like to ask your opinion on a certain matter.'

I was flattered to be asked, which was probably his intention. He delved into his satchel, searching for something.

'You see, my lady, you are close to the kind of people with whom I can never hope to be intimate. I have clients like your stepfather, Lord Hastings, men who rank far above me, but you, through your marriage to the marquess, have the good fortune to mix with duchesses and countesses and other highborn ladies. You know her grace, the queen, a lady I have never seen, only heard described as the most beautiful lady in the land. I would value your thoughts on this.'

From the depths of his satchel he brought out a single sheet, a notice of some kind, the sort you find nailed up in market squares.

'A client of mine was given this. He did not wish to keep possession of it so handed it to me.'

'Rabble rousing?' I enquired as he passed over the sheet.

'Possibly.'

My first thought was that the writing was very odd.

I looked up. 'What is this?'

'It was made on one of the new printing presses.'

'I hear there is one at Westminster.'

'There is, but I doubt this was printed there.'

I held out the sheet to pass it back but Master Catesby held up his hand.

'I would be grateful if you would read it. At the moment there are hundreds of these all over London but I'll wager in a week's time you'd be hard put to find a single one.'

The notice was in the way of a verse but as I read the words I felt my eyes widening in horror.

I looked up. 'This is treason.'

Master Catesby nodded. 'Yes, I believe it is treasonable. That is why, this evening, I shall burn it.'

'To write such things!'

'And to publish them abroad.'

What the notice said in plain words was that Elizabeth Woodville was not the king's wife. They were not married. The prince was illegitimate and could not take the throne after his father. The writer slyly suggested the king himself was not trueborn.

Master Catesby leaned forward and lowered his voice, not that there was anyone to hear other than a few servants. 'My lady, do you think the people with whom you are intimate: the ladies, the countesses, the duchesses – would they believe this?'

'Not for a moment,' I said stoutly.

'And that great lady, the queen: would she believe it?'

I thought of my mother-in-law, the perfect alabaster beauty, her face barely marked by the passing years, her calculating eyes watching Isabel at the feast at Fotheringay. Unbidden into my mind slid my mother's story of the prince who left a trail of young women in his wake, each one believing she was his wife. But that was just a story told to amuse me. It was not true. It could not possibly be true.

'She would not,' I said uncertainly.

'I did wonder.'

'Nobody would believe what is written here,' I said as a sudden wave of terror clutched at my heart, wondering if Thomas knew of this tissue of lies.

'On the contrary. In the London taverns they are already singing bawdy songs which would make unpleasant listening for her grace,' said Master Catesby. 'And out in the street, men whisper of who should be king.'

'Who would write such a calumny?'

He hesitated. 'Who indeed?'

'Do you know?'

He smiled thinly, 'No I do not but if we wish to discover the architect of this malicious muckraking, what question should we ask?'

I thought back to the days before my marriage when Master Catesby had taught me to think like a lawyer.

'*Cui bono*?'

'Exactly! To whom is it a benefit? Who do you think would benefit from spreading such slanders?'

I thought for a moment.

'The queen's enemies?'

Master Catesby gave a thin little smile. 'I could not say. I know little of court matters. I know only what I hear in the course of my business dealings and few of my clients mix with the royal family – only your stepfather. That is why I was anxious to have your opinion. It is possible the author is a person of your acquaintance.'

'No-one I know would stoop to write such disgusting lies.'

'Are you certain they are lies?' He regarded me steadily. 'What do you think, my lady? Are they lies or could they be the truth?'

I opened my mouth but no words came out. For a mad moment I thought perhaps Master Catesby had written the verse, that he was the man behind these slanders. But this was not the work of a lawyer. If Master Catesby wished to defame someone he would do it by whispers in the ear, a casual aside to someone with influence. He would not print a notice and distribute it in the street. That was not his way.

Master Catesby removed the sheet from my fingers and placed it carefully back inside his satchel. Then he fastened the straps.

'Perhaps we should file this away with those other pieces of information which we have acquired and forget about it.'

'You do not think that, do you? You want to know who wrote it?'

He laughed. 'I could hazard a guess at who wrote it, or rather, who commissioned the writing of it. But what interests me more is, why publish it now? For what purpose?'

'There is nothing there but lies.'

'Ah my lady, you have forgotten to think like a lawyer. It is not whether something is true or not which is of importance but whether it can be proved to be true. It is the same if a man chooses to tell an untruth. If you cannot prove it is an untruth, then there is no harm in others believing the lie, for it might just be the truth.'

This was the trouble with lawyers, even kind ones like Master Catesby; they twisted words round in circles, threading them in and about with backstitches until you didn't know right from wrong or truth from lies. Or what you, yourself, believed.

11

BRADGATE 1477

I hesitated on the threshold of the birthing room. The place was like an underground prison: dark and airless as a tomb. No sunlight penetrated the cracks in the shutters and the only illumination was from a single candle sconce and glowing embers in the hearth. The tapestries were suitably rich and colourful but also thick enough to muffle sounds of mice scuffling within the walls. In here, I could scream until I was hoarse and no-one outside would hear so much as a squeak.

My mother-in-law had ordered everything at Bradgate just as she had for my two previous confinements so I knew the old hag who spied for her would report the slightest deviation from her instructions: darkened room, closed widows, no music, regular readings of religious texts and on no account, admittance to any man. Not that Thomas would have dared disobey his mother, not after last time.

She had surprised him one early morning sitting by my day bed, one of his hands idly stroking my silk-clad shoulder. He had merely slipped in to give me good cheer but on that occasion her pursed lips and angry eyes betrayed her annoyance at me enticing her son into wicked ways. Neither did Thomas escape unscathed. After a sharp maternal rebuke, he had crept away like a scolded schoolboy.

This time nothing was forgotten: a low day bed, chests full of linen, swaddling bands, chairs for midwives, a birthing stool, buckets, cloths and a length of rope. I had no desire to know what use the rope might be put to. The family cradle fashioned for our first child, beautifully painted with Thomas's devices, was brought out of a store room and installed at the end of my great curtained bed.

To my profound relief it was not long before my mother arrived to share the dreariness of my confinement. She made herself comfortable on one of the chairs, looked about her, then remarked casually, 'I saw the queen a week ago.'

'Was she well?'

My mother gave a little grimace. 'Somewhat agitated.'

'Agitated?'

'Perhaps I should have said, distressed.'

'Not my doing,' I said firmly.

My mother smiled. 'No, I would not think it was but someone has upset her and, as you know, she does not take kindly to upset. When she married the king she believed her life would be one of untroubled bliss. Your Uncle Warwick's rebellion showed her she was mistaken. Now she is alert to any hint of danger.'

She rose from her chair and went over to the shuttered window. Her fingers travelled over the fine-grained wood as if looking for somewhere to gain purchase. Without turning round she said, 'One of George's squires was hanged for treason last week. A full traitor's death. I hear there was quite a crowd.'

'What had he done?' I winced as the baby shifted its position.

My mother returned to her seat, her eyes worried. 'Involved himself in a plot designed to bring about the death of the king and his eldest son.'

'Then he deserved to die.'

'He protested his innocence.'

I shrugged. 'Means nothing.'

'It was said he'd composed seditious rhymes. '

'Oh!'

My mother looked at me sharply. 'You know something?'

'It is nothing,' I said hastily. 'It is just …'

'Yes?'

'A month ago someone showed me a piece of scurrilous verse. I said I had no interest in such things.'

My mother nodded approvingly. 'That was wise. The king may appear easy-going but he is not a man careless of his safety.'

'Nor that of his queen.'

'The queen was mentioned?'

'She was,' I said, reluctantly.

'In other words, despite saying you had no interest in this verse, you read every line.'

Under interrogation by my mother, I squirmed like the small girl I'd once been.

'Yes, I read it.'

'What did it say?'

I hesitated, not wanting to admit to the words shown me by Master Catesby.

'She is not his wife. The prince is a bastard.'

'Have you told anyone?'

'Mother of God! Do you take me for a fool.'

'You did not tell Thomas.' By now my mother was perched on the edge of her seat.

'Would you tell *your* husband his mother was a whore?'

My mother gave a faint smile and subsided back against the cushions. 'No, of course you would not tell Thomas.'

She spoke as if I never confided my thoughts to Thomas, in which case she was wrong. I frequently told him my opinions, just not those concerning his mother. I was not yet ready for the battle which I knew must come. There would be a time in the future when he would have to choose between his mother and his wife and I was determined that when that day came he would choose me.

My baby was yet another boy, born two days before the feast day of St John the Baptist. We called him Thomas and my husband said he could not be more proud. He lavished praise upon me and his newborn son to such an extent that I became alarmed, wondering what he'd been doing while I'd been labouring hard to increase our family.

It was odd how a man's part in the matter of a child is completed in an evening's work beneath the bedcovers while a woman spends months of increasing nausea and discomfort culminating in hours of agonizing pain. Yet it is the man who is congratulated as if he has performed the miracle of birth entirely alone.

After the birth my seclusion for a further six weeks was irksome. I longed to walk in the sunshine and breathe clear summer air, whereas in my room the fire was kept well stoked on my mother-in-law's instructions as I and my husband's child must on no account be allowed to become chilled. Fortunately after two weeks of stifling boredom, my mother returned, unexpectedly.

'I thought you would want to know,' she said, once she had greeted me, examined the baby and seated herself beside the day bed where I lay prostrate with heat and exhaustion. 'George has been arrested and sent to the Tower.'

'What!' I tried to sit up but I was still plagued with nausea so moved with care. 'Why would the king send his own brother to the Tower?'

My mother took me by the shoulders and gently but firmly pushed me back onto the pillows. 'If you promise to lie still and not become agitated, I will tell you.'

'I am not agitated. I am shocked,' I said, feeling somewhat dizzy. The room moved and shimmered in the heat, causing a fresh bout of nausea. I put my hand to my mouth.

'My dear Ceci, you are too young to remember how George turned against the king. He believed your Uncle Warwick would get him his brother's throne.' She gave a short laugh. 'Their plan failed. All George got was Isabel as a wife.'

'He was fortunate to be forgiven.'

'He was. Sadly, it appears George has learned nothing from the experience. Your stepfather says the king suspects George of ordering the writing of those verses.'

'Does he have proof?'

My mother sighed. 'A prophecy.'

'Is that all.'

On every street corner in London there were men prophesying the end of days but I rarely bothered to listen. They were like the old crones at Ashby with their clacking voices forecasting doom and despair.

'What did the prophecy say?'

'That the next king of England will bear a name beginning with the letter G.'

'That is ridiculous!' I protested.

'It was enough to arouse the king's suspicions.'

'I cannot believe he would act on something so insubstantial.'

'Your stepfather says the king has become increasingly mistrustful of George and his intentions. There have been wild outbursts of shouting in front of the council and rumours of a waiting woman of Isabel's who George put to death in a fit of fury.'

'All the family are quick to anger, you told me so yourself,' I said.

My mother nodded. 'It is their curse. No doubt the king acted rashly in sending George to the Tower but it is done and cannot be undone.'

I frowned. 'Was this an old prophecy or one conjured up to suit the times?' I was greatly suspicious of so-called ancient writings aimed at ensnaring men's minds. Too often the ink on the parchment was barely dry.

'Nobody knows where it came from. It may be some part of the ancient Prophesy of the Kings, the story your aunt, Lady Fitzhugh, told me when I was a little girl.'

'Perhaps that is all it is, just a story. George's mind is probably unhinged after Isabel's death. I'm sure once royal tempers have cooled, the king will have his brother released,' I said, thinking the king would hardly want George imprisoned, no matter what part he'd played in having a man write foolish verses.

'It is possible,' my mother said, not sounding in the least hopeful of such an outcome.

She was right to be doubtful. As summer drew to a close and autumn gales blew in from the north-west, ripping leaves from the trees and tiles from the roofs, rattling the ill-fitting shutters and doors at Bradgate, George, Duke of Clarence, remained in the Tower.

With one potential suitor incarcerated in England, the young Duchess of Burgundy surveyed the possibilities and sensibly chose to marry Maximilian, eighteen-year-old heir of the Holy Roman Emperor. I thought marrying a Hapsburg a wise move for a woman whose neighbour was King Louis, a man whose fingers stirred every pot in Europe and was eyeing part of her duchy for his son.

Meanwhile, my stepfather, who was the source of my information, had become a prosperous wool merchant. My mother thought it amusing that the lord she'd married, expecting him to be given an earldom by the king, should instead be making a small fortune exporting wool through Calais – four thousand pells sent from England this last year by my Lord Hastings!

New building work would soon commence at Kirby Muxloe as my stepfather had great plans to transform the little manor house my mother loved into something more fitting for Lord and Lady Hastings, a grand monument to the Hastings family.

Tiring at last of the pleasures of rural life and the company of my three little boys, sweetly adorable but short on conversation, I was pleased to hear from my husband that he would like me to come to court for Christmas. His mother would be glad to see me, he said.

12

WESTMINSTER 1478

'You are back,' said my mother-in-law, smiling with her lips while her eyes priced my new gown.

'I am, your grace,' I replied. 'My husband commanded my return.'

'Your queen commanded your return,' she said glacially. 'My son does as he's bid.'

'As do my boys,' I said, knowing how she'd hate to be reminded of my success in providing Thomas with three strong sons in as many years.

Lady Donne once told me that in the first seven years of royal marriage the queen had given the king only daughters. People had muttered behind their hands how this was the king's reward for foolishly marrying a commoner. Perhaps the births of those three little princesses had also led George to believe that one day the throne would be his.

'Do my grandsons thrive?' she asked, calmly laying claim to my boys, the way she laid claim to everything that was rightfully mine. Not content with commanding my inheritance for her own purposes and making my husband dance to her tune, she now wanted my sons.

'The clean air at Bradgate keeps them safe,' I replied. 'Thomas and I prefer to keep them there, far from the stink of the city.'

She gazed at me without saying anything for a few minutes, then remarked casually, 'We shall have to consider marriages for them.'

'They are very young.'

'A child is never too young for a parent's careful planning. Dickon is not yet five but the king agrees he should wed next month.'

So the little prince was at last to marry the Mowbray heiress, daughter of the late Duke of Norfolk. At four years old, Dickon was already weighed down with titles: Duke of York, Duke of Shrewsbury and now soon to be Duke of Norfolk. I wondered what Lord Howard thought about that. Whatever he thought privately it seemed Isabel's advice had been heeded. He'd kept quiet about any rights to the Mowbray inheritance. To the king, he was still loyal and, no doubt to his profound relief, he was still alive.

The wedding of the king's second son and the daughter of John Mowbray, late Duke of Norfolk, took place ten days after the Feast of the Epiphany. I was awed at the splendour of this royal marriage but the king liked nothing better than to impress his subjects with princely magnificence.

The five-year-old bride in her heavy brocade gown showed remarkable confidence as she was led from the queen's chamber through the White Hall and into St Stephen's Chapel. Here, she was received by the Bishop of Norwich who was to perform the marriage. Blue carpets embellished with gold fleur-de-lys dazzled the eye at every turn while the king and queen and their children glittered with jewels and white cloth-of-gold beneath their golden canopy.

After the ceremony and the nuptial mass, the bride, her tiny hands engulfed by the mighty paws of the Duke of Gloucester and the Duke of Buckingham, was escorted from the chapel into the lavishly decorated king's great chamber.

Gold and silver coins were showered on the heads of the common people, and every lord, lady, gentleman and gentlewoman was in attendance. Even the king's mother, Duchess Cecily, deigned to grace the occasion with her presence, though I noticed she never once glanced at her daughter-in-law, the queen.

Only one person of high rank was missing. But nobody mentioned him. George, Duke of Clarence, under suspicion of treasonable activities, still lay in the tower while the king wrestled with the problem of what to do with his troublesome brother.

'Were you made welcome?' whispered Joan, who had not seen me since my return to my mother-in-law's chamber.

'She likes to keep an eye on me,' I replied.

'Does she fear you'll stray?'

I laughed. 'She fears her son might follow.'

We both looked to where Thomas was deep in conversation with his uncle, Lord Rivers.

'I suppose it is natural to want your family close,' Joan said.

'If they get much closer, we'll drown.'

It was true. The queen's family dominated every gathering. Wherever you looked, a Woodville shone like a star in the heavenly firmament, eclipsing lesser mortals – and there were so many of them! Each of the sisters had married advantageously while the brothers had been promoted beyond what anyone thought reasonable. Lionel was in Holy Orders, soon to become a bishop, and the two younger brothers, Richard and Edward, had found favour in the king's service. Only Anthony Woodville, Lord Rivers was well-respected, a man who would have risen high, no matter who his sister was.

'My Lady Buckingham seems out of sorts,' Joan remarked, eyeing the duchess who was sitting at the high table.

'She wishes to return to Brecknock. She's nearing her time.'

'Why does she not go?'

'The queen has refused her permission. Says she must attend today's wedding. After that she can go to the devil for all she cares.'

'A tempest?'

I laughed. 'You could hear them down in the courtyard. The duchess screaming it will be the queen's fault if she gives birth on the road.'

Joan put her hand over her mouth to stifle her giggles.

The wedding feast was interminable. We ate plovers and larks and curlews and richly spiced cakes. and drank enormous quantities of good red wine. The married couple, ridiculously young, were perched on gold satin cushions at the high table flanked by the king and queen who smiled at each other in triumph for having secured this most breathtaking of matrimonial prizes. Now all that remained was to secure a splendid foreign marriage for their eldest son.

I was seated at a table with other senior ladies, squeezed between two of the queen's sisters. I turned to Viscountess Bourchier who sat on my right, the extravagance of her crimson and silver robes threatening to eclipse my own carefully chosen plum-coloured velvet.

'This is a most splendid occasion,' I remarked. 'I've not seen the like before.'

'Oh, this is nothing,' she said, with a toss of her head. 'At the queen's coronation, my sister, Catherine, and her husband, Harry Stafford, were carried shoulder-high. The queen said she wanted her family to be admired by everyone for we were her most honoured guests.'

'A marriage made in Heaven,' I murmured, knowing it was nothing of the sort.

She gave a great sigh. 'Do you know, Lady Cecily, when my sisters and I first came to court, every family in the land vied to have one of us as a bride for their heir.' She laughed. 'We were considered most desirable.'

'You were indeed blessed.'

She smiled beatifically. 'Of course, you only have boys. You cannot know what it is like. My mother said it was the proudest day of her life.'

Having successfully navigated a conversation with the viscountess, I turned to the Countess of Pembroke. Since the birth of a daughter, she had blossomed from a complaining young woman into a comfortable matron who found little fault with the world. We spent an enjoyable time comparing the progress of our children. Naturally, her daughter proved exceptional whereas my three boys were considered quite unremarkable.

After the feasting, I went to pay my respects to Lady Catherine. She sat, scowling into a dish of winter pears, her hands laid protectively over her huge belly. When she saw me, her face lit up.

'Marchioness! I was hoping to see you. Sit here.'

'You wish to see me, duchess?' I said, somewhat taken aback at her enthusiastic greeting.

She lowered her voice to a confidential whisper. 'Lady Cecily, in the past I have not been your friend. It was wrong of me and I beg your forgiveness.'

She was pleading like Mary Hungerford did, trying to worm her way back into my favour. Undoubtedly she wanted something.

I paused for a moment, then said graciously, 'There is nothing to forgive, Lady Catherine.'

She leant closer and put her mouth to my ear. 'It is my husband, you understand. I have to save him.'

Harry Stafford, the noble Duke of Buckingham, did not appear to be in any danger. Having played a prominent role in today's royal nuptials, he was now talking to a couple of other lords. He produced a coin from his purse, tossed it in the air, caught it, slapped it on the back of his hand and laughed.

'Does he need saving, Lady Catherine?'

'Harry says he will be next.'

'Next?' I raised my eyebrows questioningly.

She stamped one of her elegant little feet on the floor. 'Do you not understand! Harry quarrelled with the king when they were in France. Since then he has been ignored. Now he is brought back. Why? Why does the king want him close?'

Why indeed, I thought.

'To honour him?' I suggested. 'To show forgiveness?'

'The king never forgives.'

'Perhaps he has forgotten about France.'

'The king forgets nothing. He keeps a tally of the doings of each man to use against them.'

'He forgave his brother, George.'

She rolled her eyes heavenwards as if I had said something stupid. 'Not this time.' She clutched at my sleeve as she glanced round to make certain we were not overheard. 'You know he is to have him killed,' she whispered.

'Lady Catherine, the king is not a monster.'

'No? You think not? You know nothing about him. He is full of suspicion. He sees treasons everywhere, even in the most innocent of actions.'

'A king needs to be careful,' I said, thinking of the verse shown me by William Catesby. 'Why would he be suspicious of your husband?'

'He fears Harry will aim for the throne.'

'Duchess! I do not think …'

'I do not need your thoughts,' she hissed. 'I need your help.'

'I have no access to the king. Perhaps if you asked the queen.'

She gave a derisive laugh. 'All my sister wants is to be rid of George.'

I wondered what punishment my mother-in-law planned for George: exile? A life of perpetual imprisonment?

'I could speak to my husband?' I volunteered.

'Thomas is no use to man or beast; surely you know that by now.'

'What would you have me do?' I said, biting my tongue on the words I'd have liked to say.

'Ask Lord Hastings. He has the king's confidence. I must know, Lady Cecily, I beg of you. A son will be no good to me without a father. If anything were to happen to Harry, my son would be taken away. '

She managed a tremulous little smile, betraying the real fear she felt, the fear all women face as their time draws near.

'Very well,' I said, kindly. 'I shall ask Lord Hastings. When I have an answer, I shall write. In the meantime I pray you have an easy birth.'

As I made my way back to my seat I noticed Lady Norfolk, dowager duchess and mother of the bride, making her way from the high table through a crowd of chattering women, coming in my direction.

She was about my mother's age but a woman much diminished by the death of her husband and the loss of her daughter to the queen. Her shoulders sagged beneath the splendour of her dark grey velvet robes, and even carefully applied paints and powders could not disguise her advancing years. My mother said she had no-one to care for but her household, no other children, her sister long dead, and a disinclination to remarry. Perhaps like many a widow she would retire into a religious life.

To my surprise she approached me.

'Duchess,' I murmured with a gracious incline of my head.

'Marchioness,' she replied, looking a if she was unsure of her reception. 'I have come to beg a favour.'

'A favour, my lady?' I was quite taken aback. What could Lady Norfolk possibly want from me. I had no connection with her kin. I could offer her nothing.

'Your mother tells me you are often with her grace, the queen.'

'Yes, that is true, my lady. It is my duty as well as my pleasure to attend her grace. I have no other occupation. My children are very young. They remain with their nursemaids in the country and my husband is mostly in attendance on the king.'

'Lady Cecily, you have seen how young my daughter is. I am loath to part with her but was given no choice.' When she looked into my eyes I saw a great hurt. There was no doubt she was suffering.

'Lady Hastings, your mother, understands how it is. She was given no choice in the decision to give you in marriage to the marquess. It was a royal command. She suggested I ask you to watch over my daughter. I realise it is much to ask but if you could see your way to grant a mother's wish I am sure you will find a just reward in Heaven.'

She looked as if she might start weeping at any moment.

'I should be honoured,' I said hastily, wondering how difficult it could be to keep an eye on a well-behaved five-year-old. 'Does the queen intend your daughter to live in the royal nursery?'

'She tells me nothing.' A single tear escaped from her eyelashes and ran in a line down her cheek. She lifted a hand and brushed it away.

'You must be pleased at the great honour done to your daughter, your grace.'

She hesitated. 'Lady Cecily, you know perfectly well why the queen wanted my daughter for her son. It has nothing to do with honour. A title and a great fortune are highly desirable when, like the queen, you are a woman raised in obscurity. If I could have saved my daughter from this travesty of a marriage, I would have done so. I mourn the unborn son I lost and wish my daughter had been born a plain gentleman's daughter. Then she would be beneath the queen's notice.'

'But to marry a prince is every girl's dream,' I said, encouraging her to see advantages of the match.

'Lady Cecily, when I was young, my sister and I were told that to understand dreams, requires guidance. It may be my daughter dreamed of marrying a prince but mistook what she saw in her vision. In the dream world it is impossible to know what is true from what is counterfeit.'

'I understand, your grace,' I said, not understanding why she needed to twist a young girls natural desire into something complex.

'My husband would grieve for our daughter, were he alive.' She clutched at the jewel she wore at her throat and whispered, 'I warned him to be careful, but he refused to listen.'

I frowned. 'Careful of what, your grace?'

She started as if surprised by what she'd said. 'Nothing! It is nothing, nothing at all.'

I moved my gaze away to give her a moment to recover her composure and happened to spy William Catesby's black-clad figure move through the crowd seeking out John Zouche who was with a group of men laughing at somebody's joke. I smiled.

'Who have you seen?' Her voice was sharp.

I looked back. 'No-one of importance, your grace; only a Master Catesby.'

Lady Norfolk's eyes widened. 'You know William Catesby?' she said accusingly.

I was taken aback by her vehemence.

'Yes, I do,' I said.

'How do you know him?'

'He is, on occasion, employed by my stepfather, your grace.'

I could see the constriction in her throat as she swallowed. 'Forgive me, I was unaware.'

'He is known to your grace?' I enquired, wondering what it was about William Catesby that so alarmed her.

She shook her head. 'My sister had a connection with his family, that is all,' she said quickly as if that explained everything.

I was certain that was *not* all but Lady Norfolk had her hand held to her mouth as if she would sew up her lips to prevent herself saying more unguarded words.

'His wife is a friend of mine,' I explained, inflating my single summer's friendship to a lifetime of attachment, not that I thought Meg would mind.

Lady Norfolk ignored my explanation. 'Lady Cecily. Before I return to my house at Broken Wharf, will you grant this grieving mother a favour? Will you have a care for my daughter?'

'Certainly, your grace,' I said, politely. 'I should be honoured. If I see anything amiss, be assured, I shall send word.'

On Thursday, as part of the celebrations, there was a great tournament. My husband and his younger brother, Richard Grey, took part as did some of the queen's brothers. Lord

Rivers, armed in the habit of a white hermit, caused a ripple of interest amongst the ladies. He was a handsome man like all the men in my mother-in-law's family. Since the loss of his wife he had remained unwed, a state of affairs which caused several women to readjust their gowns, gazing playfully in his direction, hoping to catch his eye.

'Will you take a wager on my brother?' the queen enquired, smiling.

As with everything my mother-in-law said, I wondered if there was a hidden meaning in her words.

'Your grace, he is matched against your son. As a good wife, should I not place my money on my husband?'

She laughed, a tinkling bell-like sound which belied the steeliness of her gaze. She enjoyed baiting me but since the birth of my third son I had become more adept at avoiding her barbs.

I picked up my embroidered purse, looking to see how many coins I had left. 'Will his grace, the king, not accept your wager?' I said brightly. 'I fear you might bankrupt me if I were to lose.'

The king, who had been sitting with his chin in his hand, staring moodily at nothing, turned at the mention of his name. His eyes were, like those of Lady Norfolk, full of pain.

'Her grace may place her money where she likes,' he said flatly. 'The queen is fortunate to have a brother who is loyal to us.'

Still smiling, the queen leant across and placed her slim white hand on the king's sleeve. 'Anthony will always be your most obedient and devoted servant, my lord. He will never let you down.'

It would be a foolish man who would be disloyal when he'd been given the king's eldest son to raise, and Lord Rivers was far from being foolish. He was elegant, well read, said to be kind and just, a sober man who took his duties seriously. Yet my stepfather did not trust him.

The king stood up. Close to, his famed good looks were not as glorious as they'd once been. When I first saw him, that day my mother took me to Westminster, I thought him the most handsome man I had ever seen. But he'd grown stout in the loins these past four years and his face had come to resemble, not so much a beautiful young prince, but an old boar we'd once kept at Ashby: flabby, jowly, with little piggy eyes. His glittering jewels and rich robes disguised the unpalatable truth and the crowd saw only what they expected to see: an imposing regal figure, clothed magnificently, accompanied by his beautiful queen and surrounded by a family of handsome children.

With a signal from the king, a fanfare of trumpets sounded to announce the start of the jousts.

Thomas fought with a degree of skill but no matter how cunning, could not best his uncle. He carried my favour tucked hidden in his breastplate and smiled, then quickly looked away when he noticed me gazing at him. The queen, making it obvious where her preferences lay, tapped her sister, the Viscountess, on the arm and relieved her of the last of her coins. I could have told Viscountess Bourchier not to waste her money because my mother-in-law always played to win.

That night Thomas came to my bed but seemed distracted.

'Is something amiss?' I asked.

'No,' he said shortly, throwing off his robe and climbing into bed.

'You acquitted yourself well this afternoon,' I said, moving closer into the warmth between us.

'Parliament is to resume tomorrow,' he said, not looking at me.

'You will attend?' It was not really a question. It was a man's duty to be at the parliament if he received a summons.

'Naturally.'

'Will it last many more weeks?' I asked, idly placing my hand on his bare arm, thinking how beautiful his muscles were.

'My mother says the king is to lay charges against his brother,' he said flatly.

I withdrew my hand. 'What charges?'

'There is to be a bill of attainder.'

'Against the Duke of Clarence?'

Thomas turned his head to look at me. 'The king is intent on reducing George to nothing.'

I remembered my mother's tales of how Mad Henry had raised a bill of attainder against my Nevill grandparents. My grandfather had slipped away to Calais, while my grandmother, left alone at Middleham, had fled to Ireland with nothing but the clothes on her back and the shoes on her feet. If she'd been caught they would have burned her as a traitor.

'He'll not have him killed, surely.' There was silence. 'Thomas! He cannot order his brother killed.'

'No,' my husband said hesitantly. 'I believe he will be merciful.'

Despite the words, he sounded unconvinced.

'Why act now? George has been in the Tower for months.'

Thomas began fiddling with our bedcover, teasing out tufts of fur and rolling them into knots. He sighed. 'The king has had word from France. You remember how last summer George sought the hand of the Duchess of Burgundy?'

'I remember.'

'It seems he planned to make himself King of England.'

Dear God! If George had tried for the throne it would have been brother against brother: more battles, more bloodshed, more deaths. If George, with the might of Burgundy at his back, had triumphed, what would have happened to us? The king dead, the queen's power destroyed and Thomas, if he'd survived death in battle, would almost certainly have been executed. To think I had taken so lightly those verses shown me by Master Catesby.

Above our heads, the shimmering crimson Florentine silk changed its shape. In the wavering light of the night candle I saw, not seductive folds of bright red cloth, but sinister slow-moving rivers of blood.

I shook my head. It did not do to become fanciful. The plot had been dealt with and, as Thomas said, the king would not kill his brother.

13

LONDON 1478

During the remaining days of the parliament, my stepfather proved particularly elusive. One moment he was sitting with other lords in Westminster Hall, busy with matters of great concern to the kingdom; a day later he was in conference with the king and his chancellor and could not be disturbed. Then it was reported he'd gone to the Tower to see Sir John Sutton on the king's business but when my man went there, he was told Lord Hastings was with the elderly Archbishop of Canterbury, Cardinal Bourchier.

'At Knole?' I queried, surprised my stepfather would journey so far to see Archbishop Bourchier.

'No, m'lady. At his grace's house at Lambeth.'

How stupid of me. The archbishop would be here for the parliament. Where else would he be.

Eventually after three weeks of waiting and searching, I was told Lord Hasting would be at his house by Pauls Wharf that afternoon and would see me there.

He was sitting in his chair, reading, when I was shown into his room. For a moment I was transported back to my childhood, to the little closet at Ashby where my stepfather went to be private. When I escaped my nursemaid, I would sidle in through the door and stand at his shoulder, trying to see what he was doing. He would lift me onto his knee and let me trace the words with my finger. If there were pictures, he would talk to me about them: the young man with his hand out picking a large red apple from a tree, and two strange brown animals with humps on their backs. Best of all was the picture of Mother Mary in her bright blue cloak, a golden glow around her head and a tiny baby held in her arms.

He looked up and smiled. 'Ceci!'

I saw new lines of worry on his face, and hair which was increasingly grey. He was well gone into middle age and, despite all his riding hither and thither on the king's business, he had grown somewhat stooped.

I walked across the room and kissed his cheek. He might not have fathered me but in every other way he was my father and I loved him. I could not imagine life without him.

We talked for a few moments about home, my mother and my children. He worried in case I'd felt abandoned by him, he was so often away in Calais. Above all, he was anxious to know was I content in this marriage he had never wanted for me.

'Truly,' I said. 'I am content.'

He smiled. 'Are you here on behalf of your husband?'

'No, I am come from the Duchess of Buckingham.'

He let out a great sigh. 'Ah, Buckingham! What a trouble Harry Stafford is. What does his wife want? I thought she had returned to Brecknock.'

I blushed, nervous at asking my stepfather to divulge what he might want kept secret. 'She has, but she is afraid. She believes the king is planning harm to her husband, perhaps to have him killed. Is it true?'

My stepfather walked over to the fire and stirred the crumbling logs with the toe of his boot. Then he bent down, picked a large piece of apple-wood out of the basket and threw it on the glowing pile of embers.

'You can assure the duchess, the king has no plans to kill her husband. On the contrary, he has found a use for him.'

I sighed with relief. 'She will be pleased. What position is he to have?'

My stepfather straightened up, turned and looked at me bleakly. 'Chief executioner!'

I could think of nothing to say; I just stared at him in horror.

He came and placed his hands gently on my shoulders. 'Ceci, you must understand how it is. Parliament wishes sentence on the Duke of Clarence carried out without further delay. So the king must order it. He has no choice. He is sending young Buckingham to the Tower to ensure the execution is done as required.'

I could not believe the king would subject his brother to the horrors of hanging, gutting and beheading. It was too awful to contemplate. No matter what George had done – and I accepted he was guilty of treason – he had once been Isabel's husband. He had lain with her. She had held him in her arms. He was the father of her two little children.

'Is it to be a traitor's death?'

My stepfather gave a bitter laugh. 'As a token of his mercy, the king has allowed his brother to choose the manner of his death. The fool has asked to be drowned in a barrel of malmsey.'

'Drowned?'

'The guards have been instructed to fetch up a barrel and in accordance with their orders, to hold him head first in the wine until he is dead.'

The picture he painted was awful, unbelievable.

'Dear God! When?'

'Tomorrow.'

I shivered in horror. 'How can the king bear to kill his own brother?'

My stepfather shrugged. 'He says he has no alternative.'

'Do you believe him?'

'Ceci, he is the king. I know where my loyalty lies; where it will always lie.'

'But to kill his brother!'

'Brother or no, friend or no, George is a traitor. He was forgiven once. He cannot be forgiven a second time.'

He put his arms round me. holding me against his shoulder while I wept for this man I barely knew who was a traitor to his king.

After a while I wiped away the last of my tears.

'Go home to your husband,' my stepfather said, gently. 'And Ceci.'

'Yes?'

'Tell him to look to his own affairs. The king is not in a forgiving mood.'

By the time I disembarked at our landing stage, the filth which festooned the muddy foreshore when the river was low, had disappeared, hidden beneath the incoming tide. I gave a cautious sniff – nothing but the smell of sodden greenery; the advancing water had smothered the stench which might have drifted up from the quays at Queenhithe.

A servant stood by with a lantern as the barge drew alongside. The watermen in their blue and white livery appeared from nowhere, ready to secure the ropes, allowing me to step ashore without mishap. I hurried up the path to the steps leading into the house, aware that the onset of evening had brought a steady cold drizzle from the west.

'Where is the marquess?' I asked our steward as I relinquished my layers of damp clothing to my maid.

'Upstairs in his chamber, m'lady.'

I ran my gaze across the men in the hall, most busy setting up tables and benches for supper, two of them carrying in the napery. Everything was at it should be so I walked towards the stairway.

'M'lady.'

I turned, surprised, one foot already on the lower stair. 'Yes?'

'It is the marquess, m'lady.'

'What of him?'

The steward shifted awkwardly in the way of a man with something to hide. 'He is not himself, m'lady. He appears, how can I put it, out of sorts.'

'Has he asked for his physician?'

'No, m'lady.'

'Then I shall see to him myself.'

The man heaved an audible sigh of relief.

Out of sorts? An odd way to describe my husband. To the men of our household, Thomas was an exemplary master: a cheerful, uncomplicated man, fond of the pleasures of life, a little wild like most young men but never ill-tempered in the way of some lords. His habit of passing difficult tasks to others rather than deal with them himself might appear the mark of an idle man, but if he failed to beat his servants it was more to do with his sunny temper than to laziness. Provided he had money in his purse, his estates turned a profit and his stable was a credit to his house, he seldom complained. So why was he out of sorts. No wonder the steward was concerned.

I hurried up the stairs. The servant who brought in the candles at dusk was nowhere to be seen but I caught a glimpse of two boys with a basket of logs disappearing round a corner. At the entrance to Thomas's room I knocked and, not waiting for a reply, pushed open the door. A single candle in a silver candlestick threw a meagre pool of light onto the floor, otherwise the room was in darkness. A sudden draught from the open door caused the candle to gutter as a shadow leapt across the wall.

My husband stood at the window with his back to me, his shoulders hunched like a bedraggled heron sheltering from the rain. He had removed his doublet and was dressed in only a loose linen shirt over his hose. Outside, in the gathering gloom, a few lights bobbed merrily up and down – boats taking young men across the river to sample the delights of Southwark.

From what I'd gleaned, most husbands learned their business from the painted ladies of Southwark, their apprenticeships underwritten by their older kinsmen. I was curious to know if a young Thomas Grey had frequented the stews and if so, who had paid for his education. But this was not a question a wife could ask her husband.

I walked softly across the floor until I stood behind him. He did not turn round.

'Thomas,' I said quietly.

He did not reply.

'Thomas,' I said again, this time a little louder.

He still said nothing. I touched his arm.

'Thomas, is something wrong? Are you sick?'

'Go away!' he said in a low, flat voice.

I removed my hand from his sleeve but stayed where I was.

After a little while he spoke again in the same dull voice.

'I tod you – go away. There is nothing you can do.'

I hesitated, then said, 'You cannot know that. Please, Thomas, tell me what is wrong.'

Slowly he turned until he was facing me.

His face was drawn and stained with what might have been tears. His hair, usually so sleek, stuck up in spikes. His breath held the whiff of sour wine and the sight of an empty jug lying by the table told me he'd been drinking.

For a long time he just stood there saying nothing, his eyes half closed, while I tried to think what I should do. Then he began to sway as if his legs might give way beneath him.

I took his arm. 'Thomas! Please, sit!'

As if obeying a tutor's orders, he sat down heavily on a nearby stool. He remained there with his hands hanging loosely between his knees, his eyes fixed firmly on his boots. He refused to look at me. That was when I knew he was in serious trouble because Thomas would always look me in the face, even when telling me a lie. He had such an open, honest expression it had taken me more than a year of marriage to discover that he was capable of telling lies. At the time I'd been shocked but perhaps not as shocked as I should have been.

I knelt down in front of him, sitting back on my heels.

'Thomas. I beg of you, tell me what is wrong. It may be I can help.'

At this, he glanced up. His mouth trembled. 'I cannot tell you.'

'Why not?'

He returned his gaze to his boots.

'Thomas! Please!'

'Too horrible,' he mumbled, clasping and unclasping his hands.

'Nothing can be that horrible,' I said gently, wondering what awfulness he'd involved himself in.

'You'd not understand.'

'How can I understand if you will not say?'

He shook his head.

'Thomas, I cannot help unless you tell me.'

By now I was afraid this was something to do with the Duke of Clarence's treason. Had Thomas stupidly involved himself with the Oxford men who'd been casting horoscopes or with George's squire who'd written those verses. With the king in his present mood, it was no wonder he was frightened. I tried to think who, if anyone, he might have taken into his confidence.

'Have you spoken to your mother?'

His head jerked up in alarm. 'No! And you cannot tell her. Whatever you do, you must promise never to tell her.'

By now he was almost wild with fear. Whatever he'd done, he wanted it kept secret from his mother. I hugged a small triumph. Even if he refused to tell me there was joy in knowing he'd not confided in her.

With the tips of my fingers I touched his hands. They were shaking. 'Thomas, I promise she will hear nothing from my lips. Not a word. Whatever this is will be between you and me, as it should be with husband and wife. No-one else need know. But I beg of you, tell me what has happened.'

I could see him weighing up if I could be trusted. He wanted to confide in someone but was frightened I might betray his secret. He chewed his bottom lip as he wrestled with indecision.

'I promise, I shall tell no-one,' I said again, very quietly.

There was a long pause. '... woman,' he mumbled.

I felt a wash of relief. Of course it was a woman! What had I expected. My husband was not a man to involve himself in plotting treason. There was no reason for him to do so. In my dreams I might hanker after a dukedom for him but he was content with the rewards he'd already been given. He was not greedy in that way, understanding that Thomas Grey owed his success to his mother's royal marriage not to his services to the king. Without his mother's efforts he might not even be heir to his grandmother's lands at Groby. It was no wonder he felt obligated to her, a young man unable to step out from the maternal shadow.

'Tell me,' I said.

It took him a long time. It was a tawdry little tale of the kind which might happen to any careless, free-spending man with an eye for an attractive young woman.

There were a dozen such time-wasters amongst Thomas's acquaintances: idlers and boasters with little to recommend them other than an appetite for drink and a fondness for gaming, young men who might easily fall prey to a brazen schemer. But on this occasion there were dangerous forces at play which my foolish husband had chosen to ignore.

'She was so pretty, such fun,' he said, lamely, almost begging me to agree.

'Free with her favours?'

He gazed at me with that innocent look which could still disarm me. 'No, she was not like that. She was a respectable married woman.'

There followed a long rambling account of how my husband had come to meet this respectable married woman. The words tumbled from his lips as he tried to explain how it had been. He wanted to tell someone and, although I was his wife, I was as good a listener as any.

The father had been a respected city alderman; the husband, a mercer named William Shore, well-known amongst the London merchant community. It was a marriage arranged for her by her father.

'She confided in me.'

I was astounded. 'In you?'

'It was a most private matter.'

'Mistress Shore chose to confide this most private of matters to you, a virtual stranger.'

'I was not a stranger,' my guileless husband said. 'She looked upon me as a friend.'

'A married woman should confide in her women friends,' I remarked coolly, wondering what this woman had hoped to gain from befriending my husband.

'She said she was too ashamed to tell anyone.'

'Ashamed? Of what?'

I sat with a face like stone while he told me. The story with its stops and starts, endless prevarications and numerous hesitations, took a long time in the telling. It was like a confessional, a baring of the soul, an attempt to justify his actions. I would have preferred to stop my ears and cease to listen but I had no choice. I had asked him to tell me and could hardly complain when he did.

The details were utterly disgusting. It seemed that the unfortunate Master Shore, despite marrying a pretty and willing young wife, was unable to do the deed. He showed no interest in what was expected of him between the sheets, and Mistress Shore, for all her allure and tentative efforts at intimacy, remained untouched by her husband. The bed they shared was a cold and joyless place and their marriage, outwardly so successful, continued unconsummated.

After several years of this sorry state of affairs, Mistress Shore wished for an annulment of her marriage so that she could take another husband and fulfil the purpose for which God created her, namely, to be a proper wife to some man and bear his children.

'Very worthy,' I said tartly.

'I wanted to help,' Thomas said, eagerly. 'That was all. Just be a good friend. I sought no reward, not for myself. She was such a deserving young woman. You'd like her if you met her.'

I very much doubted that.

'What did you do?' I asked, wondering what reward he'd expected from this deserving young woman.

It transpired that my obliging husband, as well as providing support and guidance to the likeable Mistress Shore, had retained a lawyer to take the her case to the Court of Arches. But the dean of the court had wisely thrown out the case. Three times they tried without success. Fortunately my husband had baulked at the vast expense of paying for the case to be taken to the papal court, the only course left open to Mistress Shore if she wanted her marriage annulled.

'Did she have no other rich friends?' I asked. 'Pretty young women whose husbands cannot oblige them in that way usually find others with fat purses who will.'

Thomas looked at me uncomfortably. 'I told you; she was not like that. She was chaste.'

I very much doubted that Mistress Shore was chaste, but kept my opinion to myself.

'What happened?'

Thomas looked at me properly for the first time. 'So many times since that day, I have regretted what I did, but at the time I truly thought it for the best.'

'What did you do?'

He told me how he had recounted the story of this pretty young woman to the king, thinking to entertain his audience, knowing how the king would laugh at the failings of the miserable husband. The king enjoyed the story so much that he ordered Thomas to bring Mistress Shore to him so that he could see for himself what kind of woman would fail to excite passion in a husband. Naturally the inevitable happened. The king's interest was piqued and within a matter of weeks Mistress Shore was ensconced at the king's side at those special entertainments arranged just for the king and his favoured companions.

In the months that followed there were numerous private visits to the houses of the king's friends, hunts for game in the greenwood and picnics amidst the leafy bowers at Havering. It was there, far from the watchful eyes of the queen, that Mistress Shore would ride with her king, sup with her king, laugh with him, dance for him and doubtless oblige him in whatever way he wished. If the queen knew, she said nothing, which was why until now, I'd not heard of the enchanting Mistress Shore.

Of course the story did not end there. Once she had obtained the costly annulment of her marriage and was a free woman again, Mistress Shore invited my husband to call on her at the house she now owned in one of the fashionable streets off Cheapside. She wished to thank him for all he had done for her.

'You went?' I lifted my eyebrows in surprise.

He looked at me in bewilderment. 'Naturally I went. What harm was there in visiting an old friend?'

'Oh, no harm at all. But, tell me – exactly how did this old friend of yours propose to demonstrate her gratitude?'

Thomas flushed, looked at me in confusion, hesitated and then mumbled something about an offer of certain intimacies.

'You accepted?' I asked, holding my breath, not wanting to know.

'Yes,' he said, very low.

My heart lurched. I had surely known this was where the story was leading but to hear it from his own lips was like a blow to my body. For a moment the pain was so great I was unable to breathe.

'Did you not think it unwise, knowing her involvement with the king?' I said in a voice quite unlike my own, a voice which was not quite steady.

'I didn't think.'

No. He didn't think. He didn't think of me, his wife and he didn't think of his lord, the king. How shaming of him not to think of me, but how foolish not to think of the king because a king has spies everywhere. He makes it his business to know everything concerning a woman in whom he is interested. I doubted Mistress Shore could look in the mirror to pin up her hair without the king being informed.

'How often did you visit her?' I asked, very quietly.

He shot a glance at me and then dropped his gaze. 'Twice.'

My husband would not have been counting. I guessed it was many more times than twice.

'And then?'

'She said we must cease, the king was suspicious.'

'When was this?'

'Last summer.'

'While I was confined at Bradgate having your child?'

'Yes.' He had the grace to look ashamed at his betrayal of our marriage.

A silence filled the space between us as the air I breathed grew colder.

'And now?' I thought of my stepfather warning me that Thomas should look to his own affairs.

His gaze, at last, met mine. 'The king is settling old scores.'

I nodded. 'Yes, he is. Lord Hastings says the Duke of Clarence is to die.'

'You see! First George; then me.'

'The king knows about you and this Mistress Shore?'

He covered his face with his hands and cried, 'I do not know! That is the worst of it. I do not know. But she is bound to have told him.'

How easy it would be for this pretty young woman to twist the encounter at her house, to say my husband had forced his attentions upon her then threatened he would tell her royal lover unless she continued to submit.

I doubted Mistress Shore had done that. She would have been much too afraid of what the king might do to her. Perhaps she had already experienced an outburst of royal temper. I'd not seen one of the king's rages but my mother said even my stepfather would turn pale and pretend he was elsewhere. I thought a woman in Mistress Shore's position would do everything in her power to keep her royal lover sweet – and ignorant of her dalliance with my husband.

I closed my eyes against the image of Thomas enjoying himself in the arms of pretty Mistress Shore.

'Lord Hastings says the king is not in a forgiving mood,' I remarked, purposefully twisting the knife hard, intending the pain which I knew would follow.

Thomas gave a moan. 'I knew it! Dear God, Ceci! You said you would help. What shall I do?' He gripped my hands. 'I beg you. Help me!'

Help was not what I wanted to give. I wanted to hurt him. And hurt him badly. Scratch out his eyes, pull out his hair, take a knife to his clothes. I would slit every one of his embroidered doublets into small pieces, rip those rich fur linings out of his robes, tear his fine silk shirts into shreds.

At that moment, if I'd had the means, I would have killed him.

I was a good wife. He could not have wanted better. Yet he had insulted me. He had betrayed my love and betrayed our marriage. He was a cheat, a liar and a fornicator. And I hated him.

When I married, I'd not expected a knight from the romances, a handsome young man clad in shining armour ready to slay my dragons. But what he'd done, the hurt he'd so carelessly inflicted, altered my perception of him as a man worthy of my love. If my stepfather was the standard I set for a husband then Thomas had failed. He had shown himself lacking in qualities I expected and I was unsure what I should do. Part of me just wanted to die. I was seventeen years old, yet at that moment felt as miserable and lost as a sour old dowager of seventy.

I'd lived with Thomas long enough to know he was far from perfect and I knew few men were faithful to their wives. Separations, the natural consequence of a man's rise in the world, could be lengthy and husbands proved disappointingly susceptible to temptation. But in its fundamental nature I'd thought our marriage was different. Lady Donne had warned me of his youthful indiscretions but I'd believed that was all they were. I thought he'd shed them when he married me. Idle flirtations and promises of undying love were part of a young man's armoury and Thomas had always enjoyed the company of women but I'd believed his marriage vows would keep him faithful. What a fool I was!

Of course I was too young to understand how much my pride had been damaged; not just my pride in myself but my pride in Thomas. I'd been taught that a wife should regard her husband as her superior, someone she could look up to, someone who gave her standing in the world. To have him disappoint me so gravely had broken something inside me. My heart felt bruised.

But I knew this was no time to feel sorry for myself. Thomas had allowed me to see him unmanned by fear. He would not forget. In a few days time he would look back on this evening and resent me for witnessing his failings, re-imagining our conversation, painting me as a heartless shrew. I would not be the loving companion who had offered help but a suspicious wife seeking revenge for his efforts in supporting a deserving young woman. He would convince himself that he was not at fault, not in any way.

At this moment I might hate him but, if I wanted to rescue our marriage, I must let him believe he *could* be that knight in shining armour from the romances, that there were other dragons to slay and that, if he was stalwart and true, I would be his princess in the high tower, waiting to be rescued.

We were young, we could do this together if only I could make him believe in himself as a man. But first I must beguile him back to my side, let him see me as a young woman who desired him as other women desired him, not simply as a wife doing her regular wifely duty. I must make him want me as he'd wanted Mistress Shore and if I needed to use low tricks for that, then that was what I would do.

I blinked away my tears, hiding the hurt I felt, swallowed hard and set to work.

'Do you remember the summer we travelled to Kirby to visit my mother?' I asked in as pleasant a voice as I could muster.

'Of course I do,' he muttered.

'The boy who called out, "Is that the king?" as you rode by.'

He gave a brief smile. 'Yes, I remember.'

'You are a most handsome and courtly man, Thomas. People admire you. It is no wonder Mistress Shore was tempted.'

'That is how it was,' he said mournfully. 'If she'd not been so desirous, so eager – you understand, it was *she* who was eager.'

How easily men fool themselves, I thought, thrusting to the back of my mind the picture of my husband drawing an eager Mistress Shore into his arms.

'Naturally she was eager and she will not have meant to put you in danger. But you must be careful. When the king finishes with her – as he will – you cannot go near her again. He may offer her to you, which I believe is his custom with the women he discards, but it would be unwise to accept.'

He nodded sadly. 'Yes. You are right. I see that now. But what if he already suspects I have been …?' He blushed. 'That she and I …'

I dug my nails into the palm of my hand to stop myself from thinking too much about what she and he had been doing together, of the whispered intimacies they had shared in the warmth and comfort of her bed.

'We should leave,' I said crisply. 'We must remove you from the king's presence before he decides to remove you himself.'

Thomas was almost falling over himself in his haste to agree. 'Yes, that would be wise. If I am absent from court he will not think of me. He will forget. And there are plenty of other men to take my place.'

I gave a small smile. 'We might go to the West Country; inspect my inheritance. What could be more natural?'

He gave me a glimmer of a smile in return. 'You have always wanted to see Shute, have you not?'

I touched his hand so that he would know we were in agreement. 'I have, but more than anything, I want you kept safe.'

'I cannot just go; not without leave. The king will suspect I am running away.'

I leaned forward and kissed him lightly on his mouth to seal our bargain. His lips tasted of stale wine and falsehoods.

'There is no question of running. I shall send the queen a note; say one of the children is unwell and you are taking me to Bradgate. Ask her to make your excuses to the king. Once we are away from London, we can make our way westwards. No-one will think to ask questions.'

We remained where we were: Thomas silent on the stool, me on my knees on the floor. After a while, I laid my head in his lap and he began to stroke my hair.

My mother said that each man had a particular set of ideals by which he orders his life and a wife's duty was to nurture those ideals and hold her husband to account should his standards show signs of slipping. Anne's husband lived according to his belief in loyalty – once bound, Richard of Gloucester, she said, was incapable of being disloyal. My stepfather believed in honour. He was true to his word. If he promised a man a favour, he would not let him down.

I had yet to discover what inner belief moved my husband beyond his need to survive in a world he perceived as inherently hostile. Perhaps this crisis in our marriage would allow me a small window into the soul of the real Thomas Grey.

But first, there was work to be done.

I looked up at him and said softly, 'Shall we go to bed?'

14

LONDON 1483

I stood at the water's edge as the river advanced slowly across the shingle, a voracious invader intent on pillage, consuming everything within its path. Downriver, beyond the jumble of rooftops on London's bridge, lay the Tower where, five years before, Cousin Isabel's husband had drowned in a butt of Malmsey wine. Five years in which I had grown up, leaving behind that prideful young woman who thought her heart was breaking, becoming more sober, more forgiving, more aware of what was important and what was not.

It had been a long hard winter. Since Christmas the rain had been relentless. Our steward at Shute wrote of ferocious gales battering the coastline, rivers breaching their banks, whole villages washed away and low-lying cottages swept into the sea. Fears of a miserable summer loomed.

But by Eastertide, our lives were greatly enriched. The first sign of spring warmth came with the death of Thomas's grandmother, a spiteful old woman who'd done her best to stop Thomas receiving his rightful inheritance, wanting the lands to go instead to the children of her second family. It was a comfort to know she'd been defeated, her death delivering Astley and the rich Groby estates into my husband's hands. An even greater triumph was our acquisition of the huge Exeter fortune when Parliament finally agreed that little Anne St Leger was the rightful heir. The child was Thomas's ward and lived in the nursery at Bradgate, marked as a valuable future bride for young Tom.

Water slid closer to the toes of my boots.

'Looking for dead bodies?'

A familiar voice – John Zouche! I turned slowly with a smile on my face,

'In a way.'

He gave a slight bow.

'Thought as much. You always were a bloodthirsty young woman.'

I laughed. 'If you're seeking the marquess, he is with the king.'

'I thought he might be at the Tower.'

The position of Deputy Constable of the Tower had been an unexpected honour, passed to Thomas by his Uncle Anthony. It seemed that this year the king was being more than generous to his wife's family.

'The marquess tells me Lord Dudley is too feeble to keep a privy pit secure, let alone the Tower,' I laughed.

'Dudley's seventy if he's a day. The king needs someone younger to do the work.'

'While Lord Dudley sups in his slippers, reminiscing with his chaplain.'

John came and stood at my side, both of us staring towards the distant walls of York Place where the bend in the river hid the king's great palace of Westminster.

'What news from the council chamber?' he asked. 'Are we to invade France this summer? If we are, I'd best set my men to sharpening their weapons. They are sadly out of practice.'

I picked up a stone from the shingle, then hurriedly stepped back as a ripple of water threatened to soak not only my boots but the hem of my skirts. 'There is talk of war. The marquess says the king is furious at the loss of his pension. He is looking for someone to blame.'

'I hear Lord Hastings received a tongue-lashing.'

'That was Lord Rivers. He accused my stepfather of wanting to sell Calais to King Louis.'

John stooped down and picked up a stone. 'Rivers is a fool. Lord Hastings would never betray the king. He is the most loyal man I know.'

'Of course he is but Lord Rivers will do anything to have my stepfather brought down. There is a chasm between them as wide as the Narrow Sea and it's filled with mutual hostility.'

John sent his stone skimming across the water.

'What was it this time? Keys to open the gates to the enemy?'

My mother believed the king had caused great offence to the queen's family when he gave the captaincy of Calais to my stepfather. She said it was the only significant honour awarded to the queen's father and having once given it to the queen's brother, to take it away had been most unwise.

I sighed. 'Lord Rivers drips poison into the king's ear and no-one gainsays him. My stepfather trusts none of the queen's family.'

'Not even the marquess?'

I shrugged. 'He is diplomatic in his dealings with my husband but they are not friends, nor ever likely to be.'

John picked up another stone. 'I did hear talk of a quarrel.'

'More than one.'

'What does the lovely Lady Hastings say?'

I smiled. 'My mother rarely comes to London. She hears what my stepfather chooses to tell her.'

'And you?'

'I am a good wife, John. I take my husband's part in all things.'

He laughed. 'My brother-in-law speaks very highly of you.'

'Your brother-in-law?'

'Will Catesby.'

'Oh yes, Master Catesby!' I smiled. 'I've not seen him since the Christmas celebrations. Not that there was much to celebrate this year once the king had news of the treaty between France and Burgundy.'

John stared moodily into the distance. 'To think a few years ago our world seemed settled and peaceful.'

It was true. The death of the young Duchess of Burgundy had changed everything. Her widower, the beleaguered Duke Maximilian, panic-stricken at French aggression on his borders, had signed a treaty of peace with King Louis. With the duchy in his pocket, Louis saw no reason to continue paying the English king a pension. Why would he? To rub salt in the wound, all hope of a French marriage for Princess Elizabeth disappeared as soon as the ink on the peace treaty was dry.

We turned and ambled slowly back to the house, avoiding numerous puddles on the path. I wondered where Thomas was. He said he'd return from Westminster by yesterday evening but there'd been no word. It was not that I mistrusted him, those days were far behind us. Our marriage was mended and to the casual observer there were no signs of where it had once been torn apart. The stitches I had carefully applied to the damaged seams were visible to no-one but myself and, like many a patched garment, the fabric was stronger than before. Our households ran smoothly, my husband's favourite dishes were served when he was at home and if most of the careful stitching had been done in the confines of our marriage bed, Thomas was none the wiser.

These past five years I had worked tirelessly at being the woman he would want above any other, the one who intrigued and delighted him. I had prevented our intimacy from growing stale by devising new ways to please him. Even when confined at Bradgate, I had ensured he was made welcome. And if the means of my welcome shocked my confessor, I deemed it a necessary sin.

My mother, that most perceptive of women, guessed what I was doing.

'The Church will have you damned six times before breakfast,' she remarked casually as she tickled the toes of my latest baby daughter.

I gave an elegant little shrug. 'Some sins are forgivable.'

'Are they?'

'The end must surely justify the means?'

She sighed. 'That is what all sinners say.'

'And what do you say?' I asked her.

She gave me one of her sideways looks. 'Be careful! Do not trust him. Never forget he is his mother's son.'

I laughed. 'Look at me! Do you think I am dissatisfied with the way he treats me?'

My mother shook her head. 'You young people understand nothing. You have never been tested. You think your lives a continual summer picnic under the trees; endless sweet pastries and cool spiced wine. You should remember that summer never lasts.'

She was wrong. Thomas and I knew all about the cold winds of winter which threaten a man and his wife. The loss of our first two sons in an outbreak of plague, the year after we visited Shute, might have ripped our marriage apart but for the new-found strength of our togetherness.

I faced the sight of those two pathetic little bodies with the fortitude expected of a wife and mother and despite my own sorrow found the strength to comfort my husband when he collapsed to his knees, sobbing like a child. I held him in my arms and stroked his hair, reminding him that God remained above in heaven and we were young and would have other sons.

Even the queen's insistence on his presence at Windsor for the burial of two-year-old Prince George, did not prevent Thomas from returning to be with me at Bradgate the following day. We wept for our two little boys, prayed together and then, despite fearing sensual enjoyment was somehow wrong at such a time, resolutely set about increasing our family once more. When a wave of desire overrode my all-encompassing grief, stirrings of guilt led me to weep on Thomas's shoulder as if my heart would break. Some men would have been justly angry but Thomas was kind, gathering me close, murmuring that between husband and wife this was a God-given act.

I ignored my mother's warnings, refusing to pass my days enumerating Thomas's sins on my fingers. Instead I flattered him for the qualities I wished to foster: his pleasant conversations with the men who frequented our table, his kindness to ancient grandmothers who tottered in to request a favour from their lord, and his pride in our children.

He was not a clever man like my stepfather who had made himself indispensible to his king, nor was he skilled at finding men to covet his good lordship. He was generous but impetuous and gullible, not qualities men looked for in a leader. His followers valued his company, though few were the kind of men you would want at your side in a crisis. I comforted myself in the knowledge that together we had overcome not one but two disasters and our marriage was stronger and more secure for having been tested.

Yet sometimes, in the dead of night, when owls called to each other in the darkness and small creatures scuttled about behind the panelling, when winter gales blew from the east and sleet hurled itself against the windows, I would wake amidst fears that the knots I had so painstakingly tied to make our life perfect might one day start to unravel.

It was late when I heard a commotion and an unfamiliar voice in the hall. The new boy, an undersized lad from Leicestershire, cousin to one of Thomas's valets, had just brought in the candles. The child was careful in his work and if instructed properly, without too much violence, would do well. I made it my business to take an interest in the younger servants as I knew how easily a growing boy could acquire bad habits.

When the knock came, I allowed the child to open the door, a task he performed commendably, despite an unfortunate gawping at the sight of a tall stranger in the doorway.

It was a messenger from Westminster but not one of my husband's men.

He fell to one knee. 'I come from my mistress, Lady Donne,' he said, fumbling for the letter in his pouch.

I was surprised as it was only a week since I'd seen my stepfather's sister at the Easter celebrations. I took the sealed packet. It was more a note than a letter, only a few hastily scribbled words.

"Come at once to Westminster. It is urgent."

I looked up in alarm. 'Has something happened to the marquess?'

'I do not know, m'lady. My mistress did not say.'

'Lord Hastings?'

The man shook his head. 'I was told nothing, m'lady; just to bring you to my mistress.'

I cursed the man. Why did he not know? Did he not have eyes? Did he not listen? What kind of dolt was he?

I knew the quickest way to Westminster was by boat but the tide had turned and was flowing out fast. It would soon be dark so we would need to be careful. I gave orders for the smaller barge to be made ready, for two armed men to accompany me and for my maid to fetch my warmest cloak.

Joan offered her services but she was grey with fatigue so I said I would take one of the maids. In no time the oarsmen were ready and the barge was heading upriver with a lantern on the prow as a warning to others of our coming. Like a bad omen, a sharp little wind had blown up from the south-west, throwing spatters of rain into my face and creeping under the folds of my cloak. I would be lying to say I was not nervous.

15

WESTMINSTER 1483

Despite the lateness of the hour the outer courtyards of the royal palace were crowded with shadowy groups of figures. Torchlight flared across walls, illuminating men gathered near the gatehouse, waiting for friends to arrive. Our entry attracted no attention: a woman with her maid and three menservants was of no interest.

With a nod from the guards, we passed into the inner courtyard, then up steps to the main doors of the palace where a brief scrutiny of our faces and the men's livery badges, allowed us through. Once inside, Lady Donne's manservant instructed my men to wait below while he led me on a circuitous route, up a back stairway, though a dozen empty chambers, up a few more steps until we arrived outside a narrow door. Lady Donne had two rooms, both, I noted with an instinctive satisfaction, considerably smaller than mine.

'What has happened?' I asked as she moved forward, looking beyond my shoulder as if I might have brought a couple of dozen intruders.

Once the servants were dismissed, she clutched my arm.

'It is the king!' she whispered, her fear unmistakeable.

A worm of unease was uncoiling in my stomach. I thought – Thomas! Then I thought – my stepfather! I feared for them both. A king who had executed a beloved brother might harbour misgivings as to any man's loyalty. Once under suspicion a man would be watched until one small slip, one careless word, one falsehood whispered into the king's ear would be enough to warrant arrest and imprisonment. And everyone knew what happened to men who were sent to the Tower. With a king who knew his own strength, no man was safe, not even my stepfather, his oldest and closest friend.

'What of the king?' I asked cautiously.

'He is dying.'

Everything stopped. For a moment I was unable to breathe or to speak.

Lady Donne's voice was bleak. 'A week ago, at Easter, he fell sick. Some thought he would die There was panic. But he recovered. This morning at dinner he was his usual self, weak but cheerful. Now he has been struck down a second time.'

I clung on to some shreds of common sense. 'Surely if he recovered once then he will recover again.'

'This time it is worse. The royal physicians say they can do nothing.'

I swallowed hard, trying to stop my mind from whirling about in panic. 'Is Lord Hastings with him?'

Lady Donne put a hand to her face in movement of distress. 'Yes.'

'And the marquess?'

She nodded. 'And Bishop Morton.'

If the king was gravely sick, why had news not seeped out into the city? Why were prayers not being said for his recovery? Why the secrecy?

'Yesterday the king asked for Lord Howard.' Lady Donne spoke as if that settled the matter.

'What of the Duke of Gloucester?'

'I do not know.'

I tried to marshal my thoughts. The king's brother was in the north. The roads in Yorkshire were known to be dreadful. Bridges might have broken in the floods. It could be weeks before he arrived. What would happen if the king died? A funeral? What else? All of a sudden I remembered that the prince, our heir, was half the country away on the marches of Wales with his guardian, Lord Rivers.

'Has word been sent to Ludlow?'

Lady Donne shook her head. 'Her grace has not asked for me. I know nothing other than what my maid heard from two of the king's body servants.'

I reached for her hands which were shaking uncontrollably. 'Perhaps the woman misunderstood. Perhaps this sickness is nothing more than an ague.'

'I fear it is not. The servants say he is dying.'

'Then the council will know what to do. It is not for you to worry.'

She pulled her hands away and walked quickly across the floor to her chest which stood by the wall. It was carved oak with an unusual design – probably brought back from Calais. Her husband had a fine eye for beauty. Out of the chest came her jewel box. She opened it and selected a small locket.

She placed the locket in my hand. Set in the gold was a tiny painting of a man in a bright blue doublet with a glimpse of white at the collar. The artist had captured the essence of his subject: the kindness, the honesty and the humour. I looked more closely. The man resembled my stepfather.

'It is beautiful,' I said.

'My brother gave it to me on the day I left home to be wed. It was to remind me of him.'

She replaced the locket in the box and put the box in the chest. With her back to me, she straightened up and said, 'What do you think will happen to Lord Hastings should the king die?'

I thought for a moment, trying to imagine a future without our golden York king. 'He will serve the king's son.'

She closed the lid of the chest and turned to face me.

'He will be killed.'

I gasped. 'No!'

'Do you imagine the queen's family will let him live? They loathe him.'

'I know Lord Rivers is his enemy but he cannot simply order him killed. There would have to be charges and a trial.'

Lady Donne looked at me sadly, her eyes full of unshed tears.

'Ask yourself – from where does Lord Rivers draw his power? Whom does he control? Whom does he guide?'

'The prince.'

'Exactly.'

'The prince is his father's son. He would not agree to the killing of his father's friend.'

Lady Donne shook her head. 'You are mistaken. The boy is a Woodville through and through. He may carry his father's name; he may resemble his father in height and looks; people may see a York heir; but he is *her* son and her brother's apprentice. They will have taught him well.'

I sat down on a stool. 'I cannot believe this is happening.'

Lady Donne knelt on the floor beside me. 'Ceci, I beg you, go to your husband, plead for your stepfather. The marquess will listen to you.'

'I think you overestimate my influence,' I said sadly.

'You are his wife. Persuade him Lord Hastings will be loyal to the prince. He poses no threat.'

We looked at each other, both knowing this to be untrue. My stepfather would always be a threat to the queen's family. From their early entanglement over her fight for the Groby lands, the queen had disliked my stepfather. As her husband's friend, she had mistrusted him. They had disagreed on matters of policy as well as the king's private affairs, his dalliances with other women which my mother-in-law blamed squarely on failings of the king's chamberlain. He was, in her eyes, a bad influence on her husband. If it had been in her gift, she would have had him destroyed long ago.

'I shall petition the king's brother, the Duke of Gloucester,' I said firmly. 'He will not allow this.'

'You think they will wait for him?'

'They must. They can do nothing without him. The prince is not yet of age and the duke is his royal uncle.'

'Come with me.'

Lady Donne rose, took my hand and led me to the narrow window which overlooked one of the stable yards. 'What do you see?'

I peered through the tiny panes of glass. In the gloom the stable yard appeared empty. The horses were safely stabled for the night, the grooms somewhere, gossiping or drinking.

'I see nothing.'

'Do you see a sign of Richard of Gloucester's men?'

'No.'

'The queen has not sent for him.'

'But a matter this important cannot be hidden. The council will insist the duke is told.'

Lady Donne took my hand and led me away from the window.

'We must pray for a miracle, for the king to recover.'

'And if he does not?'

She raised her gaze to mine. 'May God help us.'

He died next morning. I was with my mother-in-law in the queen's apartments when Archbishop Rotherham arrived. The moment I saw his grave face, I knew. It was as we'd all feared. I placed my hands neatly in my lap and held my breath, noting how some women crossed themselves, others snuffled, while a few seemed utterly stunned. The queen, or dowager queen as she now was, sat white-faced, her lips moving in what I presumed was prayer.

For a week she had known her husband to be gravely sick yet I was surprised at her composure. She made a short speech thanking the archbishop, then retired dry-eyed to her private chamber accompanied by a single maid.

If I'd been a betting woman I'd have wagered she was not at her prie dieu but having her clerk write letters. That is not to say she was not a pious woman, because she was;

but at this moment there were more important matters to attend to in this world than the care of her husband's soul in the next. Her survival and that of the rest of the Woodville family would depend on what she did. And she knew it.

Around me, women were sobbing in the way only foolish women can, wailing and dabbing their eyes, not one of them considering the implications of the king's death. I felt a light touch on my arm. It was Lady Margaret Stanley. She nodded her head towards the others.

'God expects prayers from us at a time like this, not tears. Will you accompany me, Lady Cecily?'

I inclined my head, wondering why I'd been chosen. Despite having little in common beyond a keen intellect, Lady Margaret made no secret of wanting my friendship.

It was not until we'd knelt in the chapel for a good hour that Lady Margaret decided our prayers had been sufficiently well-received by God although, to my eternal shame, I'd been thinking not praying. As we walked back to the queen's apartments with our heads bowed she said quietly, 'Do you think he was poisoned?'

I almost choked.

'Lady Margaret!'

She looked at me coolly. 'Do not pretend the thought has not occurred to you. He was not old, There was no disease. What else could it be?'

'He was loved. No-one wanted him dead,' I said firmly, wondering why the thought had not occurred to me.

She gave the ghost of a smile, noting more than a slight movement of her lips. 'You think not? How naive you are, Lady Cecily. It is well known that all men have enemies. They may even nurture a viper in the bosom of their family.'

Did she mean ... but no, that was impossible! Unbidden came the image of the king cavorting with the delightful Mistress Shore. Did my mother-in-law fear her influence waning as she was supplanted in her husband's affections by younger, more beautiful women. What of her Woodville family? For them it would be oblivion if she was set aside.

Lady Margaret continued smoothly, 'Of course it could be God's doing: a licentious life, overindulgence in the sins of the flesh, a man who failed to attend to his sins.'

'You are close to talking treason Lady Margaret.'

She raised a hand in front of her mouth to hide her smile. 'My husband tells me Lord Rivers has lately requested confirmation of his powers to raise an army should he deem it necessary.' She paused. 'Do you think it might be necessary, Lady Cecily?'

An army! Dear God!

'I do not know, Lady Margaret. Why should it be necessary?'

We walked across the courtyard in silence. At the door, she turned and said soberly, 'I think I shall write to my son, Henry Tudor. He values news from England.'

Before Christmas, Lady Margaret had negotiated a pardon for her son. He was to be restored to his father's titles and have the right of succession to his mother's estates. It had been a generous gesture from the king yet the young man was still in Brittany.

'Will the king's death delay his return?' I asked politely.

She lifted one eyebrow. 'Are you asking if I trust the dowager queen to adhere to our private agreement?'

This was strange news indeed. I'd heard nothing from my usual sources of any private agreement with my mother-in-law. Political or personal or both, I wondered. Lady Margaret was always careful in what she said so why was I being told?

'Her grace is an honourable woman,' I ventured.

Lady Margaret brushed an insect from her sleeve, 'Naturally, but now the king is dead, everything is different, is it not, Do you play chess, Lady Cecily? Yes, of course you do. A game of great skill where one is required to plan carefully and prepare for the unexpected. I believe there are certain strategies which, if deployed, may wrong-foot an opponent.'

'I do not think it seemly to play games at a time like this,' I replied, my mind circling wildly. Which opponent was to be wrong-footed?

'Indeed no, but I did wonder if a game is already in progress. And if so, who do you imagine is moving the pieces?'

That evening, Thomas came straight from the council chamber to my room. He was exhausted. I'd not expected him and was in my nightgown, having just said my prayers. His face was covered in sweat and grime but he rejected offers from his valet to fetch water. 'Just get me out of these clothes,' he ordered.

While the man attended to my husband, my maid helped me into bed. I noticed that under the guise of turning back the covers she stole a glance at my husband. Once the valet had placed a robe over his shoulders, Thomas dismissed all the servants.

'Make sure those boots are polished. I'll need them tomorrow,' he yelled as the door closed.

Outside, bells were still tolling, the dismal sound, echoing in my ears.

Thomas stumbled towards the bed like a drunkard. 'Dear God! I'm so tired I can barely think.'

'Was it dreadful?'

'On Sunday I was asked to embrace Lord Hastings,' he said, dropping his robe on the floor and clambering in beside me.

'Which you did?'

He gave a wry smile. 'Naturally.'

'So you are friends?'

He rolled over and pulled me against him. It was nine days since we'd been together and I'd missed him.

'I would be friends with you too, dearest wife, if you would be kind to me,' he murmured, reaching for the hem of my nightgown.

I gave an inward sigh. I had questions, dozens of them, but for the moment they would have to wait. Wifely duty came first and placating a needy husband was of more importance than discussing council policy. I wound my arms round his neck and whispered into his ear, 'Then let us be friends.'

It was Archbishop Rotherham who informed the dowager queen of arrangements made by the council for her husband's funeral. The king's near-naked body was already on view to the lords and the mayor and aldermen of London, a custom which Lady Stanley said was done for the avoidance of doubt should anyone claim afterwards the king was still alive. Once the embalmers had completed their business, the corpse would be wrapped in cerements, clothed as befitted a king and taken to St Stephen's chapel where it would lie in state, watched over by royal officials.

'Who is to lead the funeral procession?' My mother-in-law's voice was colourless, her face white, I presumed with grief, but her eyes kept sliding sideways as if seeking an enemy hidden beneath the archbishop's robes.

'I myself, your grace,' the archbishop replied. 'Lord Howard will walk in front of the bier. He is to carry the late king's banner.'

'The burial will be at Windsor as my husband requested?'

'Yes, your grace. As you know, the king's tomb was made ready when the chapel and choir were constructed. It is as magnificent a resting place as any mortal man could desire.'

'How long until you leave?'

Archbishop Rotherham blinked like a startled owl, taken aback by the question. 'Er, the procession is to leave within the week, your grace. The interment will be two days later. But I do not think …'

The dowager queen cut him short. 'Thank you, my lord archbishop.'

'Your grace.' The archbishop stood his ground, drawing upon his dignity, unwilling to be dismissed.

'Yes!' Up went my mother-in-law's chin.

'The matter of the Duke of Gloucester. If his grace, the duke, is delayed, the Earl of Lincoln will step in, but I think …'

We were treated to one of my mother-in-law's famous icy smiles. 'Do not concern yourself, my lord archbishop. Everything has been arranged.' Her voice was equally frosty.

'It might not be ...'

'As I said, everything has been arranged.'

I remembered Lady Donne's words – "You think they will wait for him?" With Richard of Gloucester in the north, a delay of even a few days, would be sufficient for the dowager queen's family to execute whatever plans they had. A man cannot fly from Middleham to the council chamber and in the duke's absence, decisions were already being taken.

But who were these people taking decisions? Did they have the authority? Surely the king would have wanted his brother to play a part in the ruling of England. He had entrusted him with the North and keeping the Scots at bay. It was inconceivable that he would have promoted his wife's family and ignored his brother.

Yet my mother-in-law behaved as if she had both the moral and legal right to dictate the course of events. This tallied with Thomas's account of the king's final wishes: the boy was to remain in the care of his mother's family: the queen and her brothers would lead his government – a Woodville regency in all but name.

I was not sure any of this was legal but I was no lawyer. Surely the council and parliament should decide who was to govern, not those hovering at a dying man's bedside whose recall of words spoken might well differ in their essentials. The man I needed was William Catesby. Unfortunately I had no idea where he was. He might be out of London on business. He might even be in Yorkshire.

After some thought, I wrote a careful letter, saying I wished to see him and dispatched it with my most trusted servant. His instructions were to find Master Catesby wherever he might be and not return without a reply. All I could do then was wait.

16

LONDON 1483

He looked the same as ever, though more prosperous. New boots, a new gown, a costly velvet cap, but the same battered old satchel for carrying documents.

'Marchioness!' He bowed. 'You sent for me.'

'I did, Master Catesby, I have questions. I think you may have answers.'

He gave a cursory glance round the hall, noting our servants.

He gave a slight nod. 'I shall do my best. However I suggest we might be better served by removing ourselves to somewhere more private. Your garden perhaps? I see some spring sunshine has favoured us this morning.'

What I liked about William Catesby was how I never needed to explain myself. It was as if he could read my mind. He waited patiently while my maid fetched my jacket, then we stepped outside to a secluded spot where a bench stood near the wall separating our pleasure garden from the orchard. Three large pots of early flowering lavender screened us from passing river boats yet we could be seen from the house which would calm my steward's sensibilities. On his instructions, a servant had run ahead with cushions, laying them carefully on the bench. I sat down and invited Master Catesby to be seated. He placed his satchel at his side, then turned to me.

'Now, my lady. What exactly is it that you wish to know?'

'I wish to know who is to rule? The young king …' I hesitated. 'Is it correct to call him king when he is not yet crowned? Which title should it be – king or prince?'

He gave a dry chuckle. 'A difficulty faced by many. Why not say, "the son of our late king". No-one can gainsay that he is his father's son.'

I smiled. 'That would be sensible – the son of our late king. Master Catesby, he is only a boy. I know he is heir to the throne but he is not yet of an age to rule. Who decides what should be done? Who will rule for him? Do your books tell you?'

He nodded. 'I commend you, my lady. There are few who perceive the depths and complexity of the problem we face. As you know, inheritance is not a simple matter. There is a moment when the world is fluid, when darkness ebbs and the sun has not yet risen, when we cannot know if day will come for we do not understand the secret workings of the heavens.'

'Master Catesby, the sun always rises.'

He smiled. 'Let us pray you are right, my lady. Yet that moment when a man might harbour doubts may be likened to an interregnum – the space between the death of one king and the coming of the next – a most dangerous time. No man has yet claimed the ground. No man's standard has yet been raised. Anything can happen.'

I listened carefully. As so often with Master Catesby, there was more to his words than first appeared. It took me a moment to understand exactly what he meant.

'Are you saying I should be careful?'

'My lady, I am saying you should be *extremely* careful. As I told you once before, the world you walk in is a dangerous place. You should trust no-one.'

I hazarded a small joke. 'Not even you?'

He gazed at me, his eyes serious, his mouth unsmiling.

'If I give you advice, my lady, you can be assured it is designed for your own safety.'

'I thank you. But you have not answered my question – who will rule? Will the dowager queen rule on behalf of her son?'

He leant back a little. 'Let me tell you a story. Many years ago when the Henry that was then king, lost his senses, his queen offered to rule in his stead. She wished power put into her hands but the king's council would not hear of such a thing. They did not trust her. Of course part of the reason was that not only was she a woman, but a Frenchwoman.'

'Whereas our dowager queen is an Englishwoman.'

'Margaret of Anjou was royal.'

'Ah! So you think the council will not permit the dowager queen to rule because she was born the daughter of a gentleman.'

He hesitated. 'I did not say that. I suspect – though of course without knowledge of the lords in question it is difficult to be certain – but I would imagine it is more a question of the lady's family.'

'They do not trust her family?'

'I would imagine not.'

I was not surprised. My own stepfather did not trust my mother-in-law's family. He believed they were working for his downfall.

'Do they trust my husband, the marquess?'

'I am unable to say, my lady.'

'Unable or unwilling?'

'I do not know the marquess, my lady. But if you want my opinion I would say that every man is his mother's son and some mothers hold tight to the leading rein all their lives. Whether the dowager queen is such a woman, I am unable to say.'

I recalled my mother's words at Bradgate when talking of my husband – "Do not trust him. He is his mother's son." I certainly did not trust my mother-in-law but did that mean I should not trust my husband.

'Master Catesby, if the council were to prevent the dowager queen and her family from taking power, would they choose the late king's brother, the Duke of Gloucester?'

'A prince of the blood with a strong sword arm, known to be just, a man well-suited to guide a boy until he is old enough to rule on his own. Certainly there are many who would welcome Richard of Gloucester.'

I smiled. 'You sound as if you are a supporter.'

He laughed. 'You flatter me, my lady, I have no influence. I have done a little work for the duchy but I do not have a seat on the council. No-one takes notice of what I say.'

'Other than me. And you know many highborn people. Even Lady Norfolk mentions you.'

The hesitation was so slight I might have missed it had I not been concentrating.

'You know Lady Norfolk?' His voice held a note of caution.

'A little. She is a sad lady. I once did her a small service.'

'Ah! I see – a small service.'

'And you?'

'I too, a small service. A long time ago.'

I wanted to ask more about that long-ago small service and why Lady Norfolk had been so alarmed to see him but he appeared disinclined to talk about the connection. It was odd how in every mystery I tried to unravel, the threads invariably led back to Lady Norfolk and her family.

I had nothing more than a passing acquaintance with the dowager duchess and had never met her husband, the late duke. My mother had known Lady Norfolk and her sister when they were young but I was unsure if the friendship continued or if, like so many, had withered with the passing years. Yet it was my mother who had suggested Lady Norfolk approach me with regard to her little daughter.

Master Catesby picked up his satchel. 'If that is all, my lady, I would beg you to excuse me. I have work to do.' He rose to his feet as if to go but the lavender attracted his attention.

'May I?'

'Certainly. I shall ask one of the servants to gather some for you?'

He smiled. 'I'll not steal your bounty, my lady. All I seek is a single stem. See!'

Like that time long ago at Ashby, he deftly plucked a sprig, lowered his face to inhale its scent, then tucked the flower inside his satchel.

He walked away along the path, adjusting his black gown as he went. All seemed well but it was odd how he had suddenly been in such a hurry to leave. I wondered if I had pressed him on that small service he'd done for

Lady Norfolk, would he have told me the truth or would he have lied.

People turned out in their thousands to say farewell to their king. The Duke of Gloucester had not yet arrived from the north so the chief mourner, walking behind the bier, was the young Earl of Lincoln, John de la Pole, the late king's nephew. The funeral procession set out from Westminster for Charing Cross, then to the abbey at Syon where it rested overnight. Next morning it was to go to Eton and then Windsor where the burial would take place. I saw nothing of Thomas, nor did I expect to, as he had onerous duties laid on him by the council which kept him away from home.

At some point in those days after the funeral, I sent one of my men out amongst the Londoners to find out what was being said.

'Great stew of "I remember men", m'lady. Towton. Barnet. Ye should've seen the witch's mist. Fought like a lion he did. Never see the like of him again. That sort of thing. One old knight, been at Picquigny, told anyone who'd listen how the king had bowed so low his forehead near touched the ground.'

'And the common folk?'

The man chuckled. 'Beggin' your pardon, my'lady; 't'was all snigger, nudge and wink. Not what a lady like yourself be used to. Had a good run wi' Will Shore's wife; paid his way, mind you. Wore out I reckon he were. Lewd sort of stuff.'

Hmm! Nothing new there.

'What do they say of the dowager queen?'

'The womenfolk pity her. Say she were ill-used. Jewels be all very well but what's the good of a man who's always in some other woman's bed.'

'And the men?'

'A bit of talk how she'd given him a breakfast he'd not liked.'

'Poison?'

'Reckon so. Some said she'd got what she'd wanted all along. One or two spoke more kindly but not many.'

Very much what I'd expected. Londoners had never cared for Elizabeth Woodville. My mother thought it was envy but I reckoned they'd taken her measure a long time ago.

'What of the marquess?'

The man hesitated. 'Beggin your pardon, m'lady. I've no liking to speak against the marquess.'

'I'm not interested in what you like or don't like, I wish to know what is being said. So tell me, and do not hold anything back.'

The man slid his eyes to his hands. 'They do say he'm got over-proud since the king died, m'lady. Thinks hisself a big man. Boasts he can do what he likes. They're waiting for Duke Richard to show him who's master. They do say if he don't watch his step, Lord Hastings will throw him in the Thames.'

That tallied with what I'd observed of my husband since the funeral. If he'd spoken at council meetings the way he'd been speaking to others, I was not surprised men thought him boastful. He'd also stopped confiding in me; he took everything to his mother, brought nothing home to me.

When I asked were the rumours true about his mother's brother, Edward Woodville, being appointed Lord Admiral of the Fleet, he said discussions in council meetings were none of my business, they were solely a matter for the family.

It was shaming – after nine years of marriage, six children, and my continued support, he did not consider me a member of his family.

My manservant was waiting, passing his hat from hand to hand looking unhappily at the floor.

'Is there something else?' I enquired.

'It be only what I heard, m'lady. It may not be true.'

'What is it?'

'As I said. It be only words.'

'What kind of words?'

He hesitated, 'I were at the Swan, just off the Cheap. 'Tis a fine place. There be two men having a drink, nothing secret like. The bigger one I recognised. He were in the cloth trade.'

'What were these men saying?'

'The big man, the one I recognised, he said the marquess be – beggin' your pardon, m'lady – be sniffing round Will Shore's wife again now she'm back on the market.'

I kept my face blank as my heart sank into the pit of my stomach. Some part of me had always known this would happen but that did not lessen the pain.

'And the other man?'

'Laughed. Said the marquess were wise to get his foot in the door before the rush.'

'That was all?'

'Yes, m'lady.'

'Is what they say true?'

The man shifted from one leg to the other.

'Is it true?'

'I don't rightly know, m'lady. 'Tis only what I heard.'

London gossip was not always right in its particulars but the generalities were usually correct. I thought it more than likely my husband was pursuing Mistress Shore. With the king dead, she'd be looking for a new protector and his attention to me these past few weeks had been noticeably lacking. I'd thought he was too busy, too tired, too worried about council matters – but it seemed I was wrong.

'You have heard nothing else?'

'I did hear Mistress Shore were tossed out o' the palace on her ear, m'lady, but that be well known.'

I doubted Mistress Shore had waited for my mother-in-law to toss her out. A clever woman would make herself scarce and Mistress Shore, whatever else she was, did not appear to be stupid.

'This is what you will do,' I said crisply, refusing to think about what I now suspected. 'Go to Mistress Shore's house near the Cheap. I wish to know who visits her. I need names, dates, particulars – everything. Set more than one man if necessary. Do you understand?'

'Yes m'lady.'

'I wish to know any rumours concerning her, every detail of what she is doing and what is being said. You will report back to me and you will say nothing about this to the marquess.'

My mother would have said this was an old story, the inevitable failure of a man to live up to his promises, of a husband who having once strayed, was unable to remain faithful. Yet I had truly believed that I'd triumphed, not only over pretty Mistress Shore and her offers of intimacies, but also over my mother-in-law. I thought I had severed the leading reins. It seemed I was wrong on both counts. Somehow this past month the Thomas Grey I thought I knew had slipped through my fingers like a tickled trout disappearing into the fast-moving waters midstream.

It was late next afternoon when I set off for Westminster. We'd barely slid out into the middle of the river to catch the incoming tide when I saw my stepfather's barge tied up outside his house at Paul's Wharf. It was a beautiful old house, mellow and peaceful, settled into its gardens and orchards as if dozing between the noise and bustle of the city and the slow-moving waters of the Thames. There was no sign of my stepfather but his boatmen were idling about on the landing stage, clearly expecting him to stride down the path at any moment.

'Pull in,' I ordered.

The oarsmen altered course and our barge slid alongside the wooden pier.

'Is Lord Hastings at home?' I called out.

'Aye m'lady.'

'Is anyone with him?'

'No, m'lady. Just the servants. His men are at Westminster.'

I held out my hand for someone to help me ashore and stepped carefully onto the damp boards.

I found my stepfather in his closet surrounded by his papers, a cup of wine and a small meal of bread and cheese.

He looked worried. The death of the king, had aged him, heaping new problems onto his shoulders. He had lost not only an old and valued friend but, more crucially, his access to the centre of power. He had been left rudderless, bereft of the man who had made him what he was. Now there was no-one to protect him from the cold Woodville winds blowing through the chambers of the royal palaces.

'Should you be here, my lady marquess?' he enquired.

I gave him a broad smile. 'Probably not. But who is to know?'

'I'd say anyone who recognises the Dorset barge. It is hardly inconspicuous with all that gilding and blue paint.'

'My husband is busy and I doubt my mother-in-law is out on the river. She sent a message to say she expects me at Westminster.'

He rose from his chair and kissed me. 'It is a pleasure to see you, Ceci, you know that, but I urge you to be careful. Your husband would not approve of your visiting me. You should not risk his displeasure, nor that of his mother.'

I made a little movement of my shoulders, almost a shrug. 'I do not care whether or not I have their approval for they most certainly do not have mine.'

He gave a sad smile. 'You ought to care. You are dependent on their goodwill. We none of us know how this business will be resolved. I fear it may not end well and do not want you dragged into the turmoil.'

I leaned against him the way I had as a child. He was a more solid man than Thomas, not stout like the king had been. but comfortably sturdy. He wore mourning black even though it was ten days since the king's funeral.

'Is the Duke of Gloucester on his way?'

'With God's blessing, yes. You know the dowager queen failed to inform the duke of his brother's death – make of that what you will – but I sent a letter. I warned him the dowager queen would try to subvert his brother's wishes. I urged him to make haste before she succeeded in destroying the old nobility.'

'Lord Rivers?'

My stepfather smiled. 'Ah Lord Rivers! A particularly dangerous man for all his so-called piety. He was planning to bring the prince to London with as large a force as he could muster.'

I gasped.

He patted my arm. 'Never fear, Ceci. The council may wish to see the prince succeed his father in all his glory but not at the head of an army.' He gave a short laugh. 'I threatened to raise the Calais garrison if they permitted such folly. They knew what that meant so they put a stop to Lord Rivers' plan. A retinue of two thousand has been agreed. I doubt the noble lord is pleased. His plans have been scotched and he will have had to disband his army.'

'I do not know what to wish for,' I said gloomily. 'I am not sure on which side of the divide I stand. As a wife I am bound to take my husband's part yet I need you to be safe. Lady Donne warned me of the danger you are in and I could not bear to see you harmed. Yet, whatever happens, I need my husband to prosper.'

'Ceci, you know the kind of man you married. He will not prosper under any but his family's rule. He has not the ability. He struts and crows and puffs out his chest, but no-one is deceived. When Richard of Gloucester wrote to the council urging that nothing be done contrary to law and the late king's desire, the marquess boasted how he and his family were so important that even without the young king's uncle they could make and enforce any decision they liked.'

It was easy to imagine my foolish husband bragging how powerful he was when all he held in his hand was an illusion.

'He plays with fire and does not see the danger,' I said sadly. 'His mother encourages him. I fear he has no more sense than either of our sons but he will not listen to me.'

'I thought you had his ear?'

'Not since the king died. He has others in whom he confides.'

My stepfather, who knew all the London gossip was too careful of my feelings to mention any rumours about Mistress Shore but I could tell from the look in his eyes that he'd heard what was being said.

'We men rarely confide in our wives, Ceci. Our lives are full of brutal and bloody compromises. We wish our wives to be sheltered from the ugly bargains we make with other men. We keep our wives safe from harm and they, in return, provide us with comfort and nurture our children.'

'Will my husband be safe?'

'There is no reason why not, provided he gives way to Richard of Gloucester. The marquess must remember he is not of royal blood, merely a man whose mother made a good marriage.'

'And you?'

He sighed. 'Edward should not have died first. It was not what I imagined. When he was twelve years old, I was already a grown man. I remember the day the old duke asked me to keep watch over his son. Edward was a golden boy, so much promise. I pledged myself to his service, body, heart and soul for as long as I lived. Yet he is gone and I am still here.'

'He loved you.'

'He made me. I am not so vain as to imagine men attached themselves to me for my good looks. They would say what a grand fellow William Hastings is, but it was my closeness to the king they sought. It was that which gave me my following and my fortune. Now Edward is no more.'

'Will you retire?'

He laughed. 'Ah Ceci, you do not understand how this works. If I step back they will eat me alive.'

'The dowager queen's family?'

He nodded. 'Elizabeth Woodville and I have never been friends, not since the day I told her that her son was not worthy to marry my stepdaughter. Of course we neither of us knew then that she would one day be queen. But she remembers how I had the best of our bargain. She has not forgiven me and if she can, she will destroy me. She has assured the council she means me no harm but I do not believe her.'

'Is there no way to protect yourself?'

'If Richard of Gloucester becomes protector for the young king, I should be safe. I have an understanding with him and he knows I will serve him well as I did his brother. He is an honest man and the lords in the council are agreed they will back him.'

'Has anything been decided?'

'The coronation is set for Sunday.'

'So soon!'

'Four days away. Pray God, Richard arrives in time.'

'Perhaps he has gone to Ludlow?'

My stepfather shook his head. 'I advised him to come straight to London.'

'Are Lord Rivers and the young king on their way?'

'They were due to leave Ludlow six days ago. They should be here on Friday, the day after tomorrow.'

Friday. Two days away. The guildsmen would soon begin building their displays, city wives would put finishing touches to their finery and children would go out into the fields to pick flowers. The coronation of a young king would please Londoners. But my stepfather did not look pleased.

'If the duke arrives and Lord Rivers comes with the young king, then everything will be settled, yet you look worried,' I said.

'Of course I am worried. Word is about that the dowager queen is raising an army. Elizabeth Woodville may speak of peace but she does not mean it. I sent your mother back to Kirby. I swore I would keep her safe, whatever it cost me.'

I smiled. 'And you are a man of your word.'

'I should hope so. Why not have your husband send you to Bradgate?'

'I would but my mother-in-law has ordered my attendance at Westminster. I was on my way when I saw your barge at the landing stage.'

'Coronation robes, I suppose,' he said morosely. 'She'll want you decked out like a proper Woodville.'

'I am not a Woodville,' I said stoutly. 'Neither is my husband; he is a Grey.'

My stepfather placed his hands on either side of my face and looked hard into my eyes. 'Your husband may have been born a Grey but he was raised a Woodville. None of us can escape from our early years, they inform the rest of our lives. You, my dear, were born a Bonville yet I truly believe you to be as much my daughter as my little Annie.'

I turned my face sideways and kissed his hand. 'I have always been proud to be your daughter, my lord. I love you as if you were indeed my father.'

He kissed my forehead. 'All those years ago, when the king gave me your wardship, I thought only of the fortune I would make from your land holdings. I never for one moment imagined the great joy you would bring me.'

We stood like father and daughter, hands touching, the warmth of a life shared and the softness of lips in a kiss. Yet we both knew we could no longer be truly close. We were divided by loyalties which threatened to pull us apart.

17

SANCTUARY 1483

I stayed too long. When I arrived at the palace, I expected the company to be at evening prayers. Instead, the dowager queen's apartments were like Ashby market square on fair day. A babble of noise greeted me at the entrance: women carrying coffers, screaming for others to follow; men bent almost double, huge bundles on their backs, shouting for people to get out of their way; three men on ladders in the throes of removing one of the great tapestries from the wall, yelling to those below to mind their heads. Two grooms rolling up a large red turkey rug, a third calling, 'To the left! To the right!'. A maidservant rushed by with a velvet cloak over her arm, turned on her heel and ran back to where a young girl in cap and apron was picking up cushions and stuffing them into a chest.

'Not that one, you fool!' she shrieked.

The girl burst into tears and began hauling the cushions out again.

Chairs in piles by the doorway were knocked over by four burly men trying to manoeuvre a large settle with gilded arms though into the outer chamber. At the far side of the room a man was lifting a cross studded with jewels into a carved chest with gilded handles.

'What is happening?' I asked a harassed-looking maidservant.

'Don't know, m'lady' she said, bobbing a curtsey while attempting not to drop a huge pile of sheets held in her arms. Two boys staggered by, weighed down by a box of books, followed by two smaller boys, one carrying a pewter bowl, the other a shallow tray of silver spoons.'

I'd never in my life seen such disorganisation. I walked through to the inner room where the chaos was even greater. Curtains, gowns, bed covers, lengths of cloth and blankets were strewn over the floor in great heaps while maidservants picked them up and folded them haphazardly into a row of stout chests. Two stools had been upended and placed on top of a table where a box containing shoes had fallen onto its side, spilling half the contents onto the floor.

In the middle of the mess was Princess Elizabeth, sitting on top of a low chest looking perfectly composed as if nothing was amiss.

'Princess! What is happening?'

She looked up and flashed me a small smile. 'My mother is going into sanctuary, Lady Cecily.'

'Sanctuary? But what of the coronation?'

'Her grace has decided she is no longer safe. Now that my royal uncle is coming she intends removing herself into sanctuary at Westminster, taking her children with her.'

'But why?'

Princess Elizabeth tapped her foot on the floor. 'Have you not heard?'

'I have heard nothing.'

She looked at me with a gleam in her eye, almost as if she was enjoying herself.

'My Uncle Richard has seized my brother, the king.'

I stood there with my mouth open. 'Seized the king? Are you sure, Princess?'

'Oh yes. A man in my brother's train rode to bring us the news. He was there when it happened. He saw it all.'

'Why would your royal uncle seize your brother?'

She shrugged. 'How should I know? My mother tells me nothing.'

'Has he abducted him?'

'It would seem not. I am told they are coming to London, the two of them – my Uncle Richard and my brother, the king.'

'What of your uncle, Lord Rivers, is he to accompany them?'

'He has been arrested.' She paused. 'It is not good, is it, Lady Cecily? My brother seized and my Uncle Anthony arrested. You would think we were at war.'

The word was like an obscenity in her mouth.

'Princess, I am sure there is a simple explanation.'

'Oh, I'm certain there is but I suspect it may be one not to my mother's liking.'

'Was there violence?'

She tipped her head back and laughed. 'When is there not violence? I do not think my Uncle Anthony will have welcomed the removal of his royal charge by another. He would say my father placed my brother under his protection. He would say Richard of Gloucester had no right to take my brother. Perhaps he did not. Do you think it is treason to dispute these matters?'

'Princess, I do not know.'

'My mother says my Uncle Anthony has the power to raise an army. I wonder if he brought his army with him. If so, I would certainly imagine there was violence because my royal uncle is said to have the men of the north at his back.'

I recalled my stepfather's threat to raise the Calais garrison if Lord Rivers brought an army to London and how the council had agreed to a retinue of only two thousand men. Had Lord Rivers disobeyed the council. An icy chill crept up my spine as the hairs on the back of my neck begin to prickle. I remembered the nights at Ashby I'd spent cowering in my bed, terrified of armed intruders climbing the stairs in the darkness. I might be older and wiser, the candles might be lit and the rooms full of servants, but the threat of an army marching on London still had the power to undo me.

'Princess, I think I must go to her grace.'

'Go by all means. She will tell you we are all about to be murdered. She is quite certain of it. If we are to be shut away in sanctuary, do you think I should take my lute? My sisters might enjoy some music.'

I smiled nervously. 'Princess, you must do as you think best.'

'In that case, I shall stay here. I have no wish to flee. I do not think my Uncle Richard will harm me.'

I regarded her golden prettiness, the way she spoke and moved, the delicacy of her features, her natural intelligence, and thought – you are correct; no man in his right mind would harm you.

The dowager queen's privy chamber looked like a shopkeeper's stall at the and of a day's trading, nothing left but the least desirable objects, the ones no-one wanted.

'I wondered when you'd turn up,' my mother-in-law remarked sourly. 'I suppose Princess Elizabeth has told you.'

'Yes, your grace, but I do not understand how such a thing can have happened.'

She paused to give instructions to one of the women emptying her jewel boxes.

'It is very simple. Richard of Gloucester wishes to be rid of me and all my family. He has no use for us. He has arrested my brother, Lord Rivers, and my son, Richard Grey. By now he will have dispatched them north to one of his castles. He will say it is to keep them safe but you and I both know that safety is not what he has in mind. He plans to have them killed. I would not be surprised if he has already given the order.'

'Your grace!'

'You can stand there gawping if you like but it will do you no good. Do you not understand what is about to happen? There can be no accommodation with Richard of Gloucester – none! He will murder my family in the same way your Uncle Warwick murdered my father and my brother John.

'Your grace, I am certain the duke means you no harm.'

'Are you? I'm not!'

'Your grace! If you pleaded with him.'

'Plead? You think I would crawl on my knees to Richard of Gloucester. I, an anointed queen!'

'The duke is an honourable man, your grace. He will not harm you. And he will not harm your daughters. Princess Elizabeth says …'

'Elizabeth is young. She does not know men like I do. And if you think we would be spared then you are more stupid than I thought.'

I swallowed the insult, telling myself she was distraught

and women who are distraught say things they do not mean.

'Your grace, even in war, men do not visit violence upon women.'

She laughed. 'Oh you child! Ask your mother! Ask the women raped by the Scots army brought by Margaret of Anjou. Ask those who thought themselves protected by their vows of chastity, dragged out of their convents and defiled. Let them tell you how men do not visit violence upon women.'

At Ashby I'd heard women gossip about such savagery but thought it just stories to frighten young girls and keep us in order, evils visited upon our enemies who were not under God's protection.

Then I remembered my mother's story of her encounter at Shute.

'Where is my husband? Is he safe?'

She shrugged. 'This is war. My son Thomas will take his chances with the rest of us. Would you have him run? Do you think him a coward?'

'I have never thought him a coward.'

'But you have not given him his due. Has my son not raised you up? Given you children? Yet you choose to place a barrier between him and his family.' She held up her hand. 'Do not deny it! I have watched you since the day you first entered my chamber, your proud little nose wrinkling with displeasure as if my son was not worthy of your attentions.'

I bit back the words on the tip of my tongue and raised my chin. If this was to be a battle I'd not be the one to drag us down into the gutter.

'Is my husband in the palace?'

'You will find him in his apartments. But do not imagine you can persuade him to follow you to whatever hole you have prepared. He is *my* son and he knows his duty. Now, forgive me, I must go. I have no wish to be here when Richard of Gloucester arrives. I shall not give him that pleasure.'

I gave a brief curtsey and turned away. A maidservant with a large bundle was blocking the doorway. Seeing me, she hesitated and dropped the bundle. Behind me I heard my mother-in-law's voice. 'You fool! Get someone to help you!'

I ran back through the palace, avoiding, as best I could, lines of men laden with the queen's possessions making their way to the abbey's sanctuary. At the entrance to Thomas's rooms, I stopped, appalled at the scene in front of my eyes. Like my mother-in-law's chambers, his were in chaos. Clothes and linen were being hastily folded and crammed into chests; boots and hats and gloves, tossed in anyhow.

He was standing. watching.

'My lord!'

He turned round.

'Ah! My lady wife! What a pleasure. You are just in time to bid me farewell.'

Gritting my teeth, I greeted him as a wife should though I felt like throttling him.

'Where might you be going, my lord?' I enquired coolly.

'Sanctuary – with my mother and my sisters and my brother, Dickon.'

This was what I had feared, that in the end he would desert me, choose to go with his mother. She had jerked the leading rein and he had obediently lowered his head and prepared to follow.

'Pray why are you taking yourself into sanctuary?'

'Because I do not wish to be decapitated by Richard of Gloucester.'

My heart gave a lurch at the image conjured up by his words.

'You exaggerate. Richard has no intention of harming you.'

'You think not? Do you imagine we are having a polite disagreement over who controls my royal brother. Are we to sit round the council table and discuss what should be done and who should do it? Do you imagine the duke will agree to share power with my mother? Or with me? I tell you, Richard of Gloucester plans to be rid of every Woodville he can lay his hands on.'

'You are not a Woodville, my lord. You are a Grey.'

His lips gave a twitch. 'In this, I am my mother's son. I have placed myself at her side.'

As he said the words, I felt the abyss between us widen until I feared we might never find our way back to each other.

'My lord, you do not have to do this. Fleeing into sanctuary is the act of a guilty man. Stay and prove your innocence.'

'You think in Richard's eyes I will be judged innocent?'

'You have done nothing wrong. He will be merciful.'

'Will he be merciful to my Uncle Anthony? To my brother, Richard Grey?'

'I do not know.'

'Yes you do. You know as well as I do that he will have them killed. He will have his executioner butcher them in the same way your uncle butchered my Woodville grandfather and my Uncle John. Richard of Gloucester will wade through the blood of any Woodville who opposes him. He thinks of nothing but gaining power. That is why we must stop him.'

'In sanctuary you will be powerless.'

'Believe me, we shall not. My mother has a plan.'

I remembered rumours of the queen raising an army, my fear of what might happen.

'What has she made you do?'

He seized my shoulders. 'She seeks only to protect our family.'

'With an army brought by Lord Rivers?'

'You think Richard of Gloucester has not also brought an army?'

'I think your mother would start a war.'

He thrust me from him. 'Go away! You understand nothing.'

I pulled on his arm. 'I understand that my husband is abandoning me, deserting his wife and his children, leaving us to fend for ourselves. What will happen to us if you are found guilty of fomenting armed conflict? What do you expect me to do?'

He shrugged his shoulders. 'Go home. Care for our children.'

'With a husband who has admitted his guilt by skulking in sanctuary?'

He sighed. 'There is nothing more I can do. You will be

perfectly safe. Nobody is going to harm you. But you must see the danger I am in.'

I regarded him angrily. 'You are faithless, just like before. I should have known you would choose her over me. You always have and you always will.'

He flushed red and began to bluster. 'You are wrong. It meant nothing, nothing at all. And it was only once, I swear it. Just for old times sake.'

I laughed scornfully. 'Not your harlot, my lord! You are welcome to her. I was talking about your mother.'

He frowned, wrong-footed, misunderstanding the accusation. 'I am a good son.'

'And a poor husband.'

He came close and hissed, 'If I was not in such haste I would take you home and beat you for that. Be certain I shall not forget what you have said.'

'And I shall not forget what you are about to do,' I retorted. 'Go on! Run back to your mother! She of all people must not be kept waiting.'

For a long moment we stood there, glaring at each other. Then I turned and walked away, tears streaming down my face, a knot of hard cold anger in my heart.

18

LONDON 1483

I struck my hand flat against the wall. 'How can he be such a fool?' I raged.

Joan sat perfectly still, watching as I paced up and down the room. The maids were huddled in a corner. cowering. I picked up one of my shoes and threw it as hard as I could across the floor; then for good measure, picked up the other and sent it flying.

'What am I to do?'

'Lie down?' suggested Joan.

I flung myself face down on the bed, thrust my fists against the pillows and sank my teeth into the satin cover to stop myself from screaming.

I heard Joan send the maids away, then her footsteps tapping across the floor towards the bed. The mattress sagged as she sat herself beside me.

Her voice was unsympathetic. 'Shrieking does not help. Do you wish the whole household to know you and the marquess are at odds.'

'At odds! I could strangle him,' I muttered.

'Really! Is that what you want?'

I pushed myself round and sat up. 'I want him to come to his senses and behave like a man. What will happen to *me* if he is in sanctuary? How will our children fare if their father is disgraced?'

'You could go and ask him to come out of sanctuary, meet with the duke.'

I laughed derisively. 'Have you seen the sanctuary at Westminster?'

Joan admitted that she had not.

'It is not the kind of place you go visiting. They call it the abbot's house but It is more like a prison than a palace: a vast jumble of outbuildings and a massive house with an undercroft, built to withstand a siege. He could hide in there for months.'

'You should make the effort. We could go this morning, take the barge. There is still time. It is only Thursday.'

'What would I say to him that I did not say yesterday?'

Joan pursed her lips. 'Behaving like a fishwife is hardly going to encourage the marquess to return home. He needs careful handling. A husband's pride is easily bruised – you should have learned that by now.'

She was right. I knew she was right but nobody ever thought about *my* pride, nobody bothered to handle *me* with care. I'd sacrificed my future when I married Thomas Grey, my hopes of marriage to a man whose family held an ancient pedigree, a man who might have been a duke.

Thomas was nothing but the son of a country knight and a gentleman's daughter. Whereas my mother was a Nevill and that meant something because Nevills had done more than anyone to put King Edward on his throne. My father was a Bonville, the sole heir to his father's and grandfather's vast holdings in the West Country and in the north-west. I was a young woman of importance. Now I was to be subjected to further humiliation. It was unfair!

Reluctantly I agreed to go with Joan. We took the barge to Westminster and pushed our way through the milling crowds in the precincts, walking briskly towards the sanctuary at the far end of St Margaret's churchyard. As we approached the abbot's buildings we saw Archbishop Rotherham and his escort, hurrying away.

'What is the Archbishop of York doing here?' said Joan.

'Rushing to offer the dowager queen his support, I would imagine,' I said sourly.

Joan looked shocked. 'Is that wise, considering the situation? If it is a matter of taking sides, why would the archbishop wish to pit himself against the Duke of Gloucester?'

'Doubtless, like my husband, he is so witless he has not thought of the consequences.'

We approached the gate. It was a solid affair, more iron than wood: thick heavy baulks of timber covered with iron bands, huge square-headed nails and a door with a small metal grille which protected what must be a sliding wooden shutter on the inside. There were no windows in the walls and from what I could see, this was the only way in or out. Anyone wanting access must pass through this gate be he archbishop, a man bearing delicacies for the dowager queen, or Richard, Duke of Gloucester.

'Sorry, m'lady. No visitors; not without the dowager queen's say-so.' The man had come from behind me. He gave the impression of bulk: wide shoulders, strong arms, thick legs in large boots and a fleshy bearded face. He wore a padded jacket which made him look even more intimidating.

I fixed him with a cool stare. 'I am the Lady Marquess. Open this door immediately. My husband is within.'

'Sorry, m'lady. You could have a dozen husbands in there – it's still no visitors.'

'Did you not understand? You will inform my husband that I am here.'

'Can't go nowhere, m'lady. My job's to guard the gate, along with these man 'ere.' He indicated a half-dozen other burly men lolling against the wall.

At that moment I realised how powerless I was. There was no man's name I could invoke to get me past this oaf. With my husband holed-up with his mother, my stepfather reduced in influence and the Duke of Gloucester still a day's ride away, I had no-one to call on. My Hastings brother was not yet of age and my Nevill uncles were all dead. I was truly alone.

'Come away, my lady,' said Joan quietly. 'These men mean business and the crowds are becoming restless. I'd not want you here if trouble breaks out.'

She tugged on my arm and led me back through the precincts to the river. Our journey had been a waste of time but I had received an important lesson in the limits of my power. From now on I would have to rely on subtlety and subterfuge and avoid confrontation, because confrontation without a man at my back, would get me nowhere.

By Thursday afternoon, London was seething with rumour and panic. Our servants reported fights breaking out all over the city with shopkeepers closing their doors and locking their shutters. Gangs of apprentice boys roamed the streets looking for trouble while the urchins who lived on the riverbank mingled with the crowds, stealing anything they could lay their hands on. Youths were reported throwing stones at respectable townsfolk who were hurrying back to the safety of their houses and from our walls we could see a crowd running through the alleyways, chasing a sighting on the word of some scuttlebutt. Nobody knew what was happening and everyone was afraid.

Armed men were gathered outside my stepfather's house with more near the city gates. The servants were saying a huge army had been mustered at Westminster for the dowager queen but I had it on good report that the numbers at Westminster were few. Support for the Woodvilles was not forthcoming. It seemed men were refusing to fight for a woman who, it was rumoured, wanted power for herself by trying to exclude Duke Richard and the old families. As my stepfather had said, there were lords openly hostile to my mother-in-law now she no longer had her husband to lend her position legitimacy.

Next morning the mayor and aldermen rode out to Horney Park in their finest scarlet to welcome the young king to London. It must have been a wonderful sight with the citizens who'd accompanied them all clothed in violet.

'I am torn into shreds,' I wept. 'As a wife I must obey my husband yet he has deserted me.'

Joan put her arm around me. 'Let us go up to the roof of the gatehouse, see if we can view the procession.'

Taking the greatest of care, we climbed the steps of the gatehouse as far as we dared. We were sorely tempted to scramble up the remaining stone slabs to the very top but were afraid of falling. Joan's condition meant she must take no risks.

We could hear the roar of the crowd long before we had our first sight of the procession winding its way through the streets to St Paul's. First into view trundled four wagons displaying Woodville devices, laden with weapons and armour, accompanied by officials in royal livery. There'd been rumours about these armaments but to see them revealed like this was proof, if proof were needed, that Lord Rivers and the queen had been planning an armed insurrection to get rid of Richard of Gloucester and anyone else who opposed their avowed intention to rule.

After the wagons came the rest of the procession. The young king wore deep blue velvet and was flanked by his royal uncle on one side and the Duke of Buckingham on the other. Behind them, rode a retinue of several hundred men, all dressed in black lest anyone should forget that this was a royal prince who had just lost his father and we were a country which had just lost its king.

Despite this solemn reminder, the crowds were joyous and the noise tremendous. I'd only seen Harry Stafford, Duke of Buckingham once and wondered why he had such a prominent position.

'He has thrown his support behind Richard of Gloucester,' Joan said, knowledgably.

'He was hardly likely to give it to my mother-in-law,' I laughed.

In a way I felt sorry for Lady Catherine who must now find herself, like me, in a world with divided loyalties.

People said her husband had always disliked his wife's family and with the king's death had turned his dislike into action.

'They are taking the young king to the Bishop of London's house,' Joan said, standing on the tips of her toes to get a better view.

'I wonder if Duke Richard will lodge there or if he'll come to Baynard's Castle?'

He did neither. Later that evening I was told the duke had gone to his townhouse, Crosby Place by Bishopsgate.

Days dragged by, one after the other. Twelve days after the dowager queen fled into sanctuary, Joan heard from her husband that the royal council had officially appointed the Duke of Gloucester as protector. His grand title was Protector and Defender of the Realm and Church in England and Principal Councillor of the King. The Bishop of Lincoln, was to be new chancellor.

'John says Archbishop Rotherham was removed as chancellor because of his foolishness in showing support for the dowager queen.'

'And the young king?' I asked, aware of the shame of scrabbling for bits of news from my friends.

'He is to move into the royal apartments in the Tower.'

'Is there a new date for the coronation?'

'Two days before midsummer's day. Five weeks away.' Joan touched my arm. 'You must not worry. There is ample time for the dowager queen to come out of sanctuary and make peace with the duke.'

'Yes – ample time,' I repeated, knowing that what we both wanted would not happen.

'I trust it will be soon,' Joan said, looking embarrassed. 'My position here is somewhat awkward.'

'Say it!' I said flatly, having expected this moment for a week or more. John Zouche was a loyal supporter of Duke Richard so Joan's position as my lady companion would be seen by many as unwise. My husband was increasingly being viewed as a traitor.

'John understands your situation, truly he does, but ...'

I sighed. 'His wife cannot be seen to support the wife of the marquess.'

Joan placed a hand on my arm. 'If it was just me, you know I would stay; of course I would. There would be no question. But I must obey my husband. And there is the baby.'

Ah yes! The baby! We both knew that childbirth waited for neither councils nor convenience and for Joan, this baby provided an excuse to remove herself from my side.

I smiled at her. 'I understand. Go Joan! It is better for you to leave me.'

She was close to tears. 'I shall pray for you. Perhaps afterwards, I may come back, if you will have me.'

'If God wills.'

My stepfather was right – this was not going to end well. Whatever happened, whoever triumphed, I feared bloodshed and only God knew how bloody the chaos would be or whose blood was going to be spilt.

Without Joan, I filled my days meeting with my receiver and others who managed the business of our estates. Previously I had sat with Thomas while he dealt with my inheritance as these were farms and manors I knew well, by name and repute if not by sight. With my husband absent, our men continued what they had always done, only now they brought their problems to me.

My friends had deserted me, either by their own volition or at the insistence of their menfolk. A few acquaintances came seeking information about what was happening to the dowager queen – information I did not possess. It was as if my husband and my mother-in-law had dropped through one of those holes in the ground which the wise woman at Ashby said led to purgatory.

As the month of May wore on, decisions made by the council were whispered into my ear by those who thought I should know: Bishop Stillington of Bath and Wells and Dr Morton, Bishop of Ely, were retained on the council and the young king's tutor John Alcock, Bishop of Rochester, was also given a seat. Steps had been taken to reinforce the south coast ports against possible French attacks and the protector had sent an envoy to the French to talk peace. Did I think there would be war? A question to which I had no answer.

I was told the Duke of Buckingham was garnering great rewards for his support of the protector: the lordships in the Gower and a slew of Welsh castles: Conwy, Caernarvon, Ludlow, Aberystwyth – all required to obey and assist Harry Stafford. Soon there would not be a single castle, manor or town in the whole of Wales or the marches which was not subject to the authority of the Duke of Buckingham. The protector had not forgotten the northern border: the defences of Berwick were to be strengthened and Harry Percy, Earl of Northumberland was confirmed by the young king as warden of the east and middle marches.

'See how wisely the protector is governing', these well-meaning people said, smiling behind their hands, looking to see if I showed any discomfiture. They told me the protector and Archbishop Bourchier had pleaded with the dowager queen to come out of sanctuary. They murmured that surely by now her grace must be weary of the place; it was not as if there was much in the way of entertainment. What did she do all day? And my husband? Had I heard from the marquess? No? How very peculiar!

By the time they left, none the wiser for their efforts to prise nuggets of information from my lips, I was weary of it all. After a month my anger had cooled, I even found myself missing Thomas. Without him I had no-one. For all his faults he was still my husband and the father of my children. It was my duty to give him my obedience and if once I had loved him, surely I could do so again.

I would have liked to talk with my mother but she was at Kirby with her master mason, overseeing building works. My stepfather was beyond my reach, sticking close to Richard's side, always at meetings with the council. I was surrounded by members of my household yet felt utterly alone.

19

LONDON 1483

It was at the end of the first week in June when I was visited by Lady Stanley. I was surprised to see her diminutive figure making its way down my garden path as we'd not spoken for weeks and I assumed she was avoiding me as were so many of my acquaintances. The hazy mid-afternoon sunshine softened the dark cloth of her gown and lent colour to her face, smoothing the frown etched between her eyes, making her look less severe than usual.

We greeted each other warily, both uncertain where the other's loyalty lay. Lord Stanley had a seat on the council. He and his brother were said to be supporters of the protector but Lady Margaret had always struck me as a woman whose limited passion was reserved strictly, and in that order, for God and her son.

I'd not heard her make any comment, favourable or otherwise, about Richard of Gloucester but was certain she had an opinion. My mother believed Lady Margaret's loyalties were suspect despite years of faithful service in the queen's chamber. She said Lady Margaret's Beaufort lineage marked her as someone any York king should keep under close observation.

'I was grieved to hear of your troubles, Lady Cecily,' she said, honouring me with a prim little smile which did nothing to change my impression of her as a dour woman.

'It cannot be easy being parted from your husband in such difficult circumstances. The pain of separation cuts deep for a woman, does it not?'

'Indeed it does, Lady Margaret. I thank you for your kindness,' I replied, wondering why she'd come.

She gazed across the water of the Thames, to the barges making their slow way downriver. From the quays came the salty smell of the sea, borne in on the breeze which had arrived with the turning of the tide.

'The letters I receive from my son, Henry Tudor, give solace to my heart in a way only a mother can understand.'

'Naturally you miss him, Lady Margaret. Is there no word of his return?'

She paused a moment before answering. 'Lord Stanley will ask for the favour when matters are more settled.'

'Then we must pray your hopes come to fruition.'

'What of you, Lady Cecily, do you have hope?'

'Hope of what, Lady Margaret?'

'Why, of seeing the marquess.'

I smiled like a woman without a care in the world. 'As you know, Lady Margaret, the marquess is with the dowager queen at Westminster. He has not informed me of his plans.'

'But you are able to communicate with him. Surely by now you have found a way to pass messages.'

I wondered if this was why she had come, to discover how I communicated with my husband.

'Sanctuary at Westminster is strictly observed, Lady Margaret. The prior would have it no other way.'

'Naturally he is careful. I hear the protector has asked his friends in the north to send men. Did you know?'

I murmured that no, I had not heard.

'I wonder why he should want more men?'

'Perhaps he has discovered he has enemies,' I remarked, thinking of my husband and his mother plotting in sanctuary.

Lay Margaret smiled pityingly. 'The Duke of Gloucester is no fool. He knew he had enemies long before he set foot in London. What, I wonder, could have happened to make him afraid?'

'Is he afraid?'

'Oh yes. My husband says the protector sees danger at every turn.'

'You seem very well-informed, Lady Margaret.'

Her smile was as serene as St Helen's in the church at Ashby, a curved splash of red on a smooth pale face.

'I pray for guidance from God.'

The Almighty had not created Lady Margaret as a woman for idle gossip but I will say she made an effort. We talked about women we knew who had served in the queen's chamber, what they were doing now that my mother-in-law was no longer there to be served, but in truth she knew very little. She'd heard no tittle-tattle and her clumsy attempt at female intimacy made me suspicious.

Having disposed of the whereabouts of the dowager queen's sisters she returned to her musings about my mother-in-law.

'It must be a comfort for her grace to have a grown son at her side but for a young man caught in that situation, the question of when to return is a difficult one. Will he be welcome? Does he have sufficient support? He cannot know what is happening in the world beyond where he finds himself trapped. He may hear occasional bits of news but should he trust what is being said? Naturally those who care for him will prepare the ground in advance, carefully removing any obstacles to his reinstatement but even with their help he may walk into danger.'

She looked at me enquiringly.

'I am certain you are right, Lady Margaret,' I said, giving no hint as to whether I had made preparations for Thomas's return, whether I even believed he *would* return.

She gave a fleeting smile. 'For the young man there can be only one attempt. If that should fail ...' She left the acrid stench of failure hanging in the air, the horror which would overtake Thomas should he emerge from sanctuary to be met by the executioner's axe.

I swallowed hard but said nothing.

It was only later, long after she departed, that I wondered if Lady Margaret had been talking, not about my husband, but about her son.

Henry Tudor, lineal descendant of old King Edward's third son, was in Brittany under the protection of Duke Francis. I tried to imagine what Brittany was like but the only place I had visited overseas was Calais: Calais with its bustling harbour, steep cobbled streets and huge defensive walls.

My stepfather had once stood me on top of the walls to show me the vast extent of the marshland which protected the town. He told me how, if you travelled south beyond the marshes, you would find yourself in the clutches of

King Louis, but if you travelled east along the road to Gravelines you'd be in the lands of the Duke of Burgundy.'

'What if you go that way?' I had asked, pointing out to sea where a hazy grey smudge lay along the horizon.

'England and home. But if you follow those sandy beaches over there and sail south-west, keeping your ship close to shore, you will reach the rocky coastline of Brittany.

'John Zouche says there are pirates in Brittany.'

My stepfather had laughed. 'John Zouche is right.'

'What if you go further than Brittany?

'Ah! If you sail west towards the setting sun? Nobody knows. Perhaps you would fall off the edge of the world like this.' He seized me round the waist and pretended to push me into the void. For a dizzying moment I saw the ground far below and thought I was falling. From behind me I heard my governess gasp and Mary Hungerford give a single scream of fright.

But my stepfather had me held tight.

'Beyond the great ocean, men say there is an unknown land.' he whispered into my ear,

'Impossible!' I said, catching my breath, wishing my heart would stop racing.

'With God's grace, nothing is impossible. A man can be anything he sets his mind to.'

'And a woman?'

He had smiled. 'Only if her husband permits.'

I walked back to the river's edge, considering Lady Margaret's loyalties. Although she was polite, I'd sensed a dislike of my mother-in-law, a feeling I believed was reciprocated. Besides, why would Lady Margaret support a woman in sanctuary who no longer had any power. Unless she believed the woman might one day achieve power.

We both knew that Richard of Gloucester was the one who would decide whether or not Henry Tudor was permitted to return to England. If he could bring himself to ignore her unfortunate Beaufort lineage, the protector would approve of Lady Margaret: a quiet, pious and obedient wife to her husband. Or so it seemed.

Having disposed of the problem of Lady Margaret and her troublesome son, I turned my thoughts to my own children. There seemed little I could do for my husband by remaining in London so perhaps I should journey to Bradgate. The couple I'd appointed to take charge of the children's household were sensible but occasionally a wise mother should see for herself that rules were being obeyed.

Young Tom gave me cause for concern. At six years old he was inclined to rudeness and obstinacy, sticking out his bottom lip in a surly way. According to his tutor, no amount of punishment had any effect but I suspected the man was too gentle. Boys needed a firm hand with the rod or they grew up wayward like my brother who had been outrageously spoiled in his early years. I wondered how Mary Hungerford was faring in her marriage.

I was thinking I should make the effort to visit Mary when I heard the sound of footsteps coming down the path. I turned and to my amazement saw the plump figure of my steward staggering towards me, a hand clutching his chest. He called out, 'My lady! Oh my lady! Come quickly!'

My heart lurched. 'What is it?'

'Lady Hastings, my lady!'

'My mother!'

'Yes, my lady. Oh my lady, she is in such distress.'

Without waiting to hear more, I picked up my skirts and fled back to the house, ignoring the startled servants.

'I have put her in the parlour, my lady!' The steward's voice floated up the path in my wake.

I threw open the parlour door and forgetting everything, flung myself at her feet. She was crouched on one of the smaller chairs, weeping. I took her hands and kissed them. Her gloves lay in her lap, her fingers were icy cold.

'Mother! What is it? What has happened?'

She raised her face to mine. Tears were streaming down her cheeks.

'Is it Annie?' I asked gently.

My sister was twelve years old but had not yet left my mother's care.

Mutely, my mother shook her head.

'My stepfather?'

She still said nothing.

I was almost too frightened to put my fears into words. 'Is he dead?'

She shook her head again.

'Oh Ceci!' she burst out. 'He will not listen. He is deaf to everything I say. I cannot make him understand. He says I am mistaken, that it cannot be so.'

One of the maids coughed. My mother's head jerked up like a deer scenting danger.

'Get rid of them,' she said in a low voice. 'Then lock the door.'

I shooed the maids out, checked there was no-one immediately outside, instructing one of the men to stand guard. Then I came back, closing the door behind me and turning the key.

'The window!' whispered my mother.

I went to the window, peered through the panes. No-one was there.

It was only when I returned to kneel beside my mother that I noticed she was wearing her travelling clothes.

'Are you leaving?' The servants said she'd arrived in London the previous evening. They'd seen her riding towards Paul's Wharf with her escort.

'Yes, I am returning to Kirby.'

'But what of the coronation?'

She looked at me, her eyes full of tears.

'There will be no coronation.'

Then words came tumbling out of her mouth, words which made little sense. They were interspersed by gasps and sobs and mutterings of danger. She spoke rapidly as if there was no time to lose. She spoke of people I'd not heard of and places I did not know; of doings and deceptions far in the past which had no meaning for me. Who were these people and why were they important?

When the telling became too much for her she stuffed her knuckles in her mouth and began to weep again, this time in earnest. I thought it best to let her weep. I waited until the sobs lessened.

I said gently, 'Is the young king sick?'

'No, he is not sick.'

'Then why will there be no coronation?'

She sighed the way she used to, when explaining something simple to Mary Hungerford. 'When Richard discovers the truth, he will not allow it.'

I frowned. 'What truth?'

She paused as if what she wanted to say was too difficult to put into words.

'When he discovers the boy is a bastard.'

'Which boy?'

'Edward's son. The boy who would be king.'

I gave a nervous laugh. 'Mother, is this a joke?'

'No, Ceci, it is not a joke.'

'How can the young king be a bastard?'

She gave a slight shrug of her shoulders. 'In the usual way – his parents were not married.'

'That is ridiculous!'

She looked at me levelly. 'Is it?'

'Mother, you know it is. It is laughable. Everyone knows the king and the queen were married. You told me so yourself. It was a private ceremony at her father's house. There were witnesses. The queen's mother was a witness.'

My mother-in-law's marriage was the stuff of legend: a handsome young king, a poor but beautiful widow, a love affair, a wedding and a coronation.

My mother corrected me. 'I did not say the ceremony was not performed as it should have been, or that the witnesses were not credible.'

'Then you admit they were married?'

'I admit there was a marriage ceremony.'

'If there was a marriage ceremony how can you say they were not married?'

She sat silent for a moment, staring at the floor. Then

she lifted her head, looked straight into my eyes and said. 'Edward was not free to marry. He had a wife.'

I felt as if I'd been knocked sideways.

'A wife?'

'Yes.'

'That is impossible!'

'Such things happen.'

'Mother, you must be mistaken. If there'd been a wife – which I cannot for a minute believe there was – someone would have said. The priest would have asked if there was an impediment.'

'Nobody knew; no-one who was present on that day in May when Elizabeth Woodville thought she'd netted a king.'

'The king must have known.'

My mother gave a wry little smile. 'Oh yes, he knew. But like so much else in Edward's life, it was an inconvenient truth, one to be swept aside and forgotten.'

Yes, I thought, a wife still living would have been a very inconvenient truth – if indeed she had existed.

'Who was she, this wife?'

My mother took both my hands in hers. 'You must understand that later, Edward thought he was safe – a secret, known to only two people and one of them dead. But somebody else knew. Somebody talked.'

'Does the protector know about this so-called other wife?'

'I would imagine someone will tell him.'

The difficulty I was having was in believing any of this. The story smacked of gossip emanating from the courts of Europe designed to blacken the name of the York king.

My stepfather, who knew the late king better than any other man, clearly believed my mother deluded. He had said as much. Yet, as a wife, I was well aware that husbands lied.

'What will the protector do?'

My mother shrugged. 'Ask for proof. But first he will send for Lord Lisle.'

'Lord Lisle? What has he to do with this?'

'He is your husband's uncle.'

'I know he is Thomas's uncle but why would the protector wish to see him?'

She sighed. 'Lord Lisle is married to Lady Norfolk's niece.'

I had the sense of pieces of a long-forgotten puzzle gradually moving into place and at the puzzle's centre was the figure of Lady Norfolk. Like my mother all those years ago at Shute, Lady Norfolk had lost everyone she once cared for: her husband, her daughter, her sister. Sadly diminished, she was said to take solace in prayer. My mother had been rescued by my stepfather and given a new life but no-one had rescued poor Lady Norfolk.

I felt my eyes widening as the most impossible thought crept into my mind.

'Mother! Was King Edward married to Lady Norfolk?'

'No, not Lady Norfolk.'

'Then, who?'

'Her name was Lady Eleanor Butler.'

I considered the name but it meant nothing to me.

'I've not heard of Lady Eleanor Butler. She must have been a nobody.'

My mother gave a glimmer of a smile. 'Lady Eleanor was far from being a nobody. She was the widow of Lord

Sudely's son, Sir Thomas Butler. She was born Eleanor Talbot, daughter of the old Earl of Shrewsbury. She was Lady Norfolk's sister.'

'Oh!'

'She died some years ago, when you were still a child. Now you understand why Richard will wish to speak with Lord Lisle. He will want to know if the Talbot women have knowledge of this story.'

As she spoke I remembered William Catesby telling me how truth was often not what it seemed, how a man's testimony could be purchased for a handful of coins.

'If I were the protector I would want more proof than what people remember.'

'Doubtless he will gather proof. Richard was ever a careful man. He will not halt the coronation without being certain.'

'Mother, what exactly did my stepfather say?'

My mother shook her head sadly. 'He is loyal to Edward's memory and to Edward's son. He says it is all a pack of lies.'

'And you?'

She gave a crooked smile. 'It may be that my memories of Edward are somewhat different to his. Edward was my cousin, the handsomest young man you could imagine. Like all the girls I was half in love with him.'

'And he with you?'

She laughed. 'Oh no! He barely noticed me. And when I married your father I understood that what I'd felt for Edward was a young girl's fancy, not love at all.'

'And he married this Lady Eleanor. Mother, how was that possible? To marry with no-one being aware.'

'I do not know. But all women carry secrets. Some they share, perhaps with a close friend or a sister, some they keep locked in their hearts. I have secrets, ones I've not told your stepfather.'

'To do with your cousin, Edward?'

She gazed at her hands where they lay twisted in her lap.

'We were young. Not yet twenty. You cannot imagine what it was like in those days: Nevills and Yorks pursued by the armies of Mad Henry and his she-wolf wife. We breathed danger every moment. I slept with a dagger in my hand. Twice Edward asked me to lie with him. First when we were alone together at Shute. He was only half serious and I was married and in love with your father. But the second time I was a widow, living in my brother's house, and Edward was king. On that occasion he was prepared to use force to get what he wanted. He made his desires quite explicit and when I refused, he used your wardship as a lever to make me agree. Even then I hesitated, so he offered to marry me.'

I gasped. 'The king offered to marry you? Mother! You would have been queen.'

She smiled. 'I think not. All he wanted was to possess me. You forget, I knew what he was like. Once his lust was satisfied he would have cast me aside and denied the marriage.'

'Is that what happed to Lady Eleanor?'

My mother shrugged. 'I know nothing about what occurred between them. I merely tell you how he behaved with me.'

I remembered the story my mother had once told me of the young prince who'd searched high and low for the perfect wife; how he seduced every pretty young woman he met until he found the one he liked best.

Had Elizabeth Woodville been the last in a long line of conquests? I didn't know, but my mother's tale made me doubt the love story my mother-in-law had woven about her courtship with the king. Had she been cleverer than the others or more desirable or had she, as her enemies said, used enchantments? In Paris they said she'd drawn a blade to repel the English king's advances which made him so mad with lust that he married her – and her a commoner!

I stayed there on my knees, thinking.

'Does my mother-in-law know?'

'I think she has known for some time. Naturally she will have told no-one. Whom could she tell?'

'The king?'

'Maybe she discussed it with Edward.' My mother smiled. 'A difficult conversation, I imagine, accusing your husband of deception.'

'Could they not have married – after Lady Eleanor died?'

'Possibly, but their sin was of long-standing and, as you know, the Church is unforgiving and Rome moves slowly. It would have been an ugly affair, dangerous for a king whose crown was not as secure as he might wish. The scandal would have been immense.'

I wondered what Thomas would think of his perfect mother, if he knew.

'This will not affect my husband, will it? Or our children?'

My mother put her hand gently on mine. 'Your husband's birthright is sound. So is your marriage.'

I thought of my mother-in-law, hidden in sanctuary, living a lie, and all the years she had knowingly lived that lie. Why had nobody known? Or had they? Was any of this true?

'If there was no true marriage, was her coronation sound?'

'Ceci, you are asking me questions to which I have no answer. I would imagine not, but I do not know.'

I tried to sort through the muddle in my mind, to find a path to the truth. William Catesby had taught me to reason but this was a conundrum not even he could not have imagined.

'If the young king is set aside will his brother be king?'

My mother shook her head. 'All Edward's children with Elizabeth Woodville are illegitimate.'

'Even Princess Elizabeth?'

'Yes.'

Until then the true enormity of what was at stake had not sunk in. The king's children, raised to take for granted the deference of others, the trappings of royalty; the daughters in their white silk gowns, the sons wearing velvet doublets fastened with pearl buttons. Now they would be disregarded, named as bastards before the world.

My mother rose to her feet leaving me kneeling on the floor. 'Ceci, I must go.'

'But Mother! Who will be king? England must have a king?'

My mother shrugged. 'I do not know.'

'Richard of Gloucester,' I said quietly to myself. 'That is what will happen. The protector will make himself king.'

20

PATERNOSTER ROW 1483

On hearing a knock I told my maid to see who was there. Since supper I'd been sitting in the parlour half-heartedly listening to a reading by one of the young women in my care while pondering on my mother's revelations. For two days I'd been arguing with myself over who to believe: my mother or my stepfather. I had reluctantly come to the conclusion that my stepfather was right; the story was a fabrication and whoever had fed my mother this fanciful tale of a clandestine wedding was either a mischief maker or someone wishing harm to the Woodvilles – and yet, and yet, and yet – what if it was true.

My steward came through the door, his fleshy face creased in a troubled frown.

'A man, m'lady. Refuses to give a name. Says he has a message for you.'

I raised an eyebrow. 'Do you know whose man he is?'

The steward sniffed. 'No, m'lady. Dressed plain, but tidy. Don't talk much.'

Peculiar, but the times were unsettled so an anonymous messenger was perhaps to be expected. It might be a man sent by my husband though I thought it more probable my mother-in-law had forbidden all contact.

I rose from my seat. 'It is very late but I shall see him in the hall.'

The man was of medium height, brown hair, a crooked nose in a narrow face. He wore dark clothing, shabby boots and a sturdy leather belt. Not someone I knew.

He gave a bow. 'Lady Harington?'

The use of that name made me doubly suspicious. He should have addressed me as "My Lady Marquess". Why ask for Lady Harington.

'I am Lady Harington.'

He held out a packet: something small wrapped in a piece of cloth, tied with narrow ribbon.

'This is for you, m'lady. I've been told you will recognise it.'

'Who sent you?'

'I cannot say, m'lady. My master prefers we do not use his name.'

More and more curious. A mysterious packet and a mysterious sender, a man who knew me as Lady Harington.

I untied the ribbon and peeled back the cloth. Inside was what looked like the remains of a dried flower. I lifted the bundle to my nose. The scent was unmistakeable – lavender! I was about to ask why anyone would send me sweepings from his floor when I remembered: two months earlier, soon after King Edward's death, when I'd sent for William Catesby. We had sat in the garden and he'd asked my permission to pluck some lavender.

I eyed the man. 'What does your master want? Why send you? Why not come himself?'

'He cannot come here, m'lady. It is too dangerous. He wishes to speak with you, said to tell you that it was in your best interest, not his.'

Typical lawyerly words! So Master Catesby wished to speak with me. I wondered what he wanted. He was wise to be careful. As my husband's wife, my house would be kept under observation. Doubtless Master Catesby would prefer not to be known as one of my associates.

'Where is your master?'

The man shifted awkwardly. 'I was told not to say, m'lady.'

'An unknown destination! Is it far distant?'

'No, m'lady, not far.'

If our destination was not far, I assumed Master Catesby was somewhere within the city walls.

'How are we to proceed?'

'On foot, m'lady. My master advises you wear something sober.'

'And why should I appear other than as my rank dictates?'

'For your safe-keeping, m'lady.'

It could be he was right. The streets were hazardous. Too many malcontents and, after my mother's warnings, who knew what other dangers. Or perhaps it was the notice of my unseen watchers, Master Catesby wished me to avoid.

'Very well. Wait here.'

'My lady!' he called as I turned away.

'Yes?'

'Have your maid dress plain as well.'

There was some comfort in knowing Master Catesby expected me to bring a maidservant. At least he was not intent on abduction.

Half an hour later we set out into the long summer twilight. As well as Master Catesby's man, whose name I discovered was Matthew, there was one of my own men – a well-built fellow who my steward assured me was handy with a club and who carried a lantern for our return, in case darkness came early.

I wore a plain cloak belonging to my maid and a pair of old leather boots. My hair was out of its henin, stuffed into a clean linen coif. I thought I looked sufficiently shabby to please Master Catesby. On Matthew's advice, I kept my hood up and my face lowered. It would not do, he said, to be recognised.

We made our way past the king's Great Wardrobe by Blackfriars Priory, up Creed Lane and into the warren of streets beyond Paternoster Row. I lost track of the twists and turns. In the fading light all dwellings looked similar: narrow, dark and uninviting. Eventually we stopped in front of a blue painted door but this could not be where Master Catesby lived; the house was too small and too mean. I suddenly realised I might have been mistaken about the lavender but it was too late to change my mind.

With a quick glance up and down the street, Matthew gave three sharp knocks followed by two more. I heard the sound of bolts being drawn, then the door opened a crack. After a murmured conversation, the door opened wider and I was ushered in.

We stood in a tiny low-ceilinged room, bare but for a stool and a table. The man who had opened the door was small, half-witted, gawping at us as if we were foreigners. Matthew walked towards a door at the back of the room indicating that I should accompany him. As my two companions made to follow, he said sharply, 'Only m'lady. You lot, stay here!'

He tapped on the door before pushing it open. William Catesby stood by the empty hearth, his face turned towards us, watching. I noted the look of naked relief on his face when he saw it was me.

He made a small bow, then dismissed Matthew.

'I pray you forgive the subterfuge, my lady,' he said with that familiar twist of his thin lips which in earlier days had passed for a smile. 'These are dangerous times. It would serve neither of us well for this meeting to become common knowledge.'

I held out the sprig of lavender which I'd concealed in my purse. 'A courtly gesture for a lawyer, Master Catesby. Most elegantly done.'

A slight flush rose into his cheeks. He looked down at the spread of documents on the table. When he raised his head, the colour was gone.

'I needed you to know who you were being asked to meet. I could think of no other way.'

I thought this unlikely. The lavender had not lain in a chest of clothing to be grabbed at the last moment but had been carefully pressed between the pages of a heavy book, kept for a particular reason. A most unlawyerly avocation.

'Well, Master Catesby,' I said brightly. 'You have me captive. What is it you wish to say?'

But he was not to be hurried. 'Pray be seated, my lady. I have wine if you would care for some.'

'Thank you, that would be most agreeable.'

He filled two goblets with wine from an enamelled jug while I settled myself into a chair. The outer room was as bare as a convent cell but this inner chamber was pleasantly furnished, with touches which demonstrated an improvement in Master Catesby's situation since the death of his father. His inheritance must have been substantial to afford fine gilt-silver goblets like the one I held in my hand.

'How much do you know, my lady?'

'About what?' I said, startled by the question.

He regarded me steadily as if he would read my mind, again that slight smile teasing the corners of his mouth.

'We are friends, are we not, my lady? Friends have no need for pretence. You know what I mean.'

Now it was my turn to blush. I bit my lip in embarrassment, unsure how much of what my mother told me could possibly be known by William Catesby.

'I know nothing.'

'My lady, I think you do and I think that what little you know, worries you. I thought I might help alleviate your concerns.'

'I do not see how you can do that, Master Catesby. My concerns involve persons of great importance and you told me once you have no dealings with the highest in the land.'

'Perhaps my fortunes have improved since then.'

I squashed a desire to laugh, wondering with whom Master Catesby had dealings these days.

'Master Catesby, if you consort with those who have risen high, you will know there is discussion in the council concerning arrangements for the coronation.' I thought I was on safe ground as the words were suitably vague.

'And Lord Lisle?'

My heart leapt.

'He is my husband's uncle,' I said cautiously.

'So you will have heard of his wife, Lady Lisle?'

I hesitated. 'Yes.'

'And of Lady Lisle's aunt, the Lady Eleanor?'

By now the ground was no longer safe and I found myself caught in a tangled thicket of my own making.

'I believe I may have heard of her.'

He smiled again, this time broadly, making his face look more attractive. He had put on flesh in the years since I'd first met him at Ashby and the added weight suited his height, making him a more handsome man. Together with his inheritance, perhaps Meg had not done so badly for herself.

'I assume you know the Lady Eleanor's story.'

'You may assume what you like, Master Catesby.'

'I always thought you a clever young woman, my lady. May I ask who told you?'

'You may ask, Master Catesby but I shall not tell you.'

This time he laughed aloud. 'Touché!'

I smiled at his approval. I enjoyed the role of apt pupil to his learned tutor, a game we'd played many times and one at which I seldom bested him.

'Master Catesby, it was you who taught be to be careful. I do not know what you know or from whom you have your information; nor do I know to whom you are loyal. You say you have my best interests at heart but how can I be certain you are telling the truth when you pretend one thing yet manifestly do another.'

'My lady, you are the one whose loyalties are conflicted, not I. Your husband is in sanctuary, plotting God knows what treasons against the protector, while your stepfather,

Lord Hastings, sits on the council. These two men, to whom you profess your allegiance, are sworn enemies. Unless they form an unholy alliance, which I think unlikely, you will have to choose.'

Like the clever lawyer he was, he had exposed the contradiction at the heart of my fears. The late king had exercised his power personally, controlling disputes between his wife's family and his old friends with a mixture of charm and coercion. Now that he was dead there was no-one to prevent the warring factions from trying to destroy each other. My stepfather and my husband were sworn enemies. It had always been thus but now they were unconstrained.

'I am unable to choose, Master Catesby. That is my dilemma.'

'Then let me help you. I can do nothing for your husband, nor would I wish to. The qualities he exhibits are not those I admire. I regret you are yoked to such an unworthy individual. But I have a regard for Lord Hastings. He is an honourable man. Perhaps he does not realise the danger he is in. I have warned him but he is obdurate.'

'He says the intelligence is false.'

'In that, he is wrong.'

'Master Catesby, I do not wish to be rude, but how would you know?'

Again, that sly, thin-lipped smile. 'My lady, you have not being paying attention. You told me yourself you knew of the Lady Eleanor, therefore you must know who her sister is. Two months ago I informed you of the small service I once did for Lady Norfolk. Did it not occur to you that I might also have served other members of her family?'

'I did not think,' I said lamely.

He shook his head. 'An unforgivable error.'

'If Lady Norfolk and her sister needed a lawyer, why would they choose you?'

He placed his hands on the table, fingering one of the documents.

'A family connection of longstanding. My father, Sir William Catesby, was an advisor to the old Earl of Shrewsbury. When my mother died, my father married again. The lady he chose as his new wife was the earl's niece. The second Lady Catesby, my stepmother, was Lady Eleanor's cousin. They were friends.'

My eyes widened. Master Catesby was not the man I thought he was. His eyes brightened in amusement at the look of dawning amazement on my face. I felt a fool for not having known. I had assumed he came from a family of parvenu pen pushers, men with ink-stained fingers who'd pulled themselves out of a humble existence by diligence and good fortune, whereas his father had been a man of substance.

William Catesby leant closer as if we were conspirators hatching a plot, his breath warm on my face, rich with the wine he'd just drunk.

'My father often helped with the lady's legal affairs, conveyances of land and suchlike. I attended him on his visits to Kenninghall although I cannot claim I knew the Lady Eleanor well. I was a very junior apprentice-at-law.'

'You were you privy to this connection with a certain person.'

He looked down at the document, trying not to laugh at my carefully chosen words.

'Lawyers are often asked to attend when a family crisis arises, especially where the matter concerns the legality of a contract. Even more so when the other party involved is a man of, shall we say, high standing. Naturally the final decision rests with the family but a lawyer might suggest that the most obvious course of action may not be the wisest.'

'You were there?'

'I may have been.'

Did that mean he was or he wasn't or that I was not to be told.

'You have documents relating to this connection? '

'My lady, you know how we lawyers admire the written word. It is our life's blood, for what is written carries greater weight in court than hearsay. My father was with Lady Eleanor the summer she died. He was one of the witnesses to the disposal of her estates and her testament.'

'This is where your so-called proof comes from?'

'It may do but a good lawyer always looks for more than one source when searching for the truth.'

'Another witness.'

He smiled approvingly. 'Naturally it would be valuable if a witness could be found, one more proximate to the event in question.'

More proximate! Did he mean someone who was present when the Lady Eleanor married King Edward, someone whose testimony would admit to the truth.

'Who?'

He laughed at my eagerness. 'I cannot tell you that, my lady. I have already told you more than I should.'

'Why bother telling me anything at all?' I said rudely.

'I thought you should know.'

'You could have written a note. Why drag me halfway across London?'

He paused, considering his answer, then said, 'I wanted to see you.'

'Why?'

He sat there watching me, his eyes fixed on mine. Gradually his lips curved into a smile and his eyes warmed.

'If you do not know the answer to that you are less perceptive than I thought.'

I felt my cheeks redden as I remembered the sprig of lavender and the look on his face when he'd seen me enter the room.

'I think,' I began and then stopped, lost for words. What he had just inferred was unbelievable, impossible, yet if I was honest, I'd known for some time that our friendship was of a different quality to any other, more personal, more intimate.

He spoke quietly. 'We shall not see each other again after tonight and for that I am more than sorry for I have enjoyed your company. But your husband has chosen the path of treason and it would be unwise for me to be seen with his wife. So this must be our last meeting.'

I felt a momentary panic at the thought of losing this man I thought of as more than a friend.

'It need not be.'

'I'm afraid it must, my lady.'

'But who will advise me? Who shall I turn to?'

'There are other lawyers.'

'I want you.'

The baldness of this statement was entirely inappropriate, not at all the kind of words a young lady should say to a man who was not her husband. William Catesby looked away and fumbled with his papers while I made a great show of getting ready to rise from my chair.

'Lady Cecily.' He stopped. He had just used my given name when I'd not given him permission.

'Yes?' I whispered.

'You must go before I say something I should not.'

He turned away so that his face was hidden.

'Will you come if I send for you?' I asked in a small voice.

He sighed and turned back. There was a look of great sadness in his eyes. 'You know I cannot.' He must have known what I was thinking, seen the tears glisten on my eyelashes, because he added, 'But I shall think of you often.'

After that there was silence.

There was nothing more I could say without betraying us both. With those few unguarded exchanges he had given me a glimpse of the real William Catesby; not the dull, dry lawyer forever standing in the shadows, carefully weighing up the advantage of any given situation; but a clever, sensitive man who might one day risk everything for a single shot at the sun.

William Catesby, lawyer and friend, opened the door. I walked slowly across the threshold, my arm brushing his. I heard him instruct Matthew to see me safely home.

He followed me to the outer door.

He took my hand, lifted it to his mouth and kissed it. The touch of his lips made me shiver.

'Farewell, my lady,' he murmured, very softly.

'Farewell, Master Catesby,' I whispered, close to tears, not wanting to leave yet knowing I must.

The presence of the others in the crowded room prevented me from saying more but I knew he was watching as I was hustled out into the street.

21

WEST CHEAP 1483

Dusk had given way to darkness, a single star visible in the narrow path above the overhanging roof tops. We walked quickly through empty streets towards the bulk of Baynard's Castle standing stark against the night sky. To my relief we encountered no-one other than a couple of youths running for shelter in fear of patrols ordered by the protector.

'We shall call at Lord Hastings' house by Paul's Wharf,' I informed Matthew.

'I was ordered to see you safe home, m'lady,' he protested.

'You may see me home after I have spoken with Lord Hastings,' I said firmly.

With the current state of unease prevailing in the city, a guard had been set at the gates of my stepfather's house. I was worried we might be refused entry but fortunately one of the men recognised me and I was allowed to pass through.

The main door was a sturdy relic of the days when the house had first been acquired for the Austin Canons of St Bartholomew and, like the stone walls, had mellowed into its surroundings. Matthew yanked on the bell pull. After a moment or two the door creaked open to reveal one of my stepfather's servants. Behind him I saw the pallid face of the steward.

'Lord Hastings is not here, my lady,' he said, frowning at my odd attire. He peered over my shoulder, trying to account for my companions, clearly worried by our appearance at this late hour.

'I have to see him.'

'Forgive me, my lady, he left some hours ago.'

I wanted to weep in frustration. My stepfather had slipped from my grasp just when I needed him most.

'Where has he gone?' I demanded.

'I cannot say, my lady.'

'Cannot or will not?'

The steward coughed to cover his embarrassment .'If you will excuse me, my lady, I shall see if his lordship's whereabouts are known to anyone in the house.'

With that, he melted away into the shadowy back reaches of the hall. I heard a murmured conversation in an adjoining room and after a few moments the steward reappeared with my stepfather's valet, a tall, fair-haired young man.

'You wish to see Lord Hastings, my lady?' he said smoothly, showing no surprise at seeing me dressed in my maidservant's clothes.

'I do. The matter is urgent.'

'I regret, Lord Hastings is not here, my lady. We expect him some time tomorrow. He has a meeting with the protector in the morning and will return for supper unless he is detained on business.'

I felt like stamping my feet.

'That will not do. I need to see him tonight.' I could hear my voice rising at the stupidity of these men. Did they not understand how important this was?

'I am afraid that is impossible.'

'Make it possible! This is a matter of life and death.'

'My lady, I cannot tell you what I do not know.'

'Someone must know!' By now I was shouting.

The two men exchanged a swift look which told me they both knew where my stepfather had gone but were unwilling to tell me. I had a great desire to bang their heads together to make them talk.

'Listen!' I said urgently. 'I do not care who he is with or what he is doing but I have to see him tonight. If you have a care for his safety you *must* tell me where he is.'

The fair-haired man nodded. 'Please to wait here, my lady. I shall see what I can find out.'

The moments were slipping by and, if what Master Catesby had said was true, every heartbeat meant greater danger for my stepfather.

After what seemed an age, the man returned with a scrap of paper in his hand. Somewhat reluctantly, he passed it to me.

'I think you may find Lord Hastings here, my lady. But I urge discretion and would ask you not to divulge from whom you had this intelligence.'

I glanced at the writing. A street off Cheapside, not far.

I flashed a grateful smile, saying I would remember their good service. Then I hurried out of the house and back past the guards. I handed the note to Matthew.

'Can you find this house?'

He squinted at the words. 'Yes, but, m'lady, it is not right for you to be out at this late hour. Can this not wait until tomorrow?'

I ignored his dithering. 'You have a pass?'

He nodded. Yes, m'lady.'

'Then we shall be perfectly safe. Now, hurry!'

With the lantern lit we made our way along Thames Street in the gathering gloom, past the gates to my husband's house and up Bread Lane into Cheapside. Without the bustling crowds which usually thronged the Cheap, the street felt eerily quiet. A cat padded silently by, slinking off into the darkness of a narrow alleyway, intent on some feline business of its own. Twice I stumbled over a pile of rubbish left by a careless stallholder and only Matthew's arm saved me from disaster.

Just before we reached the Hospital of St Thomas where the mercers held their guild meetings, we turned left. New houses were springing up each week in this maze of streets off West Cheap, built for wealthy townsmen who'd prospered in the peace of these last few years. Unfortunately it was too dark to see much but the smell up here was sweeter by far than where we'd been earlier in the evening near Paternoster Row.

Matthew stopped in front of one of the larger houses, its upper storeys built out across the road almost blotting out the night sky. He asked for the lantern to be lifted so that he could check he had the right place.

'Are you certain this is where Lord Hastings' man meant, my lady?' he queried.

'Of course I am certain. Do you know who lives here?'

He said nothing but neither did he move forward. Behind the shutters I could see a flicker of candlelight. I walked up to the outer gate and banged hard. The face of a boy about twelve years old peered though the peephole.

'I have come to see Lord Hastings,' I said firmly. 'Open the gate.'

There was a rattling of chains and the sound of a bolt being shot back, then the wicket gate opened and I stepped through.

Inside, a torch threw sufficient light to show a path lined with what looked like pots of herbs leading up to a door. On either side of the door were large windows, the glass panes, well-shuttered. Standing in the shadow of the porch, was another boy, this time a little older. I thought I recognised him as one of my stepfather's servants. I repeated that I had come to see Lord Hastings. The youth turned and rapped gently on the door. By now my courage was deserting me and I'd begun to feel distinctly nervous.

The door opened. Inside stood a man wearing an old-fashioned tunic, clearly a servant of the household. Behind him I could see a smallish woman, not young but with one of those fresh complexions that all women envy. I must have interrupted her preparations for bed as she was partly *déshabillé*, clothed in a simple gown of costly grey silk cut low at the neck, a mass of lustrous copper-coloured hair tumbling loosely about her ears. This must be the lady of the house.

'You wish to see me, Mistress?' she enquired in a low sweet voice.

'Lady Harington,' I said, thinking it might serve me better to use my own title rather than one people might think tainted by my husband's treason.

She immediately inclined her head and made me an elegant curtsey.

'I am Mistress Elizabeth Shore. You are very welcome, Lady Harington. Please, come in.'

I stood there staring at her, unable to move.

'You are Mistress Shore?'

'Yes.'

The door to one side of the hall was ajar. From the room beyond, a man called out, 'Who is it, Liz?'

It was my stepfather!

She turned her head in the direction of his voice. I heard footsteps and the door opened wider. There stood my stepfather. His doublet was unbuttoned and the ties at the neck of his shirt were undone.

I was too shocked even to gasp.

'Ceci!' he said into the silence. 'What in God's name are you doing here?'

'What in God's name are *you* doing here, my lord?'

I was too horrified by the implications of my stepfather's presence in a state of undress to think how unforgivably rude I was being. I had never spoken to him in such a way in my life.

Seeing that both my stepfather and I were rooted to the spot, unable to speak, Mistress Shore took charge of the situation.

'I believe Lady Harington has come to see *you*, William. Please, Lady Harington, come and sit in here. Lord Hastings will stay with you.' She turned to my stepfather. 'Go back into the parlour, William, if you please. You and Lady Harington will have privacy there. I shall fetch refreshments.'

My stepfather said sourly, 'I think Lady Harington might prefer a knife, Liz, judging from the expression on her face.'

He took my arm but I shook it off. How dare he touch me when he'd been with *that woman*!

He seized me firmly by the shoulders, steered me into the parlour and pushed me into a chair. I had no time to note the comfortable but elegant furnishings which spoke of a wealthy and educated woman; all I could see was this man who had raised me, who I'd thought decent and honourable, who I'd believed loved and respected my mother, who in one single horrible moment had revealed himself to be a lecher, a philanderer, a hypocrite and a liar. I felt a deep sense of betrayal.

As soon as the door closed on Mistress Shore, my stepfather went on the attack. 'Stay where you are, young lady. Keep your mouth shut and listen to me. I know what you're thinking and you're wrong. Mistress Shore is a friend, a good friend.'

'And what else?' I muttered.

'Ceci, be careful! I have always indulged you but I will not allow you to insult Mistress Shore. She is a respectable woman.'

'She is your whore!' I spat.

He slapped me! Hard across my cheek! I jerked back. I was so surprised I barely felt any pain. I put my fingers up to my cheek and gingerly touched the place where his handprint still stung.

He looked at me coldly. 'I warn you, I am not in the mood for insults from a foolish young woman who has no understanding of what is at stake here.'

My mouth trembled. I swallowed and said mutinously, 'Does she?'

'If by "she" you mean Mistress Shore, then yes, she does.'

'More so than your wife?'

'Yes.'

That was more than I could take from him.

'How dare you say that! My mother left in tears because you would not listen to her. She knows exactly what is at stake but you could not be bothered to understand what she was trying to tell you. I have never seen her so upset. You sent her back to Kirby and the moment she was gone you came here to be with that woman.'

'Your mother knows nothing. Nothing!'

I glared at him, surprised how love could so quickly turn to hatred.

'How could she when you never came to see us at Ashby?'

He sighed. 'Oh Christ's blood! Don't you understand anything? My life was with Edward. I owed my entire good fortune to his friendship. I was closer to him than any other man alive and he trusted me. I could not have been the man I was if I'd been for ever running back to Ashby to be with my family. Your mother understood that.'

'You could have brought her to court,' I muttered.

'She preferred Ashby. She did not care for court life.

'And you preferred to keep her at Ashby so you would not be inconvenienced by the presence of a wife.'

My stepfather gave an exasperated sigh. 'What a child you are. I was not living a life of idle pleasure. It was hard work. The king was a demanding friend.'

'What was it he demanded that meant you could not come home?'

'He was easily bored. Without a war to wage he needed constant diversion. He enjoyed his pleasures. It was my duty to devise entertainments and share in them.'

'Women?'

'Sometimes.'

'And as you were away from your wife, these women were a pleasure for you too.'

He smashed his fist onto the arm of his chair and shouted, 'Christ's teeth! Of course I had women. I'm not a bloody monk.'

'That much is abundantly clear, my lord.'

For a moment I thought he was going to hit me again but somehow he brought his anger under control.

'You mother understands and so should you. You're a married woman.'

'It is not my business to pry into your marital arrangements, my lord,' I said in my coldest voice.

'No, it is not. You'd do better to look to your own.'

A gentle knock at the door and Mistress Shore entered carrying a tray. On it were two cups and a jug of wine. She looked anxiously at my stepfather. 'Is everything alright, William? You were shouting.'

He smiled and touched her hand. 'A small disagreement, my dear, but it is past. There is no need to worry. Lady Harington has so far declined to use violence on me.'

'I was not concerned for you, William. I know you can look after yourself. I thought Lady Harington might need assistance. You can be very intimidating.'

He laughed. 'Can I?'

She was so welcoming, so kind, so gentle and undemanding, it was hard to dislike her. I had to keep reminding myself that this was the woman who had lured my husband into her bed, not just once but several times.

The woman who, after the king died, when she was looking for a new patron, offered herself to him again. Now it was apparent she had shared her favours with both men in my life.

I watched as she poured wine. She was not beautiful like my mother-in-law but possessed a prettiness which was all the more powerful for being understated. She moved gracefully, the curves of her body accentuated by the silk gown which shimmered in the candlelight.

She turned to me. 'The hour is very late, Lady Harington. May I offer you a bed for the night?'

'I thank you, no,' I said frostily.

'Then I shall leave you and Lord Hastings to talk.' She turned to my stepfather. 'Be kind to her, William.'

I could have slapped her for the way she spoke to my stepfather as if she was his wife.

'I thank you, Mistress Shore but I do not need you to speak for me.'

My stepfather placed his hand on her arm again, that possessive touch telling me everything I needed to know about their relationship. He looked up at her, a slow smile softening the lines on his face. 'Thank you, Liz, I shall bear that in mind when she pulls out her knife. God willing, I shall see you later.'

We both watched as Mistress Shore walked out, closing the door quietly behind her.

The interruption by Mistress Shore had calmed my stepfather but I was wary of another outburst of temper. This was a side of his nature I'd not witnessed before, yet it must always have been there, lurking beneath the surface of the affable Lord Hastings I'd come to know and love.

My mother praised him for his tenderness; others described him as a fine man and to me he'd shown nothing but kindness. Yet this was the same man who had frequented the bed of a known harlot in preference to that of his wife and who'd lashed out when I had protested.

He spoke coldly. 'Why have you come, other than to be unforgivably rude both to me and to Mistress Shore?'

'I hardly know why I bothered,' I said nastily. 'I believed you were in danger but I see there is no cause for concern. You have no need of my help nor that of your wife. You have your friend Mistress Shore to provide you with all the comforts you require.'

He leant forward and it took all my courage not to flinch. But this time he had no intention of hitting me, his whole body was tense and his eyes held a calculating look. 'I have been in danger from the moment Edward died. Since yesterday, I thought I was in less danger, not more. Why now?'

'What happened yesterday?'

He smiled grimly. 'A messenger went north carrying warrants for the execution of Lord Rivers and Sir Richard Grey.'

I brought my hand up to my mouth. 'Execution!'

'What else! Did you expect them to receive honourable pardons?'

'No.'

'If their plan had succeeded, the protector and I would be dead; Buckingham too. But as the wife of the marquess, perhaps that slight inconvenience does not worry you.'

'Does the dowager queen know?'

'Not yet but she will. She cannot have expected anything else.'

I thought of my mother-in-law's fury and a cold mass of dread filled the pit of my stomach. After this there would be no going back for any of us. My mother-in-law had already lost her father and one brother to her husband's family. The protector's killing of her second son and her favourite brother would be beyond forgiveness. From everything I knew of her character she was the kind of woman who would seek revenge.

'So tell me,' he said, 'where is this new danger?'

I looked him straight in the eye. 'The young king cannot take the throne. He is a bastard.'

To my surprise, he tipped back his head and laughed.

'Christ's blood! Will the old spider never stop weaving his damn lies.'

'It is not a lie; it is the truth,' I protested.

He shook his head. Listen to me, my lady marquess who thinks she knows everything. You were four years old when King Louis passed a joke around the French court, smearing the English king. Six feet tall he'd been told, unbelievably handsome, every inch a royal prince. Not so, said Louis. The mother's a whore. She cuckolded the Duke of York with an English archer named Blaybourne while the husband was away from Rouen. The English king is nothing but a bastard. The joke did the rounds of Paris and doubtless caused much merriment but when the story reached Edward's ears, he was angry, not for himself but for the slur it cast on his mother, Duchess Cecily.'

'I know about that slander,' I said.

'Then you will understand that this is simply more dross. It was the same after Picquigny: vulgar songs about how the English had been driven out of France by venison pasties and fine wines. This will have been dreamt up by someone close to King Louis. You should know by now that a man's enemies always aim their darts at his weaknesses and Louis was well aware of Edward's interest in beautiful women. There is no truth in it. What your mother believes is a well-crafted lie.'

I frowned. What he said made perfect sense but so did what William Catesby had said.

'Are you certain?' I asked, unsure which man to believe.

'Of course I am certain. I would stake my life on it. Remember, I knew Edward better than anyone.' He gave a short laugh. 'I knew him better than he knew himself.'

'What if there is proof?'

I thought I saw a flicker of doubt in his eyes.

'That is impossible.'

'What if ...'

He let go of my hands and stood up. Somehow he was even more frightening when standing at a distance than when sitting beside me, glaring into my face.

'Let us not quarrel, Ceci. In ten days time, Edward's son will be crowned and I can rest easy. I do not wish to hear any more nonsense. The coronation is a matter for discussion by the protector and the royal council. It is not a subject for mischief makers and idle gossips spouting treason against Edward's son.'

'But ...'

He put his finger to my lips. 'The matter is closed. I am weary. I shall see you out and then go to my bed.'

'Doubtless Mistress Shore will join you,' I sneered.

He gave me an amused smile. 'Doubtless she will.

Now, stepdaughter, I bid you a good night and may God keep you safe.'

He opened the door and informed the steward who'd been hovering outside, probably listening to every word we'd said, that I was leaving and to see me into the care of my escort.

As I stepped out into the darkness I realised I had forgotten to mention Master Catesby's warnings of danger. I told myself it was of no importance. I would tell him next day when he came to beg my forgiveness, and if he did not come, I would go to his house and beg *his* forgiveness. I'd no wish for us to be at odds.

What I failed to understand and could not have known was that the tomorrow I imagined would never come, and I would never see my stepfather again.

22

THE TOWER 1483

On Friday, after an early meal where I picked at my food, I settled down to attend to a complicated piece of estate business. My receiver laid various documents in front of me but I found myself unable to concentrate. I watched splashes of sunlight move slowly across the floor, edging closer to the wall as the sun rose higher, wondering about what I'd been told. Eventually, unable to ignore the insistent questions running round and round inside my head, I dismissed my receiver and began to think.

Was what William Catesby had told me, the truth? The answer was that I did not know. If it *was* the truth then my stepfather was either lying or mistaken. I pondered on the closeness of the relationship of these men. Master Catesby had been employed for several years on my stepfather's business, valued as diligent and trustworthy. But my stepfather's closeness to King Edward was well-known and of long standing: closer than brothers, closer than man and wife. It was inconceivable that my stepfather would not have known of the king's clandestine marriage to Lady Eleanor Butler – if it had taken place.

If my stepfather knew and William Catesby knew and this mysterious other witness William Catesby had mentioned, also knew, I wondered who else might know. That brought me to my mother. Who had told her? In the shock of hearing the story for the first time I had failed to ask. Clearly it was not my stepfather as he denied the truth of the Butler marriage. And it was not Master Catesby because otherwise he'd have guessed who had told me. Who else might it have been? Who knew my mother intimately enough to entrust her with what was an extremely dangerous secret?

At this point in my deliberations, my steward came hurrying self-importantly through the doorway. He gave a small bow and said, 'My lady. The man who accompanied you yesterday evening, has come with news. He reports a great commotion in the streets. He says a dozen armed men led by Sir Thomas Howard are making for Cheapside. There is to be an arrest. Word is that it is the woman you visited.'

He looked at me expectantly. I felt an immediate lurch of fear. Not for Mistress Shore – she could burn in Hell for all I cared – but for my stepfather. He should have been with the protector for a meeting, or so his valet had said. What if he had returned to Mistress Shore's house? What if it was he who was to be arrested? I told myself not to be foolish; the protector had no reason to arrest my stepfather; he was my stepfather's friend, not his enemy.

I turned to my maid. 'Bring me my cloak.'

'My lady, you cannot go out. It is much too dangerous,' the steward fussed. 'There could be violence.'

'Then fetch me two strong men and make sure they are armed with cudgels, and as you are concerned for my welfare, you had better accompany me.'

I decided we would walk towards the Tower, then up through Dowgate and Walbrook to the bottom of Corn Hill rather than risk encountering Friday crowds thronging the Cheap. I'd thought mine a good plan but before we reached the turning where the German merchants did business, we were stopped by a small group of men and women hurrying in the opposite direction.

One of the women called out, 'I'd not go this way if I were you, mistress; there be trouble at the Tower.'

'Aye,' the taller man agreed 'Protector's gone mad. Killing everyone!'

The smaller man added, 'Archbishop's dead. We heard 'im scream.'

The woman hanging on his arm, said, 'Fair turned my stomach it did, mistress. Told my sisters we'd best make for Paul's Cross.'

''Do you have proof?' my steward said, pompously.

'What proof d'you want, good fellow,' the tall man said. 'A bloody head?'

Another group of people came running from the direction of the Tower, shouting there'd been an uprising. The protector had armed men on the streets.

'That is a nonsense,' I said. 'I doubt the skinners and tallow-makers of Dowgate are in arms on a Friday. We are perfectly safe.' With that I walked resolutely onwards followed by my little entourage.

By the time we reached Mistress Shore's house the crowd was ten deep. There was so much shouting I found it impossible to understand what was going on. It was the usual mix of workmen in leather aprons, apprentices out for some fun, old women, worried shopkeepers, assorted beggars in varying degrees of infirmity, a few merchants and the odd gentleman in satins and velvet, surrounded by servants.

'Here, my lady!' My steward was guarding the entrance to a short fight of steps. 'There be a good view from up top,' he said, offering his hand.

Over the heads of the crowd I could see the gate to Mistress Shore's house. Today it was wide open, guarded by four armed men with wooden staves. Two men emerged, carrying a table with gilded legs. The crowd howled their appreciation as the table was heaved onto a nearby wagon. Next came a brocade-covered settle and a large box containing what looked like silver candlesticks.'

'Has they brought out her bed, yet?' shouted a woman standing in front of the steps

'Nay, mother,' said a hulk of a lad.

'Shame! I'd like ter see where she lay with the king.'

'Not choosy who she pleasured, was Will Shore's wife,' sniggered another woman. 'As long as 'e 'ad the tackle.'

'You looking for a bit a pleasuring yerself, Meg Wantall?' leered a stocky man with a large nose and an eyepatch.

Another roar, even louder than the first, greeted the sight of Mistress Shore being marched out of the gate. A cascade of copper curls tumbled untidily over her shoulders, a sight which might have appeal to some men but not to the two guards holding tight to her upper arms. She stumbled but was jerked upright by her captors, allowing the crowd a view of a long jagged tear down the front of her gown where someone had tried to wrench it off. Either that or she'd put up a fight when the men sent to arrest her decided to have some sport.

A great cheer erupted from the crowd as she was shoved unceremoniously into an enclosed cart and the door slammed shut and bolted by one of the men. I could just make out her pale face staring out of the barred window at the back of the cart and wondered if she knew why she'd been arrested.

Out of the gate strode Sir Thomas Howard, resplendent in a blue and red cape. He was the heir of Lord Howard, the man who'd been deprived of his rightful inheritance by my scheming mother-in-law. Since Richard of Gloucester had come south in the spring, the middle-aged Sir Thomas was known as one of his most loyal enforcers. He waved a gloved hand to the crowd as if the cheer had been for him, which perhaps it was. I had no idea of the loyalties of these fickle Londoners.

Sir Thomas looked around as if checking that order had been restored, then mounted his horse and gave the signal for the little procession comprising cart and contingent of guards to move off. The men left behind resumed the removal of the rest of Mistress Shore's goods from her house Once their wagon was fully loaded, the gate to the house was closed and the men moved off, following in the wake of Sir Thomas and his prisoner.

A collective sigh of disappointment spread through the crowd as they realised the entertainment was over. Instead of drifting off in small groups back to their daily employment, people suddenly charged off, calling on neighbours to follow. They were making for Lombard Street where the goldsmiths had their shops.

'What is happening?' I called down to my steward who was hovering at the bottom of the steps.

'Proclamation!' he called up. 'Herald said to be riding out of the Tower.'

'Find out what it's about,' I ordered.

Proclamations were usually nothing more than ways of informing citizens of what they already knew. This one would concern the arrest of Mistress Shore but it would be interesting to know why the protector had decided to have her taken up.

I sat on the second step, wondering what the upset at the Tower was about. If there was one thing I'd learned about Londoners, it was their propensity to exaggerate. A tiff between husband and wife would, in the mouths of neighbours, quickly become a marital fight with pots and pans where one spouse was brutally murdered with a poker. If I believed every story I'd heard from my more credulous friends the streets would be full of dead bodies.

The stone step was cold and I was beginning to regret my decision when I saw my steward hurrying back up the street. By now the crowds had thinned considerably with only a handful of people remaining to gawp at Mistress Shore's house in hope of a resumption of this afternoon's fun.

I stood up and smoothed my skirts. 'What was the proclamation?'

The man was panting as if short of breath and as he drew nearer I saw his face, usually ruddy like an overripe plum, had turned the colour of bleached bone. He reminded me of the man in the stream in the marshes beyond Calais.

'Oh, my lady, my lady, the most dreadful of news!'

'What is it?'

His eyes began filling with tears.

'What has happened?' I said, tendrils of terror beginning to uncurl in my stomach.

'I … I …'

'What?'

'Oh my lady!'

'What?' I screamed.

He covered his face and began sobbing.

'If you do not tell me, I shall beat you myself with one of these cudgels.'

'It is Lord Hastings, my lady.' His words came in a rush, accompanied by more sobs.

'What of Lord Hastings?'

'The protector had him killed, my lady. Lord Hastings is dead.'

I have no recollection of how I came home. I was trapped in a cloud of swirling fog unable to comprehend any words, unable to speak. Nothing made any sense. From somewhere far away, a man's voice said, 'He was plotting against the protector. He has been executed.'

This could not be true. Black rage like bile rose up in my throat.

'Who dares say Lord Hastings is a traitor?'

'The protector, my lady. The proclamation is his.'

I remember a babble of noise, a woman screaming and my maid weeping. Voices in my ears were trying to burrow themselves into my consciousness, each one a shout of, "Traitor!" "Back-stabber!", "Judas!". An insistent torrent of lower voices speaking of plots to kill the protector and secret meetings with others of like mind. They were just words, they meant nothing. None of it made any sense.

Somehow the women of my household got me to bed. Someone forced a foul-tasting draught between my lips, a liquid which brought blessed oblivion. Twice in the night I woke to darkness, panic-stricken, calling for my stepfather and once I woke with tears wetting the pillow where I slept. I feared waking, feared knowing that my stepfather was no longer alive in this world.

Next morning I listened stony-faced while I was given a full explanation of what had happened, or as full an explanation as anyone who was not present, could give. The protector had uncovered a plot against his life, the chief plotters being Lord Hastings, Archbishop Rotherham and Bishop Morton. In the middle of a meeting of some council members in the Tower, accusations were made and the protector threatened. Soldiers were called, Lord Hastings was arrested, taken outside and executed on the protector's orders. A man whose cousin was an eye-witness said it happened so quickly there was no time to build a proper scaffold, the executioner made do with a baulk of timber. Archbishop Rotherham and Bishop Morton were spared execution on account of respect for their order, but were detained. The protector, it was said, expressed regret at the loss of life.

'It is not true,' I said firmly. 'Lord Hastings was loyal to the protector. He would not have plotted his death.'

'There was evidence, my lady,' explained my steward patiently. 'Documents, letters, witnesses. The protector is a careful man. He would have insisted on proof.'

Echoes of my mother's words rang in my head: Richard of Gloucester was ever a careful man. Yet the killing of my stepfather was not that of a careful man. It was intemperate, hasty, cruel and wrong. If the protector had believed my stepfather was a traitor than someone had fed him a litany of lies. Someone had hated my stepfather sufficiently to contrive evidence against him, evidence which that someone believed would bring about his enemy's downfall.

I knew how these things worked. Master Catesby had told me. Letters could be altered, a man's words bought for the price of a silver coin and in doing so, the truth was undone and remade. But nothing could undo this. My stepfather was dead and I had to live the rest of my life without him.

Into this fog of misery, I received a note from my stepfather's steward at Paul's Wharf. He wished me to know that a letter had been sent to Lady Hastings at Kirby from the senior men of the household, a final act of loyalty to a man they had loved and respected. My mother had been informed of the circumstances of my stepfather's death. His will and testament was in safekeeping, though the steward regretted he could not say what would happen to my stepfather's property. In this most unfortunate of situations, this must be a matter for the protector and the parliament.

The day dragged on with meaningless routines: meals, prayers, letters, orders to be given, people to be seen. I was almost thankful when it was time for bed although sleep meant a return of my dreams: the protector grown twice in size, so enormous he could crush a man in his fist, hissing "Traitor!" as he advanced on my stepfather lying bound and gagged on a stone slab.

Finally I fell into a deep sleep and when morning came, woke to the sound of someone singing and my husband's kiss on my lips, his warm body nudging comfortably against mine. I reached for him, for comfort, only to find my hands touching empty air. There was no-one there.

Sunday the 15th of June. Another day. My steward came, cap in hand, to make a request.

'The woman as was taken up on Friday, m'lady – Mistress Shore.'

'What of her?'

'She be to do open penance today. She be being made to carry a lighted taper in her hand. 'Twill start at St Paul's. They say she'll be barefoot and dressed in naught but her kirtle. The men were asking if they might go and watch, my lady. 'Twill be a rare sight for I recall her as being something pretty. 'Tis not often the men get to see a woman like her walk barefoot though the city streets and 'twould be good to see her profess sorrow for her sins.'

'Very well,' I said, too weary to say otherwise though I doubted they'd be curious about Mistress Shore's soul, more likely lusting after her body.

With the house almost empty, I went outside into the garden and stood weeping for my stepfather, for my mother and for myself until there were no more tears left to shed

It was, so I was told afterwards, a fine affair: Mistress Shore walking so fair and lovely and looking so comely, especially when she blushed, that men cheered to see her.

'Seems a shame to shut such a lovely woman away,' remarked the steward.

'Where has she been taken?'

'Ludgate, my lady.'

It seemed Mistress Shore had been given the choice of her place of incarceration. Certainly the upper rooms at Ludgate would be more comfortable than most prisons.

After the steward had gone, the man I'd once sent to spy on Mistress Shore's house, asked if he might see me. He was as awkward as ever, never taking his eyes off his boots.

'What is it?' I was no longer interested in London gossip about Mistress Shore but must carry on with my duties as mistress of the household. I had given this man a commission and must listen to whatever filth he had unearthed.

'I did as you bid m'lady. I been visitin' the taverns, ones where men gossip 'bout what's goin' on and suchlike and I thought you'd want to know, seein' as it concerns the marquess.'

That made me pay attention.

'What about the marquess?'

'There be a rumour he be out of sanctuary, m'lady. Slipped away like.'

For more than six weeks I'd heard nothing of my husband. I'd stopped expecting news but at last it seemed he had broken cover.

'What is being said?'

'The protector's sent men to Westminster, m'lady. They be searchin' the fields and woods for 'e. But one old man says the fields behind the abbey be deep in standing corn so if the marquess be hid there, they'll like as not use dogs.'

'They've not found him?'

'No, m'lady. Not yet. Would you wish me to go there, m'lady? Make enquiries? I could take a few men?'

I shook my head. 'You'd be wasting your time. The marquess will have made good his escape. He'll not have lingered.'

Had the half-dream I'd had on waking that morning, been a sign? The touch of Thomas's mouth on mine had felt real, the warmth of his body reminiscent of those years when I believed us happy together.

My mother-in-law had supporters in the city so my husband was not exactly friendless, but he would have to be careful. Coming here would be foolish because the protector had set men watching the house and he would not have gone to Mistress Shore's because she was in prison.

'Go to Clerkenwell,' I said. 'There is a woman the marquess knew before I became his wife. See if she knows anything. But be discreet.'

He bowed and withdrew, taking with him the stench of my husband's many infidelities. I faced the unwelcome truth that Thomas had likely never been faithful to me, that this woman in Clerkenwell had probably been a continuing amusement throughout our marriage. My stepfather's betrayal of my mother had opened my eyes to how even the most honourable of men behaved and Thomas, regrettably, was far from being honourable.

Next day while I was waiting for the man to return, there was a great commotion out on the river. I ran outside, my heart pounding, fearing Thomas had been caught, but it was Archbishop Bourchier's barge travelling downriver followed by a great multitude of little boats, people cheering and waving swords and staves. I could make out the elderly archbishop sitting beneath his canopy and beside him a small boy of about nine years old dressed in a blue doublet.

'It's the little prince!' my maid exclaimed.

Even at this distance I recognised young Dickon, his face bright with enjoyment at this taste of freedom after so long in sanctuary. I wondered had the boy been forcibly taken or had my mother-in-law willingly let him go to join his brother in the royal apartments in the Tower.

The household were laying bets as to whether the dowager queen would now come out of sanctuary for the coronation on Sunday but of course they didn't know what I knew, that there would be no coronation.

I wanted to see my mother but with my husband loose somewhere, I could not easily leave the city. I would have to apply to the protector for permission to travel to Kirby and feared that under the circumstances he would refuse.

I decided my best hope was to see my cousin, Anne. She had a kind heart and as the protector's wife must have a little influence. If she could assure him I would not have contact with my husband, that the sole purpose of my visit was to console my mother, perhaps he would grant me a safe conduct.

Next morning, Tuesday, I wrote a note to Anne and gave it to a servant, instructing him to go first to Crosby Place and if the duchess was not there, to Baynard's Castle. After that I could do nothing but wait. In the circumstances waiting was difficult but, like grief, had to be endured.

There had been no information about my stepfather's burial or about arrangements for his widow and I was worried. By now, news of his death must have reached

Kirby and for the second time in my mother's life violence had robbed her of a husband she had loved.

I thought about the day she'd heard of my father's death, wondering if this second bereavement was worse. Her first marriage had been loving but brief whereas she'd been my stepfather's wife for more than twenty years. Was a woman's sorrow greater if her love was longer or was the raw grief of youth, sharper. I believed I mourned my dead father whereas in truth I had no memory of him, just an imaginary ideal; whereas my stepfather had been part of my life for as long as I could remember. My sorrow for the loss and the manner of his death, cut deep.

I gazed at the empty chairs in my solar. It was weeks since any of my friends had visited. Husbands, whether supporters of the dowager queen or the protector, suspected my loyalties, and my stepfather's death on an accusation of treachery had driven away everyone else. With Thomas implacably set against the protector, possibly raising men to arms, nobody wanted to know me. There were no notes and no-one called to offer condolences upon my stepfather's untimely death because nobody could afford to be a friend to a woman close to a traitor.

One person did come. Margaret Beaufort, Lady Stanley, came silently, with very little fuss. One moment my room overlooking the river was empty of visitors, the next she was seated neatly in the chair opposite mine, her sombre dark grey gown not exactly the colour of mourning but close enough to bring me a degree of comfort. I was pathetically grateful for her presence.

'Lord Stanley informed me of the circumstances of Lord Hastings' death,' she said, once she had finished explaining to me how God's Will was often mysterious but how we are fashioned in His image to bear such loss with resignation and dignity.

'How kind of him,' I said, acknowledging my own lack of resignation, wondering if Lady Margaret thought my grief, undignified.

I noticed how the deeper folds of her skirt appeared black now she sat perfectly still.

'Lord Stanley said there was much bad feeling that day and not a little violence,' she remarked.

I looked up. 'Lord Stanley was there at the meeting with Lord Hastings?'

She put her hand on mine. It was a small hand, the fingers delicate like a child's. Her voice became quieter, a low, intimate murmur.

'I thought you might want to hear the truth.'

I smiled weakly. 'Yes, I do want the truth.'

'That is what I thought. Often it happens that words are put into men's mouths, words which were never said, and who is to know? Clerks make mistakes, people misremember, men imagine doings which never took place. It is commonplace.'

Her description of what had occurred was broadly similar to what I already knew. Some members of the council came for a pre-arranged meeting in the Tower. Other councillors were at Westminster discussing arrangements for the coronation but there was so much to deal with in such a short time that the protector had convened two meetings.

Everyone was cheerful. It was a sunny day. The protector suggested Bishop Morton might send for strawberries from his garden at Holborn so they could all enjoy the first fruits of summer.

While they waited for Bishop Morton's man to return, the protector was called away. He was absent for about an hour. When he returned, his mood was savage. He accused Lord Hastings, Archbishop Rotherham and Bishop Morton of plotting against him. Heated words were exchanged, chairs were overturned and when things became ugly, the protector called in the guards. There was a brief struggle. Lord Hastings was arrested by Sir Thomas Howard, led down to the yard and beheaded on the protector's orders.

'But why?' I said.

'Treachery, my dear Lady Cecily, treachery. A man like Richard of Gloucester could in no way stomach treachery from one he believed was loyal.'

'Lord Hastings *was* loyal.'

She smiled pityingly at me. 'Are you certain?'

'Lady Margaret, he told me how pleased he was when the Duke of Gloucester became protector.'

'Ah yes, but a man may be pleased for more than one reason. Lord Hastings would not have wanted the Woodville family in power. His quarrels with Lord Rivers and with your husband, were well known. Richard of Gloucester could be relied on, not only to protect Lord Hastings from the dowager queen's family, but also to see the late king's son crowned king.'

'All the more reason for Lord Hastings to be loyal,' I cried.

Lady Margaret folded her hands in her lap and put her head slightly to one side as if considering how to say what she thought needed to be said.

'Lady Cecily, let me pose a question. Consider this: a man has information which he fails to divulge when it is not only right but vital that he should do so. A sin of omission? Certainly. And we know what the Bible says about sins of omission. A man's guilt is measured not only by the dignity of the virtue and the magnitude of the precept to which this omission is opposed, but also by the length of time he has kept the secret.'

'Lady Margaret, are you telling me the protector believed Lord Hastings was withholding information?'

'That is what Lord Stanley says, and he, we must remember, was present during this fracas. He has a bruise where his head hit the table.'

'What if the protector was mistaken? What if Lord Hastings did not have this information?'

Lady Margaret smiled, nothing more than a slight upturn of her thin lips.

'Ah, Lady Cecily, I think we both know that he did. We both know exactly what the information was that he'd been trying so hard to conceal. Doubtless he would have prayed for guidance. We can only imagine his distress when he discovered his will ran counter to that of God.'

I stared at her, trying to gauge from what she'd said and that enigmatic smile on her face, if she knew everything or if she was merely trying to get me to show my hand.

When I made no reply. she said, 'Of course, he would not have known about the others?'

I blinked in surprise. 'What others?'

'The others who were privy to the secret. Lord Hastings was a sensible man. He'd have been more careful if he'd known there were others. I think for that we have to blame the late king. He must have told Lord Hastings the secret was safe, the lady was dead; there was no-one else who knew. But he'd forgotten there were others who were privy to his secret.'

'Does the protector know?'

She raised one eyebrow slightly. 'Lord Stanley says the protector has asked to see Lord Lisle.'

She must have registered the shock in my eyes. 'Ah, so the name is familiar to you?'

'Lord Lisle is my husband's uncle.'

'Oh come, Lady Cecily, we both know Lord Lisle has not been summoned because he is your husband's uncle. His wife, Lady Lisle, is a granddaughter of the old Earl of Shrewsbury and that would be of great interest to the protector. Such an intriguing family. Naturally Richard is conflicted, but I fear the boy cannot be crowned king – not now. It would be impossible.'

She knew! A secret kept for so long and at such cost, opened up to the unforgiving light of day.

'Lady Margaret, did your husband say if Lord Hastings died well?'

She knew exactly what I was asking and, in that matter, she was kind.

'Yes, he died well. He was given time to make his confession. It was quick – one blow of the axe.'

I sat there, swimming in grief with tears rolling down my cheeks, quite unable to thank her for telling me, quite unable to make a dignified farewell.

23

BAYNARD'S CASTLE 1483

On the Thursday, two days after Lady Margaret's visit, I had my maid lay out my best mourning gown of patterned black silk. I chose my longest sleeves, the elegant ones which partly concealed my hands, and beneath my gown I wore a dark grey kirtle. I deliberately shunned jewels except for a narrow gold chain around my throat and the ruby and gold ring given to me by my mother on my wedding day. A sheer floating veil fell from my black velvet henin, brushing the tops of my shoulders.

I was the embodiment of a woman who indulged in fashionable clothing yet looked suitably demure and grieving. It was necessary to dress well for I would gain nothing from my cousin's husband if I arrived tear-stained and dishevelled.

I reddened my lips, took a last hasty look in my mirror and set out for a meeting with the protector's wife: my cousin, Anne, Duchess of Gloucester.

The message, brought by a liveried servant said I should attend on the duchess at Baynard's Castle at noon when I might be received. Compared to the scrawled note of eight years before. when Isabel was still alive, this formal invitation was chilly in the extreme and did not promise much in the way of cousinly affection.

The room, where I was left to wait, was one of those vast presence chambers where petitioners hover, hoping to catch the eye of some great man as he walks through to the inner rooms. The benches were hard but the decorative paintings were magnificent, a reminder of how great a patron of artists Duke Humphrey had been. It must have been fifty years since a Florentine artist lifted his brush and depicted the hunting scene on the wall; yet the white stag, hiding in the darkness amongst the trees, was as vibrant as the day he'd been first painted.

I watched as men passed to and fro, some carrying packages, others sheaves of documents or bowls of fruit. As the hours passed I wondered what Anne was doing, why she'd not sent for me. In earlier times I would have demanded to be taken to her chamber but my position now was one of weakness so I would have to be patient.

Eventually a man walked, soft-footed, towards me. He was young, dressed in a dark brown doublet, fine woollen hose and elegant shoes, clearly someone of greater importance than a lowly servant in my cousin's household. He gave a bow which barely bent his back, a mere incline of the head and shoulders.

'Duchess Anne, regrets she is unable to see you today, my lady.' His face was impassive.

'I was told to come,' I protested.

'As I said, my lady, the duchess is unable to see you but if you would care to follow me, the dowager duchess of York, has agreed to give you a few minutes of her time. It is a great honour, my lady,' he said with a smirk. 'I hope you appreciate that.'

I wanted to slap his smug face but instead said sweetly that the dowager duchess was most kind.

I followed this swaggering popinjay out of the archway at the far end of the chamber, up a short flight of steps and through two more rooms until he stopped before a pair of gilded doors. They were guarded by two men holding halberds. Seeing my companion, they stood aside while two other men opened the doors.

I remembered this room from my last visit: a cold ill-lit chamber with an old-woman's smell, fusty and over-perfumed. Duchess Cecily had shrunk since our last meeting, her aging bones shrivelled beneath her dark blue gown. Weighing heavily on her shoulders was a thick fur-lined mantle, fastened by a jewelled clasp.

Her expression was austere but I noticed the glint of emeralds on her fingers. She still wore the old-fashioned horned and rolled headdress but in a nod to vanity she'd had her maid pluck her hairline. Her women stood behind their mistress, merging imperceptibly into the shadows.

She leaned forward slightly, narrowing her bright little eyes. 'Brought down a trifle, eh, Lady Harington?'

I curtsied and said nothing. It was clear I was not yet required to speak.

'I liked Lord Hastings,' she continued. 'He was a good man. Shame he was so attached to the Woodville boy.' She snapped her fingers and one of the women sidled forwards. 'A chair for Lady Harington!'

Words were passed backwards into the gloom and after a few moments an elderly man tottered forwards carrying a chair. I looked at the spindly legs and lowered myself gingerly onto the seat, wondering if the ominous creaking preceded total collapse.

'I expect you are worried for your mother.'

'I am, your grace,' I murmured politely.

'Very laudable. She is a good woman and deserved better. But that is the way of the world: men make mistakes and women suffer.'

'Yes, your grace.'

Her emeralds winked as she flexed her bent fingers. I tried to keep my expression humble.

'Help me up!' Two of the women moved forwards. 'Not you, you fools,' the duchess barked. 'You, Lady Harington! Give me your hand!'

Both hands were needed to lever the old lady out of her chair and, once she was more or less upright, she leant heavily on my arm, wheezing.

'Over there!' she nodded into the shadows where I could just make out the outline of a door. The man who had brought my chair, hurried to open it. Beyond the threshold was Duchess Cecily's private chamber, dominated by a vast bed, its curtains embroidered with the red, blue and gold arms of the Yorks. On one wall was a fine wide fireplace with a carved overmantel.

We made slow progress across the floor towards a chair, placed near the fireplace, beside a large wooden chest.

Amidst the rustle of blue brocade I heard a grunt of pain as I helped Duchess Cecily into the chair.

'Go on!' she said irritably. 'Raise the lid!'

I expected a silver coffer containing jewels but instead found a man's jacket. It was padded, similar to the ones

Thomas wore when jousting. And it was old. At first I thought the jacket was black but quickly realised the blackness was dried blood. I turned my face to Duchess Cecily.

'Put it here, on my lap.'

Carefully I lifted up the garment. It was stiff with age and crackled as I laid it across the old lady's knees.

Her lips moved as if in prayer, then she said, 'You know whose coat this was?'

I didn't know but I could guess.

'The Duke of York, your grace? Your husband?'

She ran her fingers slowly over the jacket as if caressing her dead husband's body.

'He was wearing this when he died.'

She lifted the garment up and for a moment I thought she would place her lips on the blood of her dead husband, but instead she held the cloth against her cheek.

'D'you know why he died?' she said.

I was unsure what answer she expected. Supreme folly was what my mother believed. In the circumstances a more sensible answer might be courage.

When I hesitated, Duchess Cecily, answered her own question. 'He died because he trusted a man who was disloyal.'

'I did not know that,' I said, cautiously, although my mother had told me the story of what happened near Wakefield the winter after I was born.

'One single act of disloyalty and I lost my husband, my son, Edmund; your mother lost her father, her favourite brother, her husband and her father-in-law. Now do you understand the damage disloyalty can cause. My son, Richard, knows this as well as any man.'

'Your grace, I cannot believe Lord Hastings was disloyal.'

She handed me the jacket which I replaced carefully in the chest and closed the lid.

As I helped her out of her seat, she said, 'Lady Harington, when you have lived as long as I have, you will understand that men who have been given God's blessing of untold advantages, behave in ways they should not. My husband saw in William Hastings qualities valuable to our family, but in the end Lord Hastings proved false. He allowed my son, Edward, to squander his advantages on a worthless marriage. That woman brought him nothing but trouble and their marriage will be recognised for what it was – a sham.' She turned her face to me. She was smiling. 'My son Richard will do better. He will make a fine king.'

We shuffled back into the other chamber where her women were visibly fretting at their mistress's absence. The moment she reappeared they swooped with cushions and towels and the other accoutrements of old age while they arranged Duchess Cecily back in her chair.

'What is it you want, Lady Harington?' she said, once settled to her women's satisfaction.

''I should like to visit my mother, if that is possible, your grace. She is alone at Kirby. Might the protector, in his goodness, give me leave to travel there?'

She was silent for a moment.

'Where is your husband?'

'I do not know, your grace.'

She raised her eyebrows. 'How careless of you to lose him.'

'I have had no contact with my husband since he decided to defy the protector, your grace.'

'Yet you are bound to obey him.' Her mouth twisted into a gargoyle's smile. 'How difficult for you, Lady Harington. You are a young woman who has been brought low by your husband's foolishness. Perhaps prayer might help subdue your natural inclination to pride. In the meantime, I shall see what can be done.' She smiled benignly, like a queen dispensing favours.

'Thank you, your grace. You are very kind.'

She gave a distinct sniff as if kindness was not on offer.

'I do this, not for you, but for your mother. She is my niece and I care for my kin. Your unfortunate connection with the Woodville woman makes it impossible for me to ask my son to grant *you* any favours.'

I lowered my head, trying to look as meek as possible, a woman who expected nothing and was grateful for any crumb which might fall from the protector's table.

Duchess Cecily regarded me in the way I suspected she did her lowliest servants, as if I was barely worthy of her attention.

'My son is not a man to make war on women. He will see Lady Hastings is cared for and will not suffer for her husband's treachery. She was born a Nevill. My son is aware of the great debt he owes her family. Since you are concerned for your mother, I shall make it my special task to bring the matter to his attention.'

I thanked her yet again and was dismissed, just like one of those lowly servants.

In the days following my visit to Baynard's Castle, rumours began circulating in the city that the coronation was to be delayed. The young king was sick. Men who'd come for the coronation and for the parliament which was to follow, were bewildered to find no preparations had been made for either event. Then without warning, the city exploded into chaos.

It was on Sunday, nine days after my stepfather's death, the day on which the coronation was supposed to have taken place, that the secret surrounding the late king's marriage was suddenly and shockingly made known.

Dr Shaw, brother of the Mayor of London, preached a sermon at Paul's Cross, proclaiming to the assembled crowd that the sons of Edward IV could not legally inherit the throne. All across the city, sermons were given, spreading the word that the sons of King Edward were bastards because he had contracted a marriage with one Lady Eleanor Butler before his marriage to Dame Elizabeth Grey.

Before the crowds could wonder what this might mean, it was explained that as the blood of George, Duke of Clarence, had been attainted, no certain or uncorrupted lineal blood could be found of the late Duke of York, except in the person of Richard, Duke of Gloucester.

I thought few would understand a word of this, riven as it was with complex legal words. In my household there was incredulity. Could this be true? Had King Edward truly married another? Did the dowager queen know this lady? Was the Duke of Gloucester to take the throne? What of the little princes?

From the men of the household, I heard mutterings about seditious and disgraceful proceedings, suspicions of a plot hatched by this other wife to steal the throne for herself. My steward was of the opinion that the French had a hand somewhere in the proceedings. I lost count of the wild tales from across the city which came to roost in my hall, and became weary of explaining how, if there was proof, the men must believe what they were told.

On the Tuesday, Midsummer's Day, instead of the usual celebrations, Harry Stafford, Duke of Buckingham, went to the Guildhall to talk at length with city officials and with the nobility. I knew no-one who could tell me what had been said but as there was no sign of further trouble I presumed the duke had satisfied his audience that what had been said in the sermons commissioned by the protector, was true. The boys were bastards; George's son was barred by his father's attainder and therefore Richard, Duke of Gloucester, being his father's undoubted son, was the true king.

With the city simmering with rumour and speculation, I expected no word from Baynard's Castle, and none came.

24

THE RIVERSIDE 1483

The next day was overcast and darkness came early, small scuds of rain blowing upriver as the light disappeared. I said my prayers and climbed into bed, thankful to have survived another day. I was about to tell my maid to put out the candles when there came a knock at the door. I sighed, slid out of bed, threw a light shawl across my shoulders and told the girl to see who it was.

A man stood on the threshold holding his cap in his hands – one of our outside servants. Then I noticed the particular colour of his jacket and breeches. He was one of the watermen who guarded the landing stage.

I was about to order his removal from my private chamber when he muttered that he'd been sent to fetch m'lady – secret like!

'It is the middle of the night,' I remarked, coolly. 'Who wishes to see me at this hour?'

'I was told not to say, m'lady. He said wear summut dark and tread silent.'

Dear God! This sounded suspiciously like another assignation with William Catesby. Only *he* would require my presence at this hour in such mysterious circumstances. He'd said we would not meet again but apparently he'd changed his mind. I felt a slight shiver of anticipation, the same any woman would feel in such circumstances.

'Wait for me downstairs,' I ordered, wondering, like the foolish woman I was, what I should wear.

There was no time for elaborate gowns so I simply slipped my feet into a pair of shoes and fastened a dark woollen cloak around my shoulders. The hood, I pulled up to hide my hair which was plaited ready for bed. Aware with one part of my mind that my clothing was somewhat *déshabillé*, I crept down the stairs into the hall, expecting to see the familiar figure of William Catesby. But apart from the waterman waiting by the empty hearth and a couple of lads asleep in a corner, the hall was deserted. Even my steward was nowhere to be seen.

'He be waiting down by the river,' whispered the man. 'If it please ye to come with me.'

I followed him through a side door which was held open by a small boy who couldn't stop yawning.

The rain from earlier had ceased, a crescent moon now casting a veil of silver across the sky, but the path to the river remained in darkness. My companion had no lantern making our progress slow. I should have worn a more substantial pair of shoes as twice I nearly stepped in a puddle. Soon I heard a gurgling of water from the muddy foreshore. Suddenly the man halted. I could just discern the outline of the small building where we sometimes sheltered while awaiting our barge.

'He be in here, m'lady,' whispered the man.

I looked at the dark shape with trepidation. 'Why is there no light?'

'Too dangerous, m'lady.'

'Am I safe?'

I saw his teeth gleam as he smiled. 'No need to worry, m'lady. I be nearby.'

I wondered why William Catesby chose to make our meetings quite so clandestine, why he was unable to call at the gate like any other visitor. Nervously, I pushed open the door. The wood felt damp to the touch. I stepped across the threshold and heard the door swing shut behind me. My senses were immediately alert. The room was infested with a musty smell and I could hear someone breathing.

I stood perfectly still. I could see nothing but as my eyes grew accustomed to the darkness I could just make out the figure of a man. His shape was instantly recognisable. It was not William Catesby. It was my husband!

'Thomas?' I whispered, suddenly, overwhelmingly, glad to see him.

We neither of us moved, constrained perhaps by our last encounter and everything that had come after. He had deserted our marriage, choosing his mother over me and in the chaos which followed the queen's flight into sanctuary, I had lost my beloved stepfather. Yet Thomas, too, had suffered. He had lost his brother and an uncle to whom he had once been close. He had thought he would be a great man with a royal brother on the throne. Then power was snatched away. It was enough to unman even a veteran courtier.

He stepped forward.

'Ceci.'

He slipped his arms beneath my cloak and pulled me close. I could feel the beat of his heart against mine, the familiar contours of his body. We said nothing. Being together, the simple acknowledgement of our names, was enough. Both of us were aware that words alone could not heal the breach between us. It would take something more.

Over the years since our wedding day, Thomas had come to me in many guises: the dutiful son, the confident marquess, the faithless husband, the frightened penitent and, in our bed, the skilful lover. Only once had he allowed me a glimpse of the man he really was, that night on the journey to Kirby when he'd talked of his father.

I had been buffeted by bouts of mistrust, when words were difficult to decipher, when lies and half-truths tripped readily from his tongue. Now, in the darkness, I was unsure which of these men was here, holding me in his arms.

'Do you remember our first night together?' whispered the lover, stroking his hands up the length of my back, reminding me of the power he exercised over me. Not just the power of a husband who could command my compliance whenever he wished, but as a man who made me dizzy with desire. I recognised the familiar steps of our courtship dance: advance, retreat, advance again, then engagement and finally, abject surrender. I told myself it was not love, it could never be love. I tried hard to disguise my need for him, but he knew. A man as experienced with women as my husband would never be deceived by a pretence of indifference.

When at last after a lengthy engagement the music stopped, I found myself lying on the floor on my cloak, my husband breathing deeply at my side, one leg still entwined with mine. He was not asleep. A hand inched its way slowly across my breasts, fingers idly stroking my damp skin. I shivered.

'Did you miss me?' he whispered.

I smiled into the darkness. 'Can you not tell?'

He laughed then rolled over and kissed me on my mouth.

'Why are you here?' I asked, disentangling myself from his arms.

'Why do you think?'

'I doubt you came for wifely embraces.'

'Do you think I did not enjoy them?'

'No, I do not think that. But it is dangerous. Richard has men watching the house.'

'I shall be gone long before anyone knows I am here.'

I felt a shaft of disappointment although I'd known from the start he would not stay.

'Have you heard what is being said?' I asked, wondering how much he knew of what had happened these past weeks.

He paused. 'I know my brother and my Uncle Anthony are dead and I know Richard of Gloucester has both my royal brothers in the Tower. I pray they are safe.'

'Thomas, he will not harm them. He is not unkind to children.'

'When my mother heard about Lord Hastings, she knew they would come for Dickon. That is why I left. She made me go.'

His casual mention of my stepfather was like a sharp jab from a blade.

'You know what they are saying about your mother's marriage?' I said quietly.

'Yes.'

'Is it true?'

For a moment I thought he'd refuse to answer but he said, 'No, it is not true.'

I laid my hand on his chest feeling the rise and fall of his breathing.

'People say there is evidence: documents, sworn statements.'

He raised himself up on his elbow.

'Ceci, it is a lie.'

'Your mother says it is not true?'

He hesitated. 'She says my brother is the rightful king, his father's trueborn son.'

Of course she would! What else could she say. She could not back down, not now, not after so much blood had been spilt in order to make the boy, king. If she told the truth, she'd be admitting she planned to put a bastard boy on the throne. I wondered would that be treason? I did not know but what I *did* know was that the punishment for a woman found guilty of treason was death by burning.

'What will you do?'

He gave a short laugh. 'See how many friends I have. Rescue my brothers.'

'Thomas, that could be very dangerous. Men are flocking to Richard's side. He has the support of Buckingham. They say my stepfather's men are now all Buckingham's men. Could you not make your peace with Richard?'

'Ceci, Richard is not the rightful king. Would you have me abandon my brothers?'

'No. But I do not want to lose you.'

He smiled and touched my cheek. 'You will not lose me. I have a great care for my own skin.'

I could feel him slipping away from me, the pull of his mother's family too great to resist. Perhaps he was right, he had gone too far in this matter to draw back. He had no choice but to go forward.

'What can I do for you?' I whispered.

'Go to Bradgate. Care for the children. I shall send word if there is anything I need from you. Meanwhile, I have a little time before I must go. What d'you think, wife? Shall we? Again?'

The day after Thomas left I saw men from the city arrive at Baynard's Castle. The mayor in his furred robes came with a group of aldermen in blood-red hoods, accompanied by men in gowns of violet silk. These were representatives of the guilds come to pay their respects to the Duke of Gloucester. They were followed by liverymen in gold-braided blue robes and a large cheering crowd.

Three months ago these men would have acknowledged our presence with a salute but now they passed our gatehouse without so much as a glance, wanting nothing to do with those suspected of treachery. From the direction of St Pauls came a small procession of lords led by the Duke of Buckingham, also headed for Baynard's Castle.

It took a while to discover what was happening but I heard later, in the excited chatter which followed every movement of men in the city, that Richard had been asked to take the throne. To me it was no surprise. From the moment I'd first heard of the late king's marriage to Lady Eleanor Butler, I feared this was where it would end.

Nobody knew what would happen to the two princes who were no longer princes but bastards, or if my mother-in-law would come out of sanctuary and make peace with Richard who was not her kinsman by marriage, merely the brother of her one-time royal lover. Wisely, most people kept their thoughts to themselves and said nothing.

In one way the transfer of power seemed natural as Richard had been governing the country since the beginning of May but a coronation was surely a different matter? Yet most people seemed content to have a strong king with a son to follow him rather than a bastard foisted on them by an unpopular queen who was not a queen at all, merely a cleverer woman than Mistress Shore.

As soon as Richard's decision was made known, I was allowed to organise my departure for Kirby. I had a letter sent to me by Duchess Cecily as well as a formal safe conduct from the man I must learn to call King Richard. Anyone from whom I begged assistance on my way to Kirby was to know that my journey had been sanctioned by the king. I was glad to leave London because, since Thomas's disappearance, my status was uncertain. Was I still my lady marquess or was I, as Duchess Cecily had called me, plain Lady Harington? I did not know and there was no-one to ask. Besides, I was tired of hiding away.

25

KIRBY MUXLOE 1483

Our journey towards Leicester was plagued with people asking for news. We were stopped several times on the road by merchants anxious to know if rumours coming out of London were true. Was it safe for them to proceed or should they turn back. In towns there was great suspicion of all travellers but my stepfather's name still carried weight as most people had yet to hear of his death.

The closer we got to Leicester the more I began to dread the forthcoming meeting with my mother. She would have received word of my stepfather's execution but I could not decide how much I should tell her of his activities in those final days or of what I had discovered.

Our horses waded through the muddy ford where the road crossed the River Soar and soon we were among the familiar villages of my childhood. We passed the great oak at Enderby and, at last, reached the twisting tree-lined approach to Kirby Muxloe.

I had forgotten the beauty of Kirby, a little gem shimmering in the heat of an English summer. To the west was a vista of endless woods and fields of corn, and to the east, unseen behind trees, the high walls and towers of Leicester. As I rode towards my mother's house the only sound I heard over the clopping of our horses' hooves was the squawking of a flock of hens as they scattered at our approach. flapping wildly in a frenzied attempt to hide in the bushes.

For a moment it was possible to believe that the last three months had never happened, that my stepfather was here with my mother waiting to greet me, surrounded by my brothers, little Annie and my stepfather's wards; dozens of gentlemen in my stepfather's train, jostling for a prominent position; servants lined up by the bridge, all known by name: women straightening their caps, smoothing their skirts, men bracing their shoulders, puffing out their chests, boys from the kitchen grinning with pleasure at the sight of Milady Harington coming home.

But a blink of the eye and it was gone. It was a lost world and the deafening silence told me it had gone for ever.

As I rounded the last bend, the red brick walls of my stepfather's glorious new building came into view. My mother was standing facing away from me, staring at the gatehouse, at the patterns of black bricks: my stepfather's initials "WH" and images of his devices. But why were there no sounds of a busy building site, no hammering and banging? Where were the masons and carpenters? Where were the labourers who made the bricks? And why were there no small boys scampering around running errands? The great engine for lifting the bricks had gone and there was no scaffolding. Like my stepfather's life, the construction of his house at Kirby had been cut short.

At the sound of our horses, my mother turned. She was dressed in mourning clothes as I had expected, her face ashen and lined. At the edge of the drawbridge, one of her maids hovered, looking anxiously at my escort. Then from under the gatehouse came several men carrying weapons but when they saw who it was, they lowered their cudgels and stood aside. I gave orders for my escort to proceed across the bridge and for my groom to take my horse. Unaided, I slid from the saddle and walked up to my mother. I made her a greeting, then wrapped her in my arms. She felt as insubstantial as a feather. Her head drooped onto my shoulder. I heard her whisper, 'Why?'

Later, we sat together and I told her of Duchess Cecily's letter: how Richard would be generous; Lady Hastings and her family would not suffer. She said my stepfather was to be buried as he had wished, at Windsor, next to his old friend the king. Then I told her what I knew of the events of those dreadful days. Of necessity my story was as riven with holes as a moth-eaten blanket because there were conversations I could not repeat and secrets I would rather she did not know. However, my mother was no fool and even in her present state of distress she realised I was keeping much from her. Yet how could I tell her of that night at Mistress Shore's house, of what had been said, the possessive way my stepfather had looked at his whore and how when I left, I'd known she would go to his bed?

'You need not spare me,' said my mother quietly. 'I was well aware of your stepfather's relationships with other women. It made no difference to how we were together. Why should it? I was his wife and in every respect he kept the bargain we made when we married. He provided for me, he visited when he was able, he gave me my children and he loved us. What more could I ask?'

'Were you not jealous?'

She smiled. 'Jealousy is a destructive emotion as you must know. When we married I knew his life would be with Edward. In that company it would be hard for a saint to be chaste and whatever else he was, William was no saint. But yes, in the early years I fretted about the women he met and whether I would lose him. There were times when, God save me, I was even jealous of Edward. He had so much of my husband while I had so little. But William always came home to allay my fears. He was a kind and generous man.'

I nodded. 'He was kind to me.'

She picked up a piece of paper from the table and put it into my hand. It was a drawing of a wondrous house, one built of red brick, one even more glorious than Ashby.

'John Cowper, my master mason, returned this to me two weeks ago when he left. This was to be your stepfather's final gift, the house he had promised me.' She smiled with a small tilt of her lips. 'You see, he thought I would refuse his proposal of marriage and asked what he could offer to persuade me to accept.'

'You chose a house?' I was surprised. This would not be the first choice of most women.

'Not just any house. A very particular house, one I'd seen as a girl at my brother's wedding: Lord Cromwell's magnificent house at Tattershall. But it was more than the house – I wanted to know if he cared enough.'

I gave her back the drawing. 'And he did?'

'Yes, he did.'

We talked some more about the past and just when I thought she would not ask, she said, 'Did they tell you what happened at the Tower that day?'

I hesitated. 'Lady Stanley came to see me.'

'Margaret Beaufort?'

I nodded. 'Lord Stanley was there that morning. He saw it all.'

My mother gripped the arms of her chair as if afraid she might fall. 'Tell me. You need not worry. I'll not faint.'

So I told her what Lady Margaret had said. I mentioned the friendly mood of the meeting, Bishop Morton's strawberries, how the men laughed and Richard had seemed at ease with everyone. My mother said not a single word until I reached the point where my stepfather was taken down to the yard and made to kneel with his head on a baulk of timber. Then she gave an anguished cry and buried her head in her hands.

'It was quick,' I said hastily. 'Lady Margaret said he did not suffer.' I hoped it was not a lie.

After that we talked of why Richard had acted as he had. My mother believed it was done for political reasons because Richard knew my stepfather would never agree to the young king being set aside.

'Your stepfather believed in loyalty. He had pledged himself to Edward and to Edward's son and could not go back on that promise. Richard must have known how much support William had in the country. Perhaps he feared it would be used against him.'

I bit my lip and ventured, 'Lady Margaret believes it was the treachery Richard could not stomach.'

'What treachery? William was not plotting. He was an honourable man.'

I thought of the gossip I'd received from the men in my household who'd been out and about in the city streets.

'Some people believe my stepfather and Bishop Morton were plotting with the dowager queen.'

My mother made a dismissive gesture. 'William would as soon deal with the devil as with Elizabeth Woodville. You know that. They loathed each other.'

'Then why was Bishop Morton detained? My stepfather was friendly with him.'

'William may have counted Morton as a friend but he did not trust him. A man who turns his coat once should never be trusted and there was a time when Bishop Morton was a supporter of Mad Henry and Margaret of Anjou. Your stepfather would not have plotted with him, not even for a bowl of strawberries.'

I thought of what Lady Margaret had said about the sin of omission.

'Mother, you knew about the king's first marriage. I did not ask you at the time but I ask you now – who told you?'

My mother sighed. 'I hoped you would never ask. You must understand she did not intend to tell me. I believe it was a moment when, if you know a secret, you inadvertently let something slip out, something you did not mean to say. Easily done and once said, the words cannot be called back. It was a few years ago. As old women do, we were discussing death. Oh not the way the Church would have us consider our mortal end but more practical matters. I mentioned the oddity that she as a widow was free to make a will whereas I as a wife, could only do so with my husband's permission.'

'Mother, who were you with?

She looked surprised. 'Did I not say? Lady Norfolk. She said her sister had died a wife for all the good it had done her. Just that, nothing more.' My mother looked up. 'You remember who Lady Norfolk's sister was?'

'Lady Eleanor Butler.'

'Yes. At the time I thought nothing of it but later, I pondered on what she'd said and asked William if he knew who the widowed Lady Eleanor had married. I thought it likely that he'd know because he knew everyone. He told me there had been no marriage and that I should not gossip. But Lady Norfolk and I had been childhood friends when she was a Talbot and I was a Nevill. I knew she would not have made a mistake so when we met at Christmas, I asked her. Poor woman! Such a dreadful secret to carry. She believed she was the only person who knew, other than the king. She was frightened lest he silence her the way her husband had been silenced.'

'The Duke of Norfolk!'

'It was a family secret but he was her husband so she'd told him. Then, when he died so unexpectedly, she feared he'd been poisoned.'

'So she said nothing.'

'Naturally she said nothing. Who could she tell? However she found it necessary to do whatever the king asked of her.'

'Like agreeing for her little daughter to marry the young prince?'

'That was a tragedy for her. So much loss. But with all her family dead, she wanted someone to know, so she told me.'

'In case she met with an unfortunate accident.'

'Yes.'

They say a secret is a secret only if two people know and one of them is dead. Yet the more I discovered about King Edward's dangerous secret, the larger became the number of people who were privy to the details. The king had probably shared his knowledge with his close friend, my stepfather, and it was now evident that, when the king failed to honour his promise, the Lady Eleanor had confided in her sister. Lady Norfolk had told her husband and had later told my mother.

Then there was Master Catesby. He knew and said he had written proof. He'd been present at a family conference, or so he'd led me to believe. Was Lord Lisle there too? Who else? The priest? Master Catesby had not told me who the priest was or if he was still alive but if the man was not in his grave, Richard would by now have had him summoned. As everyone said, Richard was ever a careful man.

'Richard is to be crowned king,' I remarked, watching my mother's face.

She was silent for a moment and then said, 'What has he done with the boys?'

'The boys?'

'Dame Elizabeth's bastard sons.'

'They are in the royal apartments in the Tower.'

My mother nodded. 'He will have to get rid of them.'

She said the words coolly in the way she spoke of clearing the store rooms of rats.

'My husband says he will have them rescued,' I proffered, not caring to wonder exactly what my mother had meant.

'Ah yes, your husband! Where is the gallant Thomas Grey?'

'Gone.'

'And left you alone?'

'He said I should go to Bradgate, to the children.'

My mother raised her eyebrows a fraction. 'So you should. Children should not be left motherless as well as fatherless. I doubt there is anything you can do for your husband. He has made his choice. It was foolish of him but his mother will have applied pressure.'

I thought of those last moments with Thomas, when he'd held me tight and told me to be brave; though in truth I think he was talking to himself. I doubted anyone would harm Cecily, Lady Harington, whereas Thomas Grey, Marquess of Dorset was in the gravest of danger and he was not the most courageous of men.

'Mother, you know Richard. the kind of man he is, the way he thinks. What will he do?'

'To your husband?'

'No, to those boys.'

She considered the question for a few moments. 'If he wishes to be safe on his throne he has two choices but both are paths strewn with danger. He can send them far away from London, overseas or to one of his northern fortresses, so that people forget they exist. Or he can have them killed.'

It was the way she said the words, so calmly as if disposing of a misshapen dropped foal.

'Dear God! Has it come to this, that a man must murder children to be safe?'

She shook her head 'You do not understand. Richard knows their very existence threatens him.'

'If he kills them, my mother-in-law will never forgive him, nor will my husband.'

'If he lets them live they may well be the seeds of his destruction.'

'What if he cannot bring himself to murder his brother's sons?'

She smiled grimly. 'His mother will arrange matters for him.'

'They are her grandsons!'

'To your Aunt Cecily, they are the young of the serpent, the bastard sons of Elizabeth Woodville.'

I covered my face with my hands. Rather than think of two boys facing imminent death because their father was unprincipled and their mother grasping, I thought of my own children and what I could do for them.

'Mother, I must return to London for a few days until after the coronation. Then I shall come to Bradgate. If you remain at Kirby we shall see each other often.'

Her face lit up. 'It will be a joy to have you close now that Mary has gone.'

I'd not realised Kirby was at last free of the whining voice of Mary Hungerford, now a Hastings bride.

'Where has my brother taken her?'

'Ashby. He wishes to stake his claim.'

'He is not yet of age.'

My mother sighed. 'He may not be of age but he is very angry.'

'With whom?'

'With me, with his father, with Richard, with God.'

'But not with Mary?'

My mother laughed. 'You know Mary.'

I thought of little Mary Hungerford all those years ago in the marshes of Calais being comforted by my stepfather in a way he rarely comforted me, all because she had squeezed out a few tears. Perhaps Mary did the same for my brother, tearful and woebegone, seeking his protection. Such behaviour would make him feel manly though, personally, I thought tears a sign of feebleness in a woman.

I took my mother's hand. 'I shall stay for two more days, then go back to London. If I stay longer my brother might decide to be angry with me!'

26

LONDON 1453

My return to London went unnoticed, or so I thought. Riding through the city streets I was surprised at the speed of preparations for Richard's coronation. Wooden stands had sprung up along the processional route from the Tower, and at every corner, carpenters were busy building stages for plays performed by the guild merchants to welcome the king.

I'd been a small child when my mother-in-law was crowned and did not remember the occasion but if fate had dealt me a better hand, this time I'd have been present in the abbey itself. Instead, as the wife of a man who was conspiring against the king, I must hide away.

I told the steward to allow everyone to go and watch the procession, but warned him about the wearing of livery badges. I'd no wish for my household to become embroiled in fights with supporters of others. Drunkenness and rowdy behaviour were to be expected on such a momentous occasion but not broken bones and pools of blood in the street.

I sat in my solar feeling particularly sorry for myself, thinking of my cousin. It was Isabel who had wanted to be queen, not Anne, yet here was Anne on the eve of her coronation, the most important day of her life. Tomorrow she would be crowned Queen of England.

My maid insinuated herself through the doorway to tell me I had a visitor.

'I seen her afore, m'lady.'

'Name?' I said, wondering why it was so difficult to train these girls in the simplest of tasks.

She screwed up her face trying to remember what she'd been told but was saved a slap by the arrival of Lady Donne.

'I guessed you'd be here,' she said, settling herself down beside me.

Her face was shadowed by the tragedy of my stepfather's death, yet she was dressed in rich damson silk with cream satin panels. Her finery told me her husband had not suffered in any way from the fall of his brother-in-law.

'Have you come for the coronation?' I was unable to prevent an edge of bitterness in my voice.

She took my hands in hers. 'Ceci my dear, you know William would not want any of us to suffer for what he did. He was unfailingly kind to his family. Both my other brothers have been left untouched and my husband has retained his offices. Richard has been exceptionally generous.'

Wherever I went, people spoke of the generosity of King Richard but I doubted he'd be generous to Thomas.

We talked of what happened at the Tower that day in June but Lady Donne had no more idea than I did why Richard had ordered my stepfather killed. As for late king's great secret, she was not in the least surprised.

'Men do not change. He enjoyed the company of women and did not like to be refused. What man does?' She shook her head. 'As for Lady Eleanor Butler? I am certain the queen knew. Someone will have told her.'

'But who?'

'Someone who wanted her to know that they knew.'

'Why would a friend do that?'

'Perhaps it was not a friend. Perhaps it was an enemy. Think of the power a man would hold if the queen knew a single word from him would destroy her.'

'Perhaps it was a woman.'

'Whoever it was, it was a dangerous game to play with someone like the queen.'

I smiled. 'Queen no longer. After tomorrow it will be Queen Anne.'

'So it will. May God grant her a more tranquil reign than Dame Elizabeth.'

We talked a little of our children, of my mother and later of the future for my mother-in-law's daughters who still languished in sanctuary at Westminster. Lady Donne's opinion was that Richard would find them suitable marriages. They might not be legitimate but they were still his brother's daughters.

'And the two boys?'

The silence was deafening. Neither of us liked to speculate on what Richard might do, nor would I betray Thomas's hopes of a rescue for his brothers.

I wanted her to stay to keep me company but she was expected at Westminster to meet with Sir John who had come from their house at Horsenden. At our parting we clung to each other, two sad women, cast adrift in a new world they had never expected to see.

That night in the privacy of my bed, I wept for everything I had lost.

Early next morning, the day of the coronation, I had another visitor.

'The Duchess of Buckingham,' announced my steward, preening himself at the thought of the Duke of Buckingham's wife gracing us with her presence.

Lady Catherine swept in as if she owned the house, scanning the room for evidence of my fall from grace.

'Your husband is not here?'

I priced her outfit from glorious headdress to well-shod toe, reaching a figure so enormous I had to revise my impression of the duke. Expending money on his wife's wardrobe had not figured highly on Harry Stafford's previous list of priorities.

'Lady Catherine, you know perfectly well the marquess is no longer in London.'

She smiled conspiratorially. 'You can tell me where he is. I promise Harry will not hear a word from my lips.'

It was as I thought: the duke had ordered her to visit, hoping to discover Thomas's whereabouts. Harry Stafford was said to have a poor opinion of women, doubtless imagining I'd be eager to confide in his wife. But poor Lady Catherine was not an accomplished liar and I was much too clever to fall for her husband's tricks.

'It is getting late, Lady Catherine. Should you not be at the abbey?'

'I am not permitted.' she said crossly.

'By whom?'

'My husband. He says no Woodville would be welcome. He is sending me to Brecknock.'

This was no surprise. Harry Stafford was preparing to make a very public show of revenge for being married to a

Woodville wife he despised for her low birth. He'd had no say in their marriage and disliked the queen who for years had kept him tied to her skirts while she lived off his lands.

'It is not personal,' Lady Catherine assured me. 'It is my sister. Harry says her plotting makes it impossible for me to me seen at his side on a public occasion.'

Face-saving was one of Lady Catherine's great abilities so I said nothing, contenting myself with praising her husband.

'The duke has been well rewarded for his support of the king.'

'So have others less deserving,' she said, sniffing in disgust.

I waited to see if she would tell me who had earned the resentment of Harry Stafford. He was a man who, according to my mother, felt each slight as a mortal blow. He had begrudged his long exclusion from royal favour. Now that he was high in Richard's favour I thought he would be satisfied but like all greedy men, he wanted more.

'Bishop Morton says it is a disgrace,' Lady Catherine said.

'Bishop Morton who was arrested in the Tower?'

'The same. Harry is his custodian so we have the pleasure of the bishop's company at our table. He is very learned.'

'What exercises the good bishop's mind?'

'The offices the man has received: constable of Rockingham Castle! And if that was not enough for someone like him, Richard has made him chancellor of the Royal Exchequer. Bishop Morton says it is sinister and does not bode well for Harry.'

'Who has been favoured so highly?'

I thought she would name one of the Howards but for once I was mistaken.

'William Catesby. I suppose you know the name. Harry says he worked for Lord Hastings.'

William Catesby! It was a long time since Lady Catherine had surprised me. While I digested her news she carried on prattling about injustices done to her husband.

'Harry says it is enough to make you wonder what the man has done for Richard. He's only a lawyer. He has no title.'

Yes, I thought to myself. What *did* William Catesby do for Richard to be so richly rewarded?

'And that is not all, Lady Cecily. Master Catesby has a seat on the council. It is a monstrous insult to men like my husband. Does Richard expect them to share their private thoughts with this upstart?'

While Lady Catherine continued to expound on the iniquity of promoting a man like William Catesby to the small group of senior men who counselled the king, I tried to think of what value he might have been to Richard. He did not have a vast following to call on to give assistance on the field of battle. He had married well, inherited his father's properties and had more than sufficient for his needs. I'd noticed how he lived that evening when I'd visited him in his house behind St Pauls, but there was not enough wealth there to proffer much in the way of loans.

There were, of course, other sources of wealth, as Master Catesby had taught me all those tears ago. Information was valuable and lawyers were well-placed to acquire information, some of inestimable value in the right hands. William Catesby possessed such secret information. He had known about Lady Eleanor Butler. Had he been the one to tell Richard?

I was unsure, but the one gift William Catesby had given me was teaching me to think logically. Most women were like Lady Catherine, their minds in a muddle with no idea of how to winnow grain from chaff. Despite the panic in my belly I forced myself to marshal my thoughts.

William Catesby knew about Lady Eleanor and the secret marriage. He said he had documents. No – he inferred he had documents relating to the marriage. Perhaps he was lying. He'd told me to warn my stepfather to speak to Richard. So he knew that my stepfather also knew about the secret marriage. Yet my stepfather denied this. I'd been flattered by Master Catesby's attentions and had failed to take care the way a young woman should. Had he been playing with me from the moment we first met? I remembered the way he'd teased me in the garden at Ashby, how I'd blossomed under the warmth of his interest.

I woke in the middle of the night with the answer on my lips. It was William Catesby who had betrayed my stepfather and he had done it for gain. He had gone to the Tower that morning in June and told the protector what he knew, showed him the proof and feigned surprise that Lord Hastings had not already spoken of the late king's secret marriage.

"Perhaps, Lord Hastings is plotting with the dowager queen," he would have said. "I know his stepdaughter visits him. Doubtless she sends messages to her mother-in-law in sanctuary at Westminster. She is greatly enamoured of both her stepfather, Lord Hastings, and her husband, the marquess. There is also the Shore woman. whore to both men. She may be involved in this conspiracy against you, your grace."

Bile rose up into my throat at the way William Catesby had used me, making me complicit in my stepfather's death, sharing his secret knowledge then sending me out into the dark like a conspirator, knowing I'd not find my stepfather at home.

I fell asleep, wondering what I should do.

But daylight brought the realisation that there was nothing I could do. It was too late to change what had happened. Richard was king, my stepfather was dead and William Catesby had got what he wanted.

27

BRADGATE 1483 – 1484

A cold bright November moon hung in the sky when I first heard of Harry Stafford's death. The news came to Bradgate with a man travelling from the West Country who had stopped for the night in Salisbury. He'd been amongst a crowd in the marketplace when a miserable figure was led to the scaffold, unbelieving when some fellow told him the man in tattered finery, weeping and wailing like a goodun, was the powerful Duke of Buckingham. But the townspeople assured him it was so. A foul traitor, they called the duke, the most untrue creature living.

'Did he make a good end?' I enquired.

The man lifted his cup of ale. 'Mumbled some words. Three blows of the axe it took. Never seen so much blood, Mistress. S'pose it may be that they dukes has more blood in them bodies than we common men. I knows they has more silver in them purses.'

I'd known about the rebellion which cost Harry Staford his life. A month earlier word had come out of Leicester that the king was raising an army. He'd been told of trouble in the southern counties with rumours spreading about the fate of the two princes who, it was said, had died a violent death in the Tower though it was not known how. If that was not enough to make Richard a worried man, there was news of stirrings on the border with Wales where

Harry Stafford was holed up in his castle at Brecknock. He was said to have repented his former conduct and turned his coat – a traitor to King Richard.

My mother thought it likely that Harry Stafford, with his Lancastrian heritage, nurtured hopes of taking the throne for himself. We agreed that Bishop Morton, comfortably ensconced at Harry Stafford's side at Brecknock, might well have been whispering in his custodian's ear, encouraging him to believe he had more support for his claim than he did. Of course neither man would have reckoned on the rain which washed away bridges and swelled rivers to torrents, making a foray into England well nigh impossible.

My mother had shocked me by suggesting that Margaret Beaufort, Lady Stanley might have had a finger in this particular pie, not in suborning Harry Stafford but in providing encouragement to others who hated Richard. I should remember, she said, what a wealthy and influential figure Lady Margaret was. Furthermore, I should not forget the ambitions of her son.

I knew five hundred marks was the price the king had placed on my husband's head, the same as for Bishop Morton, but the man who had in the end betrayed Harry Stafford's hiding place in a poor man's cottage, received a bounty of one thousand pounds. That showed how much the duke was reviled.

I asked our guest if there'd been news of the Marquess of Dorset, but he'd heard nothing.

'Where has he gone?' I lamented to my mother.

'Overseas if he has any sense.'

'But where?'

'Brittany, I would imagine.'

'To Henry Tudor? Surely not?'

I may have been wandering around with my mind in a fog but my mother was a woman who saw things clearly.

'Ceci, you have forgotten your husband's lineage? His father fought for Lancaster as did his Woodville grandfather. Henry Tudor claims to be a Lancastrian. Besides, it is your husband's best hope. He cannot stay here, not after Richard denounced him.'

I'd tried to put out of my mind the words used against Thomas in the king's proclamation. They were utterly disgusting. My husband was accused of not fearing God nor the peril of his soul. He had, it was claimed, without shame, devoured, deflowered and defouled many and sundry maids and widows and wives. In particular he was denounced for holding the unshameful and mischievous woman called Shore's wife in adultery.

No wife should have to listen to such a litany of crimes committed against her marriage by a man she had sworn to love and obey. The words were read aloud to the townspeople of Leicester, some of whom were men and women I knew well.

On the day I returned from Leicester, I discovered my son Tom was missing. When questioned, the servants said the Lord Marquess had taken the boy. He had left me a note:

"I have taken my heir to safety. I beg you pray for us."

As my confessor told me on numerous occasions, it was not my place to criticise my husband's behaviour or in any way be other than a dutiful and submissive wife as God would wish, but when I read those words, I thought

Thomas was fortunate to have fled. In my fury I might have done him bodily damage.

I knew I was being petulant but my mother refused to let me wallow in self-righteous misery. 'You are not stupid Ceci, you must know what Richard will do next?'

I lifted my gaze to my mother. 'He has deprived us of the Exeter inheritance. Can it be any worse than what he has already done?'

She shook her head sadly. 'Yes, it can be very much worse. Richard will issue a bill of attainder, naming your husband as a traitor. His title and his lands will be confiscated by the Crown. There will be nothing left for you. Your sons will be given to a family loyal to Richard. They will raise them, not you. That is why your husband has taken his heir, to keep him out of Richard's clutches.'

Despite the quaking in my belly I lifted my chin in defiance. 'I have my own lands, my own inheritance. I know what they are worth. The king cannot deprive me of what is rightfully mine.'

My mother sighed. 'You are forgetting that a king is all-powerful. A woman whose husband is attainted may find herself left with nothing but her life and the gown on her back.'

'Is that what my grandmother faced?'

My mother shook her head. 'For her it was worse. She was in danger of losing her life.'

I remembered the story of my Nevill grandmother who'd fled to Ireland to escape Mad Henry and his evil wife. In the horror of what was happening to me, I felt close to her, wishing I could remember her face, but I was three years old when she'd died.

'What will become of my daughters?'

'The Crown will not see them starve but you will be dependent on Richard's charity.'

'I do not want his charity,' I screamed. 'I want what is mine.'

My mother slapped my face. 'Do not behave like a child. This is no time for tantrums.'

Her reproof crushed me. How little I knew of a woman's rights when she came up against the power of the Crown. William Catesby had once explained to me how a wife had no legal rights independent of her husband, how the law regarded the two as one body. I was merely my husband's shadow. He had smiled when he said it was not until a woman became a widow that she could exercise some control over her property and her future, but he doubted I would wish my husband dead. I had replied that certainly I did not want my husband dead. That conversation was in the early days of our marriage before I discovered the full extent of my husband's infidelities and treasons. Perhaps now I was better informed, I might take a different view.

'If Thomas were to die, would I keep my lands?'

My mother was horrified. 'May God forgive you for such a thought, Ceci. He is your husband. No matter what he has done, your place is to stand by him. My sister Margaret stands by her de Vere husband. She has endured years of poverty and isolation, ignored by her Nevill family because of her husband's adherence to Mad Henry's cause. She is a dutiful wife.'

I thought it wisest to say nothing more. I wished I had Master Catesby to advise me, to tell me the best way to keep safe what was mine, the inheritance I'd cherished from the day my mother first introduced me to Shute, but I had forsworn William Catesby. He, like my husband and my son Tom, was lost to me.

I called for more logs and for the children to be brought to see their grandmother. The nursemaids bustled in with their charges, anxious lest my mother would find fault with their care. I thought that unlikely as my mother loved her grandchildren. She played with my youngest, admiring her gummy little smile, while Dorothea and the two little boys vied with each other to see who could climb on their grandmother's knee. I sat there thinking what a terrible legacy my children would be left by their father if what my mother said was true.

They came in February on a day when warmth had returned to Bradgate like a long-absent guest, doubly welcome for knowing the visit would be short. Outside the parlour a bird chirped uncertainly in the bare branches of a tree, doubting this unexpected harbinger of spring.

For more than a week I'd known they would come but despite being forewarned I was unprepared for the sight of an orderly column of men making their way across our park. Bringing up the rear were four large wagons, the kind used by Richard when he'd escorted the young king into London with a cache of Woodville arms. I wondered if the wagons were painted with royal devices or if the king's man had borrowed them from some obliging merchant in Leicester.

As the party came nearer I saw there were at least two dozen of them, brawny individuals in dark padded jackets, mostly armed, which showed this was no friendly visit. I'd already ordered my steward that none of our household were to offer resistance, no matter the provocation, and I'd warned my women to keep out of the way.

As the horses passed under the gatehouse and emerged into the courtyard I looked to see which of the king's friends he'd sent to turn me out of my house. I ran my gaze over the group and to my amazement saw the solid figure of Master William Catesby. He was still wearing black and apart from a magnificent cloak with a jewelled clasp, looked very much as when I'd last seen him in London. On his head was a brimless black hat: less the duplicitous lawyer, more a respected member of the king's council.

After he was helped down from his horse by one of his men, he stood appraising our buildings. The house had been built by Thomas's grandmother for the use of a steward and did not provide the kind of accommodation I'd expected. Thomas said he would build something grander, with room for our growing family, but events had overtaken him, so the children and I still lived in what was quite a modest house. At that moment I wished it was a palace.

William Catesby spied me at the top of the steps and gave a perfunctory nod, barely more than a slight movement of his head. I stayed where I was, glad to be wearing my best winter gown. I wanted no pitying looks from Master Catesby. After a brief word with his men he climbed up the steps until he was standing in front of me.

'Master Catesby.'

He removed his hat but instead of a bow, gave another nod of his head as if I was a woman of no consequence.

'Lady Harington.'

To show I was not afraid, not of him or of anything he could do to me, I allowed a few moments of silence. Beneath his cloak I saw glimpses of an elegant new doublet with pearl buttons.

'To what do I owe the pleasure of this visit?' I said calmly.

He paused, smiled thinly, then said, 'My lady, I think you know. My appearance today can hardly be unexpected.'

I smiled with equal lack of enthusiasm. 'I was expecting a band of ruffians to bundle me and my children out into the cold, not one of the king's trusted councillors.'

He regarded me soberly. 'These men are not ruffians, my lady. You know I would not allow you to be subject to any ill-treatment.'

'No? Then why are you here?'

'To ensure your safety.'

I choked on a laugh.

'You find that amusing?'

'Do you know, Master Catesby, I have never known a man so capable of telling a lie with a straight face. Not even the marquess can better you and he lies in his teeth for a pastime.'

He took a step forward as if to touch me. I stood my ground even though I was terrified; not so much of him but of finding myself with nowhere to go and no roof over my head. Until that moment, having my home taken from me was a nightmare which would happen to some other woman, not me. I willed myself to stop trembling, clenched my fists, holding them against my skirts, wishing I had a guard rail to cling to.

For a moment he seemed at a loss, then retreated, frowning.

'My lady, I do not lie to you. It is just that sometimes you misunderstand what I say.'

'What is it you are saying now?'

He let his eyes wander over what lay beyond the gatehouse: rocky moorland, trees and streams, a few fields, a wide stretch of parkland for hunting, and in the far distance, black clouds gathering on the horizon. I doubted he was admiring the view, more likely estimating the land's value.

'Bradgate is not yours, my lady. You know that. Bradgate belonged to your husband and is thus forfeit to the Crown, as are all your husband's properties.'

To hear it said starkly was worse than seeing the written order. That had arrived a week earlier. After reading the document twice I'd consigned it to the flames as if by destroying the words I could pretend they did not exist.

I tilted my head up, staring straight into his face. 'You may take my husband's lands, Master Catesby, but I pray, do not forget his chattels. We have some particularly fine horses in our stable which I believe will be of interest, knowing how you covet anything of value which belongs to another. I trust your men will make an inventory of what they take, I should not like you to be accused of thievery when the marquess returns to reclaim what is his. Item: one silver bowl a gift from the late King Edward to his wife's son. Item: one cradle, decorated with heraldic devices and lined with ivory silk. Item: two chests, beautifully carved, spacious enough for a woman's gowns. Item: a bed of red velvet, embroidered with silver leaves and golden birds, together with red silk curtains. And do not forget, item: one wife, a little worn but still serviceable.'

Tears were filling my eyes but I was determined not to weep at the thought of so much loss.

William Catesby put out his hand as if to comfort me but I snatched my hand away. His touch would have been like the bite of a viper.

'My lady, please!'

'Please what, Master Catesby? Do you intend to offer me pity as I trudge from door to door seeking shelter for myself and my children? No, I forgot. You have orders to take my children too. How could I be so foolish as to imagine the king would allow me to keep my children. Who knows what treasons I might teach them.'

This time he caught my wrists before I had time to step away. 'Listen to me, my lady! You will not be destitute. I would not let that happen.'

'No? How will you prevent it? Are you to make me a gift of one of those valuable manors you acquired? Perhaps one that Lord Hastings owned. Think how singular that would be. Or perhaps a pension from your own purse. Is that how it works? I am new to this game and have little understanding of the rules. I know that men expect a return on their money and a woman in my position cannot afford to be choosy. So, what will you ask in return?'

'My lady, you do yourself an injustice. If in the past I have offered friendship, it was done with no expectations on my part.'

'You tricked me.'

'No, my lady, I did not.'

'What is this if not a trick?'

He gazed at me, unblinking. 'In better times, you and I have discussed the matter of a wife left in this very situation. I found you a particularly apt pupil so please, my lady, do not disappoint me by feigning ignorance. You know perfectly well that a woman whose husband is adjudged a traitor, needs a powerful man who will influence the king on her behalf if she wishes to keep her lands. You have no powerful man so your situation is indeed dire.'

He paused to let me digest the full extent of the miserable circumstances in which I found myself.

'However you are fortunate, my lady. The king in his mercy has agreed you shall not be destitute. You may remain on your own lands and you may keep your children.'

He still had hold of my wrists but I ceased to struggle. 'Shute?' I said warily, not believing what I was hearing.

He smiled. 'Yes, Shute. It is, I believe, the manor you favour most.'

I bit my lip. 'This is not a jest?'

'No, it is no jest.'

I still did not trust him. He let go of my wrists, delved into the bag he had slung over his shoulder and extracted a document.

'Read this, my lady, and you will see I do not lie.'

The document bore the royal seal. I read it slowly, expecting some sleight of hand, some careful wording which could change the meaning if read in a certain way. The writing was difficult to understand but from what I could see there was no trickery.

'I did not expect such generosity. Master Catesby, not from Richard of Gloucester. How do I express my gratitude to the king?'

He nodded in satisfaction. 'You do not need to thank the king, my lady, you may thank me. King Richard would have taken everything: your lands, your chattels, your children and your freedom. With your husband known to be in Brittany with Henry Tudor and your mother-in-law plotting in sanctuary, he sees you as a potential threat. It took a lot of persuasion to have him agree to you living at Shute.'

'You did this for me?'

Up went the corner of his mouth in that strange little half smile he sometimes gave. 'I did.'

'Why?'

'You know perfectly well why.'

I remembered that evening in his house behind St Pauls when I'd opened my eyes to the game we'd been playing in the years since we'd first met. A feeling of warmth began uncurling as I realised the implications of what he'd done.

'I cannot give you anything?'

'I do not ask for anything.'

What a strange contradiction this man was. He was devious, greedy for reward, uncaring as to who got hurt as he clawed his way up to the top. But there was another William Catesby, the man who hinted at what we both knew could never be, a man who would go to great lengths for a young woman, yet expect nothing from her in return.

He paused for a moment while he went down the steps to give an order to one of his men. When he returned he took my hands in his.

'My lady, you need to know that the king has made one stipulation with regard to your situation.'

'Which is?' I said, still suspicious.

'You will not hold your lands yourself. They will be held by someone appointed by the king to manage on his behalf.'

'So they are not mine. They belong to the king.'

'Yes. But you will be permitted to live at Shute with your children. There will be a governor who will be in charge and will ensure you are kept in a suitable manner.'

'A keeper?'

'I prefer to call him a governor.'

'But we are his charges, as if we were prisoners.'

'You will live comfortably.'

'A comfortable prison.'

'My lady, be reasonable. The king cannot allow you access to your income. You might send it overseas to help your husband who is close to Henry Tudor. This way gives protection to you and also protects the king.'

I snatched my hands away. 'Of course, how could I be so stupid!'

'My lady, I know you are angry but consider this: many wives in your situation find themselves separated from their children. You could have been placed in a convent at the king's pleasure. This way allows you a degree of freedom and you keep your children. And if some day your husband was to die, you would be able to petition the king for the return of your lands.'

I had a tremendous urge to push him down the steps but first I needed to know more.

'This governor will live with us at Shute, as if the manor was his.'

'No, the governor has other duties but will appoint a trustworthy man as his deputy. *He* will occupy the house at Shute. You will be his honoured guests.'

'Who is this governor appointed by the king who will have access to my income and decide who lives at Shute? I presume you have been told.'

He smiled as if I had said something amusing.

'King Richard has appointed me to be in charge of the fees and income from the manor of Shute and ensure the good behaviour of you and your children.'

I leaned back against the wall of the house and began to laugh.

'What a triumph for William Catesby! At last you have me exactly where you want me. I presume you will visit?'

His face betrayed nothing. 'Naturally if I find myself in the neighbourhood I shall ascertain that all is well at Shute. I should not want you to feel neglected. And, if you wish, you may write to me. All your correspondence will, of course, be read, just in case you should be tempted to contact your husband. But I doubt you will say anything indiscreet when writing to me.'

28

SHUTE MANOR 1484

In its own way, Shute was lovely beyond words: a solid refuge of grey stone where I and my children could shelter from the storms raging over our heads as a result of my mother-in-law's ill-judged opposition to Richard. She foolishly imagined she was securing continued influence for herself and her family. Instead she had brought heartbreak and chaos into our lives.

In a county of little flat land, my ancestor had chosen the position with care, building his house at the head of a shallow valley backed by low hills. As a defensive situation it could not be bettered: protected from the east by a steep rise of beech and lime, and from the west by broad expanses of dense woodland. Marshes, where a man might sink up to his knees, deterred incursions from the south thus the only way for a party of armed men to approach in relative safety would be along the east bank of the river, well within sight of Shute's defenders.

The house itself was not grand like Ashby or Kirby, more like a small version of Bradgate, but would, I thought, be comfortable enough for our purposes. In my exiled state I would hardly be entertaining visitors so there was no need for guest chambers or extensive stabling and no requirement for indoor rooms for games. No one would expect a tennis court at Shute.

The hall was long and narrow with a huge hearth which some long-ago Bonville lord must have built to impress his neighbours, although if I'd been him I would have added a tower to accommodate his lady. In my absence I had forgotten how pokey and inconvenient the private rooms were, tucked away at the top of a set of winding stone steps: icy cold in winter, unbearably hot and stuffy in the height of summer. This was where I would live with the children, where we would pass our days in enforced seclusion until someone came to our rescue or the king saw fit to have me released.

Our immediate keeper was an elderly knight who, at first glance, resembled a kindly grandfather but was, I soon discovered, not so kindly disposed towards us. He refused to stray one inch from the orders passed down by William Catesby, which were doubtless modelled on those demanded by the king.

On our arrival he explained to me in a gruff voice how we were to conduct ourselves. It was quite simple. I was to be a guest in my own house, with no duties to perform other than to care for my children and be obedient to the king's will. The servants were not mine to order although if I needed anything I was at liberty to ask.

Within the house I had complete freedom to go where I wished although it would be better for everyone if I refrained from disturbing the men at their work. I was permitted to walk in the gardens and along the short path to the church but no further. There would be no riding out, no visiting and no intercourse with Shute's neighbours. I was to take my meals in private with my children when a servant would attend on us. Two maids would be provided to help care for my children, and the services of the laundress were at my disposal.

If I required any womanly necessaries from town, such as needles or thread, I was to ask, and if the items met with my keeper's approval, they would be provided. If I wished to write, ink and parchment would be brought but I should remember that the punishment for any servant found secretly taking a letter or a message from me would likely be hanging, so I should think carefully before attempting any such ruse. Apart from that I was free to pass my days as I wished although prayer and contemplation were much to be recommended. And I would keep the services of my confessor.

I wanted to spit in his face!

Idleness did not suit me in the way I suspect it would suit few women. I had been raised to be useful, to manage a large household, to entertain visitors of importance, to improve myself in those attributes so prized by a husband, to dispense remedies for those in my care who were ailing, to teach my daughters what was expected of them, and to see to my husband's business affairs when he was absent. I had not been raised to twiddle my thumbs in some out of the way place where nobody visited and there was no proper conversation.

Time dragged, each dreary day passing exactly like the one before until I wanted to scream. Our keeper proved unwilling to converse or perhaps, like many men, it was not in his nature to talk to women. He avoided my company, mostly keeping to his room. I knew nothing about him and on the odd occasion we met he resolutely refused to answer questions about himself or what his life had been before he came to Shute.

Any attempt to talk to the steward was met with an embarrassed excuse of work which urgently needed doing elsewhere, if my lady would please forgive the haste. In desperation, like many a woman before me, I turned to religion.

The house at Shute had no chapel so every morning I fell into the habit of walking the short distance to the little church to hear the priest celebrate Mass. On seeing my approach a small child would scamper off to what I presumed was the priest's cottage, returning a few minutes later with an elderly man hastily fastening his flapping robes. After a few weeks of listening to his tuneless mumblings, he asked was I like to come every morning to hear Mass. It was only then that I realised how remiss in his duties he had become.

'Is it not usual for you to celebrate Mass each morning?' I enquired.

He smiled a sweet, almost toothless, smile. 'Ah lady, the Lord has visited me with a palsy and oftimes 'tis hard to rise from my bed.'

I looked at his bent frame, wondering how old he was. All of seventy I guessed. 'Has the vicar not sent someone to assist you?'

'Nay, not since young Nicholas took sick and died a few months back. But there be no family at the house till you came so it may be he saw no need.'

'The villagers have need?'

'Aye, they have a great need, but I do manage the Sabbeth.'

The unclean state of his robes, the stench of stale urine and the stubble on his chin spoke of a man who needed more care than he was getting. If there was a housekeeper, she should be beaten for allowing the old man to sink into such a disgusting state.

'Did you know the family when they lived here?' I asked delicately, moving slightly away from him.

'That be a long time ago, but yes, I knew them.'

For a moment I held my breath, afraid to ask the question in case the answer was not what I wanted to hear. 'Did you know the young Lord Harington, Sir William?'

'Oh aye, I knew he. And his father afore he, and the old man, the grandfather. Knew them all. 'Twas a rare tragedy what happened.'

'And the Lady Kathryn?'

'He smiled at my eagerness. 'Handsome lady, she were, Lady Kathryn. Naught but a young girl but what courage she had. I remember when the men of Colcombe came up the valley. Brave as a lion she were. Put heart into our men knowing she were here.'

He ended his words with a bout of wheezing, which turned into convulsive coughing and spluttering which shook his whole body. After a few minutes, when he had recovered his breath, I dared to ask, 'Do you remember the Lady Kathryn's baby, the one who was born in the house?'

Very slowly he nodded. 'Aye, I remember. Fine chile she were.'

'That was me,' I said, smiling. 'I was that baby.'

'Aye, a fine chile and you be a fine lady; I see that. Be you come home now?'

It was like a golden sun rising on a midsummer's morning, chasing away the darkness of night, as a flood of warmth filled my heart. Whatever else was miserable in the world, whatever misfortunes assailed me, this was an inescapable truth: of all the grand houses where I had lived, the royal palaces and elegant castles, the little manor house of Shute was home. Here was where my life began and perhaps, if God decreed this was all there was to be, where it would end.

'Yes,' I said, smiling. 'I have brought my children with me. We have come home.'

As the months passed, I stopped glaring resentfully at my shoes, blaming Thomas, the king and William Catesby in equal measure for how I found myself, and raised my eyes to my surroundings. I began to notice the many inconveniences of the old house – not just the steepness of the stairs, the endless draughts, the crooked walls and the inadequate number of hearths, but the lack of light from windows which were too narrow and too few. Even at noon I needed a candle if I wished sew fine embroidery.

There was so much here that could be improved to make life more pleasant. I'd seen the drawings my stepfather commissioned for his new buildings at Kirby and thought I might do likewise for Shute. I would ask for pen and ink and spend my days designing new buildings, a different, grander future for Shute.

It was considerably more difficult than I first thought and my early failures ended up crumpled on the floor where they'd been thrown in frustration. Why could I not translate what was in my mind's eye onto the parchment?

Why could I not draw lines that were straight or curves that were graceful?

Gradually as the weeks went by I acquired some little skill and my designs became more intricate: a vast hall with a painted ceiling and glazed widows on both sides to let in the light; a new aisle for the church to be built in memory of my father, with an elegant fan-vaulted roof like the one I'd admired in Canterbury.

From my window, beyond the walls of my prison, I noticed the changing seasons. Gone were the overcast skies and dull hues of winter. Already the meadows had lost their tired yellows and on the other side of the valley, trees were gaining mantles of bright gauzy green. Spring was here again. I had been at Shute for a whole year. There had been little news from outside although we'd heard of the death of the king's little son, only eight years old. My heart bled for my cousin, Anne, who'd not had much joy from being queen.

I was at my desk, surrounded by my latest designs for an ambitious range of private rooms which I would build to one side of the hall. I was attempting the difficult task of marrying up roof lines when William Catesby walked in. I was so amazed to see him that I just sat there, staring. Then I remembered my dishevelled state: my old woollen gown, my hair scraped back under a cap, my fingers liberally covered in ink. Instinctively I put my hand up to straighten my cap, feeling heat creep into my cheeks.

'Lady Harington, God give you a good day,' he said, politely, with no hint of surprise at finding me dressed like one of my maids.

'I was not expecting you,' I said, trying to gather my wits, immediately wishing I was more suitably gowned.

He hesitated. 'I apologise if my coming is unwelcome.'

'No, no, not at all, it is just that I am unused to visitors. It is very quiet here at Shute.'

He smiled. 'I did not come for the dancing.'

'Just as well as I have no musicians.'

He shook his head, still smiling. 'To think I left mine behind.'

The past twelve months had drained away most of my anger, leaving me in that state so desirable to men, of a seemingly submissive woman, but the sight of William Catesby standing there in his elegant new riding attire making teasing remarks, proved an unexpected irritant. It aroused my latent combative instincts.

'I suppose you've come to check on the penury to which I have been reduced,' I said sharply. 'As you see, I am suitably constrained. I have no contact with anyone and no money of my own so am unable to assist my husband should he ask for my help. I do not even know where he is.'

'Have no fear, Lady Harington, we know exactly where your husband is. He is no longer in Brittany. The duke was preparing to deliver Tudor and his band of traitors into the king's hands, so they fled across the border hoping to find firmer friends in France. I doubt they will succeed. We also know you have had no contact with him, which was wise of you.'

'If you know everything, why bother to come?'

His smile widened. 'Seeing you is always enjoyable, Lady Harington. There are few people who afford me such pleasure.'

'I am glad to be of some use.'

At that moment we were interrupted by the arrival of one of the servants with a jug and two goblets, followed by another with a plate of wafers.

'I took the liberty of ordering some refreshment. I trust that meets with your approval?'

'You may do as you wish, Master Catesby. Or am I wrong. Has the king seen fit to raise you up? Am I speaking to Sir William or even Lord Catesby?'

He laughed. 'I remain what I have always been. I do not seek a title. What would it bring but the envy of others?'

'Does Meg not hanker after being Lady Catesby?'

'My wife is content with me as I am, as I am with her.'

'You paint a picture of perfect domestic bliss.'

'Is domestic bliss not what every man seeks?'

'I would not know. I am not a man.'

Without asking, he seated himself in the only other chair, reminding me, as if I needed reminding, that this was not my house and I was not the chatelaine.

'Lady Harington, do you not think your husband would rather be here with you than alone in France?'

'Master Catesby, we both know the marquess is unlikely to be alone in his exile. He is a man who enjoys company and if his wife is imprisoned in England he will surely amuse himself elsewhere.'

'But you would prefer it if he was with you?'

'Naturally.'

'There is nothing natural about it. Many a husband and wife prefer to live apart, seeing as little of each other as can be managed. Once sons have been raised past those hazardous early years, a man and his wife need not even share a bed. Lawyers are often called in to draw up financial arrangements, the aim being to set each party free within the bounds of matrimony. That way, conventions are maintained and few are the wiser.'

'I am more interested in other kinds of freedom.'

'Which brings me to the purpose of my visit.'

'I thought your purpose was to have sight of me?'

One side of his mouth twitched but he ignored my jibe.

'Lady Harington, you have been here for more than a year. I think it is time you considered your future.'

'I thought *this* was to be my future.'

'Not if you were to wish it otherwise.'

His very pleasantness made me suspicious. In my limited experience, men who went out of their way to charm a woman wanted something in return. Yet every time I had assumed we were bargaining to my disadvantage, he disarmed me by saying he wanted nothing.

'And if I did?'

He smiled but if he thought he'd caught me in his net he was very much mistaken. I had learned to be wary of William Catesby.

'There is no future for your husband in allying himself to Henry Tudor. You know that. Tudor has already made one unsuccessful attempt to bring an army. If he makes another he will be killed. He cannot succeed against King Richard's army. He does not have the support. If your husband were to survive any battle there would be no mercy from the king. He would be executed.'

'You paint a bleak picture for the future of my marriage.'

'There is no future. You would be a widow.'

'A widow who could sue for the return of her lands.'

'I doubt the king would return them.'

I felt as if I'd been punched in the stomach.

'You said …'

'I said that a woman in your position has need of a powerful man to plead her case.'

So we were back to where we'd started. If I wanted freedom I must put myself into the hands of William Catesby, a man who said he was content in his marriage yet stirred dark undercurrents between us, our connection no longer a light-hearted flirtation between teacher and pupil but something more oppressive and dangerous.

'Are you offering me a way out?'

'If you wish to take it.'

Did I wish to take what was being offered? Did I wish to place my future in William Catesby's hands? Did I trust him?

'What would I have to do?' I said carefully.

'Take a ride with me.'

'Are we to ride for pleasure or do you have you a destination in mind?'

He smiled, sure now of victory. 'To ride with you, Lady Harington, will always be a pleasure but yes, I do have a destination in mind and I think you will find the visit instructive.'

The temptation was too great to resist, a taste of freedom, albeit one in the company of the man who was my chief gaoler. I wondered how far we were going.

'Am I to prepare for a lengthy absence?'

He rose to take his leave. 'A week and a day should suffice. We leave first thing in the morning.'

And that was that. Eight days, unrestrained by the chains which kept me at Shute, in the company of a man who was not my husband. It felt deliciously reckless, almost a treat to be savoured.

29

HEYTESBURY 1485

It was an illusion of freedom, not in any way real, but the pretence was heady stuff. By the time we'd gone a mile beyond Honiton, I found myself singing. My cheerfulness infected our escort who joined in, their deep rumbling voices a happy counterpoint to mine.

We travelled east in a leisurely fashion until on the third day we turned north onto a track which meandered along the banks of a pretty little river. From the clean clear water rippling over the stones and the steep white escarpments on our right I guessed we were in chalk country but had no idea exactly where we were.

William Catesby had proved himself an exemplary companion on our journey, never presuming to trespass upon my privacy yet making pleasant conversation when I was weary of my own thoughts. By mutual consent we did not discuss my situation at Shute, nor did we talk of what was happening at the court of King Richard and Queen Anne.

He joined me each evening at supper, which I found oddly comforting as I had, for too long, eaten my meals in loneliness with only my children for company. Being scrupulously discreet and naming no names, he entertained me with amusing stories culled from his early legal career: tales of missing wills, disappearing heiresses and cases of mistaken identity. I ate better than I had for months and actually began to enjoy myself.

'Where are we?' I asked when we halted to water our horses.

He turned in the saddle, seeking a landmark. 'I'd say not far short of our destination.'

Master Catesby chose not to enlighten me further but when, after a few miles, we stopped at a pair of solid gates, I realised our host for the night must be a man of means. We turned in though the gates and rode up towards the house which lay long and low in front of a stand of trees.

The first person I saw was a woman, strolling idly in the garden, a basket on her arm. From a distance she looked remarkably like … but no, that was not possible! It could not be. The woman looked like my mother-in-law.

'Is that …?

William Catesby looked round to see who had caught my eye. 'Why yes, I do believe it is.'

'I thought she was in sanctuary in Westminster.'

He chuckled. 'She was but Dame Elizabeth is a sensible woman except when she allows her heart to rule her head.'

I resisted the temptation to remark on my mother-in-law's absence of heart, instead asking, 'Why is she here?'

'She has made her peace with the king. After the collapse of her ill-judged attempt to foment rebellion with her Stafford brother-in-law, she saw there was nothing to be gained by continued resistance. In this way, she has allowed her daughters a future. The two eldest are at court. They serve Queen Anne.'

'That is impossible.'

'No Lady Harington, the king has made it possible. I hear her daughters are enjoying their freedom. They are pretty young women, particularly the elder. The king has promised to arrange marriages for them both.'

'Despite the circumstances of their birth.'

'They are still the daughters of a king even if their parents were not married. King Richard will find suitable gentlemen who will be only too pleased to marry a royal bastard.'

'Is my mother-in-law also welcome at court?'

The skin round his eyes crinkled in amusement at the thought. 'I do not think Queen Anne would want that. Dame Elizabeth lives here at Heytesbury in comfort with her younger daughters in the care of one of the king's loyal supporters.'

'Constrained.' I guessed that far from being free, my mother-in-law had to all intents and purposes, exchanged one prison for another, even if her new circumstances allowed her liberty to stroll in the gardens.

'Lady Harington, does Dame Elizabeth have the appearance of a woman who is constrained?'

'No,' I said slowly.

'Why not see for yourself. We shall stay two nights so you will have ample time to ask her all the questions you wish.'

'And afterwards?'

'I shall have you escorted back to Shute. Unless of course there is anywhere else you would like me to take you?'

The words were suggestive, the kind of comment a man might make to a young lady he planned to seduce.

But William Catesby was no would-be lover, his voice was perfectly polite and the look he gave me, disconcertingly steady.

Before I could think of a suitable reply we were interrupted by the appearance of our host, a man of late middle-age, who came hurrying down the steps to welcome his guests.

The visit was not the success Master Catesby predicted, or perhaps, having a tendency to deceive, what occurred was his purpose all along. Far from a warm welcome, a prodigal returned to the fold, my mother-in-law was not pleased to see me. I had two short meetings with her and on each occasion she was openly hostile, making plain she had no liking for my presence and that I might as well go back to wherever I'd come from.

I was ushered into a small private parlour where, despite the warmth of the day, a fire burned in the hearth.

'What are you doing here?' she snapped. 'I did not send for you.'

'This visit was not of my choosing,' I replied bluntly.

'How you do complain! Always buffeted by the winds of fate. Poor Cecily! One wave of his princely hand and Richard has you shut away. You must have railed against your fate.'

'A fate of your making,' I muttered.

'What a feeble young woman you are. I regret my determination to have you as a wife for my son. Of course I enjoyed defeating Lord Hastings and your fortune made you an attractive proposition, but your family was of no value to us.'

'My family is of value to me,' I retorted.

'As my son's wife, you failed to grow into your position. You remained what you always were, a spineless creature.'

That stung. 'I am not spineless and my situation is not of my making. Your son left me to care for our children while he chose to blight our future by rebelling against the king.'

Naturally, no criticism of her firstborn was allowed. 'My son was doing his duty. Richard was not entitled to take the throne.'

'My husband's so-called duty was your idea, not his.'

She glared at me with narrowed eyes. 'He did what was right and you failed him.'

'In what way did I fail?'

'Did you help him? Raise money? Men? In short did you do anything other than whine in your kennel like a lapdog missing its master?'

'How dare you!' I screamed, finally losing my temper, aware with the conscious part of my mind that this battle had been ten years in the making. 'You never wanted to let him go, did you? From the moment we were married your wishes had to be superior to mine. You trampled all over me when I was to young to fight back. You used every inch of the power you had to entice him away from me. If you'd taken him into your bed, you could not have done more to ruin my marriage.'

She hit me. The flat of her hand hard across my mouth, snapping my head back with the force of the blow.

'You little whore!' she hissed.

I felt a cold fury settle on my shoulders. 'I am not the whore here. I did not give myself to a man who was already married.'

Much later I realised I should not have said what I did but at the time I was past caring. My words were provocative even if they were true and once said there was no hope of reconciliation or of any amity between us.

This was not our final encounter, far from it, but I had driven my standard firmly into the ground of my chosen battlefield. Thomas Grey was mine, not hers and I was prepared to fight for him.

In the morning, when we were due to leave, William Catesby asked if I would walk with him awhile. He wanted to share with me arrangements that were being made for my son. The men who would escort me back to Shute would leave with six-year-old John.

'The king has arranged for him to join the household of Viscount Lovell.' He smiled. 'Lovell, as you may know, is married to your mother's Fitzhugh cousin so your boy will be well cared for. Lovell will ensure he learns his duty to King Richard.'

'I hope Lord Lovell will teach him good manners,' I said, thinking of Tom, my missing son who had merited more beatings than any of my other children.

As he proffered his arm, I turned and Master Catesby must have seen the fading red mark on my cheek. He said nothing, merely raised his eyebrows questioningly.

I gave a sigh. 'The right of a woman to chastise her daughter-in-law.'

He nodded as if he understood, although no man could understand the complicated relationship between two women, both wishing to possess the devotion of the same man.

'Was your crime worthy of rebuke?'

'She called me a whore so I told her it was not I who was the whore.'

He choked on his laughter as if levity was somehow inappropriate under the circumstances.

'Did she tell you anything of interest, that is when she was not chastising you?'

'We talked of the joys of springtime,' I said flatly.

He gave a nod of approval. 'How well you play this game, Lady Harington. You give nothing away. I should hate to be the man who presumes too much upon your good nature. So let me guess. She told you the king denies causing the death of her young sons. And she told you the rumour of a plan with Lady Stanley for Henry Tudor to marry her daughter, Elizabeth, is false.' He waited, but when I said nothing he continued. 'She will, of course, have told you how, despite the king offering your husband a safe path for his return to England, it is better he remains in France.'

'Why ask if you already know everything?' I replied crossly.

'Because Dame Elizabeth plays the game like a seasoned professional. She wagers her money on both sides. She does not know the truth about her sons and she does not know who will win if Henry Tudor comes, so she plans for all eventualities. But she does not trust you, does she? She thinks your loyalties are divided.'

'My loyalties have never been divided.'

He seized my arm roughly, in a gesture which frightened me.

'Do not take me for a fool!'

I stood perfectly still. 'Take your hands off me, Master Catesby.'

'Not until you see sense.'

'I see everything quite clearly, thank you.'

'Listen to me. Dame Elizabeth is only interested in the survival of her family and that family does not include you. Now that you have given your husband sons, you are expendable.'

This was a hard truth but one which I'd known for some time. I had been chosen to give my husband a fortune and provide him with sons. Having delivered both, I was no longer of use to Elizabeth Woodville.

William Catesby was relentless. 'Henry Tudor will come this summer. Louis has seen an opportunity. He is scouring his prisons for the worst kind of rogue, anyone able to carry a weapon who prefers to fight for the Tudor than die a miserable death in the French king's dungeons. Richard is gathering his army, one many times stronger than anything Tudor can muster. I told you before that Henry Tudor does not have the support to win. The great lords prefer Richard. They will bring their armies and Tudor will be defeated. I doubt you have seen a battle my lady, have you? They are bloody affairs with no quarter given, not like a tournament joust. If you wish to save your husband you must act now. Tomorrow will be too late.'

An image slid into my mind, of Thomas lying dead on a muddy battlefield, his sightless eyes staring up at a summer sky, pecked at by crows, his body mutilated, common soldiers, stripping off his surcoat, stealing his armour, spitting on his face. That was not what I wanted.

However angry I'd been, however much I blamed him for my situation, he was my husband and I wanted him back.

'What must I do?'

Master Catesby smiled. 'I doubt there is anything you can do. You have neither men nor resources. But *I* could perhaps arrange matters so that he does not find himself on a battlefield – if that is what you want.'

'Of course it is what I want.'

'It will be a risky venture but it is your decision. However, I urge you to think carefully because, although the married state has much to recommend it, I can envisage circumstances where a young woman like yourself might prefer widowhood to an unsatisfactory marriage.'

'Master Catesby, you insult me. Are you suggesting I should abandon my husband to his fate?'

His lips twitched in the way they did when he was tempted to smile but knew he should not. 'Forgive me if you find my words offensive, my lady. They were intended merely to shed light on the different paths you might wish to tread.'

I frowned, unsure what was being offered and what the price would be, but it was obvious what was best for Thomas – a way out. Like his mother, a bet both ways.

I felt a sudden unsettling stillness as if the air around us was being sucked into some unseen vortex. The day had grown chilly, a reminder that winter was not long past. There was no noise, just an increasingly eerie silence. The sky was growing dark as if a storm was brewing yet there was no wind, no threatening clouds, no foretaste of rain.

Then into the silence came a woman's high-pitched scream. It came from the gate into the orchard where a group of servants were gathered in a huddle, the men pointing at something over our heads. William Catesby let go of me and looked to see what had frightened them.

'May Christ in His mercy,' he said, crossing himself. His face had turned pale.

I followed his gaze. 'Mother Mary preserve us,' I gasped in horror.

Above us, high in the sky, the black shadow of some dreadful celestial being was devouring the sun, little bit by little bit, inch by inch until there was nothing left but a tiny sliver like a new moon and all around the blackness, a circle of golden fire, so bright it would blind a man if he stared at it for more than a moment.

'What is it?' I whispered, my mouth dry with fear as everything around us became submerged in near darkness.

'An evil portent.'

I was terrified. My limbs were shaking, my fingers like ice, my lips unable to form any words. I forgot who I was, everything I'd been taught and the conventions which governed my personal life, and allowed the reserved and thoroughly rational William Catesby to pull me into his arms. As I buried my face into the front of his doublet, seeking the comforting warmth of a man's body, I heard him murmur familiar words of prayer, over and over and over again: the prayers of my childhood, exhorting the saints to intercede for us and the *Pater Noster* I taught my children.

I closed my eyes, thinking of my children all alone at Shute. If disaster overtook us, what would happen to my children.

We stayed like that for what seemed an eternity, his arms holding me tight, his mouth soft on my hair, two people caught in a moment of truth – until a dog barked and he set me aside. I opened my eyes. Darkness was ebbing away, birds were twittering in the trees as they did each day at dawn. But the sunlight was not the same as before. It was colder, harsher, no longer the warming harbinger of spring, just a temporary guest who might at any moment decide to cut short their visit.

From the courtyard I heard excited chatter and nervous laughter as servants asked each other what it meant. For the first time since I'd known him, William Catesby looked unsure of himself.

'Forgive me,' he said quietly, although we both knew there was nothing to forgive, nothing to regret, nothing that I would not willingly do again.

'Was it a sign from God?'

'Men who study the heavens call it an eclipse. Doubtless they have theories as to its meaning but to me this speaks of disaster.'

'My mother told me King Edward once saw three suns in the sky,' I said uncertainly. 'That was not a sign of disaster, it heralded victory. Could this not also be a good sign?'

He touched my cheek gently with his forefinger, a silent sealing of all that had been left unsaid between us, and smiled.

'I pray so, Lady Cecily. For both our sakes I pray so.'

But he was right to be worried for the disasters were about to begin and I was wholly unprepared for what lay ahead.

30

THE PALACE OF WESTMINSTER 1485

They came for me on the eve of All Hallows, the morning after a gale swept up the valley leaving a trail of destruction in its wake: trees stripped bare of leaves, tiles ripped from roofs and fences wantonly broken.

There were six of them, all armed, all wearing an unfamiliar livery. They rode up to the gate, their horses side-stepping chaos as the Colcombe pigs charged towards the woods with a cacophony of squealing and shouting and beating of sticks such that you'd think a murder was being committed.

I'd been expecting them for weeks, ever since I realised William Catesby had been right in his prediction of disaster.

In the early days of my return to Shute, news had come of the death of my cousin, Queen Anne. She had died on the day of the eclipse. Before I had time to dry my tears and remove my mourning gown, I was told of a rumour that a man with a dragon banner had landed in Wales and was crossing into England with his followers, intent on bringing the English king to battle.

Neither event was of more than passing interest to most at Shute who went about their daily lives regardless of what was happening to kings and queens. But the most unexpected of the disasters, one that excited most comment, one that William Catesby could never have anticipated, was the defeat of the royal army.

In every town and village, proclamations were read aloud that the usurper, Richard, who called himself king, had been slain on the battlefield and that Henry Tudor was, by the Grace of God, the rightful king of England. There was a list of men dead in battle, nailed up on the Market Cross in Honiton but nowhere was there mention of Thomas Grey or John Zouche or William Catesby.

The men presented their credentials and ordered me to be ready within the hour as King Henry required my presence at Westminster. I was to be accompanied by a single maid for my comfort, but no manservant. My children were to remain at Shute. I was given no indication if I would be welcomed at court as a valued guest or condemned as a traitor by a vengeful Tudor king. One look at the men's faces told me it would be unwise to ask.

I ordered my best clothes packed and made a tearful farewell to my three children. My maid was to ride pillion behind one of the men while I was put up on a chestnut courser from the Shute stables as the journey to London would be hard and my own mare was not considered powerful enough.

I tried to ask about my husband but was told by the captain of the escort that they knew nothing. Their orders had been to proceed to the manor house of Shute, close by Axminster and there to take into their possession one Cecily, Lady Harington, who was to be brought without delay to the king's palace at Westminster. That was all they knew.

Unlike my leisurely ride with William Catesby in the spring, this was a cold and exhausting journey along roads so rutted and potholed that progress was infuriatingly slow. We set off at a punishing pace each morning, stopped only once for me to relieve myself and have a drink of ale and a bite of bread and cheese while four of the men attended to the horses; then it was back in the saddle and fast riding until signs of approaching darkness forced our captain to call a halt.

I kept my ears open at the inns and religious houses where we found a bed for the night, but all I discovered was that the coronation of Henry Tudor had taken place and every man of importance in the neighbourhood had been summoned to the king's first parliament at Westminster. One traveller kindly furnished me with names of men he'd known who had perished in the battle they were calling Bosworth, but I knew none of them.

On the afternoon of the eighth day we rode wearily into the familiar precincts of the royal palace of Westminster. In the outer courtyard I was lifted from my saddle, almost fainting with exhaustion, and ordered to follow the captain. He led me to the gates of the palace where a lengthy conversation and proffering of letters ensued, before a royal servant. dressed in the same unfamiliar livery, requested I should accompany him. He led me through rooms which were hauntingly familiar, yet utterly different. I saw no-one I recognised and began to wonder if anyone I knew was favoured by this new king or if they had all died on the field at Bosworth.

I was shown into a small room where I was told to wait. Before he left the servant looked askance at my travel-stained garments and suggested none too politely that I might care to find some fresh clothes as my lady the king's mother was particular about dress. My maid set about unpacking my gown and hanging it on one of the available perches. I was about to sink onto the stool when there was a gentle knock on the door. A middle-aged woman in sombre clothing stepped across the threshold. It was Joan's sister, Edith.

She gave a little curtsey and said in a soft voice, 'I heard you'd arrived, Lady Cecily. My mistress, Lady Margaret, the king's mother, told me to see if you had everything you required. She was unsure how many servants you'd brought.'

So Lady Margaret was here but of course that was to be expected as Henry Tudor was her son.

'That is more than kind of her.'

Edith smiled. 'My lady, the king's mother, is the kindest of women.'

Joan's sister had served Lady Margaret for many years and must be pleased her mistress had at last come into her own. She might also have news of Thomas.

'Tell me, Edith; do you know anything of my husband? I feared, what with the battle, I feared it might be that …'

Her round face creased with pleasure. 'Oh no, Lady Cecily, your husband did not take up arms. He has been in France. My lady, the king's mother, said he arrived in Calais not eight days ago. I believe he is awaiting King Henry's permission to return.'

I felt an enormous wave of relief. My fears for Thomas were unfounded. He had followed my advice and survived.

'What of your brother, Lord Dinham, Edith?'

'Safe in Calais. My lady, the king's mother, says the king bears him no ill will.'

'That is good to hear. And your sister Joan's husband, Lord Zouche?'

She shook her head. 'Joan is in a sad way, Lady Cecily. Lord Zouche has lost everything, all his wealth, all his lands, they are near destitute. But my lady, the king's mother, has a tender heart. She has promised she will intercede with the king, ask him to be merciful and pardon Lord Zouche who only did what he thought was right however misguided he may have been.'

'Lord Zouche's sister, Mistress Catesby? Do you know anything of her husband?'

'Forgive me, Lady Cecily, but I have no acquaintance with Mistress Catesby.'

I was a fool to worry about William Catesby who, when all was said and done, was nothing to me. A deviously clever man like him would have planned his escape from Richard's side. Like my mother-in-law, his bets would have been placed both ways.

'What of my mother-in-law, Dame Elizabeth?'

Edith laughed. 'She is Dame Elizabeth no longer but will be recognised as the mother of the queen, so my lady the king's mother, tells me.'

'King Henry is to wed Princess Elizabeth?'

Edith blushed as if it was through her clever offices the match had come about. 'Is it not wonderful? She is a beautiful young woman, thoroughly worthy of the honour. My husband says she will make a magnificent queen. And now if you will forgive me, Lady Cecily, I must leave you, I have much to do.'

So Princess Elizabeth was to be Henry Tudor's queen. I doubted if this was news to my mother-in-law, merely one of her many tangled plans come to fruition.

As for me, I was beginning yo see a future for myself and it was glorious: Henry would restore Thomas's lands and title. As the only remaining male kinsman of the queen, he would play an important role at court and with me beside him his career could only prosper. My friendship with Lady Margaret would open doors which might otherwise remain closed and with my lady the king's mother ruling the royal roost and showing every sign of enjoying her power, I doubted my mother-in-law's presence would be tolerated for long. A convent perhaps? Somewhere she could repent of her many sins. With a frisson of pleasure I realised that the long-fought war between us for the person of Thomas Grey was coming to an end and I was the one who had command of the battlefield.

As for my marriage which I'd once thought broken beyond repair – Thomas and I would go back to Bradgate and learn to love again. The privations of the last two years would have left both of us older and wiser, more willing to be generous and forget past hurts. True forgiveness might come slowly but there was plenty of time – I was only twenty-five. In this new Tudor world, anything was possible.

About an hour later there came a confidant knock on the door and there was Lady Catherine, widow of Harry Stafford. She swept in, dressed in a superb gown of yellow silk, decorated with knots of scarlet ribbons. Around her neck, always one of her best features, was an array of jewels and on her fingers, several heavy rings. But her face was pale and below her eyes were dark bruises as if she'd not slept.

'Lady Cecily!' She said brightly.

'Lady Catherine, you look well.'

She gave a nervous laugh. 'As a bride should, though what such a woman is doing all alone the morning after her wedding, I truly do not understand.'

'You are wed?'

'Yesterday. They have married me to Jasper Tudor, the king's uncle. Am I not the most fortunate of women?'

'It is a great honour,' I said cautiously, wondering whose idea this was. Lady Catherine and Jasper Tudor seemed an unlikely pairing.

'My sister says I am favoured yet my husband appears to have no opinion on the matter. I am his wife yet he says nothing to me.' She pouted prettily, the way she used to when complaining about Harry Stafford, an amusing affectation in a young bride but ridiculous in a woman with four children embarking on a second marriage.

'Your husband has spent the last ten years in the company of men,' I said soothingly. 'He will have forgotten how to converse with a woman. You will have to teach him.'

'Oh, he knows how to talk to a woman. He talks to Lady Margaret all the time but of course she decides everything so it is no surprise.'

A little jealousy there, I thought. Lady Catherine had never cared for Lady Margaret, king's mother or no, and clearly resented her new husband's attentions in that direction.

'Surely it is King Henry who makes the decisions,' I said.

'That is what you would think but you must understand, he knows nobody here, so Lady Margaret tells him who can be trusted and who he should promote. If you want to be accepted at Henry's court you need Lady Margaret's approval. And we are all ordered to call her "my lady, the king's mother". Is that not ridiculous! You have never seen anyone so pleased with herself. You'd think it was she who had commanded the army that killed Richard the Usurper.'

Yes, definitely jealousy.

'Hush, Lady Catherine. Do not say such things.'

'I shall say what I like for I am to be Lady Catherine no longer. I shall be Duchess Catherine. My husband is to be made Duke of Bedford. Is that not something?'

'It most certainly is.'

'Lady Margaret tells me I am to be sent to one of my husband's Welsh castles to learn my duty as a wife. She speaks as if I do not know how to be a duchess.'

'I'm certain she does not mean to be unkind.'

'Oh I am quite certain she does. You see she wanted Jasper Tudor for herself.'

'Lady Margaret is a married woman.'

She shrugged as if Lord Stanley's existence was an irrelevance, curving her lips into the smile she used when she wanted something. 'Lady Cecily, I did not come to talk of Lady Margaret but to ask you a favour.'

Sensing the need to keep Lady Catherine as a friend in this chilly Tudor court, I smiled. 'Naturally I will do anything I can do to help you.'

'It is my children. I am allowed to keep my girls but I have lost my two boys. Their wardship has been given to Lady Margaret. Edward is seven, a confident child and will not miss me but my little Henry is only five. I beg of you, Lady Cecily, watch out for my boy, see no harm comes to him. He is not brave like Edward. He still cries for his father.'

'I am certain you need not fear for their wellbeing, Lady Catherine. As you are aware, Lady Margaret is known as a pious and learned woman. She will see they are well cared for and have a good education.'

She seized my arm. 'But you will promise?'

'Yes, I promise.'

'And in return I shall give you a word of warning. Henry Tudor is a suspicious man. Be careful what you say and above all, do not speculate about my sister's boys. If Henry says Richard, the Usurper had them killed then that is what we must choose to believe.'

'And your sister's marriage?'

She smiled. 'Perfectly sound. Those scurrilous rumours put about by the Usurper were completely false, as my sister always said they were.'

'There was a bill in parliament,' I remarked in case she had forgotten.

'I expect Henry has had it removed. He will allow no slurs cast over the legitimacy of his queen.'

Happy now she had secured what she wanted and issued her warnings, the soon-to-be-Duchess of Bedford, made to leave. I thought swiftly. Jasper Tudor would have been present at the battle where Richard was killed He must have a list of those who had died.

'Lady Catherine! Do you happen to know if William Catesby, the lawyer, survived the battle?'

She looked at me in surprise. 'Mother of God! Why would you want to know about that piece of scum!' She shrugged. 'Henry had him executed.'

I allowed my face to show none of the shock I felt. Like the shreds of a distant echo, Lady Catherine's words came from far away.

How could William Catesby be dead? How could he not be somewhere in this world, waiting to reappear in my life as he'd done since that morning in the garden at Ashby when I'd first heard my mother and stepfather discussing my marriage.

Since the day of the eclipse when he held me in his arms, I had known I was mistaken. It was not my stepfather who was honourable, brave and principled but William Catesby. He had refused to commit the sin of omission but had followed God's will and told the truth. He had urged my stepfather to speak out but, finding his advice ignored, had approached the protector himself. He was no more grasping than most men, relishing his rewards, thoughtless of those damaged in the process. I doubted he knew of the flaming temper which ran through the veins of the sons of York, a passion which could erupt in a single moment, sweeping away rational thought, forcing a man into precipitate action which he'd later regret. If he had known, he might have taken more care.

Lady Margaret had spoken the truth. When faced with the dilemma of whether to speak out or keep silent, if a man discovers his will runs counter to that of God, he faces a moral problem at the heart of his being. Should he do what is right, thus risking all he holds dear; or is the sin of omission too high a price to pay. My stepfather had ignored God's will, choosing to keep faith with his friend, the late king, whereas William Catesby had faced the same dilemma and chosen to do what was right. It was too late to ask his forgiveness for doubting him, for thinking him a lesser man than he was. He had once told me I sometimes misunderstood what he said, and he was right.

My grief for the loss of William Catesby threatened to overwhelm me. I had failed to acknowledge how important to me he had become, too often dismissing him as a useful but largely insignificant acquaintance. I had failed to thank him for the care he had shown me and now it was too late.

I knew there would come a time, perhaps in a week, perhaps in a month, perhaps in a year, when I would no longer remember the sound of his voice or his odd sideways smile. I would forget the conversations we had and my fury when I believed he'd betrayed my stepfather and colluded with King Richard to have me imprisoned. But always there would be the memory of those small unasked for kindnesses from a man I now realised was so much more to me than a friend.

It snowed a little in the night but by morning, Elizabeth's wedding day was blessed with a sky the colour of a dunnock's egg and a bright winter sun which sparkled on rooftops and gold finials alike. Buoyed by the fine weather and the lure of free meat and drink, Londoners flocked in their thousands to Westminster to watch their York princess marry this unknown man who'd come to the throne by conquest – not something approved of by the commons. Richard's taking of the throne from his nephew had caused enough grumbling, but this grab by a man they regarded as a foreigner – for who I ask you had heard of Henry Tudor? – was nothing short of an assault on every Englishman's unalienable rights to be governed by one of their own.

Henry, being a cautious man would probably have preferred a small private ceremony, something less costly, hidden from curious crowds, but Lady Margaret, who was in charge of the actual arrangements, knew better. She was well aware that a public marriage was necessary, not because it gave validity to Henry's claim to the throne which we all knew was tenuous at best, but because, Elizabeth, being the undoubted daughter of King Edward, would quell disquiet in the hearts of those who would have preferred another York king on the throne.

Nobody dared speak their thoughts aloud, the danger of disloyalty to Henry Tudor was far too obvious, far too frightening, but there were several great families who, now that the dust had settled from the shock of defeat by a Lancastrian invader, would be more than happy to stake a private claim to the throne.

Elizabeth did not look radiant as, by tradition, brides are supposed to be, but pale, almost sickly which was no surprise if the gossip I'd gleaned from a maid in her chamber was to be believed: a course missed, her linen clean and a disinclination to break her fast in the mornings. Yes, Henry was a careful man.

A king newly come to the throne with a shaky thread of royal descent through his mother needed to move swiftly to make his dynasty secure and for that he required sons. A fertile wife was of utmost importance. Nobody spoke of it but Henry's secret visits to the chamber of his betrothed and the hasty exit of her maids, were known to many who would happily part with information if paid for their pains.

People admired this true-born York princess, saying how she would be a great Tudor queen. I had no doubt that Elizabeth would be a great queen. But a Tudor queen? My mother once told me of my grandmother's claim that Henry Tudor was no Tudor, the name was a sham, a pretence. She knew the truth about his father's birth and the subterfuge designed to protect a young king. She had spoken bitter words of how the power of the Church had been used to silence a poor neglected woman whose only sin was to love a man. But, as my mother said, loving a man was always a perilous business and my grandmother had many tales about the past.

And true-born? I wondered what Henry knew about the illegitimacy of his wife, what information Lady Margaret had garnered from her network of spies. My mother-in-law, who retained her superior smile, would admit to no flaw in that Maytime wedding so many years ago which had brought her a handsome husband, a crown and a clutch of beautiful children. If pressed, she would blame her subsequent woes upon Richard the Usurper who had lied and schemed to steal the throne from her sons. A convenient fiction as Richard was dead, her sons had disappeared and Henry sat on the throne.

But the truth?

EPILOGUE

JANUARY 1486

It was late in the afternoon when a man arrived from Kirby Muxloe with a gift from my mother; somewhat unexpected but pleasing nonetheless. As well as the package, which was bulky, there was a letter which the man fished out of his pouch and put into my hand.

'Lady Hastings said I was to deliver this to you in person, my lady,' he said politely. 'Not that I'd have left it with that servant who showed me your rooms, who, if I might make the observation, did not look trustworthy.'

I thanked him, assured him as to my well-being and asked him to give greetings to my mother.

As soon as he'd gone I sat in the comfortable chair I'd acquired through Lady Margaret's good offices and opened the letter. It was full of news about Mary Hungerford. Owing to Henry's benevolence, Mary was now Baroness Hungerford, a long-delayed justice that delighted my brother.

The rest of the letter contained bits of family gossip, telling me how much my mother was looking forward to seeing me and the children. The content of the package, she wrote, was a special gift which she urged me to examine closely and only in private to ensure it was to my liking. If it was not, she desired it returned to her rather than passed to someone else.

I unwrapped my gift, struggling with the cords which were knotted tightly. Inside was a length of peach-coloured silk. I placed it on the table and lifted up a corner to feel the texture. As delicate as gossamer. Holding it against the back of my hand to see if the colour suited me, I noticed something hidden deep within the folds: a small insignificant-looking packet.

I sat staring at it, aware how, even if my mother had learned to be careful, only something potentially dangerous would be so well hidden. First, the man's instructions to give the package only to me, no-one else. Then my mother's desire for me to examine the contents in private. Lastly, her insistence that the gift should not be passed to anyone else. I dropped the corner of the silk and called for my maid to run an unnecessary errand. She curtsied and scuttled out of the room, closing the door quietly behind her.

The packet was sealed with wax but there was no imprint, just a plain shiny wax. It was as if the sender did not want me to know who he or she was. Cautiously I slid my knife under the seal and opened up the packet. Inside was a letter and a soft leather bag, badly worn, tied at the neck with a length of narrow black ribbon.

I picked up the letter. There was no greeting at the top and no name at the bottom to say who it was from or where it had been written, but neither were necessary as I recognised the handwriting. Immediately I realised how wise my mother's warning had been. A letter from this quarter would put me in the gravest of danger should it be discovered and taken to Henry Tudor.

I glanced swiftly around the empty room just in case someone was hiding behind a curtain or under the table where the peach-coloured silk lay in all its innocence . But I was completely alone. I moistened my lips with my tongue and bent my head to the letter. It was short.

> *"I have left instructions that if anything happens to me, this should be given into your hands. What you choose to do with it I leave to you for I could think of none other who would make the decision with such care. I have valued our friendship over the years and hope that you have taken pleasure from our conversations. I trust that any advice I have tendered has been of use and that on the occasions when we disagreed, your displeasure has not soured the kindness you so often bestowed and which I did so little to deserve. I pray that God grants you a long life and that you achieve the purpose and contentment you seek."*

A letter from beyond the grave. William Catesby had been clever. This could have been from anyone. There was nothing to identify the sender or how the letter had arrived, and the recipient could be any person within the palace.

I placed the letter carefully on top of the silk and picked up the leather bag. It was not heavy. It took me a little while to tease the knot undone and open the neck of the bag. Inside was a piece of parchment, good quality, the kind I'd often seen used for legal documents. I lifted it out. The black ink was a trifle faded but still perfectly legible. At the bottom of the document were two small dark red seals below two signatures: one strong and flamboyant as if the signatory was proud of his name; the other small and neat, a woman's hand.

I knew what the document was but read it nonetheless all the way from the first line down to the bottom, every incriminating word. If nothing else, William Catesby had taught me to be thorough. I could hear his voice saying, "Never assume to know what a document says. Read carefully because lawyers love to slip in a single word, easily overlooked by the careless, which can change the whole meaning of a sentence."

What I held in my hand was a simple contract of marriage between Edward of York, King of England and France, and Eleanor, late the daughter of John Talbot, Earl of Shrewsbury and late the wife of Thomas Butler, knight. The place of marriage was the bride's manor of Fenny Compton in the County of Warwickshire and the date, the all-important date, was the eighth day of June 1461 in the first year of the reign of King Edward, the fourth of that name.

I almost dropped the document in my haste to be rid of it, to hide the danger so that no-one would see. I stuffed it back in the bag and then stopped.

I did as I had been taught, took a deep breath and said a brief prayer to Our Lady to guide my thoughts. Only then did I allow myself to consider what I should do. Obviously I could show this to no-one so the question was: should I keep it or destroy it. Again, William Catesby's voice whispered in my ear: "We lawyers love the written word; it is our life's blood, for what is written carries greater weight in court than hearsay."

There might come a time in the far distant future when the truth of the late King Edward's first marriage should see the light of day but at this moment the mere possession of such a document would be considered treason. And treason meant death. The safest course was to burn everything: the marriage contract and the letter.

I removed the document from the bag, picked up the letter and walked over to the tiny hearth where all that remained of the earlier cheerful fire was a pile of charred logs and a warm steady glow. I knelt down and placed the letter onto the embers. Instantly it blackened at the edges, crinkled and quickly burned to ash. I held the document towards the dying flames, all the time hearing William Catesby's voice.

What kind of woman was I? A good, obedient wife and subject of the king, or a believer in truth. Which did I want to be? Then I remembered the man on the marshes outside Calais, the would-be spy who had made a single mistake, one small slip, and paid for his carelessness with his life. It was dangerous out alone on the marshes and in the dark you could not tell right from wrong or which way led to safety.

I hesitated.

Author's Notes

Thomas Grey was eventually allowed to return to England. His lands and title were restored but Henry Tudor never trusted him, twice putting him under restraint. Thomas and Cecily had several more children. After Thomas's death in 1501, Cecily remarried. Her second husband was a man some twenty years her junior – Henry Stafford, younger son of Catherine Woodville and Harry Stafford, Duke of Buckingham.

The fate of the "Princes in the Tower" is still a mystery, but Henry Tudor's reign was plagued with pretenders, claiming to be one or other of the two princes.

After eighteen months at court, Elizabeth Woodville, withdrew to Bermondsey Abbey where she died in 1492.

Henry VII and his queen had four children who survived infancy. Elizabeth died in 1503. Henry died in 1509 leaving their second son to take the throne as Henry VIII.

Lady Margaret Beaufort survived her son's death by just over two months.

"The Dorset Aisle" in the Church of St Mary at Ottery St Mary in Devon was designed and commissioned by Cecily, Marchioness of Dorset.

Acknowledgements

Many thanks to James and Emily of Two Birds Experience at River Bourne Community Farm, Laverstock near Salisbury for an unforgettable introduction to the noble art of falconry; to volunteer Ben and my two feathered friends: Merula and Ruby.

I should like to thank the kind gentleman at St Michael's Church at Shute whose name I do not know but who took time to sit with me and tell me about the manor house and its history. Also the National Trust guide who showed me round the oldest parts of the house.

Also thanks also to Ken Cooper for coming with me to Glastonbury for a day's immersion in the world of the Wars of the Roses. We didn't get much to eat as we were last in the queue but we learned a lot about the Battle of Bosworth.

As always thanks to my daughters for their support, but most of all a huge thank you to my husband, Richard, who walks with me every step of the way.

Bibliography

*The Secret Queen: Eleanor Talbot
The Woman who put Richard III on the Throne*
by John Ashdown-Hill

Richard III: The Maligned King
by Annette Carson

Richard III and the Murder in the Tower
by Peter A Hancock

Richard III: Loyalty Binds Me
by Matthew Lewis

The Wars of the Roses
by Desmond Seward

Thomas Grey, 1st marquess of Dorset
by T.B. Pugh in Oxford DNB online

Coming Soon

THE MIRROR OF NAPLES

It is 1514 and Henry VIII has decided to marry his sister Mary to Louis XII, the elderly King of France. Accompanying Mary to her wedding is her cousin, seventeen-year-old Elizabeth Grey.

Despite a magnificent reception in Abbeville not everyone at the French court welcomes the English bride. Some, like Madame Louise, mother of Louis's heir, want Mary dead. But it is Louis who dies and Elizabeth who must twice put herself in danger to save her cousin's life.

From the menacing world of the French court and the glittering extravaganza of the Field of the Cloth of Gold to the tinder box that is Tudor Ireland, *The Mirror of Naples* is a story of the enduring power of love and the price a young woman must pay for having what she wants.

About the Author

Caroline Newark was born in Northern Ireland and as a child she wanted to be a farmer's wife, have twelve children and live in a cottage with roses round the door. Instead she became a teacher, a lawyer, a dairy farmer and cheesemaker. Other remnants of that early dream survive – she has two daughters, five grandchildren and lives with her husband, Richard, in a house in a village in the West Country with roses growing round the door.

In 1997 after her mother died, Caroline found a small, red leather-bound book lying in a drawer in a bureau. Inside were details of twenty-one generations of her mother's family starting in 1299 with a marriage between the Royal Houses of England and France. With one book for each generation, Caroline has imagined the lives of these women who lived in our past.

The Woodville Conspiracy is the eighth book in the series.

Website: www.carolinenewark.com
Contact: caroline@carolinenewark.com
Follow: Caroline Newark on Facebook